The Master of Man

The Master of Man

The Story of a Sin

By
Hall Caine

"Be sure your sin will find you out"

Fredonia Books
Amsterdam, The Netherlands

The Master of Man:
The Story of a Sin

by
Hall Caine

ISBN: 1-4101-0316-1

Copyright © 2003 by Fredonia Books

Reprinted from the 1921 edition

Fredonia Books
Amsterdam, The Netherlands
http://www.fredoniabooks.com

CONTENTS

AUTHOR'S NOTE

I wish to acknowledge my indebtedness to conversations, many years ago, with the late Karl Emil Franzos for important incidents in Chapter Forty-Four, which, founded on fact, were in part incorporated by the Russo-Jewish writer in his noble book, "The Chief Justice."

Also I wish to say that Tolstoy told me, through his daughter, that similar incidents occurring in Russia (although he altered them materially) had suggested the theme of his great novel, "Resurrection."

For as much knowledge as I may have been able to acquire of Manx law and legal procedure, I am indebted to Mr. Ramsey B. Moore, the Attorney-General in the Isle of Man, the scene of my story.

H. C.

Greeba Castle,
  Isle of Man.

The Master of Man

FIRST BOOK

THE SIN

CHAPTER ONE

THE BREED OF THE BALLAMOAR

WE were in full school after breakfast, when the Principal came from his private room with his high, quick, birdlike step and almost leapt up to his desk to speak to us. He was a rather small, slight man, of middle age, with pale face and nervous gestures, liable to alternate bouts of a somewhat ineffectual playfulness and gusts of ungovernable temper. It was easy to see that he was in his angry mood that morning. He looked round the school for a moment over the silver rims of his spectacles, and then said,

"Boys, before you go to your classes for the day I have something to tell you. One of you has brought disgrace upon King William's, and I must know which of you it is."

Then followed the " degrading story." The facts of it had just been brought to his notice by the Inspector of Police for Castletown. He had no intention of entering into details. They were too shameful. Briefly, one of our boys, a senior boy apparently, had lately made a practice of escaping from his house after hours, and had so far forfeited his self-respect as to go walking in the dark roads with a young girl—a servant girl, he was ashamed to say, from the home of the High Bailiff. He had been seen repeatedly, and although not identified, he had been recognised by his cap as belonging to the College. Last night two young townsmen had set out to waylay him. There had been a fight, in which our boy had apparently used a weapon, probably a stick. The result was that one of the young townsmen was now in hospital, still insensible, the other was seriously injured about the face. Probably a pair of young blackguards who had intervened from base motives of their own and therefore deserved no pity. But none the less the conduct of the King William's boy had been disgraceful. It must be punished, no matter who he was, or how high he might stand in the school.

1

"I tell you plainly, boys, I don't know who he is. Neither do the police—the townsmen never having heard his name and the girl refusing to speak."

But he had a suspicion—a very strong suspicion, based upon an unmistakable fact. He might have called the boy he suspected to his room and dealt with him privately. But a matter like this, known to the public authorities and affecting the honour and welfare of the college, was not to be hushed up. In fact the police had made it a condition of their foregoing proceedings in the Courts that an open inquiry should be made here. He had undertaken to make it, and he must make it now.

"Therefore, I give the boy who has been guilty of this degrading conduct the opportunity of voluntary confession—of revealing himself to the whole school, and asking pardon of his Principal, his masters and his fellow-pupils for the disgrace he has brought on them. Who is it?"

None of us stirred, spoke or made sign. The Principal was rapidly losing his temper.

"Boys," he said, "there is something I have not told you. According to the police the disgraceful incident occurred between nine and nine-thirty last night, and it is known to the house-master of one of your houses that one boy, and one only, who had been out without permission, came in after that hour. I now give that boy another chance. Who is he?"

Still no one spoke or stirred. The Principal bit his lip, and again looked down the line of our desks over the upper rims of his spectacles.

"Does nobody speak? Must I call a name? Is it possible that any King William's boy can ask for the double shame of being guilty and being found out?"

Even yet there was no sign from the boys, and no sound except their audible breathing through the nose.

"Very well. So be it. I've given that boy his chance. Now he must take the consequences."

With that the Principal stepped down from his desk, turned his blazing eyes towards the desks of the fifth form and said,

"Stowell, step forward."

We gasped. Stowell was the head boy of the school and an immense and universal favourite. Through the mists of years some of us can see him still, as he heaved up from his seat that morning and walked slowly across the open floor in front to where the Principal was standing. A big, well-grown boy, narrowly bordering on eighteen, dark-haired, with broad forehead, large dark eyes, fine features, and, even in those boyish days, a singular air of distinction. There was no surprise in his face, and not a particle of shame, but there was a look of defiance which raised to boiling point the Principal's simmering anger.

" Stowell," he said, " you will not deny that you were out after hours last night? "

" No, Sir."

" Then it was you who were guilty of this disgraceful conduct?"

Stowell seemed to be about to speak, and then with a proud look to check himself, and to close his mouth as with a snap.

" It was you, wasn't it? "

Stowell straightened himself up and answered, " So you say, Sir."

" *I* say? Speak for yourself. You've a tongue in your head, haven't you? "

" Perhaps I have, Sir."

" Then it *was* you? "

Stowell made no answer.

" Why don't you answer me? Answer, Sir! It *was* you," said the Principal.

And then Stowell, with a little toss of the head and a slight curl of the lip, replied,

" If *you* say it was, what is the use of *my* saying anything, Sir? "

The last remnant of the Principal's patience left him. His eyes flamed and his nostrils quivered. A cane, seldom used, was lying along the ledge of his desk. He turned to it, snatched it up, and brought it down in two or three rapid sweeps on Stowell's back, and (as afterwards appeared) his bare neck also.

It was all over in a flash. We gasped again. There was a moment of breathless silence. All eyes were on Stowell. He was face to face with the Principal, standing, in his larger proportions, a good two inches above him, ghastly white and trembling with passion. For a moment we thought anything might happen. Then Stowell appeared to recover his self-control. He made another little toss of the head, another curl of the lip and a shrug of the shoulders.

" Now go back to your study, Sir," said the Principal, between gusts of breath, " and stay there until you are told to leave it."

Stowell was in no hurry, but he turned after a moment and walked out, with a strong step, almost a haughty one.

" Boys, go to your classes," said the Principal, in a hoarse voice, and then he went out, too, but more hurriedly.

Something had gone wrong, wretchedly wrong, we scarcely knew what—that was our confused impression as we trooped off to the class-rooms, a dejected lot of lads, half furious, half afraid.

II

At seven o'clock that night Stowell was still confined to his study, a little, bare room, containing an iron bedstead, a deal wash-stand, a table, one chair, a trunk, some books on a hanging book-shelf, and a small rug before an iron fender. It was November and the day had been cold. Jamieson (the Principal's valet) had smuggled up some coal and lit a little fire for him. Mrs. Gale (the Principal's housekeeper), bringing his curtailed luncheon, had seen the long red wheal which the cane had left across the back of his neck, and insisted on cooling it with some lotion and bandaging it with linen. He was sitting alone in the half-darkness of his little room, crouching over the fire, gloomy, morose, fierce and with a burning sense of outraged justice. The door opened and another boy came into the room. It was Alick Gell, his special chum, a lad of his own age, but fair-haired, blue-eyed, and with rather feminine features. In a thick voice that was like a sob half-choked in his throat, he said,

" Vic, I can't stand this any longer."

"Oh, it's you, is it? I thought you'd come."

" Of course you didn't do that disgraceful thing, as they call it, but you've got to know who did. It was I."

Stowell did not answer. He had neither turned nor looked up, and Gell, standing behind him, tugged at his shoulders and said again,

" Don't you hear me? It was I."

" I know."

" You know? How do you know? When did you know? Did you know this morning? "

" I knew last night."

Going into town he had seen Gell on the opposite side of the road. Yes, it was true enough he was out after hours. The Principal himself had sent him! Early in the day he had told him that after " prep " he was to go to the station for something.

"Good Lord! Then he must have forgotten all about it! "

" He had no business to forget."

" Why didn't you tell him? "

" Not I—not likely! "

" But being out after hours wasn't anything. It wasn't knocking those blackguards about. Why didn't you deny that anyway? "

" Oh, shut up, Alick."

Again Gell tugged at his shoulders and said,

" But why didn't you? "

" If you must know, I'll tell you—because they would have had you for it next."

Mrs. Gale had found the big window of the lavatory open at a quarter-past nine, and when she sent Jamieson down he saw Gell closing it.

" Do you mean that. . . . that to save me, you allowed yourself to. . . . "

" Shut up, I tell you! "

There was silence for a moment and then Gell began to cry openly, and to pour out a torrent of self-reproaches. He was a coward; a wretched, miserable, contemptible coward—that's what he was and he had always known it. He would never forgive himself—never! But perhaps he had not been thinking of saving his own skin only.

" That was little Bessie Collister."

" I know."

If he had stood up to the confounded thing and confessed, and given her away, after she had been plucky and refused to speak, and his father had heard of it. . . . *her* father also. . . . her stepfather. . . .

" Dan Baldromma, you know what he is, Vic? "

" Oh, yes, there would have been the devil to pay all round,"

" Wouldn't there? "

" The College, too! Dan would have had something to say to old Peacock (nickname for the Principal) on that subject also."

Yes, that was what Gell had thought, and it was the reason (one of the reasons) why he had stood silent when the Principal challenged them. Nobody knew anything except the girl. The Police didn't know; the Principal didn't know. If he kept quiet the inquiry would end in nothing and there would be no harm done to anybody—except the town ruffians, and they deserved all they got. How was he to guess that somebody else was out after hours, and that to save him from being exposed, perhaps expelled, his own chum, like the brick he was and always had been. . . .

" Hold your tongue, you fool! "

Gell made for the door. " Look here," he said, " I'm going to tell the Principal that if you were out last night it was on an errand for him—that can't hurt anybody."

" No, you're not."

" Yes, I am—certainly I am."

" If you do, I'll never speak to you again—on my soul, never."

" But he's certain to remember it sooner or later."

" Let him."

"And when he does, what's he to think of himself?"

"That's his affair, isn't it? Leave him alone."

Gell's voice rose to a cry. "No, I will not leave him alone. And since you won't let me say that about you, I'll tell him about myself. Yes, I will, and nobody shall prevent me! I don't care what happens about father, or anybody else, now. I can't stand this any longer. I can't and I won't."

"Alick! Alick Gell! Old fellow. . . . "

But the door had been slammed to and Gell was gone.

III

The Principal was in his Library, a well-carpeted room, warmed by a large fire and lighted by a red-shaded lamp. His half-yearly examination had just finished and his desk was piled high with examination papers, but he could not settle himself to his work on them. He was harking back to the event of the morning, and was not too pleased with himself. He had lost his temper again; he had inflicted a degrading punishment on a senior boy, and to protect the good name of the school he had allowed himself to be intimidated by the police into a foolish and ineffectual public inquiry.

"Wretched! Wretched! Wretched!" he thought, rising for the twentieth time from his chair before the fire and pacing the room in a disorder.

He thought of Stowell with a riot of mingled anger and affection. He had always liked that boy—a fine lad, with good heart and brain in spite of obvious limitations. He had shown the boy some indulgence, too, and this was how he had repaid him! Defying him in the face of the whole school! Provoking him with his prevarication, the proud curl of his lip and his damnable iteration: "If *you* say so, Sir. . . ." It had been maddening. Any master in the world might have lost his temper.

Of course the boy was guilty! But then he was no sneak or coward. Good gracious, no, that was the last thing anybody would say about him. Quite the contrary! Only too apt to take the blame of bad things on himself when he might make others equally responsible. That was one reason the under-masters liked him and the boys worshipped him. Then why, in the name of goodness, hadn't he spoken out, made some defence, given some explanation? After all the first offence was nothing worse than being out after hours for a little foolish sweethearting. The Principal saw Stowell making a clean breast of everything, and himself administering a severe admonition and then fighting it all out with the police for school and scholar. But that was impossible now—quite impossible!

"Wretched! Wretched! Wretched!"

He thought of the boy's father—the senior judge or Deemster of the island, and easily the first man in it. One of the trustees of the college also, to whom serious matters were always mentioned. This had become a serious matter. Even if nothing worse happened to that young blackguard in the hospital the police might insist on expulsion. If so, what would be the absolute evidence against the boy? Only that he had been out of school when the disgraceful incident had happened! The Deemster, who was cool and clear-headed, might say the boy could have been out on some other errand. Or perhaps that some other boy might have been out at the same time.

But that couldn't be! Good heavens, no! Stowell wasn't a fool. If he had been innocent, why on earth should he have taken his degrading punishment lying down? No, no, he had been guilty enough. He had admitted that he was out after hours, and, having nothing else to say even about that (why or by whose permission), he had tried to carry the whole thing off with a sort of silent braggadocio.

"Wretched! Wretched! Wretched!"

The Principal had at length settled himself at his desk, and was taking up some of the examination papers, when he uncovered a small white packet. Obviously a chemist's packet, sealed with red wax and tied with blue string. Not having seen it before he picked it up, and looked at it. It was addressed to himself, and was marked " By Passenger Train—to be called for."

The Principal felt his thin hair rising from his scalp. Something he had forgotten had come back upon him with the force and suddenness of a blow. Off and on for a week he had suffered from nervous headaches. Somebody had recommended an American patent medicine and he had written to Douglas for it. The Douglas chemist had replied that it was coming by the afternoon steamer, and he would send it on to Castletown by the last train. The letter had arrived when he was in class, and Jamieson the valet, being out of reach, he had asked Stowell, who was at hand, to go to the Station for the parcel after preparation and leave it on his Library table. And then the headache had passed off, and in the pressure of the examination he had forgotten the whole matter!

The Principal got up again. His limbs felt rigid, and he had the sickening sensation of his body shrinking into insignificance. At that moment there came a knocking at his door. He could not answer at first and the knocking was repeated.

"Come in then," he said, and Gell entered, his face flooded with tears.

He knew the boy as one who was nearly always in trouble, and his first impulse was to drive him out.

"Why do you come here? Go to your house-master, or to your head, or . . . ."

"It's about Stowell himself, Sir. He's innocent," said Gell.

"Innocent?"

"Yes, Sir—it was I," said Gell. And then came a flood of words, blurted out like water from an inverted bottle. It was true that he was with the girl last night, but it was a lie that he had made a practice of walking out with her. She came from the north of the island, a farm near his home, and he hadn't known she was living in Castletown until he met her in the town yesterday afternoon. They were on the Darby Haven Road, just beyond the college cricket ground, about nine o'clock, when the blackguards dropped out on them from the Hango Hill ruins and started to rag him. It was true he smashed them and he would do it again, and worse next time, but it was another lie that he had done it with a stick. *They* had the stick, and it was just when he was knocking out one of them that the other aimed a blow at him which fell on his chum instead and tumbled him over insensible. The girl had gone off screaming before that, and seeing the police coming up he had leapt into the cricket ground and got back into school by the lavatory window.

"But why, boy . . . . why . . . . why didn't you say all this in school this morning?"

"I was afraid, Sir," said Gell, and then came the explanation he had given to Stowell. He had been afraid his father would get to know, and the girl's father, too—that was to say her step-father. Her step-father was a tenant of his own father's; they were always at cross purposes, and he had thought if the girl got into any trouble at the High Bailiff's and it came out that he had been the cause of it, her step-father . . . .

"Who is he? What's his name?"

"Dan Collister—but they call him Baldromma after the farm, Sir."

"That wind-bag and agitator who is always in the newspapers?"

"Yes, Sir."

"But, good heavens, boy, don't you see what you've done for me?—allowed me to punish an innocent person?"

"Yes, I know," said Gell, and then, through another gust of sobs, came further explanations. It had all been over before he had had time to think. The Principal had said that nobody knew, and he had thought he had only to hold his tongue and nothing would be found out. But if he had known that Stowell knew, and that he had been out himself . . . .

"And did he know?"

"Yes, Sir. He saw me with Bessie Collister as he was going to the station and he thought he couldn't get out of this himself without letting me in for it."

"Do you mean to tell me that he took that punishment to . . . . to save you from being discovered?"

Gell hesitated for a moment, then choked down his sobs, and said with a defiant cry:

"Yes, he did—to save me, and the school, and . . . . and you, too, Sir."

The Principal staggered back a step, and then said: "Leave me, boy, leave me."

He did not go to bed that night, or to school next day, or the day after, or the day after that. On the fourth day he wrote a long letter to the Deemster, telling him with absolute truthfulness what had happened, and concluding:

"That is all, your Honour, but to me it is everything. I have not only punished an innocent boy, but one who, in taking his punishment, was doing an act of divine unselfishness. I am humiliated in my own eyes. I feel like a little man in the presence of your son. I can never look into his face again.

"My first impulse was to resign my post, but on second thoughts I have determined to leave the issue to your decision. If I am to remain as head of your school you must take your boy away. If he is to stay I must go. Which is it to be?"

CHAPTER TWO

THE BOYHOOD OF VICTOR STOWELL

DEEMSTER STOWELL was the only surviving member of an old Manx family. They had lived for years beyond memory at Ballamoar (the Great Place) an estate of nearly a thousand acres on the seaward angle of the Curragh lands which lie along the north-west of the island. The fishermen say the great gulf-stream which sweeps across the Atlantic strikes the Manx coast at that elbow. Hence the tropical plants which grow in the open at Ballamoar, and also the clouds of snow-white mist which too often hang over it, hiding the house and the lands around, and making the tower of Jurby Church on the edge of the cliff look like a lighthouse far out at sea.

The mansion house, in the Deemster's day, was a ramshackle old place which bore signs of having been altered and added to by many generations of his family. It stood back to the sea and facing a broad and undulating lawn, which was bordered by lofty elms that were inhabited by undisturbed colonies of rooks. From a terrace behind, opening out of the dining-room, there was a far view on clear days of the Mull of Galloway to the north, and of the Morne Mountains to the west. People used to say—

"The Stowells have caught a smatch of the Irish and the Scotch in their Manx blood."

The Deemster was sixty years of age at that time. A large, spare man with an almost Jovian white head, clean-shaven face, powerful yet melancholy eyes, bold yet sensitive features and long yet delicate hands—a strong, silent, dignified, rather solemn personality.

He was a man of the highest integrity. Occupying an office too often associated, in his time, with various forms of corruption, the breath of scandal never touched him. He was a legislator, as well as a Judge, being *ex officio* a member of the little Manx Parliament, but in his double capacity (so liable to abuse) nobody with a doubtful scheme would have dared to approach him.

"What does the old Deemster say?"—the answer to that question often settled a dispute, for nobody thought of appealing against his judgment.

"Justice is the strongest and most sacred thing on earth"—that was his motto, and he lived up to it.

His private life had been saddened by a great sorrow. He married, rather late in life, a young Englishwoman, out of Cumberland—a gentle creature with a kind of moonlight beauty. She died four or five years afterwards and the Manx people knew little about her. To the last they called her the "Stranger."

The Deemster bore his loss in characteristic silence. Nobody intruded on his sorrow, or even entered his house, but on the day of the funeral half "the north" lined the long grass-grown road from the back gates of Ballamoar to the little wind-swept churchyard over against the sea. He thanked none of them and saluted none, but his head was low as his coach passed through.

Next day he took his Court as usual, and from that day onward nobody saw any difference in him. But long afterwards, Janet Curphey, the lady housekeeper at Ballamoar, was heard to say in the village post-office, which was also the grocer's shop, that every morning after breakfast the Deemster had put a vase of fresh-cut flowers on the writing-desk in his library under his young wife's portrait, until it was now a white-haired man who was making his daily offering to the picture of a young woman.

" Aw, yes, Mrs. Clucas, yes! And what did it matter to the woman to be a stranger when she was loved like that? "

The " Stranger " had left a child, and this had been at once the tragedy and the triumph of her existence. Although an ancient family of exceptional longevity the Stowells had carried on their race by a very thin line. One child, rarely two, never three, and only one son at any time—that had been all that had stood from generation to generation between the family name and extinction. After three years of childlessness the Deemster's wife had realised the peril, and, for her husband's sake, begun to pray for a son. With all her soul she prayed for him. The fervour of her prayers made her a devoutly religious woman. When her hope looked like a certainty her joy was that of an angel rejoicing in the goodness and greatness and glory of God. But by that time the sword had almost worn out its scabbard. She had fought a great fight and under the fire of her spirit her body had begun to fail.

The Deemster had sent for famous physicians and some of them had shaken their heads.

" She may get through it; but we must take care, your Honour, we must take care."

Beneath his calm exterior the Deemster had been torn by the red strife of conflicting hopes, but his wife had only had one desire. When her dread hour came she met it with a shining face. Her son was born and he was to live, but she was dying. At the last moment she asked for her husband, and drew his head down to her.

" Call him Victor," she said—she had conquered.

II

It was then that the lady housekeeper took service at Balla-moar. Janet Curphey was the last relic of a decayed Manx family that had fallen on evil times, and having lost all she had come for life. She quickly developed an almost slave-like devotion to the Deemster (during her first twenty years she would never allow anybody else to wait on him at table) as well as a motherly love for his motherless little one. The child called her his mother, nobody corrected him, and for years he knew nothing to the contrary.

He grew to be a braw and bright little man, and was idolized by everybody. Having no relations of his own, except " mother," and the Deemster, he annexed everybody else's. Bobbie, the young son of the Ballamoar farmer (there was a farm between the mansion-

house and the sea) called his father " Dad," so Robbie Creer was
" Dad " to Victor too.   The old widow in the village who kept the
post-office-grocer's shop was " Auntie Kitty " to her orphan niece,
Alice, so she was " Auntie Kitty " to Victor also.

"Everybody loves that child," said Janet.   It was true.   As
far back as that, under God knows what guidance, he was laying
his anchor deep for the days of storm and tempest.

During his earlier years he saw little of his father, but every
evening after his bath he was taken into the Library to bid Good-
night to him, and then the Deemster would lift him up to the picture to bid Good-night to his mother also.

"You must love and worship her all your life, darling.   I'll
tell you why, some day."

He was a born gipsy, often being lost in the broad plantations
about the house, and then turning up with astonishing stories of
the distances he had travelled.

" I didn't went no farther nor Ramsey to-day, mother "—seven
miles as the crow flies.

He was born a poet too, and after the Deemster had made a
" Limerick " on his Christian name, he learnt to rhyme to the same
measure, making quatrains almost as rapidly as he could speak,
though often with strange words of his own compounding.   Thus
he celebrated his pet lamb, his kid, his rabbits, the rooks on the
lawn, and particularly a naughty young pony his father had given
him, who " lived in the fiel' " and whom he " wanted to go to Peel,"
but whenever he went out to fetch her she " always kicked up her
heel."   Janet thought this marvellous, miraculous.   It was a gift!
The little prophet Samuel might have been more saintly but he
couldn't have been more wonderful.

Janet was not the only one to be impressed.   It is known now
that day by day the Deemster copied the boy's rhymes, with much
similar matter, into a leather-bound book which he had labelled
strangely enough, " *Isobel's Diary*."   He kept this secret volume
under lock and key, and it was never seen by anyone else until
years afterwards, when, in a tragic hour, the childish jingles in the
Judge's sober handwriting, under the eyes that looked at them,
burnt like flame and cut like a knife.

It was remarked by Janet that the Deemster's affection for the
child grew greater, while the expression of it became less as the
years went on.   " Is the boy up yet? " would be the first word he
would say when she took his early tea to him in the morning; and
if a long day in the Courts kept him from home until after the
child had been put to bed, he would never sit down until he had
gone upstairs to look at the little one in his cot.

In common with other imaginative children brought up alone
the boy invented a playmate, but contrary to custom his invisible
comrade was of the opposite sex, not that of the little dreamer. He
called her " Sadie," nobody knew why, or how he had come by the
name, for it was quite unknown in the island. " Sadie " lived with
her mother, " Mrs. Corlett," in the lodge of Ballamoar, which had
been empty and shut up since " the Stranger " died, when the
coachman, who had occupied it, was no longer needed. On returning from some of his runaway jaunts the boy accounted for his
absence by saying he had been down to the gate to see " Sadie."
He filled the empty house with an entire scheme of domestic econ-
omy, and could tell you all that happened there.

" Sadie was peeling the potatoes this morning and Mrs. Corlett
was washing up, mamma."

His pony's name was Molly and by six years of age he had
learnt to ride her with such ease and confidence that to see them
cantering up the drive was to think that boy and pony must be a
single creature. Molly developed a foal, called Derry, which
always wanted to be trotting after its mother. That suited the boy
perfectly. Derry had to carry " Sadie "—a rare device which
enabled his invisible comrade to be nearly always with him.

But at length came a dire event which destroyed " Sadie." The
master of Ballamoar was rising seven when a distant relative of the
Derby family (formerly the Lords of Man) was appointed Lieu-
tenant-Governor of the island. This was Sir John Stanley, an
ex-Indian officer—a man in middle life, not brilliant, but the incar-
nation of commonsense, essentially a product of his time, firm of
will, conservative in opinions, impatient of all forms of romantic
sentiment, but kindly, genial and capable of constant friendship.

The Deemster and the new Governor, though their qualities had
points of difference, became good friends instantly. They met
first at the swearing-in at Castle Rushen where, as senior Judge
of the island, the Deemster administered the oath. But their
friendship was sealed by an experience in common—the Governor
having also lost a beloved wife, who had died in childbirth, leaving
him with an only child. This was a girl called Fenella, a year and
a half younger than Victor, a beautiful little fairy, but a little
woman, too, with a will of her own also.

The children came together at Ballamoar, the Governor having
brought his little daughter, with her French governess, on his first
call. There was the usual ceremonious meeting of the little people,
the usual eyeing of each other from afar, the usual shy aloofness.
Then came swift comradeship, gurgling laughter, a frantic romp-
ing round the rooms, and out on to the lawn, and then—a wild

quarrel, with shrill voices in fierce dispute. The two fathers rose from their seats in the Library and looked out of the windows. The girl was running towards the house with screams of terror, and the boy was stoning her off the premises.

" You mustn't think as this is *your* house, 'cause it isn't."

Janet made peace between them, and the children kissed at parting, but going home in the carriage Fenella confided to the French governess her fixed resolve to " marry to a girl," not a boy, when her time came to take a husband.

The effect on Victor was of another kind but no less serious. It was remarked that the visit of little Fenella Stanley had in some mysterious way banished his invisible playmate. Sadie was dead —stone dead and buried. No more was ever heard of her, and Mrs. Corlett's cottage returned to its former condition as a closed-up gate-lodge. When Derry trotted by Molly's side there was apparently somebody else astride of her now. But—strange whispering of sex—whoever she was the boy never helped her to mount, and when she dismounted he always looked another way.

III

Four years passed, and boy and girl met again. This time it was at Government House and the boot was on the other leg. Fenella, a tall girl for her age, well-grown, spirited, a little spoiled, was playing tennis with the three young Gell girls—daughters of a Manx family of some pretensions. When Victor, in his straw hat and Eton jacket, appeared in the tennis court (having driven over with his father and been sent out to the girls by the Governor) the French governess told Fenella to let him join in the game. She did so, taking a racquet from one of the Gell girls and giving it to the boy. But though Victor, who was now at the Ramsey Grammar School, could play cricket and football with any boy of his age on the island, he knew nothing about tennis, and again and again, in spite of repeated protests, sent the balls flying out of the court.

The Gells tittered and sniffed, and at length Fenella, calling him a booby, snatched the racquet out of his hand and gave it back to the girl. At this humiliation his eyes flashed and his cheeks coloured, and after a moment he marched moodily back to the open window of the drawing-room. There the Governor and the Deemster were sitting, and the Governor said,

" Helloa! What's amiss? Why aren't you playing with the girls?"

" Because I'm *not*," said the boy.

" Victor! " said the Deemster, but the boy's eyes had begun to fill, so the matter ended.

There was a show of peace when the girls came in to tea, but on returning to Ballamoar the boy communicated to Janet in " open Court " his settled conviction that " girls were no good anyway."

Boy and girl did not meet again for yet another four years and then the boot had changed its leg once more. By that time Victor had made his boy-friendship. It was with Alick Gell, brother of the three Gell girls and only son of Archibald Gell, a big man in Manxland, Speaker of the House of Keys, the representative branch of the little Manx Parliament. Archibald Gell's lands, which were considerable, made boundary with the Deemster's, and his mansion house was the next on the Ramsey Road, but his principal activities were those of a speculative builder. In this capacity he had put up vast numbers of boarding-houses all over the island to meet the needs of the visiting industry, borrowing from English Insurance Companies enormous sums on mortgage, which could only be repaid by the thrift and forethought of a second generation.

Alick knew what was expected of him, but down to date he had shown no promise of capacity to fulfil his destiny. He had less of his father's fiery energy than of the comfortable contentment of his mother, who came of a line of Manx parsons, always shockingly ill-paid, generally thriftless and sometimes threadbare. Yet he was a lovable boy, not too bright of brain but with a heart of gold and a genuine gift of friendship.

At the Ramsey Grammar School he had attached himself to Victor, fetching and carrying for him, and looking up to him with worshipful devotion. Now they were together at King William's College, the public school of the island, fine lads both, but neither of them doing much good there.

It was the morning of the annual prize day at the end of the summer term. The Governor had come to present the prizes, and he was surrounded by all the officials of Man, except the Deemster, who rarely attended such functions. The boys were on platforms on either side of the hall, and the parents were in the body of it, with the wives and sisters of the big people in the front row, and Fenella, the Governor's daughter, now a tall girl in white, with her French governess, in the midst of them.

At this ceremony Gell played no part, and even Stowell did not shine. One boy after another went down to a tumult of hand-clapping and climbed back with books piled up to his chin. When Stowell's turn came, the Principal, who had been calling out the names of the prize-winners, and making little speeches in their praise, tried to improve the occasion with a moral homily.

"Now here," he said, making one of his bird-like steps forward, " is a boy of extraordinary talents—quite extraordinary. Yet he has only one prize to receive. Why? Want of application! If boys of such great natural gifts . . . . yes, I might almost say genius, would only apply themselves, there is nothing whatever, at school or in after life. . . ."

P'shew! During this astonishing speech Stowell was already on the platform, only a pace back from the Principal, in full view of everybody, with face aflame and a burning sense of injustice. And, although, when the interlude was over, and he stepped forward to receive his Horace (he had won the prize for Classics) the Governor rose and shook hands with him and said he was sure the son of his old friend, the Deemster, would justify himself yet, and make his father proud of him, he was perfectly certain that Fenella Stanley's eyes were on him and she was thinking him a " booby."

But his revenge came later. In the afternoon he captained in the cricket match, with fifteen of the junior house against the school eleven. Things went badly for the big fellows from the moment he took his place at the wicket, so they put on their best and fastest bowlers. But he scored all round the wicket for nearly an hour, driving the ball three times over the roof of the school chapel and twice into the ruins beyond the Darby-Haven road, and carrying his bat for more than sixty runs. Then, as he came in, the little fellows who had been frantic, and Gell, who had been turning cartwheels in delirious excitement, and the big fellows, who had been beaten, stood up together and cheered him lustily.

But at that moment he wasn't thinking about any of them. He knew—although, of course, he did not look—that in the middle of the people in the pavilion, who were all on their feet and waving their handkerchiefs, there was Fenella Stanley, with glistening eyes and cheeks aglow. Perhaps she thought he would salute her now, or even stop and speak. But no, not likely! He doffed his cap to the Governor as he ran past, but took no more notice of the Governor's winsome daughter than if she had been a crow.

IV

After that—nothing! Neither of the boys distinguished himself at college. This was a matter of no surprise to the masters in Gell's case, but in Stowell's it was a perpetual problem. Their favourite solution was that the David-and-Jonathan friendship between two boys of widely differing capacity was at the root of the trouble—Gell being slow and Stowell unwilling to shame him.

As year followed year without tangible results the rumour came home to Ballamoar that the son of the Deemster was not fulfilling expectations. " *Traa de liooar* " (time enough) said Robbie Creer of the farm; but Dan Baldromma, of the mill-farm in the glen, who prided himself on being no respecter of persons, and made speeches in the market-place denouncing the " aristo-craks " of the island, and predicting the downfall of the old order, was heard to say he wasn't sorry.

" If these young cubs of the Spaker and the Dempster," said Dan, " hadn't been born with the silver spoon in their mouths we should be hearing another story. When the young birds get their wings push them out of the nest, I say. It's what I done with my own daughter—my wife's, I mane. Immajetly she was fifteen I packed her off to sarvice at the High Bailiff's at Castletown, and now she may shift for herself for me."

The effect on the two fathers was hardly less conflicting. The Speaker stormed at his son, called him a "poop " (Anglo-Manx for numskull), wondered why he had troubled to bring a lad into the world who would only scatter his substance, and talked about mak-ing a new will to protect his daughters and to save the real estate which the law gave his son by heirship.

The Deemster was silent. Term by term he read, without com-ment, the Principal's unfavourable reports, with the " ifs " and " buts " and " althoughs," which were intended to soften the hard facts with indications of what might have been. And he said not a word of remonstrance or reproach when the boy came home without prizes, though he wrote in his leather-bound book that he felt some-times as if he could have given its weight in gold for the least of them.

At seventeen and a half Stowell became head of the school, not so much by scholastic attainment as by seniority, by proficiency in games and by influence over the boys. But even in this capacity he had serious shortcomings. Gell had by this time developed a supernatural gift of getting into scrapes, and Stowell, as head boy, partly responsible for his conduct, often allowed himself to become his scapegoat.

Then the rumour came home that Victor was not only a waster but a wastrel. Janet wouldn't believe a word of it, 'deed she wouldn't, and " Auntie Kitty " said the boy was the son of the Deemster, and she had never yet seen a good cow with a bad calf. But Dan Baldromma was of another opinion.

" The Dempster may be a grand man," said Dan, " but sarve

him right, I say. Spare the rod, spoil the child! Show me the
man on this island will say I ever done that with my own child—
my wife's, I mane."

Finally came a report of the incident on the Darby-Haven road.
John Cæsar, a " lump " of a lad, son of Qualtrough, the butcher
(a respectable man and a member of the Keys), had been brutally
assaulted while doing his best to protect a young nurse-girl from
the unworthy attentions of a college boy. The culprit was Victor
Stowell, and the father of the victim had demanded his prosecution
with the utmost rigour of the law. But out of respect for the
Deemster, and regard for the school, he was not to be arrested
on condition that he was to be expelled.

For three days this circumstantial story was on everybody's
lips, yet the Deemster never heard it. But he was one of those who
learn ill tidings without being told, and see disasters before they
happen, so when the Principal's letter came he showed no surprise.

Janet saw him coming downstairs dressed for dinner (he had
dressed for dinner during his married days and kept up the habit
ever afterwards, though he nearly always dined alone) just as old
Willie Killip, the postman, with his red lantern at his belt, came
through the open porch to the vestibule door. Taking his letter
and going into the Library, he had stood by the writing desk under
the " Stranger's " picture, while he opened the envelope and looked
at the contents of it. His face had fallen after he read the first
page, and it was the same as if the sun was setting on the man, but
when he turned the second it had lightened, and it was just as if
the day was dawning on him.

Then, without a moment's hesitation, he sat at the desk and
wrote a telegram for old Willie to take back. It was to the Principal at King William's, and there was only one line in it—

" Send him home—*Stowell*."

After that—Janet was ready to swear on the Holy Book to it—
he rose and looked up into the " Stranger's " face and said, in a
low voice that was like that of a prayer:

" It's all right, Isobel—it is well."

CHAPTER THREE

FATHERS AND SONS

NEXT day the Deemster drove to Douglas to meet his son coming back. The weather was cold, he had to leave home in the grey
of morning, and he was driving in an open dog-cart, but the
Deemster knew what he was doing. Ten minutes before the train

came in from Castletown he had drawn up in the station yard. The passengers came through from the platform and saw him there, and he saluted some of them. Cæsar Qualtrough was among them, a gross-bodied and dark-faced man, darker than ever that day with a look of animosity and scorn.

When, at the tail of the crowd, Victor came, in the sour silence of the disgraced, no longer wearing his college cap, and with his discoloured college trunk being trundled behind him, the Deemster said nothing, but he indicated the seat by his side, and the boy climbed up to it. Then with his white head erect and his strong eyes shining he drove out of the station yard.

It was still early morning and he was in no hurry to return home. For half an hour he passed slowly through the principal thoroughfares of the town, bowing to everybody he knew and speaking to many. It was market day and he made for the open space about the old church on the quay, where the farmers' wives were standing in rows with their baskets of butter and eggs, the farmers' sons with their tipped-up carts of vegetables, and the smaller of the farmers themselves, from all parts of the island, with their carcases of sheep and oxen. Without leaving his seat the Deemster bought of several of them and had his purchases packed about the college trunk behind him.

It was office hours by this time and he began to call on his friends, leaving Victor outside to take care of the horse and dog-cart. His first call was on the Attorney-General, Donald Wattle-worth, who had been an old school-fellow of his own at King William's, where forty odd years ago he had saved him from many troubles.

The Attorney was now a small, dapper, very correct and rather religious old gentleman (he had all his life worn a white tie and elastic side-boots), with the round and wrinkled face that is oftenest seen in a good old woman. For a quarter of an hour the Deemster talked with him on general subjects, his Courts and forthcoming cases, without saying a word about the business which had brought him to Douglas. But the Attorney divined it. From his chair at his desk on the upper story he could see Victor, with his pale face, in the dog-cart below, twiddling the slack of the reins in his nervous fingers, and when the Deemster rose to go he followed him downstairs to the street, and whispered to the boy from behind, as his father was taking his seat in front,

"Cheer up, my lad! Many a good case has a bad start, you know."

The Deemster's last call was at Government House, and again Victor, to his relief, was left outside. But when, ten minutes later, the Governor, with his briar-root pipe in his hand, came into the porch to see the Deemster off, and found Victor in the dogcart, looking cold and miserable, with his overcoat buttoned up to his throat, he stepped out bareheaded, with the wind in his grey hair, and shook hands with him, and said,

" Glad to see you again, my boy. You remember my girl, Fenella? Yes? Well, she's at college now, but she'll be home for her holiday one of these days—and then I must bring her over to see you. Good-bye! "

The Deemster was satisfied. Not a syllable had he said from first to last about the bad story that had come from Castletown, but before he left Douglas that day, it was dead and done for.

" Now we'll go home," he said, and for two hours thereafter, father and son, sitting side by side, and never speaking except on indifferent subjects, followed the high mountain road, with its far view of Ireland and Scotland, like vanishing ghosts across a broken sea, the deep declivity of the glen, with Dan Baldromma's flour mill at the foot of it, and the turfy lanes of the Curraghs, where the curlews were crying, until they came to the big gates of Ballamoar, with the tall elms and the great silence inside of them, broken only by the loud cawing of the startled rooks, and then to Janet, in her lace cap, at the open door of the house, waiting for her boy and scarcely knowing whether to laugh or cry over him.

II

Meantime there had been another and very different homecoming. In a corner of an open third-class carriage of the train that brought Victor Stowell from Castletown there was a little servant girl with a servant's tin box, tied about with a cord, on the seat beside her. This was Bessie Collister, dismissed from the High Bailiff's service and being sent home to her people. She was very young, scarcely more than fifteen, with coal-black eyes and eyebrows and bright complexion—a bud of a girl just breaking into womanhood.

Dan Baldromma had no need to say she was not his daughter. Her fatherhood was doubtful. Rumour attributed it to a dashing young Irish Captain, who sixteen years before had put into Ramsey for repairs after his ship, a coasting schooner had run on the Carrick rock. Half the girls of " the north " had gone crazy over this intoxicating person, and in the wild conflict as to who should win him Liza Corteen had both won and lost, for as soon as his ship was ready for sea he had disappeared, and never afterwards been heard of.

Liza's baby had been born in the following spring, and two years later Dan Collister, a miller from " the south " who had not much cause to be proud of his own pedigree, had made a great virtue of marrying her, child and all, being, as he said, on " conjergal " subjects a man of liberal views and strong opinions.

In the fourteen years that followed Liza had learned the liberality of Dan's views on marriage and Bessie the strength of his hand as well as opinions. But while the mother's nerves had been broken by the reproaches about her " by-child," which had usually preceded her husband's night-long nasal slumbers, the spirits of the girl had not suffered much, except from fear of a certain strap which he had hung in the ingle.

" The world will never grow cold on that child," people used to say in her earliest days, and it seemed as if it was still true, even in the depth of her present trouble.

The open railway carriage was full of farming people going up to market, and among them were two buxom widows with their baskets of butter and eggs on their broad knees and their faces resplendent from much soap. Facing these was a tough and rough old sinner who bantered them, in language more proper to the stud and the farmyard, on their late married lives and the necessity of beginning on fresh ones. The unvarnished gibes provoked loud laughter from the other passengers, and Bessie's laugh was loudest of all. This led to the widows looking round in her direction, and presently, in the recovered consciousness of her situation, she heard whispers of " Johnny Qualtrough " and the " Dempster's son " and then turned back to her window and cried.

There was no one to help her with her luggage when she had to change at Douglas, so she carried her tin box across the platform to the Ramsey train. The north-going traffic was light at that hour, and sitting in an empty compartment she had time to think of home and what might happen when she got there. This was a vision of Dan Baldromma threatening, her mother pleading, herself screaming and all the hurly-burly she had heard so often.

But even that did not altogether frighten her now, for she had one source of solace which she had never had before. She was wearing a big hat with large red roses, a straw-coloured frock and openwork stockings, with shoes that were much too thin for the on-coming winter. And looking down at these last and remembering she had bought them out of her wages, expressly for that walk with Alick Gell, she thought of something that was immeasurably more important in her mind than the incident which had led to all the trouble—Alick had kissed her!

She was still thinking of this, and tingling with the memory of it, and telling herself how good she had been not to say who her boy was when the " big ones " questioned her, and how she would never tell that, 'deed no, never, no matter what might happen to other people, when the train drew up suddenly at the station that was her destination and she saw her mother, a weak-eyed woman, with a miserable face, standing alone on the shingly platform.

"Sakes alive, girl, what have thou been doing now?" said Mrs. Collister, as soon as the train had gone on. "Hadn't I trouble enough with thy father without this?"

But Bessie was in tears again by that time, so mother and daughter lifted the tin box into a tailless market cart that stood waiting in the road, climbed over the wheel to the plank seat across it, and turned their horse's head towards home.

Dan Baldromma's mill stood face to the high road and back to the glen and the mountains—a substantial structure with a thatched and whitewashed dwelling-house attached, a few farm buildings and a patch of garden, which, though warm and bright in summer under its mantle of gillie-flower and fuchsia, looked bleak enough now with its row of decapitated cabbage stalks and the straw roofs of its unprotected beehives.

As mother and daughter came up in their springless cart they heard the plash of the mill-wheel and the groan of the mill-stone, and by that they knew that their lord and master was at work within. So they stabled their horse for themselves, tipped up their cart and went into the kitchen—a bare yet clean and cosy place, with earthen floor, open ingle and a hearth fire, over which a kettle hung by a sooty chain.

But hardly had Bessie taken off her coat and hat and sat down to the cup of tea her mother had made her when the throb of the mill-wheel ceased, and Dan Baldromma's heavy step came over the cobbled " street" outside to the kitchen door.

He was a stoutly-built man, short and gross, with heavy black eyebrows, thick and threatening lips, a lowering expression, and a loud and growling voice. Seeing the girl at her meal he went over to the ingle and stood with his back to the fire, and his big hands behind him, while he fell on her with scorching sarcasm.

"Well! Well!" he said. "Back again, I see! And you such a grand woman grown since you were sitting and eating on that seat before. Only sixteen years for Spring, yet sooreying (sweethearting) already, I hear! With no wooden-spoon man neither, like your father—your stepfather, I mane! The son and heir of one of the big ones of the island, they're telling me! And yet you're not thinking mane of coming back to the house of a common man like me! Wonderful! Wonderful!"

Bessie felt as if her bread-and-butter were choking her, but Dan, whose impure mind was not satisfied with the effect of his sarcasm, began to lay out at her with a bludgeon.

" You fool! " he said. " You've been mixing yourself up with bad doings on the road, and now a dacent lad is lying at death's door through you, and the High Bailiff is after flinging you out of his house as unfit for his family—that's it, isn't it? "

Bessie had dropped her head on the table, but Mrs. Collister's frightened face was gathering a look of courage.

" Aisy, man veen, aisy," said the mother. " Take care of thy tongue, Dan."

" My tongue? " said Dan. " It's my character I have to take care of, woman. When a girl is carrying a man's name that has no legal claim to it, he has a right to do that, I'm thinking."

" But the girl's only a child—only a child itself, man."

" Maybe so, but I've known girls before now, not much older than she is, to bring disgrace into a dacent house and lave others to live under it. ' What's bred in the bone comes out in the flesh,' they're saying."

The woman flinched as if the lash of a whip had fallen on her face, and Dan turned back to the girl.

" So you're a fine lady that belaves in the aristocracks, are you? Well, I'm a plain man that doesn't, and nobody living in my house can have any truck with them."

" But goodness me, Dan, the boy is not a dale older than herself," said Mrs. Collister. " Nineteen years at the most, and a fine boy at that."

" Chut! Nineteen or ninety, it's all as one to me," said Dan, "and this island will be knowing what sort of boy he is before he has done with it."

The young cubs of the " big ones " began early. They treated the daughters of decent men as their fathers treated everybody —using them, abusing them, and then treading on them like dirt.

" But Manx girl are hot young huzzies," said Dan, " and the half of them ought to be ducked in the mill pond. . . . What did you expect this one would do for you, girl, after you had been colloquing and cooshing and kissing with him in the dark roads? Marry you? Make you the mistress of Ballamoar? Bessie Corteen, the by-child of Liza Collister? You toot! You booby! You boght! You damned idiot! "

Just then there was the sound of wheels on the road, and Dan walked to the door to look out. It was the Deemster's dog-cart, coming down the glen, with father and son sitting side by side.

The women heard the Deemster's steady voice saluting the miller as he went by.

"Fine day, Mr. Collister!"

"Middlin', Dempster, middlin'," said Dan, in a voice that was like a growl. And then, the dog-cart being gone, he faced back to the girl and said, with a bitter snort:

"So that's your man, is it—driving with the Dempster?"

"No, no," said the girl, lifting her face from the table.

"No? Hasn't he been flung out of his college for it—for what came of it, I mane? And isn't the Dempster taking him home in disgrace?"

"It was a mistake—it wasn't the Dempster's son," said Bessie.

"Then who was it?"

There was no reply.

"Who was it?"

"I can't tell you."

"You mean you won't. We'll see about that, though," said Dan, and returning to the fireplace, he took a short, thick leather strap from a nail inside the ingle.

At sight of this the girl got up and began to scream. "Father! Father! Father!"

"Don't father me! Who was it?" said Dan.

The blood was rising in the mother's pallid face. "Collister," she cried, "if thou touch the girl again, I'll walk straight out of thy house."

"Walk, woman! Do as you plaze! But I must know who brought disgrace on my name. Who was it?"

"Don't! Don't! Don't!" cried the girl.

The mother stepped to the door. "Collister," she repeated, "for fourteen years thou's done as thou liked with me, and I've been giving thee lave to do it, but lay another hand on my child . ."

"No, no, don't go, mother. I'll tell him," cried the girl. "It was . . . . it was Alick Gell."

"You mean the son of the Spaker?"

"Yes."

"That's good enough for me," said Dan, and then, with another snort, half bitter and half triumphant, he tossed the strap on to the table, went out of the house and into the stable.

An hour afterwards, in his billycock hat and blue suit of Manx homespun, he was driving his market-cart up the long, straight, shaded lane to the Speaker's ivy-covered mansion-house, with the gravelled courtyard in front of it, in which two or three peacocks strutted and screamed.

III

The Speaker had only just returned from Douglas. There had been a sitting of the Keys that day and he had hurried home to tell his wife an exciting story. It was about the Deemster. The big man was down—going down anyway!

Archibald Gell was a burly, full-bearded man of a high complexion. Although he belonged to what we called the " aristocracy " of the island, the plebeian lay close under his skin. Rumour said he was subject to paralysing brain-storms, and that he could be a foul-mouthed man in his drink. But he was generally calm and nearly always sober.

His ruling passion was a passion for power, and his fiercest lust was a lust of popularity. The Deemster was his only serious rival in either, and therefore the object of his deep and secret jealousy. He was jealous of the Deemster's dignity and influence, but above all (though he had hitherto hidden it even from himself) of his son.

Stooping over the fire in the drawing-room to warm his hands after his long journey, he was talking, with a certain note of self-congratulation, of what he had heard in Douglas. That ugly incident at King William's had come to a head! The Stowell boy had been expelled, and the Deemster had had to drive into town to fetch him home. He, the Speaker, had not seen him there, but Cæsar Qualtrough had. Cæsar was a nasty customer to cross (he had had experience of the man himself), and in the smoking-room at the Keys he had bragged of what he could have done. He could have put the Deemster's son in jail! Yes, ma'am, in jail! If he had had a mind for it young Stowell might have slept at Castle Rushen instead of Ballamoar to-night. And if he hadn't, why hadn't he? Cæsar wouldn't say, but everybody knew—he had a case coming on in the Courts presently!

" Think of it," said the Speaker, " the first Judge in the island in the pocket of a man like that! "

Mrs. Gell, who was a fat, easy-going, good-natured soul, with the gentle eyes of a sheep (her hair was a little disordered at the moment, for she had only just awakened from her afternoon sleep, and was still wearing her morning slippers), began to make excuses.

" But mercy me, Archie," she said, " what does it amount to after all—only a schoolboy squabble? "

" Don't talk nonsense, Bella," said the Speaker. " It may have been a little thing to begin with, but the biggest river that ever plunged into the sea could have been put into a tea-cup somewhere."

This ugly business would go on, until heaven knew what it would come to. The Deemster, who had bought his son's safety from a blackguard without bowels, would never be able to hold up his head again—he, the Speaker never would, he knew that much anyway. As for the boy himself, he was done for. Being expelled from King William's no school or university across the water would want him, and if he ever wished to be admitted to the Manx Bar it would be the duty of his own father to refuse him.

" So that's the end of the big man, Bella—the beginning of the end anyway."

Just then the peacocks screamed in the courtyard—they always screamed when visitors were approaching. Mrs. Gell looked up and the Speaker walked to the window and looked out without seeing anybody. But at the next moment the drawing-room door was thrust open and their eldest daughter, Isabella, with wide eyes and a blank expression was saying breathlessly,

" It's Alick. He has run away from school."

Alick came behind her, a pitiful sight, his college cap in his hand, his face pale, drawn and smudged with sweat, his hair disordered, his clothes covered with dust, and his boots thick with soil.

" What's this she says—that you've run away? " said the Speaker.

" Yes, I have—I told her so myself," said Alick, who was half crying.

" Did you though? And now perhaps you will tell *me* something—why? "

" Because Stowell had been expelled, and I couldn't stay when he was gone."

" Couldn't you now? And why couldn't you? "

" He was innocent."

" Innocent, was he? Who says he was innocent? "

" I do, Sir, because . . . . it was *I*."

It was a sickening moment for the Speaker. He gasped as if something had smitten him in the mouth, and his burly figure almost staggered.

" You did it . . . . what Stowell was expelled for? " he stammered.

" Yes, Sir," said Alick, and then, still with the tremor of a sob in his voice, he told his story. It was the same that he had told twice before, but with a sequel added. Although he had confessed to the Principal, they had expelled Stowell. Not publicly perhaps, but it had been expelling him all the same. Four days they had kept him in his study, without saying what they meant to do with him. Then this morning, while the boys were at prayers they had heard carriage wheels come up to the door of the Principal's house, and when they came out of Chapel the study was empty and Stowell was gone.

"And then," said the Speaker (with a certain pomp of contempt now), "without more ado you ran away?"

"Yes, Sir," answered the boy, "by the lavatory window when we were breaking up after breakfast."

"Where did you get the money to travel with?"

"I had no money, Sir. I walked."

"Walked from Castletown? What have you eaten since breakfast?"

"Only what I got on the road, Sir."

"You mean . . . . begged?"

"I asked at a farm by Foxdale for a glass of milk and the farmer's wife gave me some bread as well, Sir."

"Did she know who you were?"

"She asked me—I had to answer her."

"You told her you were my son?"

"Yes, Sir."

"And perhaps—feeling yourself such a fine fellow, what you were doing there, and why you were running away from school?"

"Yes, Sir."

"You fool! You infernal fool!"

The Speaker had talked himself out of breath and for a moment his wife intervened.

"Alick," she said, "if it was you, as you say, who walked out with the girl, who was she?"

"She was . . . . a servant girl, mother."

"But who?"

"Tut!" said the Speaker, "what does it matter who? . . . . You say you confessed to the Principal?"

"Yes, Sir."

"Then if he chose to disregard your confession, and to act on his own judgment, what did it matter to you?"

"It was wrong to expel Stowell for what I had done and I couldn't stand it," said the boy.

"You couldn't stand it! You dunce! If you were younger I should take the whip to you."

The Speaker was feeling the superiority of his son's position, but that only made him the more furious.

"I suppose you know what this running away will mean when people come to hear of it?"

Alick made no answer.

"You've given the story a fine start, it seems, and it won't take long to travel."

Still Alick made no answer.

"Stowell will be the martyr and you'll be the culprit, and that ugly incident of the boy with the broken skull will wear another complexion."

"I don't care about that," cried Alick.

"*You* don't care!"

"I had to do my duty to my chum, Sir."

"And what about your duty to me, and to your mother and to your sisters? Was it your ' duty ' to bring disgrace on all of us? "

Alick dropped his head.

"You shan't do that, though, if I can help it. Go away and wash your dirty face and get something on your stomach. You're going back to Castletown in the morning."

"I won't go back to school, Sir," said Alick.

"Won't you, though? We'll see about that. I'll take you back."

"Then I'll run away again, Sir."

"Where to, you jackass? Not to this house, I promise you."

"I'll get a ship and go to sea, Sir."

"Then get a ship and go to sea, and to hell, too, if you want to. You fool! You damned blockhead! "

After the Speaker had swept the boy from the room, his mother was crying. "Only eighteen years for harvest," she was saying, as if trying to excuse him. And then, as if seeking to fix the blame elsewhere, she added,

"Who was the girl, I wonder? "

"God's sake, woman," cried the Speaker, "what does it matter who she was? Some Castletown huzzy, I suppose."

The peacocks were screaming again; they had been screaming for some time, and the front-door bell had been ringing, but in the hubbub nobody had heard them. But now the parlour-maid came to tell the Speaker that Mr. Daniel Collister of Baldromma was in the porch and asking to see him.

IV

Dan came into the room with his rolling walk, his eyes wild and dark, his billy-cock hat in his hand and his black hair ' strooked ' flat across his forehead, where a wet brush had left it.

"Good evening, Mr. Spaker! You too, Mistress Gell! It's the twelfth to-morrow, but I thought I would bring my Hollantide rent to-day."

" Sit down," said the Speaker, who had given him meagre welcome.

Dan drew a chair up to a table, took from the breast pocket of his monkey-jacket a bulging parcel in a red print handkerchief (looking like a roadman's dinner), untied the knots of it, and disclosed a quantity of gold and silver coins, and a number of Manx bank notes creased and soiled. These he counted out with much deliberation amid a silence like that which comes between thunderclaps—the Speaker, standing by the fireplace, coughing to compose himself, his wife blowing her nose to get rid of her tears, and no other sounds being audible except the nasal breathing of Dan Baldromma, who had hair about his nostrils.

" Count it for yourself; I belave you'll find it right, Sir."

" Quite right. I suppose you'll want a receipt? "

" If you plaze."

The Speaker sat at a small desk, and, as well as he could (for his hand was trembling), he wrote the receipt and handed it across the table.

" And now about my lease," said Dan.

" What about it? " said the Speaker.

" It runs out a year to-day, Sir, and Willie Kerruish, the advocate, was telling me at the Michaelmas mart you were not for renewing it. Do you still hould to that, Mr. Spaker? "

" Certainly I do," said the Speaker. " I don't want to enter into discussions, but I think you'll be the better for another landlord and I for another tenant."

There was another moment of silence, broken only by Dan's nasal breathing, and then he said:

" Mr. Spaker, the Dempster's son has come home in disgrace, they're saying."

" What's that got to do with it? " said the Speaker.

" My daughter has come home in disgrace, too—my wife's daughter, I mane."

Mrs. Gell raised herself in her easy chair. " Was it your girl, then . . . " she began.

" It was, ma'am. Bessie Corteen—Collister, they're calling her."

" What's all this to me? " said the Speaker.

" She's telling me it's a mistake about the Dempster's son, Sir. It was somebody else's lad did the mischief."

" I see you are well informed," said the Speaker. " Well, what of it? "

" Cæsar Qualtrough might have prosecuted but he didn't, out of respect for the Dempster," said Dan.

"So they *say*," said the Speaker.

"But if somebody gave him a scute into the truth he mightn't be so lenient with another man—one other anyway."

The Speaker was silent.

"There have been bits of breezes in the Kays, they're telling me."

Still the Speaker was silent.

"Cæsar and me were middling well acquaint when I was milling at Ballabeg and he was butching at Port St. Mary—in fact we were same as brothers."

"I see what you mean to do, Mr. Collister," said the Speaker, "but you can save yourself the trouble. My lad is in this house now if you want to know, but I'm sending him to sea, and before you can get to Castletown he will have left the island."

"And what will the island say to that Sir?" said Dan. "That Archibald Gell, Spaker of the Kays, chairman of everything, and the biggest man going, barring the Dempster, has had to send his son away to save him from the lock-up."

The Speaker took two threatening strides forward, and Dan rose to his feet. There was silence again as the two men stood face to face, but this time it was broken by the Speaker's breathing also. Then he turned aside and said, with a shamefaced look:

"I'll hear what Kerruish has to say. I have to see him in the morning."

"I lave it with you, Sir; I lave it with you," said Dan.

"Good-day, Mr. Collister."

"Good-day to you, Mr. Spaker! And you, too, Mistress Gell!" said Dan. But having reached the door of the room he stopped and added:

"There's one thing more, though. If my girl is to live with me she must work for her meat, and there must be no more sooreying."

"That will be all right—I know my son," said the Speaker.

"And I know my step-daughter," said Dan. "These things go on. A rolling snowball doesn't get much smaller. Maybe that Captain out of Ireland isn't gone from the island yet—his spirit, I mane. Keep your lad away from Baldromma. It will be best, I promise you."

Then the peacocks in the courtyard screamed again and the jolting of a springless cart was heard going over the gravel. The two in the drawing-room listened until the sound of the wheels had died away in the lane to the high road, and then the Speaker said:

"That's what comes of having children! We thought it bad for the Deemster to be in the pocket of a man like Cæsar Qualtrough, but to be under the harrow of Dan Baldromma!"

" Aw, dear! Aw, dear! " said Mrs. Gell.

" He was right about Alick going to sea, though," said the Speaker, and, touching the bell for the parlour-maid, he told her to tell his son to come back to him.

Alick was in the dining-room by this time, washed and brushed and doing his best to drink a pot of tea and eat a plate of bread-and-butter, amid the remonstrances of his three sisters, who, seeing events from their own point of view, were rating him roundly on associating with a servant.

" I wonder you hadn't more respect for your sisters? " said Isabella.

" What are people to think of us—Fenella Stanley, for instance? " said Adelaide.

" I declare I shall be ashamed to show my face in Government House again," said Verbena.

" Oh, shut up and let a fellow eat," said Alick, and then something about " first-class flunkeys."

But at that moment the parlour-maid came with his father's message and he had to return to the drawing-room.

" On second thoughts," said the Speaker, " we have decided that you are not to go to sea. We have only one son, and I suppose we must do our best with him. You haven't brains enough for building, so, if you are not to go back to school, you must stay on the land and learn to look after these farms in Andreas."

" I'll do my best to please you, Sir," said Alick.

" But listen to this," said the Speaker, " Dan Baldromma has been here, and we know who the girl was. There is to be no more mischief in that quarter. You must never see her or hear from her again as long as you live—is it a promise? "

" Yes, Sir," said Alick, and he meant to keep it.

CHAPTER FOUR

ENTER FENELLA STANLEY

THE winter passed, the spring came and nothing was done for Victor. His father made no effort to provide for his future, whether at another school, at college, or in a profession.

" I wonder at the Dempster, I really do," said Auntie Kitty.

" Leave him alone," said Janet—it would all come right some day.

Left to himself, Victor became the great practical joker of the countryside. Every prank for which no other author could be found was attributed to him. If any pretentious person fell into a ridiculous mare's nest people would say,

" But where was young Stowell while that was going on?"

In this dubious occupation of " putting the fun " on folks he soon found the powerful assistance of Alick Gell. That young gentleman, for his training on the land, had been handed over to the charge of old Tom Kermode, the Speaker's steward. But Tom, good man, foresaw the possibility of being supplanted in his position if the Speaker's son acquired sufficient knowledge to take it, and therefore he put no unnecessary obstacles in the way of the boy's industrious efforts not to do so. On the contrary he encouraged them, with the result that Alick and Victor foregathered again, and having nothing better to do than to make mischief, they proceeded to make it.

How much the Deemster heard of his son's doings nobody knew. Twice a day he sat at meat with him without speaking a word of reproof. But Janet saw that when report was loudest he wrote longer than usual in his leather-bound book before going to bed, and that his head was lower than ever in the morning.

At length Janet entered into a secret scheme with herself for lifting it up again. This consisted in prompting her dear boy to do something, to make an effort, to justify himself. So making excuse of the Deemster's business she would take Victor's breakfast to his bedroom before he had time to get up to it.

It was a bright room to the north-east, flooded with sunshine at that season after she had drawn the blind, and fresh, after she had thrown up the sash, with morning air that smacked of the blue sea (which came humming down from the dim ghost of Galloway), and relished of the sandy soil of Man, with its yellowing crops of rustling oats, over which the larks and the linnets tumbled and sang.

Victor was always asleep when she went in at eight o'clock, for he slept like a top, and after she had scolded him for lying late, he would sit up in bed, with his sleepy eyes and tousled hair, to eat his breakfast, while she turned his stockings, shook out his shirt, gathered up his clothes (they were usually distributed all over the room) and talked.

Victor noticed whatever she began upon she always ended with the same subject. It was Fenella Stanley. That girl was splendid, and she was getting on marvellously. Still at college " across "? Yes, Newnham they were calling it, and she was carrying everything before her—prizes, scholarships, honours— goodness knows what.

The island was ringing with her praise but Janet was hearing everything direct from Miss Green, the Governor's housekeeper, with whom she kept up a constant correspondence. That woman worshipped the girl—you never saw the like, never! As for the Governor, it was enough to bring tears into a woman's eyes to see how proud he was of his daughter. When he had news that she had taken a new honour it was like new life to the old man. You would think the sun was shining all over the house, and that was saying something there—the Keys being so troublesome. Of course he was " longing " for his daughter to come home to him, and that was only natural, but knowing how hard she was working now—six in the morning until six in the evening, Catherine Green was saying—he was waiting patiently.

"Aw, yes, yes, that's the way with fathers," said Janet. " Big men as they may be themselves, they are prouder of their children's successes than of their own—far prouder."

The effect of Janet's scheme was the reverse of what she had expected. By a law of the heart of a boy, which the good soul knew nothing of, Victor resented the industry, success and reputation of Fenella Stanley. It was a kind of rebuke to his own idleness. The girl was a bookworm and would develop into a blue-stocking! He had not seen her for years and did not want to see her, but in his mind's eye he pictured her as she must be now—a pale-faced young person in a short blue skirt and big boots, with cropped hair and perhaps spectacles!

Describing this vision to Alick Gell, as they were drying themselves on the shore after a swim, Victor said with emphasis that if there was one thing he hated it was a woman who was half a man.

" Same here," said Alick, who had had liberal doses of the same medicine at home, less delicately administered by his sister Isabella.

But where Janet failed, a greater advocate, nature itself, was soon to succeed. The boys were then in their nineteenth year, a pair of full-grown, healthy, handsome lads as ever trod the heather, or stripped to the sea, but there was a great world which had not yet been revealed to either of them—the world of woman. That world was to be revealed to one of them now.

II

It was a late afternoon early in September. The day had been wonderful. Over the bald crown above Druidsdale the sun came slanting across the Irish Sea from a crimsoning sky beyond the purple crests of the Morne mountains. Stowell and Gell had been camping out for two days in the Manx hills, and, parting at a junction of paths, Gell had gone down towards Douglas while

Stowell had dropped into the cool dark depths of the glen that led homewards.

Victor was as brown as a berry. He was wearing long, thick-soled yellow boots almost up to his knees, with his trousers tucked into them, a loose yellow shirt, rolled up to the elbows of his strong round arms, no waistcoat, his Norfolk jacket thrown over his left shoulder, and a knapsack strapped on his back.

With long, plunging strides he was coming down the glen, sing-ing sometimes in a voice that was partly drowned by the louder water where it dipped into a dub, when, towards the Curragh end of it, on the " brough " side of the river, he came upon a start-ling vision.

It was a girl. She was about seventeen years of age, bare-headed and bare-footed, and standing ankle-deep in the water. Her lips, and a little of the mouth at either side, were stained blue with blackberries—she had clearly been picking them and had taken off shoes and stockings to get at a laden bush.

She was splendidly tall, and had bronze brown hair, with a glint of gold when the sun shone on it. The sun was shining on it now, through a gap in the thinning trees that overhung the glen, and with the leaves pattering over her head, and the river running at her feet, it was almost as if she herself were singing.

With her spare hand she was holding up her dress, which was partly of lace—light and loose and semi-transparent—and when a breeze, which was blowing from the sea, lapped it about her body there was a hint of the white, round, beautiful form beneath. Her eyes were dark and brilliantly full, and her face was magnificently intellectual, so clear-cut and clean. And yet she was so feminine, so womanly, such a girl!

She must have heard Stowell's footsteps, and perhaps his sing-ing as he approached, for she turned to look up at him—calmly, rather seriously, a little anxiously but without the slightest con-fusion. And he looked at her, pausing to do so, without being quite aware of it, and feeling for one brief moment as if wind and water had suddenly stopped and the world stood still.

There was a moment of silence, in which he felt a certain chill, and she a certain warmth, and both a certain dryness at the throat. The girl was the first to recover self-control. Her face sweet-ened to a smile, and then, in a voice that was a little husky, and yet sounded to him like music, she said, as if she had asked and answered an earlier question for herself:

" But of course you don't know who I am, do you? "

He did. Although she was so utterly unlike what he had

expected (what he had told himself he expected) he knew—she was Fenella Stanley.

As often as he thought of it afterwards he could never be quite sure what he had said to her in those first moments. He could only guess at what it must have been by his vivid memory of what she had said in reply.

She watched him, womanlike, for a moment longer, to see what impression she had made upon him, now that she knew what impression he had made upon her. Then she glanced down at her bare feet, that looked yellow on the pebbles in the running water, and then at her shoes and stockings, which, with her parasol, lay on the bank, and said:

" I suppose you ought to go away while I get out of this? "

" Why? "

He never knew what made him say that, but she glanced up at him again, with the answering sunshine of another smile, and said:

" Well, you needn't, if you don't want to."

After that she stepped out of the river, and sat on the grass to dry her feet and pull on her stockings. As she did so, and he stood watching, forgetting (such was the spell of things) to turn his eyes away, she shot another look up at him, and said:

" I remember that the last time I was in these parts you ordered me off, Sir."

" And the last time I was at Government House you turned me out of the tennis court," he answered.

She laughed. He laughed. They both laughed together. Also they both trembled. But by the time she had put on her shoes he was feeling braver, so he went down on his knees to tie her laces.

It was a frightening ordeal, but he got through at last, and to cover their embarrassment, while the lacing was going on, they came to certain explanations.

Yesterday the Governor had telegraphed to the Deemster that he would like to fulfil his promise to visit Ballamoar and stay the night if convenient. So they had driven over in the carriage and arrived about two hours ago, and were going back to-morrow morning.

" Of course *you* were not there when we came," she said, " be-ing, it seems, a gentleman of gipsy habits, so when Janet (I mean Miss Curphey) mentioned at tea that you were likely to come down the glen about sunset . . . . "

" Then you were coming to meet me? " he said.

She laughed again, having said more than she had intended and finding no way of escape from it.

When all was done and he had helped her up (how his fingers

tingled!) and they stood side by side for the first time (she was less than half a head shorter than himself and her eyes seemed almost on the level of his own) and they were ready to go, he suddenly remembered that they were on the wrong side for the road. So if she hadn't to take off her boots and stockings and wade through the water again, or else walk half a mile down the glen to the bridge, he would have to carry her across the river.

Without more ado she let him do it—picking her up in his quivering arms and striding through the water in his long boots.

Then being dropped to her feet she laughed again; and he laughed, and they went on laughing, all the way down the glen road, and through the watery lanes of the Curragh, where the sally bushes were singing loud in the breeze from the sea—but not so loud as the hearts of this pair of children.

III

That night, after dinner, leaving the Deemster and the Governor at the table, discussing insular subjects (a constitutional change which was then being mooted), Victor took Fenella out on to the piazza (his mother had called it so), the uncovered wooden terrace which overlooked the coast.

He was in a dark blue jacket suit, not yet having possessed evening wear, but she was in a gauzy light dress with satin slippers, and her bronze-brown hair was curled about her face in bewitching ringlets.

The evening was very quiet, almost breathless, with hardly a leaf stirring. The revolving light in the lighthouse on the Point of Ayre (seven miles away on its neck of land covered by a wilderness of white stones) was answering to the far-off gleam of the light on the Mull of Galloway, while the sky to the west was a slumberous red, as if the night were dreaming of the departed day.

They had not yet recovered from their experience in the glen, and, sitting out there in the moonlight (for the moon had just sailed through a rack of cloud), they were still speaking involuntarily, and then laughing nervously at nothing—nothing but that tingling sense of sex which made them afraid of each other, that mysterious call of man to maid which, when it first comes, is as pure as an angel's whisper.

" What a wonderful day it has been ! " she said.

" The most wonderful day I have ever known," he answered.

" And what a wonderful home you have here," she said.

" Haven't we? " he replied. And then he told her that over there in the dark lay Ireland, and over there Scotland, and over there England, and straight ahead was Norway and the North Pole.

That caught them up into the zone of great things, the eternities, the vast darkness out of which the generations come and towards which they go; and, having found his voice at last, he began to tell her how the island came to be peopled by its present race.

This was the very scene of the Norse invasion—the Vikings from Iceland having landed on this spot a thousand years ago. When the old sea king (his name was Orry) came ashore at the Lhen (it was on a starlight night like this) the native inhabitants of Man had gone down to challenge him. "Where do you come from?" they had cried, and then, pointing to the milky way, he had answered, "That's the road to my country." But the native people had fought him to throw him back into the sea—yes, men and women, too, they say. This very ground between them and the coast had been the battlefield, and it must still be full of the dead who had died that day.

"What a wonderful story!" she said.

"Isn't it?"

"The women fought too, you say?"

"Thousands of them, side by side with their men, and they were the mothers of the Manxmen of to-day."

"How glorious! How perfectly glorious!"

And then, clasping her hands about her knee, and looking steadfastly into the dark of the night, she, on her part, told him something. It was about a great new movement which was beginning in England for a change in the condition of women. Oh, it was wonderful! Miss Clough, the Principal, and all the girls at Newnham were ablaze with it, and it was going to sweep through the world. In the past the attitude towards women of literature, law, even religion, had been so unfair, so cruel. She could cry to think of it—the long martyrdom of woman through all the ages.

"Do you know," she said, "I think a good deal of the Bible itself is very wicked towards women . . . . That's shocking, isn't it?"

"Oh, no, no," said Victor—he was struggling to follow her, and not finding it easy.

"But all that will be changed some day," said Fenella.

It might require some terrible world-trouble to change it, some cataclysm, some war, perhaps (she didn't know what), but it *would* be changed—she was sure it would. And then, when woman took her rightful place beside man, as his equal, his comrade, his other self, they would see what would happen.

"What?"

All the old laws, so far as they concerned the sexes (and which of them didn't?) would have to be made afresh, and all the old tales about men and women (and which of them were not?) would have to be re-told.

" The laws made afresh, you say? "

" Yes, and some of the judges, too, perhaps."

" And all the old tales re-told? "

" Every one of them, and then they will be new ones, because woman will have a new and far worthier place in them."

They had left the stained-glass door to the dining-room ajar, and at a pause in Fenella's story they heard the voice of the Governor, in conversation with the Deemster on the constitutional question, saying,

" Well, well, old friend, I don't suppose either the millennium will dawn or the deluge come whether the Keys are reformed or not."

That led Victor to ask Fenella what her father thought of her opinions.

" Oh well," she said, " he doesn't agree. But then . . . . (her voice was coming with a laugh from her throat now) I don't quite approve of father."

This broke the spell of their serious talk, and he asked if she would like to go down to an ancient church on the seaward boundary of the old battlefield—it was a ruin and looked wonderful in the moonlight.

She said she would love to, and, slipping indoors to make ready, she came back in a moment with a silk handkerchief about her head, which made her face intoxicating to the boy who was waiting for it, and feeling for the first time the thrilling, quivering call of body and soul that is the secret of the continued race. So off they went together with a rhythmic stride, down the sandy road to the shore—he bareheaded, and she in her white dress and the satin slippers in which her footsteps made no noise.

The ruined church was on a lonesome spot on the edge of the sea, with the sea's moan always over it, and the waves thundering in the dark through the cavernous rocks beneath.

Fenella bore herself bravely until they reached the roofless chancel, where an elm tree grew, and the moonlight, now coming and going among the moving clouds, was playing upon the tomb of some old churchman whose unearthed bones the antiquaries had lately covered with a stone and surrounded by an iron railing, and then she clutched at Victor's arm, held on tightly and trembled like a child.

That restored the balance of things a little, and going home (it

was his turn to hold on now) he could not help chaffing her on her
feminine fear. Was that one of the old stories that would have to
be re-told . . . . when the great world-change came, the great
cataclysm?

" Oh, that? Well, of course . . . . (he believed she was
blushing, though in the darkness he could not see) women may not
have the strength and courage of men—the physical courage,
I mean . . . . "

" Only physical? " he asked.

She stammered again, and said that naturally men would always
be men and women, women.

" You don't want *that* altered, do you? " she said.

" Oh no, not I, not a bit," said Victor, and then there was more
laughter (rather tremulous laughter now) and less talking for the
next five minutes.

They had got back to the piazza by this time, and knowing that
her face was in the shaft of light that came through the glass door
from the dining-room, Fenella turned quickly and shot away
upstairs.

For the first time in his life Victor did not sleep until after
three o'clock next morning. He saw the moonlight creep across
the cocoa-nut matting on his bedroom floor and heard the clock on
the staircase landing strike every hour from eleven to three.

Now that he was alone he was feeling degraded and ashamed.
Here was this splendid girl touching life at its core, dealing with
the great things, the everlasting things, attuning her heart to the
future and the big eternal problems . . . . while he!

But under all the self-reproach there was something joyous
too, something delicious, something that made him hot and dizzy
and would not let him sleep, because a blessed hymn of praise was
singing within, and it was so wonderful to be alive.

He could have kicked himself next morning when he awoke
late, and found the broad sunshine in his bedroom, and heard from
Janet that Fenella had been up two hours and all over the stables
and the plantation.

After breakfast (downstairs for him this time) the Governor's
big blue landau, with two fine Irish bays, driven by an English
coachman, came sweeping round to the front and he went out in the
morning sunshine, with the Deemster and Janet, to see their
guests away.

The Governor shook hands with him warmly, but Fenella (who
was wearing a coat and some kind of transparent green scarf about
her neck, and thanked the Deemster and kissed Janet as she was

stepping into the carriage) looked another way when she was saying good-bye to him.

He slammed the door to, and stepped back, and the carriage started, and (while the other two went indoors) he stood and looked after it as it went winding down the drive, amid the awakened clamour of the rooks, until it came to the turn where the trees were to hide it, and then Fenella faced round and waved a hand to him. At the next moment the carriage had gone—and then the sun went out, and the world was dead.

That night after dinner Victor told his father that he would like to go into the Attorney-General's office, as a first step towards taking up the profession of the law.

"Good—very good," said the Deemster.

CHAPTER FIVE

THE STUDENT-AT-LAW

FENELLA STANLEY had not awakened early, as Janet had supposed—she had never been to sleep. Her bedroom had been to the north-east, and she, too, had seen the moonlight creep across her floor; and when it was gone, and all else was dark, she had felt the revolving light from the stony neck of the Point of Ayre passing every other minute over her closed eyelids.

She was too much of a woman not to know what was happening to her, but none the less she was confused and startled. Do what she would to compose herself she could not lie quiet for more than a moment. Her blood was alternately flowing through her veins like soft milk and bounding to her heart like a geyser.

As soon as the daylight came and the rooks began to caw she got up and dressed, and went through the sleeping house, with its drawn blinds, and let herself out by the glass door to the piazza.

Of course she turned towards the shore. It was glorious to be down there alone, on the ribbed sand, with the salt air on her lips and the odour of the seaweed in her nostrils and the rising sun glistening in her eyes over the shimmering and murmuring sea. But it was still sweeter to return by the sandy road, past the chancel of the old church (how silly to have been afraid of it!) and to see footsteps here and there—his and hers.

The world was astir by this time, with the sun riding high and the earth smoking from its night-long draughts of dew, the sheep munching the wet grass in the fields on either side, and the cattle lowing in the closed-up byres, waiting to be milked. But the white blind of Victor's room (she was sure it was Victor's) was still down, like a closed eyelid, and she had half a mind to throw a handful of gravel at it and then dart indoors.

Back in the house there were some embarrassing moments. Breakfast was rather a trying time after Victor came down, looking a little sheepish, and that last moment on the path was difficult, when he was holding the carriage door open and saying good-bye to her; but she could not deny herself that wave of the hand as they turned the corner of the drive—she was perfectly sure he must be looking after them.

After that—misery! Every day at Government House seemed to bring her an increasing heartache, and when she returned to College a fortnight later, and fell back into the swing of her former life there (the glowing and thrilling life she had described to Victor) a bitter struggle with herself began.

It was a struggle between the mysterious new-born desires of her awakening womanhood and the task she had supposed to be her duty—to consecrate her whole life to the liberation of her sex, giving up, like a nun if need be, all the joys that were for ever whispering in the ears of women, that she might devote herself body and soul to the salvation of her suffering sisters.

Three months passed in which Fenella believed herself to be the unhappiest girl in the world. Moments of guilty joy and defiance mingled with hours of self-reproach. And then dear, good people were sometimes so cruel! Miss Green, her father's housekeeper, never wrote without saying something about Victor Stowell. He was a student-at-law now, and was getting along wonderfully.

Once Miss Green enclosed a letter from Janet asking Fenella for her photograph. For nearly a week that was a frightful ordeal, but in the end the woman triumphed over the nun and she sent the picture.

" Dear Janet," she wrote, " it was very sweet of you to wish for my photograph to remind you of that dear and charming day I spent at Ballamoar, so I have been into Cambridge and had one specially taken for you, in the dress I wore on that lovely August afternoon which I shall never forget. . . . "

It had been a tingling delight to write that letter, but the moment she had posted it, with the new Cambridge photograph, she could have died of vexation and shame—it must be so utterly obvious whom she had sent them to.

As the Christmas vacation approached she began to be afraid of herself. If she returned to the island she would be sure to see Victor Stowell (he must be in Douglas now) and that would be the end of everything.

After a tragic struggle, and many secret tears, she wrote to her
father to say what numbers of the Newnham girls were going to
Italy for the holidays and how she would love to see the pictures
at Florence. To her consternation the Governor answered immediately, saying,

"Excellent idea! It will do you good, and I shall be happy to
get away from 'the Kays' for a month or two, so I am writing
at once to engage rooms at the Washington."

She could have cried aloud after reading this letter, but there
was no help for it now.

Truly, the heart of a girl is a deep riddle and only He Who
made can read it.

II

In the Attorney-General's office Victor Stowell was going from
strength to strength. There was a vast deal of ordinary drudgery
in his probationary stage, but he was bearing it with amazing
patience. His natural talents were recognised as astonishing and
he was being promoted by rapid degrees. After a few months the
Attorney wrote to the Deemster:

"Unless I am mistaken your boy is going to be a great lawyer
—the root of the matter seems to be in him."

Not content with the routine work of the office he took up (by
help of some scheme of University extension) the higher education
which had been cut short by his dismissal from King William's,
and in due course obtained degrees. One day, after talking with
Victor, the Bishop of the island was heard to say:

"If that young fellow had been sent up to Oxford, as he ought
to have been, he might have taken a first-class in *Literae Hu-
maniores* and became the most brilliant man of his year."

The Attorney-General's office was a large one, and it contained
several other students-at-law. Among them now was Alick Gell,
who had prevailed upon his mother to prevail upon his father to
permit him to follow Stowell.

"God's sake, woman," the Speaker had said, "let him go then,
and make one more rascally Manx lawyer."

But neither Alick's industrious idleness, nor the distractions of
a little holiday town in its season, could tempt Stowell from his
studies. His successes seemed lightly won, but Alick, who lodged
with him in Athol Street, knew that he was a hard worker. He
worked early and late as if inspired by a great hope, a great ideal.

His only recreation was to spend his week-ends at home. When
he arrived on the Saturday afternoons he usually found his father,
who was looking younger every day, humming to himself as he

worked in an old coat among the flowers in the conservatory. At night they dined together, and after dinner, if the evenings were cool, the Deemster would call on him to stir the peats and draw up to the fire, and then the old man would talk.

It was wonderful talking, but nearly always on the same subject—the great Manx trials, the great crimes (often led up to by great temptations), the great advocates and the great Deemsters. Victor noticed that whatever the Deemster began with he usually came round to the same conclusion—the power and sanctity of Justice. After an hour, or more, he would rise in his stately way, to go to the blue law-papers for his next Court which his clerk, old Joshua Scarf, had laid out under the lamp on the library table, saying:

"That's how it is, you see. Justice is the strongest and most sacred thing in the world, and in the end it *must* prevail."

But Victor's greatest joy in his weekly visits to Ballamoar was to light his candle at ten o'clock on the mahogany table on the landing under the clock and fly off to his bedroom, for Janet would be there at that hour, blowing up his fire, turning down his bed, opening his bag to take out his night-gear and ready to talk on a still greater subject.

With the clairvoyance of the heart of a woman who had never had a lover of her own ("not exactly a *real* lover," she used to say) she had penetrated the mystery of the change in Victor. She loved to dream about the glories of his future career (even her devotion to the Deemster was in danger of being eclipsed by that) but above everything else, about the woman who was to be his wife.

In some deep womanlike way, unknown to man, she identified herself with Fenella Stanley and courted Victor for her in her absence. She had visions of their marriage day, and particularly of the day after it, when they would come home, that lovely and beloved pair, to this very house, this very room, this very bed, and she would spread the sheets for them.

"Is that you, dear?" she would say, down on her knees at the fire, as he came in with his candle.

And then he, too, would play his little part, asking about the servants, the tenants, Robbie Creer, and his son Robin (now a big fellow and the Deemster's coachman) and Alice and "Auntie Kitty," and even the Manx cat with her six tailless kittens, and then, as if casually, about Fenella.

"Any news from Miss Green lately, Janet?"

One night Janet had something better than news—a letter and a photograph.

"There! What do you think of that, now?"

Victor read the letter in its bold, clear, unaffected handwriting, and then holding the photograph under the lamp in his trembling fingers (Janet was sure they were trembling) he said, in a voice that was also trembling:

" Don't you think she's like my mother—just a little like? "

" 'Deed she is, dear," said Janet. " You've put the very name to it. And that's to say she's like the loveliest woman that ever walked the world—in this island anyway."

Victor could never trust his voice too soon after Janet said things like that (she was often saying them), but after a while he laughed and answered:

" I notice she doesn't walk the island too often, though. She hasn't come here for ages."

" Oh, but she will, boy, she will," said Janet, and then she left him, for he was almost undressed by this time, to get into bed and dream.

III

At length, Victor Stowell's term as a student-at-law came to an end and he was examined for the Manx bar. The examiner was the junior Deemster of the island—Deemster Taubman, an elderly man with a yellow and wrinkled face which put you in mind of sour cream. He was a bachelor, notoriously hard on the offences of women, having been jilted, so rumor said, by one of them (a well-to-do widow), on whose person or fortune he had set his heart or expectations.

Stowell and Gell went up together, being students of the same year, and Deemster Taubman received them at his home, two mornings running, in his dressing-gown and slippers. Stowell's fame had gone before him, so he got off lightly; but Gell came in for a double dose of the examiner's severity.

" Mr. Gell," said Deemster Taubman, " if somebody consulted you in the circumstance that he had lent five hundred pounds on a promissory note, payable upon demand, but without security, to a rascal (say a widow woman) who refused to pay and declared her intention of leaving the island to-morrow and living abroad, what would you advise your client to do for the recovery of his money? "

Alick had not the ghost of an idea, but knowing Deemster Taubman was vain, and thinking to flatter him, he said,

" I should advise my client, your Honour, to lay the facts, in an *ex parte* petition before your Honour at your Honour's next Court " (it was to be held a fortnight later) " and be perfectly satisfied with your Honour's judgment."

" Dunce! " said Deemster Taubman, and sitting down to his

desk, he advised the Governor to admit Mr. Stowell but remand Mr. Gell for three months' further study.

Victor telegraphed the good news to his father, packed up his belongings in his lodging at Athol Street, and took the next train back to Ballamoar. Young Robbie Creer met him at the station with the dog-cart, and took up his luggage, but Victor was too excited to ride further, so he walked home by a short cut across the Curragh.

His spirits were high, for after many a sickening heartache from hope deferred (the harder to bear because it had to be concealed) he had done something to justify himself. It wasn't much, it was only a beginning, but he saw himself going to Government House one day soon on a thrilling errand that would bring somebody back to the island who had been too long away from it.

Of course he must speak to his own father first, and naturally he must tell Janet. But seeing no difficulties in these quarters he went swinging along the Curragh lane, with the bees humming in the gold of the gorse on either side of him and the sea singing under a silver haze beyond, until he came to the wicket gate on the west of the tall elms and passed through to the silence inside of them.

He found the Deemster in the conservatory, re-potting geraniums, and when he came up behind with a merry shout, his father turned with glad eyes, a little moist, wiped his soiled fingers on his old coat and shook hands with him (for the first time in his life) saying, in a thick voice,

" Good—very good ! "

They dined together, as usual, and when they had drawn up at opposite cheeks of the hearth, with the peat fire between them, the Deemster talked as Victor thought he had never heard him talk before.

It was the proper aspiration of every young advocate to become a Judge, and there was no position of more dignity and authority. Diplomatists, statesmen, prime ministers and even presidents might be influenced in their conduct by fears or hopes, or questions of policy, but the Judge alone of all men was free to do the right, as God gave him to see the right, no matter if the sky should fall.

" But if the position of the Judge is high," said the Deemster, " still higher is his responsibility. Woe to the Judge who permits personal interests to pervert his judgment and thrice woe to him who commits a crime against Justice."

Victor found it impossible to break in on that high theme with mention of his personal matter, so, as soon as the clock on the landing began to warn for ten he leapt up, snatched his candle, and flew off to his bedroom in the hope of talk of quite another kind with Janet.

But Janet was not there, and neither was his bed turned down as usual, nor his night-gear laid out, nor his lamp lighted. He had asked for her soon after his arrival and been told that she had gone to her room early in the afternoon, and had not since been heard of.

"Headache," thought Victor, remembering that she was subject to this malady, and without more thought of the matter, he tumbled into bed and fell asleep.

But the first sight that met his eyes when he opened them in the morning was Janet, with a face dissolved in tears, and the tray in her hand, asking him in a muffled voice to sit up to his breakfast.

"Lord alive, Janet, what's amiss?" he asked, but she only shook her head and called on him to eat.

"Tell me what's happened," he said, but not a word would she say until he had taken his breakfast.

He gulped down some of the food, under protest, Janet standing over him, and then came a tide of lamentation.

"God comfort you, my boy! God strengthen and comfort you!" said Janet.

In the whirl of his stunned senses, Victor caught at the first subject of his thoughts.

"Is it about Fenella?" he asked, and Janet nodded and wiped her eyes.

"Is she—dead?"

Janet threw up her hands. "Thank the Lord, no, not that, anyway."

"Is she ill?"

"Not that either."

"Then why make all this fuss? What does it matter to me?"

"It matters more to you than to anybody else in the world, dear," said Janet.

Victor took her by the shoulders as she stood by his bed. "In the name of goodness, Janet, what is it?" he said.

It came at last, a broken story, through many gusts of breath, all pretences down between them now and their hearts naked before each other.

Fenella Stanley, who, since she left Newnham, had been working (as he knew) as a voluntary assistant at some Women's Settlement in London, had just been offered and had accepted the position of its resident Lady Warden, and signed on for seven years.

"Seven years, you say?"

"Seven years, dear."

The Governor had prayed and protested, saying he had only one daughter, and asking if she meant that he was to live the rest of his life alone, but Fenella, who had written heart-breaking letters, had held to her purpose. It was like taking the veil, like going into a nunnery; the girl was lost to them, they had seen the last of her.

"I had it all from Catherine Green," said Janet.

Willie Killip, the postman, had given her the letter just when she was standing at the porch, looking down the Curragh lane for Victor, and seeing him coming along with his high step and the sunset behind him, swishing the heads off the cushags with his cane.

"I couldn't find it in my heart to tell you last night, and you looking so happy, so I ran away to my room, and it's a sorrowful woman I am to tell you this morning."

She knew it would be bitter hard to him—as hard as it must have been to Jacob to serve seven years for Rachel and then lose her, and that was the saddest story in the old Book, she thought.

"But we must bear it as well as we can, dear, and—who knows?—it may all be for the best some day."

Victor, resting on his elbow, had listened with mouth agape. The flaming light which had crimsoned his sky for five long years, sustaining him, inspiring him, had died out in an instant. For some moments he did not speak, and in the intervals of Janet's lamentations nothing was audible but the cry of some sea-gulls who had come up from the sea, where a storm was rising. Then he began to laugh. It was wild, unnatural laughter, beginning thick in his throat and ending with a scream.

"Lord, what a joke!" he cried. "What a damned funny joke!"

But at the next moment he broke into a stifling sob, and fell face down on to the pillow and soaked it with his tears.

Janet hung over him like a mother-bird over a broken nest, her wrinkled face working hard with many emotions—sorrow for her boy and even anger with Fenella.

"Aw, dear! aw, dear!" she moaned, "many a time I've wished I had been your real mother, dear; but never so much as now that I might have a right to comfort you."

At that word, though sadly spoken, Victor raised himself from his pillow, brushed his eyes fiercely and said, in a firm, decided voice,

"That's all right, mother. I've been a fool. But it shall never happen again—never!"

CHAPTER SIX

THE WORLD OF WOMAN

VICTOR STOWELL spent his first two hours after Janet left him in destroying everything which might remind him of Fenella. Her picture, which Janet had framed and hung over his mantel-piece, he put face-down in a drawer. The flowers she had placed in front of it he flung out of the window. A box full of news-paper cuttings and extracts from books dealing with the hardships of the laws relating to women (the collection of five laborious years) he stuffed into the grate and set fire to.

But having done all this he found he had done nothing. Only once, since her childhood, had Fenella been to Ballamoar, yet she had left her ghost all over it. He could not sit on the piazza, or walk down the sandy road to the sea, without being ripped and raked by the thought of her. And sight of the turn of the drive at which she had waved her hand, and turned the glory of her face on him, was enough to make the bluest sky a blank.

For a long month he went about with a look too dark for so young a face and a step too heavy for so light a foot, blackening his fate and his future. He never doubted that he had lost something that could never be regained. Without blaming Fenella for so much as a moment he felt humiliated and ashamed, and like a fool who had built his house upon the sand. God, how hollow living seemed! Life had lost its savour; effort was useless and there was nothing left in the world but dead-sea fruit.

How much the Deemster had learnt of his trouble he never knew, but one night, as they drew up to the cheeks of the hearth after dinner, he said:

"Victor, how would you like to go round the world? Travel is good for a young man. It helps him to get things into proportion."

Victor leapt at the prospect of escaping from Ballamoar, but thought it seemly to say something about the expense.

"That needn't trouble you," said the Deemster, "and you wouldn't be beholden to me either, for there is something I have never told you."

His mother had had a fortune of her own, and the last act of her sweet life had been to make it over to her new-born son, at the discretion of his father, signing her dear will a few minutes before she died, against every prayer and protest, in the tragic and unrecognizable handwriting of the dying.

"It was five hundred a year then," said the Deemster, "but I've not touched it for twenty-four years, so it's nine hundred now."

" That's water enough to his wheel, I'm thinking," said Dan Baldromma, when he heard of it, and Cæsar Qualtrough was known to say:

" It's a horse that'll drive him to glory or the devil, and I belave in my heart I'm knowing which."

Two months later Victor Stowell was ready for his journey. Alick Gell was to go with him—that gentleman having scrambled through his examination and prevailed on his mother to prevail on his father to permit him to follow Stowell.

" God's sake, woman," the Speaker had said again, " let him go, and give him the allowance he asks for, and bother me no more about him."

Turning westward the young travellers crossed the Atlantic; stood in awe on the ship's deck at their first sight of the new world, with its great statue of Liberty to guard its portals; passed over the breathless American continent, where life scours and roars through Time like a Neap tide on a shingly coast, casting up its pebbles like spray; then through Japan, where it flows silent and deep, like a mill race under adumbrous overgrowth; and so on through China, India and Egypt and back through Europe.

It was a wonderful tour—to Gell like sitting in the bow of a boat where the tumult of life was for ever smiting his face in freshening waves; to Stowell (for the first months at least) like sitting miserably in the stern, with only the backwash visible that was carrying him away, with every heave of the sea, from something he had left and lost.

But before long Stowell's heavy spirit regained its wings. Although he could not have admitted it even to himself without a sense of self-betrayal, Fenella Stanley's face, in the throng of other and nearer faces, became fainter day by day. There are no more infallible physicians for the heart-wounds inflicted by women than women themselves, and when a man is young, and in the first short period of virginal manhood, the world is full of them.

So it came to pass that whatever else the young men saw that was wonderful and marvellous in the countries they passed through, they were always seeing women's eyes to light and warm them. And being handsome and winsome themselves their interest was rewarded according to the conditions—sometimes with a look, sometimes with a smile, and sometimes in the freer communities, with a handful of confetti or a bunch of spring flowers flung in their faces, or perhaps the tap of a light hand on their shoulders.

Thus the thought of Fenella Stanley, steadily worn down in Victor's mind, became more and more remote as time and distance

separated them, until at length there were moments when it
seemed like a shadowy memory.

Stowell and Gell were two years away, and when they returned
home the old island seemed to them to have dwarfed and dwindled,
the very mountains looking small and squat, and the insular affairs,
which had once loomed large, to have become little, mean and
almost foolish.

" Now they'll get to work; you'll see they will," said Janet,
and for the first weeks it looked as if they would.

For the better prosecution of their profession, as well as to
remove the sense of rivalry, they took chambers in different towns,
Stowell in Old Post Office Place in Ramsey, and Gell in Preaching
House Lane in Douglas—two outer rooms each for offices and two
inner ones for residential apartments.

But having ordered their furniture and desks, inscribed their
names in brass on their door-posts (" VICTOR STOWELL,
Advocate "), engaged junior assistants to sit on high stools and
take the names of the clients who might call, and arranged for
sleeping-out housekeepers to attend to their domestic necessities
(Victor's was a comfortable elderly body, Mrs. Quayle, once a
servant of his mother's at Ballamoar, afterwards married to a
fisherman, and then left a widow, like so many of her class, when
our hungry sea had claimed her man), they made no attempt to
practise, being too well off to take the cases of petty larceny and
minor misdemeanour which usually fall to the High Bailiff's Court,
and nobody offering them the cases proper to the Deemster's.

Those were the days of Bar dinners (social functions much in
favour with our unbriefed advocates), and one such function was
held in honour of the returned travellers. At this dinner Stowell,
being the principal speaker, gave a racy account of the worlds they
had wandered through, not forgetting the world of women—the
sleepy daintiness of the Japanese, the warm comeliness of the
Italian, the vivacious loveliness of the French, and above all, the
frank splendour of the American women, with their free step,
their upturned faces and their conquering eyes.

That was felt by various young Manxmen to be a feast that
could be partaken of more than once, so a club was straightway
founded for the furtherance of such studies. It met once a week
at Mount Murray, an old house a few miles out of Douglas, in the
middle of a forest of oak and pine trees, now an inn, but formerly
the home of a branch of the Athols, when they were the Lords of
Man, and kept a swashbuckler court of half-pay officers who had
come to end their days on the island because the living and liquor
were cheap.

One room of this house, the dining-room, still remained as it used to be when the old bloods routed and shouted there, though its coat-of-arms was now discoloured by damp and its table was as worm-eaten as their coffins must have been. And here it was that the young bloods of the " Ellan Vannin " (the Isle of Man) held their weekly revel—riding out in the early evening on their hired horses, twenty or thirty together, sitting late over their cups and pipes, and (the last toast drunk and the last story told) breaking up in the dark of the morning, stumbling out to the front, where a line of lanterns would be lining the path, the horses champing the gravel and the sleepy stable-boys chewing their quids to keep themselves awake, and then leaping into their saddles, singing their last song at the full bellows of their lungs in the wide clearing of the firs to the wondering sky, and galloping home, like so many Gilpins (as many of them as were sober enough to get there at the same time as their mounts) and clattering up the steep and stony streets of Douglas to the scandal of its awakened inhabitants.

Victor Stowell was president of the " Ellan Vannin," and in that character he made one contribution to its dare-devil jollity, which terminated its existence and led to other consequences more material to this story.

II

In his heavy days at Ballamoar, before he went abroad, his father's house had been like a dam to which the troubled waters of the island flowed—the little jealousies and envies of the island community, the bickerings of church and chapel, of town and country, of town and town, not to speak of the darker maelstrom of more unworthy quarrels. While the Deemster had moved through all this with his calm dignity as the great mediator, the great pacifier, Victor with his quick brain and wounded heart had stood by, seeing all and saying nothing. But now, making a call upon his memory, for the amusement of his fellow clubmen, out of sheer high spirits and with no thought of evil, he composed a number of four-line " Limericks " on the big-wigs of the island.

Such scorching irony and biting satire had never been heard in the island before. If any pompous or hypocritical person (by preference a parson, a local preacher, a High Bailiff or a Key) had a dark secret, which he would have given his soul's salvation not to have disclosed, it was held up, under some thin disguise, to withering ridicule.

A long series of these reckless lampoons Victor fired off weekly over the worm-eaten table at Mount Murray, to the delirious delight of the clubmen, who, learning them by heart, carried them to their little world outside, with the result that they ran over the island like a fiery cross and set the Manx people aroar with laughter.

The good and the unco' good were scandalized, but the victims were scarified. And to put an end to their enemy, and terminate his hostilities, these latter, laying their heads together to tar him with his own brush, found a hopeful agency to their hand in the person of a good-looking young woman of doubtful reputation called Fanny, who kept a house of questionable fame in the unlit reaches of the harbour south of the bridge.

One early morning word went through the town like a searching wind that Fanny's house had been raided by the police, in the middle of the night, about the hour when the Clubmen usually clattered back to Douglas. The raid had been intended to capture Stowell, but had failed in its chief object—that young gentleman having gone on, when some of his comrades had stopped, put up his horse at his job-master's and proceeded to Gell's chambers where he slept on his nights in town. Others of his company had also escaped by means of a free fight, in which they had used their hunting crops and the police their truncheons. But Alick Gell, with his supernatural capacity for getting into a scrape, had been arrested and carried off, with Fanny herself, to the Douglas lock-up.

Next day these two were brought up in the Magistrate's Court, which was presided over by his Worship the Colonel of the " Nunnery," a worthy and dignified man, to whom the turn of recent events was shocking. The old Court-house was crowded with the excited townspeople, and as many of the Clubmen were present as dare show their bandaged heads out of their bedrooms.

When the case was called, and the two defendants entered the dock, they made a grotesque and rather pitiful contrast—Gell in his tall, slim, fair-haired gentlemanliness, and Fanny in her warm fat comeliness, decked out in some gaudy finery which she had sent home for, having been carried off in the night with streaming locks and naked bosom.

In the place of the Attorney-General, the prosecutor was a full-bodied, elderly advocate named Hudgeon, who had been the subject of one of the most withering of the lampoons. He opened with bitter severity, spoke of the case as the worst of the kind the island had known; referred to the " most unholy hour of the morning " which had lately been selected for scenes of unseemly riot; said his " righteous indignation " was roused at such disgraceful doings, and finally hoped the Court would, for the credit of lawyers " hereafter " make an example, " without respect of persons," of the representative of a group of young roysterers, who were a disgrace to the law, and had nothing better to do (so rumour and report were saying) than to traduce the good names of their elders and betters.

When he had examined the constables and closed his case it looked as if Gell were in danger of Castle Rushen, and the consequent wrecking of his career at the Bar, and that nothing was before Fanny but banishment from the island, with such solace as the bribe of her employers might bring her.

But then, to a rustle of whispering, Stowell, who was in wig and gown for the first time, got up for the defence. It had been expected that he would do so, and many old advocates who had heard much of him, had left their offices, and filled the advocates' box, to see for themselves what mettle he was made of.

They had not long to wait. In five minutes he had made such play with his " learned friend's " " unholy hour of the morning," " his righteous indignation " and his " hereafter " for lawyers (not without reference to a traditional personage with horns and a fork) that the merriment of the people in Court rose from a titter to a roar, which the ushers were powerless to suppress. Again and again the writhing prosecutor, with flaming face and foaming and spluttering mouth, appealed in vain to the Bench, until at length, getting no protection, and being lashed by a wit more cutting than a whip, he gathered up his papers and, leaving the case to his clerk, fled from the Court like an infuriated bat, saying he would never again set foot in it.

Then Stowell, calling back the constables, confused them, made them contradict themselves, and each other, and step down at last like men whose brains had fallen into their boots. After that he called Gell and caused him to look like a harmless innocent who had strayed out of a sheepfold into a shambles. And finally he called Fanny, and getting quickly on the woman's side of her, he so coaxed and cajoled and flattered and then frightened her, that she seemed to be on the point of blurting out the whole plot, and giving away the names of half the big men in the island.

His Worship of the Nunnery closed up the case quickly, saying " young men will be young men," but regretting that the eminent talents exhibited in the defence were not being employed in the service of the island.

The Court-house emptied to a babel of talking and a burst of irrepressible laughter, and that was the end of the " Ellan Vannin." But the one ineffaceable effect of the incident, most material to this story, was that Alick Gell, who was still as innocent as the baby of a girl, had acquired a reputation for dark misdoings (especially with women) whereof anything might be expected in the future.

After the insular newspapers had dwelt with becoming severity on this aspect of the "distressing proceedings," the Speaker walked over in full-bearded dignity to remonstrate with the Deemster.

"Your son is dragging my lad down to the dirt," he said, "and before long I shall not be able to show my face anywhere."

"What do you wish me to do, Mr. Speaker?" asked the Deemster.

"Do? Do? I don't know what I want you to do," said the Speaker.

"I thought you didn't," said the Deemster, and then the full-bearded dignity disappeared.

Concerning Victor, although he had made the island laugh (the shortest cut to popularity), opinions were widely divided.

"There's only the breadth of a hair between that young man and a scoundrel," said Hudgeon, the advocate.

"Lave him rope and he'll hang himself," said Cæsar Qualtrough, from behind his pipe in the smoking-room of the Keys.

"Clever! Clever uncommon! But you'll see, you'll see," said the Speaker.

"I've not lost faith in that young fellow yet," said the Governor. "Some great fact will awaken a sense of responsibility and make a man of him."

The great fact was not long in coming, but few could have foreseen the source from which it came.

III

With the first breath of the first summer after their return to the island Stowell and Gell went up into the glen to camp. They had no tent; two hammocks swung from neighbouring trees served them for beds and the horizontal boughs of other trees for wardrobes.

There, for a long month, amidst the scent of the honeysuckle, the gorse and the heather, and the smell of the bracken and the pine, they fished, they shot, they smoked, they talked. Late in the evening, after they had rolled themselves into their hammocks, they heard the murmuring of the trees down the length of the glen, like near and distant sea-waves, and saw, above the soaring pine-trunks, the gleaming of the sky with its stars. As they shouted their last "Good-night" to each other from the depths of their swaying beds the dogs would be barking at Dan Baldromma's mill at the bottom of the glen and the water would be plashing in the topmost fall of it. And then night would come, perfect night, and the silence of unbroken sleep.

Awaking with the dawn they would see the last stars pale out and hear the first birds begin to call; then the cock would crow at old Will Skillicorne's croft on the " brough," the sheep would bleat in the fields beyond, the squirrels would squeak in the branches over their heads and the fish would leap in the river below. And then, as the sun came striding down on them from the hill-tops to the east, they would tumble out of their hammocks, strip and plunge into the glen stream—the deep, round, blue dubs of it, in which the glistening water would lash their bodies like a living element. And then they would run up to the headland (still in the state of nature) and race over the heather like wild horses in the fresh and nipping air.

They were doing this one midsummer morning when they had an embarrassing experience, which, in the devious ways of destiny, was not to be without its results. Flying headlong down the naked side of the glen (for sake of the faster run) they suddenly became aware of somebody coming up. It was a young woman in a sun-bonnet. She was driving four or five heifers to the mountain. Swishing a twig in her hand and calling to her cattle, she was making straight for their camping-place.

The young men looked around, but there was no escape on any side, so down they went full length on their faces in the long grass (how short!) and buried their noses in the earth.

In that position of blind helplessness, there was nothing to do but wait until the girl and her cattle had passed, and hope to be unobserved. They could hear the many feet of the heifers, the flapping of their tails (the flies must be pestering them) and the frequent calls of the girl. On she came, with a most deliberate slowness, and her voice, which had been clear and sharp when she was lower down the glen, seemed to them to have a gurgling note in it as she came nearer to where they lay.

" Come out of that, you gawk, and get along, will you? " she cried, and Victor could not be quite sure that it was only the cattle she was calling to.

At one moment, when they thought the girl and the cattle must be very close, there was a sickening silence, and then the young men remembered their breeches which were hanging open over a bough and their shirts which were dangling at the end of it.

" Get up, stupid! What are you lying there for? " cried the girl, and then came another swish of the twig and a further thudding of the feet of the heifers.

"The devil must be in that girl," thought Victor, and he would have given something to look up, but dare not, so he lay still and listened, telling himself that never before had two poor men been in such an unfair and ridiculous predicament.

At length the feet of the cattle sounded faint over the rippling of the river, and the girl's voice thin through the pattering of the leaves. And then the two sons of Adam rose cautiously from the grass, slithered down the glen-side and slipped into the essential part of their garments.

Half-an-hour later, the lark being loud in the sky, and the world astir and decent, they were cooking their breakfast (Gell holding a frying-pan over a crackling gorse fire, and Stowell, in his Wellington boots, striding about with a tea-pot) when they heard the girl coming back. And being now encased in the close armour of their clothes they felt that the offensive had changed its front and stepped boldly forward to face her.

She was a strapping girl of three or four and twenty, full-blooded and full-bosomed, with coal-black hair and gleaming black eyes under her sun-bonnet, which was turned back from her forehead, showing a comely face of a fresh complexion, with eager mouth and warm red lips. Her sleeves were rolled back above her elbows, leaving her round arms bare and sun-brown; her woollen petticoat was tucked up, at one side, into her waist, and as she came swinging down the glen with a jaunty step, her hips moved, with her whole body, to a rhythm of health and happiness.

"Attractive young person, eh?" said Victor.

But Gell, after a first glance, went back without a word to his frying-pan, leaving his comrade, who was still carrying his tea-pot, to meet the girl, who came on with an unconcerned and unconscious air, humming to herself at intervals, as if totally unaware of the presence of either of them.

"Nice morning, miss," said Victor, stepping out into the path.

The girl made a start of surprise, looked him over from head to foot, glanced at his companion, whose face was to the fire, recognised both, smiled and answered:

"Yes, Sir, nice, very nice."

Then followed a little fencing, which was intended by Victor to find out if the girl had seen them.

Came up this way a while ago, didn't she? Aw, yes, she did, to take last year's heifers to graze on the mountains. Seen anything hereabouts—that is to say on the tops? Aw, no, nothing at all—had he? Well, yes, he thought he'd seen something running on the ridge just over the waterfall.

The girl gave him a deliberate glance from her dark eyes, then dropped them demurely and said, with an innocent air,

"Must have been some of the young colts broken out of the top field, I suppose."

"That's all right," thought Victor, not knowing the ways of women though he thought himself so wise in them.

After that, feeling braver, he began to make play with the girl, asking her how far she had come, and if she wouldn't be lonesome going back without company.

She looked at him quizzically for a moment, and then said, with her eyes full of merriment,

"What sort of company, sir?"

"Well, mine for instance," he answered.

She laughed, a fresh and merry laugh from her throat, and said, "You daren't come home with *me*, Sir."

"Why daren't I?"

"You'd be afraid of father. He's not used of young men coming about the place, and he'd frighten the life out of you."

Victor put down his tea-pot and made a stride forward. "Come on—where is he?"

But the girl swung away, with another laugh, crying over her shoulder,

"Aw, no, no, plaze, plaze!"

"Ah, then it's you that are afraid, eh?" said Victor.

"It's not that," replied the girl.

"What is it?" said Victor.

She gave him another deliberate glance from her dark eyes— he thought he could feel the warm glow of her body across the distance dividing them—and said,

"The old man might be sending somebody else up with the heifers next time, and then . . . . "

"What then?"

She laughed again with eyes full of mischief, and seemed to prepare to fly.

"Then maybe I'd be missing seeing something," she said, and shot away at a bound.

Victor stood for a moment looking down the glen.

"God, what a girl!" he said. "I've a good mind to go after her."

"I shouldn't if I were you," said Gell. "You know who she is?"

"Who?"

"Bessie Collister."

"The little thing who was in Castletown?"

" Yes."

" Then I suppose she belongs to you? "

" Not a bit.   I haven't spoken to her from that day to this,"
said Gell, and then he told of the promise he had made to his father.

" But Lord alive, that was when you were a lad."

" Maybe so, but ' as long as you live '—that was the word, and
I mean to keep it.   Besides, there's Dan Baldromma."

" That blatherskite? " said Victor.

" He'd be an ugly customer if anything went wrong, you
know."

" But, good Lord, man, what is going to go wrong? "

When they had finished breakfast and Gell was washing up at
the water's edge, Victor was on a boulder, looking down the glen
again, and saying, as if to himself,

" My God, what a girl, though!   Such lips, such flesh,
such . . . . "

" I say, old fellow! " cried Gell.

Victor leapt down and laughed to cover his confusion.

" Well, why not?   We're all creatures of earth, aren't we? "

CHAPTER SEVEN

THE DAY OF TEMPTATION

FENELLA STANLEY had been two and a half years at the head
of the Women's Settlement.   Her work as Lady Warden had been
successful.   It had been a great, human, palpitating experience.
There were days, and even weeks, when she felt that it had brought
her a little nearer to the soul of the universe and helped her to
touch hands across the ages with the great women who had walked
through Gethsemane for the poor, despoiled and despairing victims of their own sex.

But nevertheless it had left her with a certain restlessness
which at first she found it hard to understand.   Only little by
little did she come to realise that nature, with its almighty voice,
was calling to her, and that under all the thrill of self-sacrifice she
was suffering from the gnawing hunger of an underfed heart.

The seven years that had passed since her last visit to the island
had produced their physical effects.   From a slim and beautiful
school-girl she had developed into a full and splendid woman.
When the ladies of her Committee (matrons chiefly) saw the swing
of her free step and the untamed glance of her eye they would say,

" She's a fine worker, but we shall never be able to keep her—
you'll see we shall not."

And as often as the men of the Committee (clergymen generally, but manly persons, for the most part, not too remote from
the facts of life) came within range of the glow and flame of her
womanhood, they would think,

" That splendid girl ought to become the mother of children."

During the first year of her wardenship her chief touch with
home (her father being estranged) had been through correspondence with his housekeeper. Miss Green's leters were principally
about the Governor, but they contained a good deal about Victor
Stowell also. Victor had been called to the Bar, but for some
reason which nobody could fathom he seemed to have lost heart
and hope and the Deemster had sent him round the world.

Fenella found herself tingling with a kind of secret joy at this
news. She was utterly ashamed of the impulse to smile at the
thought of Victor's sufferings, yet do what she would she could
not conquer it.

Her tours abroad with her father had ceased by this time, but
in her second year at the Settlement she took holiday with a girl
friend, going through Switzerland and Italy and as far afield as
Egypt. During that journey fate played some tantalizing pranks
with her.

The first of them was at Cairo, where, going into Cook's, to
enter her name for a passage to Italy, her breath was almost
smitten out of her body by the sight of Victor's name, in his own
bold handwriting, in the book above her own—he had that day
sailed for Naples.

The second was at Naples itself (she would have died rather
than admit to herself that she was following him), where she saw
his name again, with Alick Gell's, in the Visitors' List, and being
a young woman of independent character, marched up to his hotel
to ask for him—he had gone on to Rome.

The third, and most trying, was in the railway station at
Zurich, where stepping out of the train from Florence she collided
on the crowded platform with the Attorney-General and his comfortable old wife from the Isle of Man, and was told that young
Stowell and young Gell had that moment left by train for Paris.

But back in London she found her correspondence with Miss
Green even more intoxicating than before, and every new letter
seemed like a hawser drawing her home. Victor Stowell had
returned to the island, but he was not showing much sign of settling to work. He seemed to have no aim, no object, no ambition.
In fact it was the common opinion that the young man was going
steadily to the dogs.

" So if you ever had any thoughts in that direction, dear," said

Miss Green, "what a lucky escape you had (though we didn'
think so at the time) when you signed on at the Settlement!"

But the conquering pull of the hawser that was dragging hei
home came in the letters of Isabella Gell, with whom she had
always kept up a desultory correspondence.

The Deemster was failing fast ("and no wonder!"); and
Janet Curphey, who had been such a bustling body, was always
falling asleep over her needles; and the Speaker (after a violent
altercation in the Keys) had had a profuse bleeding at the nose;
which Dr. Clucas said was to be taken as a warning.

But the only exciting news in the island just now was about
Victor Stowell. Really, he was becoming impossible! Not content with making her brother Alick the scapegoat of his own misdoings in a disgraceful affair of some sort (her father had forbid-
den Alick the house ever since, and her mother was always moping
with her feet inside the fender), he was behaving scandalously.
A good-looking woman couldn't pass him on the road without his
eyes following her! Any common thing out of a thatched cottage,
if she only had a pretty face, was good enough for him now!! The
simpletons!! Perhaps they expected him to marry them, and give
them his name and position? But not he!! Indeed no!! And
heaven pity the poor girl of a better class who ever took him for
a husband!!!

Fenella laughed—seeing through the feminine spitefulness of
these letters as the sun sees through glass. So mistress Isabella
herself had been casting eyes in that direction! What fun! She
had visions of the Gell girls having differences among themselves
about Victor Stowell. The idea of his marrying any of them, and
keeping step for the rest of his life with the conventions of the
Gell family, was too funny for anything.

But those Manx country girls, with their black eyes and eager
mouths, were quite a different proposition. Fenella had visions
of them also, fresh as milk and warm as young heifers, watching
for Victor at their dairy doors or from the shade of the apple trees
in their orchards, and before she was aware of what was happening
to her she was aflame with jealousy.

That Isabella Gell was a dunce! It was nonsense to say that
the Manx country girls out of the thatched cottages expected Victor
to marry them. Of course they didn't, and neither did they want
his name or his position. What they really wanted was Victor
himself, to flirt with and flatter them and make love to them, perhaps. But good gracious, what a shocking thing! That should
never happen—never while she was about!

Of course this meant that she must go back to save Victor.

Naturally she could not expect to do so over a blind distance of three hundred miles, while those Manx country girls in their new Whitsuntide hats were shooting glances at him every Sunday in Church, or perhaps hanging about for him on week-evenings, in their wicked sun-bonnets, and even putting up their chins to be kissed in those shady lanes at the back of Ballamoar, when the sun would be softening, and the wood-pigeons would be cooing, and things would be coming together for the night.

That settled matters! Her womanhood was awake by this time. Seven years of self-sacrifice had not been sufficient to quell it. After a certain struggle, and perhaps a certain shame, she put in her resignation.

Her Committee did not express as much surprise as she had expected. The ladies hoped her native island would provide a little world, a little microcosm, in which she could still carry on her work for women, (she had given that as one of her excuses), and the gentlemen had no doubt her father, " and others," would receive her back " with open arms."

She was to leave the Settlement at the close of the half year, that is to say at the end of July, but she decided to say nothing, either to her father or to Miss Green, about her return to the island until the time came for it at the beginning of August.

She was thinking of Victor again, and cherishing a secret hope of taking him unawares somewhere—of giving him another surprise, such as she gave him that day in the glen, when he came down bareheaded, with the sea wind in his dark hair, and then stopped suddenly at the sight of her, with that entrancing look of surprise and wonder.

And if any of those Manx country girls were about him when that happened . . . . Well, they would disappear like a shot. Of course they would!

II

Meantime, another woman was hearing black stories about Victor, and that was Janet. She believed them, she disbelieved them, she dreaded them as possibilities and resented them as slanders. But finally she concluded that, whether they were true or false, she must tell Victor all about them.

Yet how was she to do so? How put a name to the evil things that were being said of him—she who had been the same as a mother to him all the way up since he was a child, and held him in her arms for his christening?

For weeks her soft heart fought with her maidenly modesty, but at length her heart prevailed. She could not see her dear boy walk blindfold into danger. Whatever the consequences she must speak to him, warn him, stop him if necessary.

But where and when and how was she to do so? To write was impossible (nobody knew what might become of a letter) and Victor had long discontinued his week-end visits to Ballamoar.

One day the Deemster told her to prepare a room for the Governor who was coming to visit him, and seizing her opportunity she said,

" And wouldn't it be nice to ask Victor to meet him, your Honour? "

The Deemster paused for a moment, then bowed his head and answered,

" Do as you please, Miss Curphey."

Five minutes afterwards Janet was writing in hot haste to Ramsey.

" He is to come on Saturday, dear, but mind *you* come on Friday, so that I may have you all to myself for a while before the great men take you from me."

Victor came on Friday evening and found Janet alone, the Deemster being away for an important Court and likely to sleep the night in Douglas. She was in her own little sitting-room—a soft, cushiony chamber full of embroidered screens and pictures of himself as a child worked out in coloured silk. A tea-tray, ready laid, was on a table by her side, and she rose with a trembling cry as he bounded in and kissed her.

Tea was a long but tremulous joy to her, and by the time it was over the darkness was gathering. The maid removed the tray and was about to bring in a lamp, but Janet, being artful, said:

" No, Jane, not yet. It would be a pity to shut out this lovely twilight. Don't you think so, dear? "

Victor agreed, not knowing what was coming, and for an hour longer they sat at opposite sides of the table, with their faces to the lawn, while the rooks cawed out their last congress, and the thrush sang its last song, and Janet talked on indifferent matters— whether Mrs. Quayle (his sleeping-out housekeeper) was making him comfortable at Ramsey, and if Robbie Creer should not be told to leave butter and fresh eggs for him on market-day.

But when, the darkness having deepened, there was no longer any danger that Victor could see her face, Janet (trembling with fear of her nursling now that he had grown to be a man) plunged into her tragic subject.

People were talking and talking. The Manx ones were terrible for talking. Really, it ought to be possible to put the law on people who talked and talked.

" Who are they talking about now, Janet?   Is it about me? "
said Victor.

" Well, yes . . . . yes, it's about you, dear."

Oh, nothing serious, not to say serious!   Just a few flighty
girls boasting about the attentions he was paying them.   And then
older people, who ought to know better, gibble-gabbling about the
dangers to young women—as if the dangers to young men were
not greater, sometimes far greater.

" Not that I don't sympathise with the girls," said Janet,
" living here, poor things, on this sandy headland, while the best
of the Manx boys are going away to America, year after year, and
never a man creature younger than their fathers and grandfathers
about to pass the time of day with, except the heavy-footed
omathauns that are left."

What wonder that when a young man of another sort came
about, and showed them the courtesy a man always shows to a
woman, whatever she is, when he is a gentleman born—just a
smile, or a nod, or a kind word on the road, or the lifting of his
hat, or a hand over a stile perhaps—what wonder if the poor foolish young things began to dream dreams and see visions.

" But that's just where the danger comes in, dear," said Janet.
" Oh, I'm a woman myself, and I was young once, you know, and
perhaps I remember how the heavens seem to open for a girl
when she thinks two eyes look at her with love, and she feels as if
she could give herself away, with everything she is or will be, and
care nothing for the future.   But only think what a terrible thing
it would be if some simple girl of that sort got into trouble on
your account."

" Don't be afraid of that, Janet," said Victor in a low voice.
" No girl in the island, or in the world either, has ever come to
any harm through me—or ever will do."

There came the sound of a faint gasp in the darkness, and then
Janet cried:

" God bless you for saying that, dear!   I knew you would!
And don't think your silly old Janet believed the lying stories they
told of you.   'Deed no, that she didn't and never will do, never!
But all the same a young man can't be too careful! "

There were bad girls about also—real scheming, designing huzzies!   Some of them were good-looking young vixens too, for it
wasn't the good ones only that God made beautiful.   And when
a man was young and handsome and clever and charming and
well-off and had all the world before him, they threw themselves in
his way, and didn't mind what disgrace they got into if they could
only compel him to marry them.

" But think of a slut like that coming to live as mistress here—
here in the house of Isobel Stowell! "

Then the men folk of such women were as bad as they were.
There was a wicked, lying, evil spirit abroad these days that Jack
was as good as his master, and if you were up you had to be pulled
down, and if you were big you had to be made little.

" Only think what a cry these people would make if anything
happened," said Janet, " wrecking your career perhaps, and making promotion impossible."

" Don't be afraid of that either, Janet. I can take care of
myself, you know."

" So you can, dear," said Janet, " but then think of your
father. Forty years a judge, and not a breath of scandal has ever
touched him! But that's just why some of these dirts would like to
destroy him, calling to him in the Courts themselves, perhaps, with
all the dirty tongues at them, to come down from the judgment-
seat and set his own house in order."

" My father can take care of himself, too, Janet," said Victor.

" I know, dear, I know," said Janet. " But think what he'll
suffer if any sort of trouble falls on his son! More, far more, than
if it fell on himself. That's the way with fathers, isn't it?
Always has been, I suppose, since the days of David. Do you
remember his lamentations over his son Absalom? I declare I feel
fit enough to cry in Church itself whenever the Vicar reads it: ' O
my son Absalom! Would God I had died for thee, O Absalom,
my son, my son.' "

There was silence for a moment, for Victor found it difficult
to speak, and then Janet began to plead with him in the name
of his family also.

" The Deemster is seventy years old now," she said, " and he
has four hundred years of the Ballamoars behind him, and there
has never been a stain on the name of any of them. That's always
been a kind of religion in your family, hasn't it—that if a man
belongs to the breed of the Ballamoars he will do the right—he can
be trusted? That's something to be born to, isn't it? It seems to
me it is more worth having than all the jewels and gold and titles
and honours the world has in it. Oh, my dear, my dear, you know
what your father is; he'll say nothing, and you haven't a mother
to speak to you; so don't be vexed with your old Janet who loves
you, and would die for you, if she could save you from trouble and
disgrace; but think what a terrible, fearful, shocking thing it
would be for you, and for your father, and for your family, and
. . . . yes, for the island itself if anything should happen now."

" Nothing *shall* happen—I give you my word for that, Janet,"
said Victor.

" God bless you! " said Janet, and rising and reaching over in the darkness she kissed him—her face was wet.

After that she laughed, in a nervous way, and said she wasn't a Puritan either, like some of the people in those parts whom she saw on Sunday mornings, walking from chapel in their chapel hats, after preaching and praying against " carnal transgression " and " bodily indulgence " and " giving way to the temptations of the flesh "—as if they hadn't as many children at home as there were chickens in a good-sized hen-roost.

" Young men are young men and girls are girls," said Janet, " and some of these Manx girls are that pretty and smart that they are enough to tempt a saint. And if David was tempted by the beauty of Bathsheba—and we're told he was a man after God's own heart—what better can the Lord expect of poor lads these days who are making no such pretensions? "

She was only an old maid herself, but she supposed it was natural for a young man to be tempted by the beauty of a young woman, or the Lord wouldn't have allowed it to go on so long. But the moral of that was that it was better for a man to marry.

" So find a good woman and marry her, dear. The Deemster will be delighted, having only yourself to follow him yet. And as for you," she added (her voice was breaking again), " you may not think it now, being so young and strong, but when you are as old as I am . . . . and feeling feebler every year . . . . and you are looking to the dark day that is coming . . . . and no one of your own to close your eyes for you . . . . only hired servants, or strangers, perhaps . . . . "

It was Victor's turn to rise now, and to stop her speaking by taking her in his arms. After a moment, not without a tremor in his own voice also, he said,

" I shall never marry, and you know why, Janet. But neither will I bring shame on my father, or stain my name, as God is my help and witness."

The rooks were silent in the elms by this time, but the gong was sounding in the hall, so, laughing and crying together, and with all her trouble gone like chased clouds, Janet ran off to her room to wipe her eyes and fix her cap before showing her face at supper.

III

Next morning the Deemster returned from Douglas, and in the afternoon, the Governor arrived. They took tea on the piazza, the days being long and the evenings warm.

5

The Deemster was uneasy about the case they had tried the day before, and talked much about it. A farmer had killed a girl on his farm after every appearance of gross ill-usage. The crime and the motive had been clear and therefore the law could show no clemency. But there had been external circumstances which might have affected the man's conduct. Down to ten years before he had been a right-living man, clean and sober and honest and even religious. Then he had been thrown by a young horse and kicked on the head and had had to undergo an operation. After he came out of the hospital his whole character was found to have changed. He had become drunken, dishonest, a sensualist and a foul-mouthed blasphemer, and finally he had committed the crime for which he now stood condemned.

" It makes me tremble to think of it," said the Deemster, " that a mere physical accident, a mere chance, or a mere spasm of animal instinct, may cause any of us at any time to act in a way that is utterly contrary to our moral character and most sincere resolutions."

" It's true, though," said the Governor, " and it doesn't require the kick of a horse to make a man act in opposition to his character. The loudest voice a man hears is the call of his physical nature, and law and religion have just got to make up their minds to it."

Next morning, Sunday morning, they went to church. Janet drove in the carriage by way of the high road, but the three men walked down the grassy lane at the back, which, with its gorse hedges on either side, looked like a long green picture in a golden frame. The Deemster, who walked between the Governor and Victor, was more than usually bent and solemn. He had had an anonymous letter about his son that morning—he had lately had shoals of them.

The morning was warm and quiet; the clover fields were sleeping in the sunlight to the lullaby of the bees; the slumberous mountains behind were hidden in a palpitating haze, and against the broad stretch of the empty sea in front stood the gaunt square tower from which the far-off sound of the church bells was coming.

Nowhere in the island could they have found a more tragic illustration of the law of life they had talked about the evening before than in the person of the Vicar of the Church they were going to.

His name was Cowley, and down to middle life he had been all that a clergyman should be. But then he had lost a son under circumstances of tragic sorrow. The boy had been threatened with a consumption, so the father had sent him to sea, and going to town to meet him on his return to the island, he had met his body instead, as it was being brought ashore from his ship, which was lying at anchor in the bay.

The sailors had said that at sight of them and their burthen, Parson Cowley had fallen to the stones of Ramsey harbour like a dead man, and it was long before they could bring him to, or staunch the wound on his forehead. What is certain is that after his recovery he began to drink, and that for fifteen years he had been an inveterate drunkard.

This had long been a cause of grief and perhaps of shame to his parishioners; but it had never lessened their love of him, for they knew that in all else he was still a true Christian. If any lone " widow man " lay dying in his mud cabin on the Curragh, Parson Cowley would be there to sit up all the night through with him; and if any barefooted children were going to bed hungry in the one-roomed hovel that was their living-room, sleeping-room, birth-room and death-room combined, Parson Cowley would be seen carrying them the supper from his own larder.

But his weakness had become woeful, and after a shocking moment in which he had staggered and fallen before the altar, a new Bishop, who knew nothing of the origin of his infirmity, and was only conscious of the scandal of it, had threatened that if the like scene ever occurred again he would not only forbid him to exercise his office, but call upon the Governor (in whose gift it was) to remove him from his living.

The bells were loud when the three men reached the white-washed church on the cliff, with the sea singing on the beach below it, and Illiam Christian, the shoemaker and parish clerk, standing bareheaded at the bottom of the outside steps to the tower to give warning to the bell-ringers that the Governor had arrived.

In expectation of his visit the church was crowded, and with Victor going first to show the way, the Governor next, and the Deemster last, with his white head down, the company from Balla-moar walked up the aisle to the family pew, in which Janet, in her black silk mantle, was already seated.

The Deemster's pew was close to the communion rails, and horizontal to the church with the reading-desk and pulpit in the open space in front of it, and a marble tablet on the wall behind, containing the names of a long line of the Ballamoars, going as far back as the sixteenth century.

The vestry was at the western end of the church, under the tower, and as soon as the bells stopped and the clergy came out, it was seen that the Vicar was far from sober. Nevertheless he kept himself erect while coming through the church behind his choir and curate, and tottered into the carved chair within the rail of the communion.

The curate took the prayers, and might have taken the rest of the service also, but the Vicar, thinking his duty compelled him to take his part in the presence of the Governor, rose to read the lessons. With difficulty he reached the reading-desk, which was close to the Deemster's pew, and opened the Book and gave out the place. But hardly had he begun, in a husky and indistinct voice, with " Here beginneth the first chapter of the Second Book of Samuel " (for it was the sixth Sunday after Trinity) when he stopped as if unable to go farther.

For a moment he fumbled with his spectacles, taking them off and wiping them on the sleeve of his surplice, and then he began afresh. But scarcely had he said, in a still thicker voice, " Now it came to pass " . . . . when he stopped again, as if the words of the Book before him had run into each other and become an unreadable jumble.

After that he looked helplessly about him for an instant, as if wondering what to do. Then he grasped the reading-desk with his two trembling hands, and the perspiration was seen to be breaking in beads from his forehead.

A breathless silence passed over the church. The congregation saw what was happening, and dropped their heads, as if knowing that for their beloved old Vicar this (before the eyes of the Governor) was the end of everything.

But suddenly they became aware that something was happening. Quietly, noiselessly, almost before they were conscious of what he was doing, Victor Stowell, who had been sitting at the end of the Deemster's pew, had risen, stepped across to the reading-desk, put a soft hand on the Vicar's arm, and was reading the lesson for him.

" Saul and Jonathan were lovely and pleasant in their lives, and in their death they were not divided . . . . I am distressed for thee, my brother Jonathan; thy love to me was wonderful, passing the love of women."

People who were there that morning said afterwards that never before had the sublime lament of the great King, the great warrior and the great poet, for his dead friend and dead enemy been read as it was read that day by the young voice, so rich and resonant, that was ringing through the old church.

But it was not that alone that was welling through every bosom. It was the thrilling certainty that out of the greatness of his heart the son of the Deemster (of whom too many of them had been talking ill) had covered the nakedness of the poor stricken sinner who had sunk back in his surplice to a seat behind him.

When the service was over, and the clergy had returned to the vestry, the congregation remained standing until the Governor had left the church. But nobody looked at him now, for all eyes were on the two who followed him—the Deemster and Victor.

The Deemster had taken his son's arm as he stepped out of his pew, and as he walked down the aisle, through the lines of his people, his head was up and his eyes were shining.

" Did thou see that, Mistress? " said Robbie Creer, in triumphant tones to Janet Curphey, as she was stepping back, with a beaming face, into her carriage at the gate.

" Thou need have no fear of thy lad, I tell thee. *The Balla-moar will out!* "

But the day of temptation was coming, and too soon it came.

CHAPTER EIGHT

THE CALL OF BESSIE COLLISTER

IT was the first Saturday in August, when the throbbing and thunging of the vast machinery of the mills and factories of the English industrial counties comes to a temporary stop, and for three days at least, tens of thousands of its servers, male and female, pour into the island for health and holiday.

Stowell and Gell had never yet seen the inrushing of the liberated ones, so with no other thought, and little thinking what fierce game fate was playing with them, they had come into Douglas that day, in flannels and straw hats, in eager spirits and with high steps, to look on its sights and scenes.

It was late afternoon, and they made first for the pier, where a crowd of people had already assembled to witness the arrival of an incoming steamer.

She was densely crowded. Every inch of her deck seemed to be packed with passengers, chiefly young girls, as the young men thought, some of them handsome, many of them pretty, all of them comely. With sparkling eyes and laughing mouths they shouted their salutations to their friends on the pier, while they untied the handkerchiefs which they had bound about their heads to keep down their hair in the breeze on the sea, and pinned on their hats before landing.

The young men found the scene delightful. A little crude, perhaps a little common, even a little coarse, but still delightful.

Then they walked along the promenade, and that, too, was crowded. From the water's edge to the round hill-tops at the back of the town, every thoroughfare seemed to be thrilling with joyous activity. Hackney carriages, piled high with luggage and higher still with passengers, were sweeping round the curve of the bay; windows and doors were open and filled with faces, and the whole sea-front, from end to end, seemed to be as full of women's eyes as a midnight sky of stars.

For tea they went up to Castle Mona—a grave-looking mansion in the middle of the bay, built for a royal residence by one of the Earls of Derby when they were lords of Man before the Athols, but now declined to the condition of an hotel for English visitors, with its wooded slopes to the sea (wherein more than one of our old Manx Kings may have pondered the problems of his island kingdom), transformed into a public tea-garden, on which pretty women were sitting under coloured sunshades and a string band from London was playing the latest airs from Paris.

The young men took a table at the seaward end of the lawn, with the rowing boats skimming the fringe of the water in front, the white yachts scudding across the breast of the bay, the brown-sailed luggers dropping out of the harbour with the first flood of the flowing tide; and then the human tide of joyous life running fast on the promenade below—girls chiefly, as they thought, usually in white frocks, white stockings and white shoes, skipping along like human daisy-chains with their arms entwined about each other's waists, and sometimes turning their heads over their shoulders to look up at them and laugh.

The sun went down behind the hills at the back of the town, the string band stopped, the coloured sunshades disappeared, the gong was sounded from the hall of the hotel and they went indoors for dinner.

They sat by an open window of the stately dining-room (wherein our old Earls and their Countesses once kept court), and being in higher spirits than ever by this time, they ate of every dish that was put before them, drank a bottle of champagne, toasted each other and every pretty woman they could remember of the many they had seen that day (" Here's to that fine girl with the black eyes who was standing by the funnel "), and looked at intervals at the scenes outside until the light failed and the darkness claimed them.

At one moment they saw the dark hull of another steamer, lit up in every port-hole, gliding towards the pier, and at the next (or what seemed like the next), shooting across the white sheet

of light from the uncovered windows of their dining-room, a large
blue landau, drawn by a pair of Irish bays, driven by a liveried
coachman. Gell leapt up to look at it.

"Vic," he cried, "I think that must be the Governor's
carriage."

"It is," said Stowell.

"And that's the Governor himself inside of it."

"No doubt."

"And the lady sitting beside him is . . . . yes, no . . . . yes
. . . . . upon my soul I believe it was his daughter."

"Impossible," said Stowell, and, remembering what Janet had
told him, he thought no more of the matter.

They returned to the lawn to smoke after dinner, and then the
sky was dark and the stars had begun to appear; the tide was up
but the sea was silent; the rowing-boats were lying on the shingle
of the beach; the yachts were at anchor in the bay; the last of the
fishing-boats, each with a lamp in its binnacle, were doubling the
black brow of the head, and from the farthest rock of it the
revolving light in the lighthouse was sweeping the darkness from
the face of the town as with an illuminated fan. The young
men were enraptured. It was wonderful! It was enchanting!
It was like walking on the terrace at Monte Carlo!

Then suddenly, as at the striking of a clock, the town itself
began to flame. One by one the façades of the theatres and
dancing palaces that lined the front were lit up by electricity. It
raced along like ignited gunpowder and in a few minutes the broad
curve of the bay from headland to headland, was sparkling and
blazing under ten thousand lights.

It was now the beginning of night in the little gay town. The
young men could hear the creak of the iron turn-stile to one of the
dancing-halls near at hand, and the shuffling of the feet of the
multitudes who were passing through it, and then, a few minutes
later, the muffled music of the orchestra and the deadened drumming of the dancing within.

That was more than they could bear, in their present state of
excitement, without taking part in the scene of it, so within five
minutes more, they were passing through the turn-stile themselves
and hurrying down a tunnel of trees, lit up by coloured lamps, to
the open door of the dancing-hall—deep in a dark garden which
seemed to sleep in shadow on either side of them.

The vast place, decorated in gold and domed with glass, was
crowded, but going up into the gallery the young men secured seats
by the front rail and were able to look down. What a spectacle!

Never before, they thought, though they had travelled round the world, had they seen anything to compare with it. To the clash of the brass instruments and the boom of the big drums, five thousand young men and young women were dancing on the floor below. Most of the men wore flannels and coloured waist-scarves, and most of the girls were in muslin and straw hats. They were only the workers from the mills and factories of Lancashire and York-shire, but the flush of the sun and the sea was in their faces and the joy and health of young life was in their blood.

Stowell felt himself becoming giddy. Waves of perfume were floating up to him, with the warmth of women's bright eyes, red lips and joyous laughter. His nerves were quivering; his pulses were beating with a pounding rush. He was beginning to feel afraid of himself and he had an almost irresistable impulse to get up and go.

II

One other person important to this story had come to Douglas that day—Bessie Collister. During the first three years after her return home from Castletown she had lived in physical fear of Dan Baldromma; but during the next three years, having grown big and strong and become useful on the farm, she had been more than able to hold her own with him, and he had even been compelled to pay her wages.

" I don't know in the world what's coming over the girls," he would say. " In my young days they were content with priddhas and herrings three times a day, and welcome, but nothing will do now, if it's your own daughter itself, but ten pounds a year per annum, and as much loaf bread and butcher's mate as would fill the inside of a lime kiln."

" Aw, but the girl's smart though," Mrs. Collister would answer.

" I'm saying nothing against her," Dan would reply. " A middling good girl enough, and handy with the bases, but imperent grown—imperent uncommon and bad with the tongue."

There was scarcely a farmer on the island who would not have given Bessie twice the wages Dan paid her, but she remained at home, partly for reasons of her own and partly to protect her mother from Dan's brutalities by holding over his head the threat of leaving him.

Mrs. Collister, who had been stricken with sciatica and was hobbling about on a stick, had by this time taken refuge from her life-long martyrdom in religion, having joined the " Primitives," whose chapel (a whitewashed barn) stood at the opposite angle of

the glen and the high road. She had tried to induce her daughter
to follow her there, but Bessie had refused, having come to the
conclusion that the " locals " on the " plan-beg," whose favourite
subject was the crucifixion of the flesh, were always preaching at
her mother, or pointing at her.

So on Sunday mornings when the church bells were ringing
across the Curragh, and the chapel-going women of the parish
were going by with their hymn-books in their handkerchiefs, and
old Will Skillicorne, who was a class-leader, was coming down
from his thatched cottage in his tall beaver, black frock coat and
black kid gloves, Bessie, in her sunbonnet and a pair of Dan's
old boots, and with her skirt tucked up over her linsey-wolsey petticoat, would be seen feeding the pigs or washing out a bowl of potatoes at the pump.

And on Sunday evenings, while the Primitives were singing a
hymn outside their chapel before going in for service, she would be
tripping past, lightly shod, and wearing a hat with an ostrich
feather, on her way to town, where a German band played sacred
music on the promenade, and young people, walking arm-in-arm,
laughed and " glimed " at each other under the gas-light.

" I wonder at herself though, bringing up her daughter like a
haythen in a Christian land," old Will would say. " But then
what can you expect from a child of sin and a son of Belial "—the
latter being a dig at Dan, whose lusty voice could always be heard
over the singing, reading aloud to himself in the kitchen the
" Rights of Man " or " The Mistakes of Moses."

Bessie was a full-developed and warm-blooded woman by this
time, living all day and every day in the natural world of the
farmyard, ready to break loose at the first touch of the hand of a
live man if only he were the right one, and having no better relief
for the fever of her womanhood than an occasional dance in the
big barn at Kirk Michael Fair.

But then came her adventure with Stowell and Gell in the glen
and it altered everything. Running down in her excitement she
told her mother what had happened, and her mother, in a moment
of tenderness, told Dan, and Dan, in the impurity of his heart,
drew his own conclusions.

" It's the Spaker's son again," he said, making a noise in
his nostrils.

The young men had camped out there expressly to meet Bessie,
and it wasn't the first time the girl had gone up to them.

" Goodness sakes, man veen, how do thou know that? And
what's the harm done anyway? " said Mrs. Collister.

" Wait and see what's the harm, woman. Girls is not to trust when a wastrel like that is about. We've known it before now haven't we?"

To one other person Bessie told the story of the glen, and that was her chief friend, Susie Stephen, the English barmaid at the Ginger Hall Inn—a girl of fair complexion and some good looks who had shocked the young wives of the parish by wearing short frocks, transparent stockings and a blouse cut low over the bosom

It was at closing-time a few nights after the event, and as the girls stood whispering together by the half-open door, with the lights put out in the bar behind them, they squealed with laughter laid hold of each other and shuddered.

The young men had gone from the glen by that time, but the August holidays were coming, so they decided to go up to Douglas on the Saturday following to dance off their excitement.

At five o'clock that day, having milked her cows, and given a drink of meal and water to her calves, Bessie was in her bedroom making ready for her journey.

It was a stuffy little one-eyed chamber over the dairy, entered from the first landing of the stairs, open to the whitewashed scraas (which gave it a turfy odour), having a skylight in the thatch, a truckle bed, a deal table for wash-stand and a few dried sheepskins on the floor for rugs.

Bessie threw off the big unlaced boots and the other garments of the cow-house, kicking the one into a corner and throwing the others in a disorderly mass on to the bed over her pink-and-white sunbonnet, washed to the waist and then folded her arms over each other in their warmth and roundness and laughed to herself in sheer joy of bounding health and conscious beauty.

While doing so she heard her step-father's voice in the kitchen below, loud as usual and as full of protest, but she had a matter of more moment to think of now—what to wear out of her scanty wardrobe.

The question was easily decided. After putting on white rubber shoes and white stockings, she drew aside a sheet on the wall that ran on a string and took down a white woollen skirt and a new cream-coloured blouse cut low at the neck like Susie's.

But the anchor of her hope was her hat, which she was to wear for the first time, having bought it the day before in Ramsey. It was shaped like a shell, with a round lip in front, and to find the proper angle for it on her head was a perplexing problem. So she stood long and twisted about before an unframed sheet of silvered glass which hung by a nail on the wall, with a lash comb in her hand a number of hat-pins across her mouth, while the floor creaked under her, and the conversation went on below.

She got it right at last, just tilted a little aside, to look pert and saucy, with her black hair, which was long and wavy, creeping up to it like a cushion. And then, standing off from her glass to look at it again over her shoulder, with eyes that danced with delight, she turned to the door and walked with a buoyant step downstairs.

III

Dan Baldromma also had made an engagement for that day, handbills having been distributed in Ramsey during the morning saying that " Mr. Daniel Collister of Baldromma " would deliver an address in the market-place at seven o'clock in the evening.

At five Dan had strapped down the lever which stopped the flow of water on to his overshot wheel and stepped into the dwelling-house, where Liza, his wife, had laid tea for two and was blowing up a fire of dry gorse to boil the kettle.

" Tell your girl to put a lil rub on my Sunday boots," he said.

" But she's upstairs dressing for Douglas," said Mrs. Collister.

" You don't say? " said Dan. " So that's the way she's earning her living? "

" Chut, man," said Mrs. Collister. " If a girl's in life she wants aisement sometimes, doesn't she? And her ragging and tearing to keep the farm going, and a big wash coming on next week, too."

" Well, that's good! That's rich! I thought it was myself that was keeping the farm going. Douglas, you say? Well, well! I wonder at you, encouraging your girl to go to such places, and you a bound Methodist. Tell her to put a rub on my boots, ma'am."

" I'll do it myself, Dan," said Mrs. Collister. " It's little enough time the girl will have to catch the train, and her fixing on her new hat, too."

" New hat, eh? "

" Aw, yes, man, the one she bought at Miss Corkill's yesterday."

" What a woman! And you telling me, when you got five goolden sovereigns out of me on Monday that she was for wearing it at the Sulby Anniversary. I wonder you are not afraid for your quarterly ticket."

" But it was only the girl's half year's wages, and the labourer is worthy of his hire. Thou art always saying so at the Cross anyway."

" Hould thy tongue, woman, and don't be milking that ould cow any more—it's dry, I tell thee."

It was at this moment that Bessie came downstairs, and Dan

who was on the three-legged stool before the fire, making wry faces as he dragged off his mill-boots with a boot-jack, fell on her at first with his favourite weapon, irony.

"Aw, the smart you are in your new hat, girl—smart tremenjous!"

"I didn't think you'd have the taste to like it," said Bessie, sitting at the table.

"Taste, is it?" said Dan. "Aw, the grand we are! The pride that's in some ones is extraordinary though. There'll be no holding you! You'll be going up and up! Your mother has always been used of a poor man's house and the wind above the thatch. But you'll be wanting feather beds and marble halls, I'm thinking."

"They won't be yours to find then, so you needn't worry," said Bessie.

"You think not? I'm not so sure of that. Man is born to trouble as the sparks fly upwards . . . . So you're for Douglas, are you?"

"Yes, I am, if you'll let me take my tea in time for the train."

"Aisy, bogh, aisy!" said Mrs. Collister.

"Well, you're your own woman now, so I suppose you've got lave to go," said Dan.

And then rising to his stockinged feet, his face hard and all his irony gone, he added, "But I'm my own man, too, and this is my own house, I'm thinking, and if you're not home for eleven o'clock to-night, my door will be shut on you."

Bessie leapt up from the table.

"Shut your door if you like. There'll be lots of ones to open theirs," she cried, and swept out of the house.

"There you are, woman!" said Dan. "What did I say? Imperent uncommon and dirty with the tongue! She'll have to clane it this time though. If she's not back for eleven she'll take the road and no more two words about it."

Mrs. Collister struggled to her feet and followed Bessie, pretending she had forgotten something.

"Bessie! Bessie!"

Bessie stopped at the end of the "street" and her mother hobbled up to her.

"Be home for eleven, bogh," she whispered. "It's freckened mortal I am that himself has some bad schame on."

"What schame?" asked Bessie.

"I don't know what, but something, so give him no chance."

"What do I care about his chance?"

"Aw, bolla veen, bolla veen, haven't I enough to bear with

thy father and thee? Catch the ten train back—promise me, promise me."

" Very well, I promise," said Bessie, and at the next moment she was gone.

Five minutes later, arm-in-arm with Susie, she was swinging down the road to the railway station for Douglas.

The little gay town, when they reached it, was at full tide, with pianos banging in the open-windowed houses, guitars twanging in the streets, and lines of young men marching along the pavements and singing in chorus. The girls, fresh from their twinkling village by the lonely hills, with the river burrowing under the darkness of the bridge, were almost dizzy with the sights and sounds.

When they came skipping down the steep streets to the front, and plunged into the electric light which illuminated the bay, they could scarcely restrain themselves from running. And when, bubbling with the animal life which had been suppressed, famished and starved in them, they passed through the turn-stile to the dancing-palace and hurried down the tunnel of trees, lit by coloured lamps, and saw the stream of white light which came from the open door, and heard the crash of the band and the drumming of the dancers within, their feet were scarcely touching the ground and they felt as if they wanted to fly. And when at last, having entered the hall, the whole blazing scene burst on them in a blinding flash, they drew up with a breathless gasp.

" Oh! Oh! "

One moment they stood by the door with blinking and sparkling eyes, their linked arms quivering in close grip. Then Bessie, who was the first to recover from the intoxicating shock, looked up and around, and saw Stowell and Gell sitting in the gallery.

" Good sakes alive," she whispered, " they're there! "

" Who? The gentlemen? "

" Yes, in the front row. Be quiet, girl. They see us. Don't look up. They might come down."

And then the girls laughed with glee at their conscious make-believe, and their arms quivered again to the rush of their warm blood.

IV

" Alick, isn't that our young friend of the glen? "

" Bessie Collister? Where? "

" Down there, standing with the fair girl, just inside the door."

" Well, yes, upon my word, I think it is! "

" I've a great mind to go down to them. Let us go."

" No? Really? In a place like this? "

" Why not, man? "

" Well, if you don't mind, I don't."

A few minutes later, in an interval between the dances, Victor, coming behind Bessie, touched her on the shoulder.

" How are those sweet-smelling heifers——still grazing on the mountains? "

Bessie, who had watched the young men coming downstairs, and felt them at her back, turned with a look of surprise, then laughed merrily and introduced Susie. For a few nervous moments there were the light nothings which at such times are the only wisdom. Then the violins began to flourish for another dance, and the two couples paired off—Victor with Bessie and Susie with Gell.

Victor took Bessie's hand with a certain delicacy to which she was quite unaccustomed and which flattered her greatly. The dance was a waltz, and she had never waltzed before, so they had to go carefully at first, but when the dance was coming to an end she was swinging to the rhythm of the orchestra as if she had waltzed a hundred times.

In the interval the two couples came together again, and there was much general chatter and laughter. Gell joined freely in both, and if at first he had had any backward thoughts of the promise he had given to his father they were gone by this time.

Another dance began and without changing partners they set off afresh, Stowell taking Bessie's hand with a firmer grasp and Bessie holding to his shoulder with a stronger sense of possession. His nerves were tingling. Turning round and round among women's smiling faces, and with Bessie's smiling face by his side, he had the sense of sweeping his partner along with an energy of physical power he had never felt before.

When the orchestra stopped the second time and they went in search of their companions, they discovered Susie on a seat, panting and perspiring, and Gell fanning her with the brim of his straw hat.

Victor's excitement was becoming feverish. He wanted Bessie to himself, and during the third dance he felt himself dragging her to the opposite side of the hall. She knew what he was doing, and found it enchanting to be carried off by sheer force.

When the dance came to an end Victor put Bessie's moist hand through his arm and walked up and down with her. Her throat was throbbing and her breast rising and falling under her low-cut blouse. They spoke little, but sometimes he turned his head to look at her, and then she turned her eyes to his. He thought her black eyes were looking blacker than ever.

The evening was now at its zenith, and the orchestra was tuning up for the " shadow-dance." The white lights on the walls went out, and over the arc lamps in the glass roof a number of coloured disks were passed, to throw shadows over the dancers, as of the sunrise, the sunset, the moon and the night with its stars. The dance itself was of a nondescript kind in which at intervals, the man, with a whoop, lifted his partner off her feet and swung her round him in his arms—a sort of symbol of marriage by capture.

When the shadow-dance ended there was much hand-clapping among the dancers. It had to be repeated, this time with a more rapid movement and to the accompaniment of a song, which, being sung by the men in chorus, made the hall throb like the inside of a drum. Many of the dancers fell out exhausted, but Victor and Bessie kept up to the last.

Then the big side doors were thrown open, and amid a babel of noise, cries and laughter, nearly all the dancers trooped out of the hall into the garden to cool. Victor gave his arm to Bessie and they went out also.

Lights gleamed here and there in the darkness of the trees, throwing shadows full of mystery and charm. After a while the orchestra within was heard beginning again, and most of the dancers hastened back to the hall, but Victor said,

" Let us stay out a little longer."

Bessie agreed and for some minutes more they wandered through the garden, in and out of the electric light, with the low murmur of the sea coming to them from the shore and the muffled music from the hall.

She was breathing deeply, and he was feeling a little dizzy. They found themselves talking in whispers, both in the Anglo-Manx, and then laughing nervously.

" Did you raelly, raelly see the young colts racing on the tops, though? "

" 'Deed no, not I, woman. But I belave in my heart I know who did."

" Who? "

" Why you! "

At that word, and the touch of his hand about her waist, she made a nervous laugh, and turned to him, her eyes closed, her lips parted and her white teeth showing, and they drew together in a long kiss.

At the next moment a clock struck coldly through the still air from the tower of a neighboring church and Bessie broke away.

"Gracious me, that must be ten o'clock. I have to catch the ten train home."

"You can't now. It's impossible," he said, and he tried to hold her.

"I must—I promised," she cried, and she bounded off. He called and followed a few steps, but she was gone.

Feeling like a torn wound he returned to the dancing-hall. The scene was the same as before but it seemed crude and tame and even dead to him now. Where was Gell? He must have gone to see the fair girl off by the ten train. He would come back presently.

Victor returned to the hotel. To compose his nerves while he waited he called for another half bottle of wine, and drank it, iced. The music was still murmuring in his ears. After a while it stopped; there were a few bars of the National Anthem, and then the pattering like rain of innumerable feet on the paved way from the dancing-hall to the promenade. It was now a few minutes to eleven, and remembering that that was the hour of the last train to the north he walked up to the station.

A noisy throng was on the platform, chiefly young Manx farming people of both sexes, returning to their homes in the country. The open third-class carriages were full of them, all talking and laughing together.

Victor walked down the line of the train and looked into each of the dim-lit carriages for Bessie, thinking it impossible that she could have caught the earlier one. Not finding her, he inquired if the ten train had left promptly and was told it had been half-an-hour late. She must have gone.

He got into an empty first-class compartment, folded his arms and closed his eyes and the train started. While it ran into the dark country the farming people, being unable to talk with comfort, sang. Over the rolling of the wheels their singing came in a dull roar, and when the train stopped at the wayside stations it went up in the sudden silence in a wild discord of male and female voices.

Victor was beginning to feel cold. He put up the window. His brain which had been blurred was becoming lucid. He recalled the scenes he had taken part in and some of them seemed to him now to have been crude and common and even a little vulgar. He thought of Bessie and felt ashamed.

When the train drew up at the station for the glen he turned his face from the direction of the mill, and to defeat a desire to look at it he opened the window at the other side of the carriage and put out his head.

The free air was refreshing to body and brain, but when his eyes had become accustomed to the darkness he saw the broad belt of the trees of Ballamoar. That brought a stabbing memory of Janet and the promise he had given her, and then of the Deemster and his conversation with the Governor.

He began to shiver, and to feel as if he were awakening from a fit of moral intoxication. To-morrow he would go home, and since he could not trust himself any longer, he would put himself out of the reach of temptation by living at Ballamoar in future.

When the train drew up at Ramsey it was half-past twelve. As he walked out of the quiet station into the echoing streets of the sleeping town he was drawing a deep breath and saying to himself:

" Thank God! "

It was all over.

CHAPTER NINE

THE MASTER OF MAN

DAN BALDROMMA's meeting in the market-place had not been the success he had expected. Standing on the steps of the town lamp, between the Saddle Inn and the Ship Store, he had discoursed on the rights of the labourer to the land he cultivated.

The Earth was the Lord's, and the fulness thereof. Therefore it could not belong to the big ones who were adding field to field— least of all to their wastrels of sons who were doing nothing but hang about the roads and the glens to ruin the daughters of decent men. The moral of this was that the land belonged to the people and the time was coming when they would pay no rent for it.

Dan's audience of Manx farmers had listened to this new gospel with Manx stolidity, but a group of young English visitors, clerks from the cotton factories, looking down from the balcony of the Saddle Inn, had received it with open derision.

Dan had ignored their opposition as long as possible, merely saying, when his audience laughed at their sallies,

" We must make allowance for some ones, comrades—children still, they've not been rocked enough."

But when at length they had called him Bradlaugh Junior and Ingersoll the Second and told him to keep his tongue off better men, Dan had looked up at the balcony and cried,

" If you're calling me by them honoured names I'm taking my hat off to you " (suiting the action to the word), " but if you're saying you are better men we'll be going into a back coort some-wheres and taking off our jackets and westcots."

6

To preserve the peace the police had had to put an end to the meeting, whereupon Dan, spitting contemptuously and snorting about " The Cottonies " and " the Cotton balls," had harnessed his horse at the Plough Inn and driven home in a dull rage.

It had been ten o'clock when he got back to Baldromma, and after unharnessing his horse in his undrained stable, and wiping his best boots with a wisp of straw, he had stepped round to the kitchen.

His wife was there, beating time on the hearthstone to a long-drawn Methodist hymn while she stirred the porridge in a pot that hung over a slow peat fire.

> " *Tell me the old, old story,* . . . .
> *Of Jesus and His love.*"

" Your daughter isn't back then? " said Dan with a growl.

" Be raisonable, man," said Mrs. Collister. " Eleven o'clock thou said, and it's only a piece after ten yet."

She poured out the porridge and hobbled to the dairy for a basin of milk, and then Dan, after a sour silence, sat down to his supper.

" They were telling me in Ramsey," he said, making noises with his spoon, " that the Spaker's son went up to Douglas to-day."

" Like enough! " said Mrs. Collister.

" I'll go bail your girl went up to meet him."

" Sakes alive, man veen, what for should thou be saying that? "

" She's fit enough for it anyway."

" But what has the girl done? Twenty-four years for Spring and not a man at her yet."

" Chut! Once they cut the cables that sort is the worst that's going. She'd be an angel itself though to stand up against a waistrel like yander."

" Bessie will be home for eleven," said Mrs. Collister.

" She'd better, or she'll find Dan Baldromma a man of his word, ma'am."

After that there was another sour silence in which both watched the open-faced clock whose pendulum swung by the wall. Tick, tick tick, said the clock. To the man it was going slowly, to the woman it seemed to fly. But hardly had the fingers pointed to eleven, or the chain begun to shake for the first stroke of the hour, when Dan was at the door, bolting and locking it.

" Will thou not give the girl a few minutes' grace, even? "

" Not half a minute."

" But the ten train hasn't whistled at the bridge yet."

" I've nothing to do with trains, Misthress Collister. Eleven o'clock, I said, and now it's eleven and better."

" But surely thou'll never shut thy door on a poor girl in the middle of the night? "

" There's others that's open to her—she said so herself, remember. She's not for coming home to-night, so take your candle and get to bed, woman."

" But the train must be late—I'll wait up myself for her."

" You might burn your candle to the snuff—she's not for coming, I tell you."

" But she promised me—faithfully promised me . . . . "

" Get to bed, ma'am. I wonder you're not thinking shame, making excuses for the bad doings of your by-child, and you a Methodist."

The woman was on the verge of tears.

" Shame enough it is, Dan Collister, when a mother has to shut her heart to her own child if she's not to show disrespect to her husband."

In the intimacy of the bedroom Dan threw off all disguise. Winding his silver-lever watch and hanging it with its Albert on a hook in the bed-post, and then sitting on the side of the bed to undress, he almost crowed over his prospects. That son of the Speaker would have to pay for his whistle this time! Baldromma would be his by heirship, and a father had a right to damages for the loss of the services of his daughter.

" There'll be no more rent going paying by me, I'm thinking," said Dan.

So that was his scheme! Mrs. Collister stood long in her cotton nightdress, fumbling with the strings of her night-cap, and wondering if she could ever lie down with the man again.

" Are you never for putting out that candle and coming to bed, woman? "

Half-an-hour passed and the mother lay still and listened. Dan was asleep by this time and breathing audibly, but there was no sound outside save the slipping of the water from the fixed wheel and the stamping of the horse in the stable. At last came the whistling of the train, and a few minutes later, Bessie's step on the " street " and then the rattling of the latch of the kitchen door.

Mrs. Collister tried to slip out of bed without awakening Dan, but her sciatica had made her limbs stiff and she knocked over the candlestick that stood on a chair beside her. This awakened her husband, and hearing the noise downstairs, he rolled out of bed, saying, in a threatening voice,

" Lie thou there—I'll settle her."

He went out to the stairhead, slamming the bedroom door behind him, threw up the sash of a window on the landing, and shouted into the darkness:

"Who's there?"

"Me, of course," cried Bessie.

A fierce altercation followed, in which Dan's voice was harsh and coarse, and Bessie's shrill with anger.

"Then find your bed where you've found your company," shouted Dan. And shutting down the window with a crash he returned to the bedroom.

The mother heard Bessie going off, and the fading sound of the girl's footsteps tore her terribly. But after a few minutes more Dan was making noise in his nostrils again and she got up and crept downstairs to the kitchen (where the dull red of the dying turf left just enough light to see by), slid the bolts back noiselessly, opened the door and called in a whisper:

"Bessie!"

No answer came back to her, so she stepped out to the end of the cobbled way, barefooted and in her nightdress and nightcap, and called again:

"Bessie! Bessie!"

Still there was no reply; so she returned to the kitchen, leaving the door on the latch, and sat for a long hour in a rocking chair by the hearth (souvenir of the days when Bessie was a child, and she had rocked her to sleep in it), fighting, in the misery of her heart, with the black thought which Dan had put there.

At length she remembered Susie and persuaded herself that Bessie must have gone to the Ginger Hall to sleep.

"Yes, Bessie must have gone to Susie."

Being comforted by this thought, and feeling cold, for the fire had gone out, she crept upstairs. It was hard to go by Bessie's room on the landing. Every night for years she had stopped there on her way to bed. And in the winter, when the wind in the trees in the glen made a roar like the sea, she had called through the closed door: "Art thou warm enough, Bessie, or will I bring thee my flannel petticoat?" And now the door was open and the room was empty!

Dan was still asleep when she got back to the bedroom and her approach did not awaken him, so she fumbled her way to the bed (knowing where she was when her feet touched the warm sheepskin that lay by the side of it) and then opened the clothes and crept in.

The cold air she brought with her awakened Dan, and he turned on the pillow and said,

" You've not been letting in that girl of yours, have you? "
" No! "

Dan made a grunt of satisfaction, and then said, with his face to the wall,

" Remember, you'll have to be up early to milk for yourself in the morning."

" Yes."

Then came a yawn, and then a snore, and then silence fell on the little house.

II

Bessie had run all the way to the station and then found that the train had nearly half-an-hour to wait for the passengers by the last of the day's steamers. The carriages were full of English visitors, but there were very few Manx people and she could not see Susie anywhere. This vexed her with the thought of having to tear herself away a good hour earlier than anybody else. It was all her mother's fault—getting her to make that ridiculous promise.

From such thoughts, as the train ran into the country, her mind swung back to the memory of Stowell. She recalled his looks, his smile, his whole person, and every word he had said to her down to the moment of that burning kiss.

What pleased her most was the certainty that he had never kissed a girl before. The trembling of his lips, when they were lip to lip, told her that. And in spite of all that had been said of him she was sure he had never had a woman in his arms until to-night—never ! "

And she?' Well, she had never before been kissed by a man. Alick Gell? She was only a child then. Kiss-in-the-ring at Michael Fair? Chut! A girl felt that no more than the wind blowing over her bare cheek.

By the clocks at the wayside stations she saw she was going to be late getting home, but she didn't care. Dan Baldromma wasn't fool enough to shut her out. But let him if he liked to! Where would he go to get another girl to work for her wages— summer and winter, as if the creatures had been her own, up all hours calving, and out before the dawn in the lambing season, when the hoar-frost was on the fields?

It was twenty minutes past eleven when she got down at the glen station, and there was Susie getting down also! Susie was in the sulks. Not only had Bessie deliberately lost her in the dancing-hall, but after she had hurried away to catch the ten train, knowing Bessie had promised to return by it, she had had to come back alone!

This added to Bessie's vexation, and when she reached the house, and found the door locked on her, it expressed itself in her hand when she rattled the kitchen latch.

Then came the scene with Dan Baldromma who shouted down at her from the upper window as if she had been a thief—it was suffocating! And when he said, " Find your bed where you've found your company," and banged down the sash on her, she flung away, crying, as well as she could for the anger that was choking her,

" So I will, and you'll be sorry for it some day."

At that moment she meant to sleep with Susie at the Ginger Hall Inn, and offer herself next day to one or other of the farmers who had so often asked for her. But she had not gone many steps before she reflected that all the farmers' houses would be full now and nobody could take her in until Michaelmas.

No matter! She might have been no better off. Those old farmers were all the same. If it wasn't the bullying of brutes like Dan Baldromma it was the meanness of old hypocrites like Teare of Lezayre, who laid foundation stones, and put purses of money on top of them, and then went home and gave his girls cold potatoes and salt herrings for supper!

That made her think of young Willie Teare. She had met him in Ramsey the day before, when he had said he was tired of slaving for his father, and meant to set up in a farm for himself as soon as he could find the right wife. But no thank you, no marrying with a farmer for her! After a woman had worn herself to the bone, keeping things together and gathering the stock, and she was doubled up with sciatica, and ought to be in bed, with some-body to wait on her, the husband was nagging and ragging her from morning to night. That was marriage! Hadn't she seen enough of it?

Bessie had reached the Ginger Hall by this time, and, seeing a light in Susie's window, she was about to call up when (with Dan's insult ' Find your bed, etc.' still rankling in her mind) a startling thought seized her and made her heart leap and the hot blood to rush through and through her. There was one way to escape from Dan Baldromma and his tyrannies—Mr. Stowell!

Mr. Stowell would return by the last train to Ramsey, having bachelor rooms there, in which he lived alone—so people were saying. If she were to meet him on his arrival and tell him what had happened he would find some way out for her. Of course he would! She was sure he would!

Ashamed? Why should she be? People had said all they

could say about a girl like her while she was a baby in arms, and who was there to say anything now?

And then Mr. Stowell wouldn't care either. He was rich, therefore he had no need to be afraid of anybody. And if he were fond of a girl he would stand up for her and defy the whole island —that was the sort of young man he was!

The last train could not reach Ramsey before midnight, and it might be later. It was only half-past eleven yet. There was still time. Why shouldn't she?

" ' Find your bed,' indeed! We'll see! We'll see! "

Three-quarters of an hour later she was approaching Ramsey. The stars had gone out; the night was becoming gloomy; she was tired and her spirit of defiance was breaking down under a chilling thought. What if Mr. Stowell did not want her? It was one thing for a young man to amuse himself with a girl in the glen or in a dancing-hall, but to become responsible for her . . . .

" If he felt like that and found me in Ramsey what would he think? "

Afraid and ashamed she was slowing down with the thought of returning to the Ginger Hall when she heard the train whistle behind her, and looking back, saw its fiery head forging through the darkness. That sent the hot blood bounding to her heart again, and within a few minutes she was walking slowly down the main street of the town, which was all shut up and silent.

She knew where Mr. Stowell's rooms were—in Old Post Office Place—and that he would have to come this way to get to them. She heard the train drawing up in the station, the passengers trooping out, parting in the square and shouting their good-nights as they went off by the streets to the north and south. One group was coming behind, on the other side of the way, laughing over something they had seen at a place of entertainment. They passed and turned down a side street and the echo of their voices died away at the back of the houses.

Then came a few moments of sickening silence. Bessie, as she walked on, could hear nothing more, and another chilling thought came to her. What if Mr. Stowell had not returned by the train and were sleeping the night in Douglas?

All her courage and defiance ebbed away, and she saw herself for the first time as she was—a miserable girl, cast out of her step-father's house, in which she had worked so hard but in which nothing belonged to her, homeless, penniless (for she had spent her half-year's wages on her clothes) without a shelter, in the middle of the night, alone!

It was beginning to rain and Bessie was crying. All at once

she heard a firm step behind her. It was he! She was sure of it! Her heart again beat high and all her nerves began to tingle. He was overtaking her. She turned her head aside and wiped her eyes. He was walking beside her. She could hear his breathing.

" Bessie! "

" Mr. Stowell! "

" Good gracious, girl, what are you doing here? "

And then she told him.

III

" The brute! The beast! Did you tell him your train was late? "

" No. He ought to have known that for himself."

" So he ought. You are quite right there, Bessie. But didn't your mother . . . . "

" Mother is afraid of her life of the man. She daren't say anything."

" Was there any other house he might have thought you would go to—any neighbour's, any relation's? "

" I have no relations, Sir."

" Ah! . . . . Then he deliberately shut you out of his house in the middle of the night, knowing you had nowhere else to go to? "

" Yes! "

" The damned scoundrel! "

Bessie, who had been crying again, was looking up at him with wet but shining eyes.

" Well, what are you going to do now? Do you know anybody in town who can take you in for to-night? "

" No."

" Then I must knock up one of the Inns for you. Here's the old Plough—what do you say to the Plough? "

" Dan Baldromma goes there—Mrs. Beatty would get into trouble."

" The Saddle then? "

" I go there myself, every market-day, with butter and eggs—people would be talking."

There was only the Mitre Hotel left, and Stowell himself shrank from that. To go to the Mitre with a girl at this time of night would be like shouting into the mouth of a megaphone. Within twenty-four hours the whole town would hear the story, with every explanation except the right one.

" But, good heavens, girl, I can't go home and go to bed and leave you to walk about in the streets."

" I'll do whatever you think best, Sir," said Bessie, crying again and stammering.

They were at the corner of Old Post Office Place by this time, and, after a moment's hesitation, he took the girl's hand and drew it through his arm and then turned quickly in the opposite direction, saying:

" Come, then, let us think."

It was still raining but Stowell was scarcely aware of that. With the girl walking close by his side he was only conscious of a return of the faint dizziness he had felt in the garden at Douglas. To conquer this and to keep up his indignation about Dan Baldromma, while they walked round the square of streets, he asked what the man had said when he finally shut down the window.

" He said I was to find my bed where I had found my company," said Bessie, stammering again and with her head down.

" Meaning that you had been in *bad* company? "

" Yes."

" The foul-minded ruffian! "

His nerves were quivering, and he knew that the hot tide of his indignation was ebbing rapidly. Suddenly an idea came to him and he felt an immense relief—Mrs. Quayle! She was a good, religious woman, who had seen sorrow herself, and that was the best kind to go to in a time of trouble. She would take Bessie in for to-night, and to-morrow they would all three go back together to Baldromma, and then—then he would tell that old blackguard what he thought of him.

" That's it, Bessie! I wonder why in the world I didn't think of it before? "

Bessie was answering " Yes " and " Yes," but her beaming eyes were looking sideways up at him, and the blood was pounding through his body with a rush.

They had got back to the corner of Old Post Office Place when Stowell stopped and said:

" Wait! Mrs. Quayle's house is rather a long way off—one of the little fishermen's cottages on the south beach, you know. I'm not quite sure that she has a second bed. And then she might be alarmed if two of us turned up at this time of night. What if I run over first and make sure? "

Again Bessie answered " Yes " and " Yes."

" But it's raining heavily now, and, of course, you can't stay out in the streets any longer. Here are my rooms—just here. Why shouldn't you step in and wait? I shall have to go upstairs for an overcoat anyway."

Bessie showed no embarrassment, and Victor felt at first that what he was doing was something a little courageous and rather noble. But as soon as they reached the door, and he began to fumble with his key to open it, he became nervous and a voice within him seemed to say, " Take care! "

" Come in," he said bravely, but when Bessie brushed him on entering the house he trembled, and from that moment onwards he was conscious of a struggle between his blood and his brain.

As he was closing the door on the inside he saw that there was a letter in the letter-box at the back of it, but he left it there, and held out his hand to Bessie to guide her up the stairs, saying:

" It's dark here. Give me your hand. Now come this way. Don't be afraid. You shan't fall. I'll take care of you."

There were two short flights and then a landing, from which a door opened on either side—on the right to Victor's offices, on the left to his living-rooms. He opened the door on the left, leaving Bessie to stand on the landing until he had found matches and lit the gas.

He was long in finding them, and while rummaging in the dark room he heard the girl's quick breathing behind him.

" Ah, here they are at last! " he cried in a tremulous voice, and then he lit up a branch under a white globe on one side of the mantelpiece.

" Now you can come in," he said, and turning to the window he loosened the cord of the Venetian blind and it came clattering down.

Bessie stepped into the room. It was a warm and cosy chamber, with a thick Persian carpet, two easy chairs, an open bookcase full of law books, a desk-table with ink-stand, writing-pad and reading-lamp (looking so orderly as to suggest that no work was done there) and a large pier-glass with a small bust of a pretty Neapolitan girl and a little silver-cased clock in front of it. The clock was striking one.

" One o'clock! It was stupid to stay out in the streets so long, wasn't it? "

" Yes."

" Your hat is dripping. Hadn't you better take it off for the few minutes you'll have to stay? "

" Should I? "

" Do; and I'll light the gas-fire—a bachelor has to have gas-fires, you know."

While he was down on his knees lighting the fire, and regulating its burning from blue to red, Bessie, with trembling fingers, was drawing the pins out of her hat—the wonderful new hat of a few hours ago, now wet and bedraggled. In doing so she pulled down her hair and made a faint cry,

" Oh! "

" Don't mind that at this time of night," said Victor. But at sight of the girl's face, now framed in its shower of waving black hair, his nervousness increased. He had always thought her a good-looking girl, but he had never known before that she was beautiful.

" My coat is wet, too. I must change it," he said, getting up and going towards his bedroom door. " It would be foolish to put an overcoat over a wet jacket, wouldn't it? "

" Yes."

" But your blouse seems to be soaking. Why shouldn't you take it off and dry it at the fire while I'm away at Mrs. Quayle's? "

" Should I? "

" Why not? "

While he was in the inner room, opening and closing his wardrobe, and changing his wet coat for a dry one, he kept on talking. Mrs. Quayle was a good creature who had lost her husband in that January gale a few years ago. She would take Bessie in—he was sure she would. But this was only to drown the clamour of two voices within himself, one of which was saying, " Must you go? " and the other " Certainly you must! Be a man and play the game, for God's sake."

When he returned to the sitting-room the breath was almost smitten out of his body by what he saw. Bessie had taken off her blouse, and was kneeling by the fire to dry it. She did not raise her eyes to his, and after a first glance he did not look at her. Opening the outer door to the landing, where the hat-rail stood, he pulled on a cap and dragged on an ulster, saying, in a nervous voice,

" It's only a hop-skip-and-a-jump to Mrs. Quayle's. I shall be back presently."

Suddenly there came a flash of lightning which lit up the dark bedroom, and then a clap of thunder, loud and long, which rattled the window frames.

" It would be foolish to go out in a storm like that, wouldn't it? " he said.

" 'Deed it would," said Bessie. She had risen with a start, but now she knelt again and held her steaming blouse before the fire.

Stowell took off his cap and ulster and dropped them on to a chair. Then he walked about the room, trying to keep his eyes from the girl, and to fill the difficult silence by talking on indifferent subjects—other storms he had seen in other countries.

After a while the thunder went off in the direction of Ireland, its echo becoming fainter and fainter in the sonority of the sea.

" It's gone—now I can go," he said.

But hardly had he taken up his cap again when the rain, which had ceased for a moment, came in a sudden torrent.

"Only a thunder shower—it will soon be over," he said.

But the rain went on and on. Good Lord, were the very forces of nature conspiring to keep him there all night?

It was half-past one by the clock on the mantelpiece, and the rain was still pelting on the pavement of the street outside with a sound like that of an army in retreat. Stowell was feeling alternately hot and cold, and the voice within him was saying, "Must you go? You would be drenched through before you got back from Mrs. Quayle's, and the girl would be as wet in getting there as if you had dropped her into the sea." After a few minutes more he said,

"Bessie, I'm afraid we shall have to give up the idea of going to Mrs. Quayle's."

"Yes?"

"But you can stay here, and I can go over to the Mitre."

"No, no."

"It's nothing—only two yards away."

Johnny Kelly, the boots, slept on the ground floor—he could get him up without ringing the bell. Of course he would have to tell the old man some cock-and-bull story—that he had lost his key or something.

"But it's the very thing. I wonder I didn't think of it before."

He half hoped and half feared she might make some further protest. But she did not, so he picked up his cap and ulster and was making for the door when he thought of the gas. Would Bessie, who had been brought up in a thatched cottage, know how to put it out?

"Well, no, no," she stammered.

"It's quite simple. You turn the tap, so . . . . ."

He had to kneel by her side to show her, and he was feeling the warm glow he had felt in the glen.

"But not being used of it . . . . ."

"Then I know—the reading-lamp!"

He leapt up to light it, and having done so, he turned out the branch under the white globe, saying, with a laugh, it was lucky he had thought of the lamp, for if old Johnny had seen the light in the window the story of the key would have sounded thin, wouldn't it?

Then she laughed too, and they laughed together, but their laughter broke into a sharp and breathless silence.

He carried the lamp into the bedroom, put it on the table by the bedside and then pulled down the white window-blind, breaking the cord by the tug of his trembling fingers. He was feeling as if another storm, a storm of emotions, were now thundering within him. " Must you go? " " You must! You shall! Good Lord, could a man of any conscience . . . . Never! Never! "

When he returned to the sitting-room Bessie had risen to her feet. She was standing at the opposite side of the mantelpiece and the intoxicating red light of the fire was over her. Stowell thought he had never seen anything so beautiful. But he could not trust himself to look twice.

" You'll be all right here, Bessie," he said, in a loud voice, snatching up his coat and cap and making for the door. " You can let yourself out of the house as early as you like in the morning; and if you decide to go back to that damned old devil at Baldromma you can tell him from me where you passed the night, and I'll stand up for you—why shouldn't I? "

Then he heard a breathless cry behind him, and then the words, " Must you go? "

He stopped and turned. Was it Bessie who had spoken? She had taken a step towards him, was breathing irregularly and looking at him with gleaming eyes.

He felt as if the floor were rocking under his feet, as if the walls were reeling round him, as if he were seeing the face of woman for the first time.

At the next moment they were clasped in each other's arms.

CHAPTER TEN

THE CALL OF THE BALLAMOARS

" WHAT a mistake! What a hideous blunder! "

Stowell, who had slept little, was awakening as from a bad dream. A dull lead-coloured light was filtering through the white window-blind.

He could not help seeing it—Bessie was not as pretty as he had thought. There was something common about her beauty when she was asleep which had been effaced by her eyes while she was awake.

Ashamed to look any longer he stepped into the sitting-room. A close odour hung in the air. The gas fire was still burning, and Bessie's blouse was lying, where she had flung it, on the floor. With a sense of moral and physical suffocation, he went downstairs and out into the streets.

The morning was fine and the dawn was breaking, but the town was still asleep. So great was the upheaval within himself that in some vague way he expected everything to look changed. But no, everything was the same—the shops, the signs, the lamps, which had not yet been put out. There was no sound except that of his own footsteps on the pavement, and to deaden this he walked in the middle of the streets.

He wanted to be alone, to leave the town behind him. Turning northward he crossed the harbour bridge and made for the red pier which stood out into the bay with a light-house at the end of it.

The tide hummed far off on the shore. It was the bottom of the ebb. Trading schooners were lying half on their sides in the mud. Seagulls were calling over it. Sand, slime, sea-wrack and the broken refuse of the town lay uncovered at the harbour's mouth, and the last draught of the ebbing water was playing about them with a guttural sound.

When he came to the light-house he saw that some fragments of stone and glass were lying about, but his mind was too confused to ask itself what had happened. He sat down on the light-house steps, looked down into the harbour-basin and tried to think.

Good Lord, what a fool he had been! To ask the girl into his rooms, being who and what she was, alone, in the middle of the night, just after he had formed the resolution to go home and put himself out of the reach of temptation . . . . what a fool!

He thought of the stories people had told of him and how he had justified the very ugliest and worst of them . . . . what a fool!

He remembered what he had said to Janet, that no girl on the island or in the world had ever come to any harm through him, or ever should. That was only a little while ago and now . . . . what a fool!

He recalled the white heat of his indignation against Dan Baldromma for what he had done to his step-daughter. That was only last night, and now he himself . . . . what a fool! What a fool!

Then the sense of his folly gave way to a sense of shame. Down to yesterday he had lived a decent life. Reckless, heedless, careless, stupid perhaps, but decent anyway. And now . . . . what shame!

The light was then clearing, and raising his eyes he saw on the south beach a one-story fisherman's cottage from which the smoke was rising. It was Mrs. Quayle's cottage. She was making her early breakfast, and presently she would go to his room to make his. He shuddered at a vision of what she would find there —the close air, the gas fire, the girl's blouse on the floor, the girl herself . . . . how degrading it all was!

He saw Dan Baldromma ferreting out the facts (as of course he would, having to find excuses for his own barbarity), and then blazoning them abroad to his own disgrace and the discredit of his class. Or worse—a hundredfold worse—holding them as a threat over his father. What a disgusting bog he had strayed into!

He saw the truth leaking out one way or other and putting an end to his career at the bar. It was not the same here as in the greater communities, where a man might commit a fault and then submerge it in the fathomless tide of life. In this little island, where everybody knew everybody, it was the man himself who was submerged.

If the story of last night became known to anyone it would become known to everyone, from the Governor himself to the meanest beggar on the roads. No position of honour or authority would ever be possible to him after that. The black fact would be a clanking chain which he would have to drag after him as long as he lived.

When he thought of this—that the event of one night might alter the whole course of his life, and bring scandal upon the Deemster, and that it was due to a miserable accident in the first instance—the accident of meeting Bessie on the streets after midnight—he was filled with a fierce and consuming rage, and for one bad moment he had an almost uncontrollable desire to return to his rooms and drive her out of them.

That horrified him. He hated himself for it, and after a while his self-pity gave place to pity for the girl.

" Good heavens, what are my risks compared to hers? " he asked himself.

The poor girl had so many excuses. Back in the past, before she was born even, she had been condemned and branded, and the damned hypocritical world had been deepening the injury every day since. If he had found her in the streets it was only because her brutal step-father had turned her from his door. And if she had come into his rooms it was because she had no other shelter.

She had been a good girl too. No other man had been allowed to lead her astray. He could hear her voice still, repeating his own words after him: " You *will* stand up for me, won't you? " and he had promised that he would. He could not cast her off now without being a scoundrel. Could the son of Deemster Stowell be a scoundrel? "

" No, by God! "

A few minutes later he saw himself going back to Bessie and saying, " Look here, my dear girl. It was neither your fault nor mine, but take this, and this, and remember if you ever find it is not enough, there'll be more where that comes from."

But no, he could not do that either. If he made the girl take money he would put her in the position of a harlot; and once a woman accepted that position there was no bottom to the unguessed depths to which she might descend.

Bessie's future stood up before him like a spectre. Other men, each more brutal than the last, quarrels, violence, all the miseries of such a life—until some day, perhaps, some hideous fact with which he had had nothing to do, would look at him with accusing eyes and say,

" *You* are responsible for this, because you were the first."

Down to that moment he had been thinking of the event of last night as a blunder, but now he saw it as a crime. To prevent the possible consequences of that crime he must keep the girl with him, take care of her, protect her as the saying was.

But no, that was impossible also. Justification for such a relation there might be—no doubt was—where law or custom or other impediment were keeping apart a man and woman who belonged together. But to put a girl into the position of a mistress, because she was unworthy to be a wife, and to hide her away behind a curtain of duplicity and lies, was to destroy her body and soul.

Again Bessie's future stood up before him as a spectre—that high-spirited girl who, but for him, might have married a decent man of her own class, and held her head proud, declining, after a few vain months of fine clothes and idleness, to the condition of a slattern, and going down to the dirt and degeneration of drink.

And then he saw that what had happened last night was not merely a crime—it was a sin.

But what was he to do? What? What?

Just at that moment the sun had come up out of the sea in crimsoning clouds, and the white mist that is the shroud of night had risen above the houses of the town, the steeples of the churches, the hills and the mountain tops, and was vanishing away in that new birth of morning light that is the world's daily resurrection.

" I know! I know! " he thought, and he leapt to his feet.

He had remembered something that Janet had said about the men of his family—that it had always been a kind of religion with them to do the right. Four hundred years of the Ballamoars and not a stain on the name of any of them! That was something to be born to, wasn't it? It was worth all the titles and honours the world had in it.

And then, in that moment of strange and solemn splendour, when the things of the other world appear to be as real as the things of this one, it seemed as if the Ballamoars were calling to him! Four hundred years of the dead Ballamoars were calling to the last of their sons—" *Do the right!* "

" I must marry that girl," he told himself.

But at the next moment there came, with the shock of a blow, the memory of his mother.

Marriage had always been associated in his mind with such different conditions. Such a different woman; somebody who would be your equal, perhaps your superior; somebody who would sustain and inspire you; somebody who would help you feel the throbbing pulse of life, and listen to all the suffering hearts that beat; somebody who, if she had to go before you, would leave behind her, for as long as your life should last, the fragrance of flowers and the halo of a holy saint.

That was marriage as he had always thought of it. And now this girl—illiterate, inadequate, with that mother, that father . . . . in the presence of the Deemster . . . . the home of Isobel Stanley . . . . Oh, God!

Then a mocking voice seemed to say,

" Good Lord, what a joke! If every man who ever made a tragic blunder (there have been hundreds of thousands of you) had acted on your exaggerated sense of responsibility, what a mess the old world would be in by this time! Why, there is scarcely a man alive who would not laugh at you and call you a fool."

" Let them," he thought, for louder at that moment than any other voice was the voice that cried,

" *Do the right!* "

The marriage need not take place immediately. Bessie could be educated. She was bright; there was no saying how quickly she might develop. That would soften the blow to his father, And anyhow the Deemster would see that he was trying to be true to his blood, his race.

" Yes, yes, I must do the right; whatever it may cost me."

But then came another chilling thought. Love! There could be no love in such a marriage. This brought, with the pain of a bleeding wound, the memory of Fenella.

In spite of all he had said to himself through so many years he had never really been reconciled to the loss of her. Down in some dark and secret chamber of his consciousness there had always been a phantom hope that notwithstanding her devotion to her work for women, and the dedication to celibacy (as stern as the consecration of the veil) which she believed to be demanded by it, Fenella would return to the island, and his great love would be rewarded.

7

That had been the real cause of his idleness. He had been waiting, waiting, waiting for Fenella to come back and make it worth while . . . . and now . . . . by his own act . . . . the consequences of it . . . . Oh, God! Oh, God!

For the first time, save once since he was a child, he felt tears in his eyes, but he brushed them away impatiently.

" It's too late to think of that now," he thought.

A duty claimed him. He must put such dreams away. Besides where was the merit of doing the right if you had not to sacrifice something? Love might be the light of life, but men and women all the world over had for one reason or other to marry without it. Millions of hearts in all ages were like old battlefields. with dead things, which nobody knew of, lying about in the dark places. And yet the world went on.

He might have struggles, heart-aches, heart-hunger, and more than he could do to keep the pot boiling, with the fire out and the hearth cold, but nobody need know anything about that. This girl need never know. Fenella need never know. Nobody need know. It was a matter for himself only.

" Yes, yes, I must do the right," he kept on saying, " whatever it may cost me."

Having arrived at this decision he felt an immense relief and got up to go back.

The windows of the town were reflecting the morning sun and the smoke was rising from the chimneys. He saw an elderly woman, with a little shawl pinned over her head and under her chin, trudging along past the storm-cone station on the other side of the harbour. It was Mrs. Quayle, on her way to his rooms. But he shuddered no longer at the thought of her. She was a good creature and when she heard what he meant to do she would help him with the care of Bessie.

As he walked towards the town he told himself he had another reason now for setting to work in earnest—he had to justify what he was going to do in the eyes of the island and of the Deemster. Therefore the event of last night might be a good thing after all, little as he had thought so.

At the mouth of the bridge he met the harbour-master, whose face wore a look of dismay.

" This is a ter'ble shocking thing that has happened in the night, Mr. Stowell."

Stowell caught his breath and asked " What? "

" Why, the light-house. Struck by lightning in the storm. Didn't you see it, Sir? "

" Oh yes, of course, certainly."

" I'm just after telegraphing to the Governor and the Receiver-General. The old light has gone out with the tide, Sir, and it will be middlin' bad for the boats coming in at night until we get a new one."

" It will, Captain, it will. Good-morning! "

His eyes were positively shining with joy as he walked sharply through the town, and as he opened his door he was saying to himself again,

" I must do the right, *whatever* it may cost me."

He was closing the door on the inside when he saw in the letter-box the letter which had caught his eye last night. Now he could open it.

It was marked " Immediate." Recognising the Ballamoar crest and Janet's handwriting, he trembled and turned pale.

> " A line in frantic haste, dear, to say I have just heard from Miss Green that Fenella is crossing by the steamer due to arrive at eight o'clock this evening. She has left her Settlement and is coming back to stay in the island for good. I thought you might like to go up to Douglas to meet her. Trust me, dear, she will be simply delighted.
>
> " Robbie Creer is taking this into town by hand, so that you may receive it at the earliest possible moment. I am frightfully excited, and oh, so glad and happy."

Stowell reeled and laid hold of the hand-rail. And when at length he went upstairs he staggered as if he were carrying a crushing load.

END OF FIRST BOOK

SECOND BOOK
THE RECKONING

CHAPTER ELEVEN

THE RETURN OF FENELLA

" Fate has played me a scurvy trick," thought Stowell. " No matter! I'll go on."

Within an hour he settled Bessie Collister temporarily with Mrs. Quayle. He told her they were to be married ultimately, but meantime (that she might feel more comfortable in her new condition) he intended to find some suitable place in which she would complete her education.

He tried to say this tenderly so as not to hurt the girl's pride, and even affectionately, so as to convey the idea that it was she who would be doing the favour. But a certain shallowness in Bessie's nature disappointed him. While he unfolded his plans she said " Yes " and " yes," looking alternately surprised and startled, but it was with a troubled face, rather than a glad one, that she went off with Mrs. Quayle, whose own face was grave also.

Two days later Stowell went up to see Gell. He had determined to say nothing about his intimate relations with Bessie. Why should he? If it was his duty to marry the girl, it was equally his duty to protect her honour—the honour of the woman who was to become his wife.

Gell was astounded. He listened, with a twinkling eye, to Stowell's story of how he had come upon Bessie in the street, after midnight, friendless and homeless, being shut out by her abominable father, and how he had taken her to Mrs. Quayle's. But when Stowell went on to say that, feeling a certain responsibility for the girl's misfortune, having been a principal cause of it (by keeping her out too late at night) and having seen something of her since, he had come to like and even to love her, and had made up his mind to marry her, Gell broke into exclamations of astonishment which cut Stowell to the quick.

" But Bessie? Bessie Collister? Do you really mean it? "

" Why not? "

" Well . . . . it is not for me to say why not. She was a sort of old flame of my own, you know."

100

Stowell flinched at this, but went on with his story. For Bessie's sake he had decided to put back the marriage until she could be educated a little. And if Gell knew of any school, not too well known, and far enough away . . . .

"Why, yes, of course I do," said Gell.

It was that of the Misses Brown at Derby Haven—a remote village at the south of the island. Two old maids who had formerly been governesses to his sisters. Only yesterday the elder of them had written asking if there was anything he could put in her way. It looked like the very thing. At all events he would go down and see. And if Stowell wished to keep things quiet for a while, as of course he would, if it was only for the sake of the Deemster, he was ready to act as go-between.

"What a good fellow you are, Alick!"

"Not a bit! It's no more than you would have done for me—less than you've done already."

Next day Stowell had a letter from Gell saying he had arranged everything. The Misses Brown, who had no other pupil at present, would be only too delighted. Bessie might be sent up at any time and he would see her to her destination.

Within a week the girl was despatched to Douglas, with such belongings as Mrs. Quayle had bought for her, and in due course Stowell had a second letter from Gell, saying,

"It's all right. I've delivered the goods! Of course I made no unnecessary explanations, and old Miss Brown, smelling a secret, thinks *I* am to be the happy man. What larks! But I don't mind if you don't. Bessie looked a little wistful when I came away, so I had to promise to run down and see her sometimes. That's all right, I suppose?"

Then Stowell set to work. Letting it be known that he was willing to accept cases of all kinds it was not long before he was fully occupied. Common assault, drunkenness, petty larceny—he took anything and everything that came his way. He did his work well. In a little while people began to whisper that he was a chip of the old block and to employ the Deemster's son was to ensure success.

Meantime he saw nothing of Fenella. Having made up his mind to do the right thing he tried his best to banish all thought of her. But everybody was talking of the Governor's daughter. She was beautiful; she was charming; she was wonderful! Oh, the joy of it all! But the pain and the misery of it, also!

One day he met Janet driving in the street, and after she had asked if he had received her letter, and he had answered no, it had arrived too late. she said.

"But of course you'll call, dear.   I'm sure she'll expect it."

The Governor sent out invitations to a garden-party in honour of his daughter's return home, but Stowell excused himself on the ground of urgent work.   A little later Fenella herself issued invitations to a meeting towards the establishment of a League for the Protection of Women, but again Stowell excused himself—a case in the Courts.

Still later he went out to Ballamoar to see his father, whom he had neglected of late, and the Deemster (who looked older and feebler and had a duller light in his great but melancholy eyes) flamed up with a kind of youth when he talked of Fenella.

"It's extraordinary," he said.   "Do you know, Victor, she is the only woman I have ever met who has reminded me of your mother?   And if I close my eyes when she is speaking, I can almost persuade myself it is the same."

Stowell began to think he hated the very name of Fenella. But there were moments when he felt that he could have given the whole world, if he had possessed it, just to look upon her face.

One day Gell came to "report progress" about Bessie.   She was getting on all right, but "longing" a little in those unaccustomed surroundings, so he had to go down in the evenings sometimes to take her out for walks.

"We'll have to be careful about that, though," he said, "for what do you think?"

"What?"

"Dan Baldromma suspects *me,* and is having me watched."

Stowell was startled and ashamed.   Where had his head been that he had not thought of this before?   He had got up from his desk and was looking vacantly out of the window when he became aware that the Governor's big blue landau was drawing up in the street below.

At the next moment there was a light step on the stairs, and at the next the door of his room was opened by his young clerk, and through the doorway came someone who was like a vision from a thousand of his dreams, but now grown in her stately height out of the beauty of a bewitching girl into the full bloom of womanly loveliness.

It was Fenella Stanley.

II

"You wouldn't come to see me, so I've come to see you."

Stowell never knew what answer he made when he took her outstretched hand: but after a moment he said.

" You know my friend Gell? "

" Indeed I do . . . . And how's Isabella? . . . . And Adelaide? . . . . And Verbena? "

While Fenella was talking to Gell, Stowell had time to look at her. She was the most beautiful woman in the world! Those dark eyes, beaming with bluish opal; those lips like an opening rose; that spacious forehead, with its brown hair shot with gold— they had not told him the half.

Gell made shift to answer for the sisters he had not seen for months, and then went off.

And then Fenella, taking the chair that Stowell had set for her, and dropping her voice to a deeper note, said,

" And now to business. You know we've established on the island a branch of the Women's Protection League? "

" I know."

" One of its objects is to protect women from the law."

" The law? "

" Yes, sir, the law," said Fenella smiling. " Your law can be very cruel sometimes—especially to women. But our first case is not one of that kind. It is a case in which the law, if rightly guided, can best do justice by showing mercy."

A young wife in Castletown had killed her husband. She had already appeared at the High Bailiff's Court and been committed for trial to the Court of General Gaol Delivery—the Manx Court of Assize.

" There seems to be no question of her guilt," said Fenella, " so we can neither expect nor desire that she should escape punishment altogether. The poor thing—she's scarcely more than a girl —will say nothing in self-defence, but when we remember how the soul of a woman shrinks from a crime of that kind we feel that she must have suffered some great injustice, some secret wrong, which, if it could be brought out in Court . . . . "

" I see," said Stowell.

Fenella paused a moment and then said, in a voice that was becoming tremulous,

" Therefore we have thought that for this case we need an advocate who loves women as women and can see into the heart of a woman when she's down and done, because God has made him so. And that's why. . . ."

" Yes? "

" That's why I've brought this first case to you."

Stowell could scarcely speak to answer her. But after a moment he stammered that he would do his utmost; and then

Fenella brought out of her hand-bag some printed papers that were a report of the preliminary inquiry.

" I'll read them to-night," he said, putting them into his breast pocket.

" Of course you'll require to see the prisoner? "

" Yes."

" She hasn't opened her lips yet, but you must get her to speak."

" I'll try."

" That's all for the present," said Fenella, rising; and at the next moment she was smiling again, and her eyes were beginning to glow.

" So this is where you live? "

" No, this is my office; I live at the other side of the house."

" Really? I wonder . . . . "

" You would like to see my living rooms? "

" I'd love to. I've always wanted to see how young bachelors live alone."

" Come this way then."

Stowell had not realised what he was doing for himself until he was on the landing, with the key in the lock, and Fenella behind him, but then came a stabbing memory of another woman in the same position.

" Come in," he cried (his voice was quivering now), and drawing up the Venetian blind he let in a flood of sunshine and the soft song of the sea.

" What a comfy little room! " said Fenella.

As she looked around her eyes seemed to light up everything.

" It's easy to see that you've been racing all over the earth, sir. That Neapolitan girl on the mantelpiece came from Rome, didn't she? "

" She did."

" And that lamp from Venice, and that silver bowl from Cairo, and that cedar-wood photograph frame from Sorrento? "

" Quite right."

" Books! Books! Books! All law books, I see. Not a human thing among them, I'll be bound. And yet they're all terribly, fearfully, tragically human, I suppose? "

" That's so."

" Gas fire? So you have a gas fire for the cold wet nights? "

" Yes, a bachelor has to have . . . . " But another stabbing memory came, and he could get no further.

" And so this is where you sit alone until all hours of the night —reading, reading, reading? "

He tried to speak but could not. She glanced at the bedroom door which stood open, and said, with eyes that seemed
to laugh,

" Is that your . . . . ? "

He nodded, breathing deeply, and trying to turn his eyes away.

" May I perhaps . . . .? "

" If you would like to."

" What fun ! "

She stood in the doorway, looking into the room for a moment,
with the sunlight on her bronze-brown hair, and then, turning
back to him with the warmer sunshine of her smile, she said,

" Well, you young bachelors know how to make yourselves
comfortable, I must say. But I seem to scent a woman about
this place."

He found himself stammering: " There's my housekeeper,
Mrs. Quayle. She comes every morning . . . . "

" Ah, that accounts for it."

She walked downstairs by his side, and said, as he opened the
carriage door for her,

" You'll do your best for that poor girl? "

" My very best."

" And by the way, the Deemster has invited the Governor and
me to Ballamoar. We go on Monday and stay a week. Of course
you'll be there? "

" I'm afraid . . . . "

" Oh, but you must."

" I'll . . . . I'll try."

" Au revoir ! "

He stood, after the carriage had gone until it had crossed to the
other side of the square, where, from the shade of the inside (it
had been closed in the meantime) Fenella reached her smiling face
forward and bowed to him again. Then he went back to his room
—now empty, silent and dead.

Oh, God, why had that senseless thing been allowed to happen !
Lord, what a little step in front of him on life's highway a man
was permitted to see !

Stowell did not return to his office that afternoon. His young
clerk locked up, left the keys, went downstairs and shut the door
after him, but still he sat in the gathering darkness like a man
nursing an incurable wound. He would never forgive himself for
allowing Fenella to come into his rooms—never !

" You fool ! " he thought, leaping up at last. " What's done is
done, and all you've got to do now is to stand up to it."

Then he lit the gas and taking the report out of his pocket he began to read it. What a shock! As, little by little, through the thick-set hedge of question and answer, the story of the wretched young wife came out to him, he saw, to his horror, that it was the story of Bessie Collister as he had imagined it might be if he deserted her.

What devil out of hell had brought this case to him as a punishment? By the hand of Fenella, too! No matter! If the unseen powers were concerning themselves with his miserable misdoings perhaps it was only to strengthen him in his resolution— to compel him to go on.

Suffer? Of course he would suffer! It was only right that he should suffer. And as for the haunting presence of Fenella's face in that room, there was a way to banish that.

So, sitting at his desk, he wrote,

"DEAR BESSIE,—Please go into Castletown to-morrow and have your photograph taken, and send it on to me immediately."

After that he felt more at ease and sat down before the fire to study his case.

III

"I must not go to Ballamoar while she's there. It would be madness," thought Stowell.

To escape from the temptation he made a still deeper plunge into the cauldron of work, going to Courts all over the island and winning his cases everywhere.

Twice he went to Castle Rushen to see the young wife in her cell. What happened there was made known to the frequenters of the "Manx Arms" by Tommy Vondy, the gaoler. Tommy, who had been coachman at Ballamoar in the "Stranger's" days, and appointed to his present post by the Deemster's influence, was accustomed to scenes of loud lamentation. But having listened outside the cell door, and even taken a peep or two through the grill, he was "free to confess" that "the young Master" could not get a word out of the prisoner.

As the week of Fenella's visit to Ballamoar was coming to a close, Stowell's nervousness became feverish. One day, as he was walking down the street, a dog-cart drew up by his side and a voice called,

"Mr. Stowell!"

It was Dr. Clucas, a jovial, rubicund full-bearded man of middle age, not liable to alarms.

"I've just been out to Ballamoar to see the Deemster, and I think perhaps you ought to keep in touch with him."

"Is my father . . . . ? "

"Oh no, nothing serious, no immediate danger. Still, at his age, you know . . . . "

"I'll go home to-morrow," said Stowell.

On the following afternoon he walked to Ballamoar. It was a bright day in early September. There was a hot hum of bees on the gorse hedges and the light rattle of the reaper in the fields, but inside the tall elms there was the usual silence, unbroken even by the cawing of the rooks.

The house, too, when he reached it, seemed to be deserted. The front door was open but the rooms were empty.

"Janet!" he cried, but there came no answer. Then he heard a burst of laughter from the back, and going through the dining-room to the piazza, he saw what was happening.

The yellow corn field which had been waving to a light breeze when he was there a fortnight before, was now bare save for the stooks which were dotted over part of it, and in the corner nearest to the mansion house a group of persons stood waiting for the cutting of the last armful of the crop—the Deemster, leaning on his stick; the Governor smoking his briar-root pipe; Parson Cowley, with his round red face; Janet in her lace cap; the house servants in their white aprons; Robbie Creer, in his sleeve waist-coat; young Robbie, stripped to the shirt; a large company of farm lads and farm girls, and—Fenella, in a sunbonnet and with a sickle in her hand. It was the Melliah—the harvest home.

"Now for it," cried Robbie, " strike them from their legs, miss." And at a stroke from her sickle Fenella brought the last sheaf to the ground.

Then there was a shout of " Hurrah for the Melliah! " and at the next moment Robbie was dipping mugs into a pail and hand-ing them round to the males of the company, saying, when he came to the Parson,

"The Parson was the first man that ever threw water in my face " (meaning his baptism), " but there's a jug of good Manx ale for his own."

The rough jest was received with laughter, and then the Deemster, being called for, spoke a few words with his calm dignity, leaning both hands on his stick:

" ' Custom must be indulged with custom, or custom will weep.' So says our old Manx proverb. The sun is going west on me, and I cannot hope to see many more Melliahs. But I trust my dear son, when he comes after me, will encourage you to keep up all that is good in our old traditions."

Then there was another shout, followed by some wild horse-play, with the farm-boys vaulting the stooks and the girls stretching straw ropes to trip them up, while the Deemster and his company turned back to the house.

Fenella, coming along in her sun bonnet (a little awry) and with her sheaf over her arm, was the first to see Victor, and she cried,

"At last! The Stranger has come at last!"

Janet was in raptures, and the Deemster said, while his slow eyes smiled,

"You are sleeping at home to-night, Victor?"

"Yes, father."

"Good!"

After saluting everybody Victor found himself walking by Fenella's side, and she was saying in a low voice, with a side-long glance,

"And how do you like me in a sun bonnet, sir? You rather fancy sun bonnets, I believe." But at that moment a wasp had settled on her arm and he was too busy removing it to reply.

At dinner that night Stowell found himself drawn into the home atmosphere as never before since his days as a student-at-law. The dining-table was bright with silver and many candles, and the wood fire, crackling on the hearth, filled the low-ceiled room with the resinous odour of the pine.

Everybody except himself and the doctor (who had arrived as they were sitting down) had dressed. The beauty of Fenella, who came in with the Deemster, seemed to be softened and heightened by her pale pink evening gown—like the beauty of a flower-bud when it opens and becomes a rose.

With Janet's complete approval Fenella had taken control of everything, and as Victor entered she said,

"That's your place, Mr. Stranger," putting him at the end of the table, with Janet and the doctor on either side.

She herself sat by the Deemster, whose powerful face wore an expression of suffering, although, as often as she spoke to him, he turned to her and smiled.

"She's lovelier than ever, really," whispered Janet, and then (with that clairvoyance in the heart of a woman which enables her to read mysteries without knowing it), "What a pity she ever went away!"

As a sequel to the Melliah the talk during dinner was of the ancient customs and old life of the island. The Deemster, who

could have told most, said little, but the Governor spoke of the
riots of the Manx people (especially the copper riot when they
wanted to burn down Government House), and Janet of the roysterers and haffsters of the Athols who kept racehorses and fought
duels—her mother in her girlhood had seen the blue mark of the
bullet on the dead forehead of one of them.

Such sweetness, such nobility, the men, the women, and the
manners! Fenella joined in the talk with great animation, but
Stowell was silent and in pain. Here they were, his family and
friends, without a suspicion that some day, perhaps soon, he would
bring quite another atmosphere into this house, this room. Visions
of the mill, the miller, his wife and his daughter rose before him,
and he felt like a traitor.

But it was not until they went into the library (it was library
and drawing-rooom combined) that he knew the full depth of his
humiliation. The Deemster, who was by the fire, asked Fenella to
sing to them, and she did so, sitting at the piano, with Doctor
Clucas (who in his youth had been the best dancer in the island)
tripping about her with old-fashioned gallantry to find the music
and turn over the leaves.

" This is for the Stranger," she said (cutting deeper than she
knew), and then followed a series of old Manx ballads, some of
them like the wailing of the wind among the rushes on the Curraghs, and some like the dancing of the water in the harbour
before a fresh breeze on a summer day.

Then the doctor brought out from a cupboard a few faded
sheets inscribed " Isobel Stowell," and Fenella sang " Allan
Water " and " Annie Laurie." And then the Deemster closed his
eyes, and it seemed to Victor who sat on a hassock by his side, that
his father's blue-veined hands trembled on his knees.

" And this is for myself," said Fenella, dropping into a deeper
tone as she sang:

> *Less than the weed that grows beside thy door* . . . .
> *Even less am I.*"

Victor wanted to fly out of the room and burst into tears. But
just then the clock on the landing struck, and Fenella rose from
the piano.

" Ten o'clock! Time to go upstairs, Deemster."

The old man seemed to like to be controlled by the young
woman, and leaning on her arm, he bowed all around in his stately
way, and permitted himself to be led from the room.

Then the Governor (being a privileged person) lit his pipe
with a piece of red turf from the fire, and Janet whispered to the
maid who had come back for the coffee-tray,

"See that Mr. Victor's night-things are laid out, Jane."

But Victor himself was in the hall, helping the Doctor with his overcoat, and saying,

"Can you take me back to town with you?"

"Certainly, if you'll wait at the lodge while I look in on the cowman's wife."

"Why, what's this mischief you are plotting?" It was Fenella coming downstairs.

The doctor explained, and Victor said,

"There's that case. It comes on soon. I must see the poor woman again in the morning."

"Well, if you must, you must, and I'll go down to the gate with you," said Fenella. And putting something over her head she walked by his side (the doctor having gone on), taking his arm unasked and keeping the step with him.

"I was just wanting a word with you."

"Yes?"

"It's about your father. You must really come back to live with him."

"Has he asked . . . . "

"Not to say asked! 'Victor doesn't come to see me very often'—that's all."

"After this case is over I'll . . . . "

"Do. You can't think how much it will mean to him."

On the way back to Ramsey, with the lamps of the dog-cart opening up the dark road in front of them, Stowell was silent, but the doctor talked continuously, and always on the same subject.

"I've seen something of the ladies in my time, Mr. Stowell, sir, but I really think . . . . yes, sir I really do think . . . . " and then rapturous praises of Fenella. They rang like joy-bells in Stowell's ear but struck like minute-bells also.

When he closed the street door to his chambers he found a large envelope in the letter-box behind it. Bessie's photograph! As he held it under the gas globe in his cold room the pictured face gave him a shock. Beautiful? Yes, but there was something common in its beauty which he had never observed before.

His first impulse was to hide the photograph out of sight. But at the next moment he tore open the cedar-wood frame on the mantelpiece, removed the portrait it contained, inserted Bessie's in its place, and then put it to stand on the table by the side of his bed.

"There! That shall be the last face I see at night and the first I see in the morning!"

But oh vain and foolish thought! With the first sleep of the night another face was in his dream.

CHAPTER TWELVE

THE DEATH OF THE DEEMSTER

THE Deemster had not intended to sit at the next Court of General Gaol Delivery, and had already arranged for the second Deemster to take his place, but when, next morning at breakfast, he heard from Fenella that Victor was to plead, he determined to preside.

" I must hear Victor's first case at the General Gaol," he said.

" We shall have to be careful, then," said Dr. Clucas. " No excitement, your Honour! No more heart-strain!"

On the morning of the trial he was up early. Janet heard him humming to himself in the conservatory as he cut the flowers for the vase in front of his young wife's picture. When he was ready to go she helped him on with his overcoat, turning up the collar and putting a muffler about his neck. And when young Robbie came round with the dog-cart he stepped up into it with surprising strength.

And then Janet, who had smuggled a brandy-flask into the luncheon basket at the back of the dog-cart, stood with a swollen heart and watched the old man as he went off in the morning mist, with the awakened rooks cawing over the unseen tops of the trees.

Three hours later, the Deemster arrived at Castletown. The sun was up, and there was a crowd at the castle gate. All hats were off as he passed through the Judge's private passage-way to the dark robing-room with its deeply recessed window. The Governor, in General's uniform, was there already, for he sat also in the high court of the island.

A few minutes later they were in the Court-house. It was densely crowded, and all rose as they entered. But at that moment the Deemster was conscious of one presence only—his own youth in wig and gown (himself as he used to be forty years before) in the curved benches for the advocates immediately below. It was Victor.

Then the prisoner was brought in—a forlorn-looking creature of three or four-and-twenty, not without traces of former comeliness, but now a rag of a woman, ill-clad and slatternly.

When asked to plead she said nothing, therefore the customary plea of Not Guilty was made for her, and without more ado the Attorney-General embarked on the history of her crime.

It was not a case for refinement; the crime was palpable; it had no redeeming feature, and for the protection of life in the island it called for the extreme penalty of the law.

Then, with the usual long pauses, the woman's story was raked out of the witnesses—her neighbours in the low streets that crept under the Castle walls, the police and the doctor. She had been an orphan from her birth, brought up at the expense of the parish by a woman who had ill-treated her. As a young servant-girl she had been " taken advantage of " in the big house she lived in, perhaps by the footman, more probably by an officer of the regiment then garrisoned in the town. Finally she had married the dead man, lived a cat-and-dog life with him (there was a dark record of drink and assaults) and at last stabbed him to the heart in a fatal quarrel and been found standing over his body with a table-knife in her hand.

Stowell's cross-examination consisted of three questions only. When the dead man was found had he anything in his hand? " Yes, a poker," said the policeman. When the prisoner was arrested were there any wounds on her? " Yes, three on the head," said the doctor. Were there any wounds on the dead man's body except the heart-stab from which he died? " None whatever."

" Ah ! " said the Deemster, and he reached forward to make a note.

When the Court adjourned for luncheon, the case for the Crown was over, and it almost seemed as if the rope of the hangman were already about the prisoner's neck.

Stowell did not leave the Court-house. He sat in his place with folded arms and closed eyes. Tommy Vondy, the gaoler, looked in on him sitting alone, and presently returned (from the direction of the Deemster's room) with a plate of sandwiches and something in a glass, but he sent back both untouched.

When the Court resumed it appeared to be still more crowded and excited than before. As the Deemster took his seat, he saw that his son's face was strongly illumined by the sun (which was now streaming from a lantern light in the roof) and that it was pale and drawn. Immediately behind Victor a lady was sitting— it was Fenella Stanley.

Then Stowell rose for the defence. There was a hush, and the Deemster found himself breathing audibly and wishing that he could pour something of himself into his son—himself as he used to be in the old days when God had given him strength.

But that was only for a moment. Stowell began slowly, almost nervously, but was soon speaking with complete command, and the Deemster, who had been bending forward, leaned back.

He did not intend to call witnesses. Neither would he put the prisoner into the box. He would content himself with the evidence for the Crown. He knew no more about the crime than the jury did. The accused had told him nothing, and degraded as they might think her, he had not thought it right to invade the sanctity of a woman's soul. That she had killed her husband was clear. If killing him was a crime she was guilty. But was it a crime? To answer that let the jury follow him while he did his best to piece together, from the evidence before them, the torn manuscript of this poor creature's story.

Then followed such speaking as none could remember to have heard in that court before. Flash after flash of spiritual light seemed to recreate the stages of the prisoner's life. First, as the child, who should have been happy as the birds and bright as the flowers, but had never known one hour of the love and guidance of her natural protectors. Next, as the young girl, pretty perhaps, with the light of love dawning on her, but betrayed and abandoned. Next, as the deserted creature, braving out her disgrace with " Wait! only wait! My gentleman will come back and marry me yet! " Next, as the badgered and shame-ridden woman, with all hope gone, saying to her despairing heart, " What do I care what happens to me now? Not a toss! " and then marrying (as the last cover for a hunted dog) the brute who afterwards had beaten her, brutalized her, cursed her, taught her to drink, and brought her down, down, down to . . . . what they saw.

Kill him? Yes, she had killed him—there couldn't be a doubt about that. But if she had three wounds on her body, and he had only the wound from which he died, was it not clear as noonday that she had been the victim of a murderous assault, and had struck back to save her life? If so her act was not murder and the only righteous verdict would be Not Guilty.

For the last passage of his defence Stowell faced full upon the jury, and spoke in a ringing and searching voice:

" Long ago, in Galilee, out of the supreme compassion which covered with forgiveness the transgressions of one who had sinned much but loved much, it was said, ' Let him that is without sin among you cast the first stone.' We have all done something we would fain forget, and when we lay our heads on our pillow we pray that the darkness may hide it. But does anybody doubt that if the all-seeing Justice could enter this Court this day another figure would be standing there in the dock by the side of that unhappy woman—a man in scarlet uniform perhaps, with decorations on his breast, and that the Deemster would have to say to him, ' *You* did this, for you were the first.' Mercy, then—mercy for the beaten, the broken, the scapegoat, the sinner."

People said afterwards that Stowell was a full half minute in his seat before anybody seemed to be aware that he was no longer speaking.

8

The spectators had listened without making a sound; the jury (a panel of stolid Manx farmers) had sat without moving a muscle; the prisoner had raised her head for the first time during the trial and then dropped it lower than before and her shoulders had shaken as if from inaudible sobs; the Governor, who had all day been drawing geometrical patterns on the sheet of foolscap in front of him, had let his pencil fall and stared down at the paper, and the Deemster had looked up at the lantern light from which the sunlight (it had moved on) was now streaming upon his face, showing at last a solitary tear that was rolling slowly down his cheek to the end of his firm-set mouth.

Then there was a rustle, as if the windows of a room on the edge of the sea had suddenly been thrown open. The Attorney-General was speaking again. After the defence they had just listened to (there being no evidence to rebut) he would waive his right of reply—the Crown desired justice, not revenge.

The Deemster's summing-up was the shortest that had ever been heard from him. There were legal reasons which justified the taking of human life, but the cases to which they applied were few. If the jury thought the prisoner had wilfully killed her husband they would find her Guilty. If they were satisfied from what they had heard that she had reasonable grounds for thinking that a felony was being committed upon her which endangered her own life they would find her Not Guilty.

Without leaving their box the jury promptly gave a verdict of Not Guilty; and then the Deemster in a loud, clear, almost triumphant voice said:

"Let the prisoner be discharged."

A few minutes later there was a scene of excitement on the green within the Castle walls. The spectators, being turned out of the Court-house with difficulty, were waiting for the chief actors in the life-drama to come down the stone steps, and from the private door to the Deemster's room.

"Wonderful! He snatched the woman out of the jaws of death, Sir!" "The Deemster's a grand man, but he'll have to be looking to his laurels!" "Man alive, that was a speech that must have been dear to a father's heart, though!"

Stowell was one of the first to appear. He looked pale, almost ill, and was carrying his soft felt hat in his hand, for the Court-house had been close and there was perspiration on his forehead still. A way was made for him and he passed through the court-yard without speaking or making sign, until he came under the arch of the Portcullis and there he was stopped by someone. It was Fenella. She was waiting for the Governor and hoping she might come upon Stowell also. Her eyes were red and swollen.

"How magnificent you were!" she said. And then with a half-tremulous laugh: "But how could you see into a woman's heart like that? I shall always be afraid of you in future, Sir!"

The Deemster came next. He was muffled in his great-coat and scarf, and was walking heavily on his stick, but there was a proud look in his uplifted face. With his left hand he grasped Victor's right, but he did not look at him, and he passed on without a word. Fenella followed, offering her arm, but he insisted on giving his—the grand old gentleman to the last.

But this time the Attorney-General had taken possession of Stowell. He had lost his case, but one of his "boys" had won it. "I've just been telling your father I always knew the root of the matter was in you, he said, and then others gathered around.

The Governor came last, having had documents to sign, and taking Stowell's arm, he carried him away, saying, "Come along—they'll kill you."

The Deemster's dog-cart had now gone, but the Governor's carriage was at the gate, with Fenella inside.

"Don't forget your promise about Ballamoar," she said.

"I'm going to-morrow," said Stowell.

Just then there was a commotion among the crowd. The liberated woman was coming out of the Castle, surrounded by a tumultuous company of her friends from the back streets. She saw Stowell by the carriage door, and breaking away from her companions she rushed up to him, threw herself at his feet, laid hold of his hand and covered it with kisses.

"That settles it," said Fenella, in a thick voice, after the woman had been carried off. "Now you know what the future of your life is to be—that of the champion of wronged and helpless women."

At the railway station, and in the railway carriage, Stowell's fellow advocates overwhelmed him with congratulations, but he hardly heard them. At last he folded his arms and closed his eyes, and, thinking he was tired, they left off troubling him.

On arriving at Ramsey his pulses were beating fast, and on going down the High Street, past the Old Plough Inn, he hardly felt the ground under his feet.

Clashing his door behind him he went into his bedroom and threw himself down on his bed. An immense joy had taken possession of him. Ambition, dead so long, had been restored to vivid life under Fenella's last words.

And then came a shock. Turning to the table by his bedside, his eyes fell on the photograph that stood upon it.

Bessie Collister!

II

The Deemster had a cheerful homegoing. Young Robbie Creer said afterwards that he had never seen the old man so strong and hearty. Driving himself, he saluted everybody on the roads, always by name and generally in the Anglo-Manx. All the way back it was " How do, John? " or " Grand day done, Mr. Killip."

Janet was waiting for him at the porch of Ballamoar.

" You must be tired after your long day, your Honour? "

" Not at all! "

" And Victor—how did he get on, Sir? "

" Wonderfully! Won his case and covered himself with honour."

At dinner (he insisted on Janet dining with him) he talked of nothing but Victor and the trial.

" He has got his foot on the ladder now, Miss Curphey, and there is no height to which he may not ascend."

Janet could do nothing but wipe her shining eyes and say,

" Aw, well now! Think of that now! " And then, with a wise shake of her old head, " But nobody can say I didn't know he would make us proud of him some day."

Night fell. Janet began to be afraid of the Deemster's excitement. She remembered Doctor Clucas's order (privately given to her) to knock at the Deemster's door between six and seven every morning, and, if she got no answer, to go into the room. She would do so to-morrow.

After Janet had gone to bed the Deemster sat at his desk in the Library and wrote for a long time in his leather-bound book. When he rose the clock on the landing was striking twelve.

He closed the book, but instead of putting it under lock and key, as he had always done before, he left it open on the desk, merely shutting the lid on it. Then with a long look round the room he put out the lamps and turned to go upstairs.

The reaction had begun by this time, and he staggered a little and laid hold of the handrail. He paused three times on the stairs, but his weakness did not frighten him. Lighting his candle on the landing, he wound the clock, extinguished the lamp that stood by it and faced the last flight with a smile. All was silent in the house now.

On reaching his own bedroom he paused again, and then

stepped down the corridor to Victor's. The door was ajar. He
pushed it open, took a step into the empty room and looked round—
at the cocoa-nut matting, the rugs, the bed in the shadow, the discoloured school trunk in the corner. And then he smiled again.
But he was breathing deeply at intervals and had the look of a
man who knew that he was doing familiar things for the last time.

The window in his own room was open, and the smell of tropical plants (especially the magnolia, with its sleep-inducing odour)
was coming up from the garden. He remembered that his own
father had brought them from the East long ago, when he was
himself a boy.

The sky was dark, but the hidden moon broke through silvery
clouds for a moment, and, looking through the surrounding black-
ness, he saw the bald crown of Snaefell, far beyond the trees and
above the glen. He remembered that he had seen it so all the way
up since he was a child.

He closed the curtains slowly and taking his candle again he
walked around the room and looked long at the pictures on the
walls. They were chiefly portraits or miniatures of Victor, at
various periods of childhood and youth—the latest being a photograph sent home to him from abroad.

That was the last oscillation of the pendulum. When he was
about to prepare for bed he found his strength exhausted, and he
was compelled to sit several times while he undressed. But he
continued to smile, and when he lay down at length and put his
head on the pillow he did it with a will.

Then he closed his eyes, and drew a deep breath, as one who
has gone through a long day's labour but has seen it finish up well
at the end. And then he closed his eyes and the surge of sleep
passed over him.

Outside the house everything seemed to slumber. It was a
night strangely calm and dark. The tall elms stood like soundless
sentinels in the darkness. Not a leaf stirred. The rivers flowed
without noise, as if a supernatural hand had been laid on them to
silence them. The only sound was the slow boom of the sea, which
seemed to come up out of the ground and to be the pulse of the
earth itself. The deep mystery of night was over all.

Towards morning there was a faint waft of wind in the trees
and along the grass. Was it the movement in the earth's bosom
of the new day about to be born? Or some invisible presence striding along with noiseless footsteps?

Within the house everything seemed to sleep. But the Deemster lay dead.

III

" Mr. Victor, Sir! Mr. Victor!"

It was Robbie Creer, who, after knocking in vain at Stowell's door in the grey hours of morning, was shouting up at his window. He had driven into town in the dog-cart and the little mare was steaming with perspiration.

Stowell threw up the window and heard the dread news. After a moment he answered, in a voice that sounded strange in Robbie's ears:

" Wait for me. I will go back with you."

When he was ready to go he wrote a message to Fenella, and left it for Mrs. Quayle to send off as soon as the telegraph office opened:

" *He has gone, heaven forgive me. I am going home now.*"

It was Sunday morning, and the sleeping streets echoed to the rattle of the flying wheels. When they got into the country (they were taking the shortest cuts) the farms were lying idle and quiet. Stowell sat with folded arms while they raced past the whitewashed cottages with thatched roofs, and scattered flocks of geese that went off with screams and stretched necks.

On arriving at Ballamoar he paused before entering the house. The pastoral tranquillity of the place was heart-breaking. The sun had risen, the rooks were cawing, the linnets were twittering in the eaves, a kitten was playing with a butterfly in the porch— it was just as if nothing had happened during the night.

Janet was in his father's room, with red eyes and a handker-chief in her hand. She did not speak, but her silence seemed to say, " Why didn't you come before?"

Stowell advanced to the side of the bed. The august face on the pillow, in the majesty and tranquillity of death, had never before looked so calm and noble, but that also seemed to say: " Why didn't you come before?" He reached over and put his lips to the cold forehead. And then, with head down, he hurried from the room.

He could never afterwards remember what he did during the rest of that day—only that to escape from the vague cheerfulness, the hushed bustle, the half-smothered hysteria, which come to a house after a death, he had strolled along the shore and past the ruined church in which he had walked with Fenella.

At length Janet came to him in the library to say " Good-night" and to sob out something about not grieving too much. And then he was left alone.

Sitting at the desk, where his father had sat the night before,

he took up the leather-bound book and read it from end to end—
not without a sense of looking into the sanctuary of another soul,
where only God's eyes should see.

It was a large volume, of some five hundred quarto pages, with
" Isobel's Diary " inscribed on its first page, and these words
below:

> " Inasmuch as I cannot believe that my beloved compan-
> ion who has died to-day is lost to me even in this life, and
> being convinced that the divine purpose in leaving me behind
> is that I may care for and guard her child, I dedicate this
> book to the record of my sacred duty."

Then followed, in the Deemster's steady handwriting, a daily
entry, sometimes only a phrase or a line, sometimes a page, but
always about his son:

> " This morning in the library, making my desk under
> your portrait his altar, Parson Cowley baptised your boy—
> Janet Curphey standing godmother, and the Attorney his
> other sponsor. We called him Victor, so the last of your dear
> wishes has been fulfilled."

Stowell looked up and around him. He was on the very spot
of that scene of so many years ago. Then came records of his
childhood, his childish talk, his childish rhymes, his childish
ailments:

> " Your boy contracted a cold yesterday, and fearing it
> might develop into bronchitis, I sat up most of the night that
> I might go into the nursery at intervals to mend the fire under
> the steam kettle, Janet being worn out and sleepy. Thank
> God his breathing is better this morning! "

Stowell felt as if he were choking. Then came the records of
his school-days; his expulsion; the slack times before he set to
work; the bright ones when he was a student-at-law; the dark
ones when he was going headlong to the dogs. After these latter
entries it would be:

> " A son is a separate being, Isobel. I can only stand
> and wait."

Or sometimes, as if for comfort, a line from one of the great
books, not rarely the Bible:

> " Thy way is in the sea, and thy path is the great waters,
> and thy footsteps are not known."

It was now the middle of the night. A dog was howling somewhere in the farm. Stowell paused and thought of the superstition about a howling dog and a dead body. When he resumed his reading he turned the pages with a trembling hand:

> "It is six months since Victor returned to the island and he has only been here twice. I had hoped he would come to live with me at Ballamoar. But I must not complain. Nature looks forward, not backward. No son can love his father as the father loves the son. That is the law of life, Isobel, and we who are fathers must reconcile ourselves to it."

Stowell felt his head reel and his eyes swim. If he had only known. If somebody had only told him!

The fire behind him had gone out by this time and he had begun to shiver. But he turned back to the book for the few remaining pages. And then came a shock. They were all about Fenella, and the Deemster's hope that she and his son would marry.

> "Never were two young people better matched to the outer eye, Isobel—that splendid girl with her conquering loveliness or your son with his mother's face. Her influence on him seems to be wonderful. She has only been a month back from London, but he is like a new man already."

Overwhelmed with confusion Stowell tried to close the book, but he could not do so.

> "A man looks for a woman who is a heroine, and a woman for a man who is a hero, and please God these two have found each other."

Then came a glowing account of the trial at Castle Rushen, and then:

> "So it's all well at last, Isobel. Your son can do without me now. He needs his father no longer. With that fine woman by his side he will go up and up. They will marry and carry on the tradition of the Ballamoars. It is the dearest wish of my heart that they should do so."

There was only one entry after that, and it ran:

> "I am tired and my work is done. Now I can rejoin you, having waited so long. When I close my eyes to-night I shall see your face—I know I shall. So Good-night, Isobel! Or should I say, Good-morning?"

The clock on the landing was striking three—the most solemn hour of day and night, for it is the hour between. Stowell, with a heavy heart, the book in one hand and his candle in the other, was going to bed. Reaching the door of his father's room he dropped to his knees.

"Forgive me! Forgive me! Forgive me!"

But after a while a light seemed to break on him. Where his father now was he would know that there was no help for it—that he, too, must follow the line of honour.

"Yes," he thought, rising and going on to his own room. "I must do the right, whatever it may cost me."

IV

On the morning of the burial, Stowell received a letter from Bessie Collister:

> "Dere Victor,
>
> "I am sorry to here from Alick about the death of the Deemster you must feel it verry much the loss of such a good kinde father everrybody is talking about him and saying he was the best gentleman that everr was thank you for the nice cloths Mrs. Quayle bought me. Alick is very kinde—
>
> "Bessie."

The poor, illiterate, inadequate, ill-spent message made Stowell's heart grow cold, and with a certain shame he read it by stealth and then smuggled it away.

The news of the Deemster's death had fallen on the Manx people like a thunder-bolt. The one great man of Man had gone. It was almost as if the island had lost its soul.

No work was done on the day of the funeral. At ten o'clock in the morning the whole population seemed to be crossing the Curragh lanes to Ballamoar. By eleven the broad lawn was covered with a vast company of all classes, from the officials to the crofters. A long line of carriages, cars and stiff carts, lined the roads that surrounded the house.

The day had broken fair, with a kind of mild brightness, but out on that sandy headland the wind had risen and white wreaths of mist were floating over the land. It was late September and the leaves were falling rapidly.

Nobody entered the house. According to Manx custom all stood outside. At half-past eleven the front door was opened and the body was brought out, under a pall, and laid on four chairs in front of it. A moment later Victor Stowell came behind, bare-headed and very pale. A wide space was left for him by the bier. A creeper that covered the house was blood-red at his back.

Somebody started a hymn—"Abide with me"—and it was taken up by the vast company in front. The rooks swirled and screamed over the heads of the singers. The bald head of old Snaefell looked down through the trees.

Then the procession was formed. It took the grassy lane at the back by which the Deemster had always gone to church. Everybody walked, and six sets of bearers claimed the right "to carry the old man home."

They sang two hymns on the way: "Lead, Kindly Light" and "Rock of Ages." Between the verses the wind whistled through the gorse hedges on either side. Sometimes it raised the skirt of the pall and showed the bare oak beneath.

When they reached the cross roads in front of the church the bell began to toll. At that moment a white mist was driving across the church tower and almost obscuring it.

The Bishop of the island was at the gate, waiting for the procession, but Parson Cowley, pale and trembling, was also there, and he would have fought to the death for his right to bury the Deemster.

"I am the Resurrection and the Life," he began in his quavering voice, as the procession came up, and at the next moment the mists vanished. The little churchyard with its weather-beaten stones, seemed to look up at the wonderful sky and out on the sightless sea. The bearers had to bend their knees as they passed through the low door.

Every seat in the body of the church was occupied, and great numbers had to remain outside. But Victor Stowell sat alone in the pew of the Ballamoars with the marble tablet on the wall behind him—four hundred years of his family and he the last of them. During the reading of the Epistle the lashing and wailing of the wind outside almost drowned the Bishop's voice.

The service ended with the singing of another hymn, "O God our help in ages past." Everybody knew the words, and they were taken up by the people outside:

> "Time, like an ever-rolling stream,
> Bears all its sons away."

Thus far Victor Stowell had gone through everything in a kind of stupor. He was conscious that the island was there to do honour to her greatest son, but that was nothing to him now. When he came to himself he was standing by the open vault of the Stowells. A line of stones lay over the closed part of it, some of them old and worn and with the lettering almost obliterated. But a cross of white marble, which had been dislodged from its place, lay at his feet, and it bore the words:

> " *To the dear memory of Isobel, the beloved wife of Douglas Stowell, Deemster of this Isle.*"

Victor's throat was throbbing. He was losing (what no man can lose twice) his father and greatest friend, whose slightest word and wish should be as sacred to him as his soul.

He heard the words " dust to dust " and they were like the reverberation of eternity. Then came a dead void, after Parson Cowley's voice had ceased, and it was just as if the pulse of the world had stopped.

And then, at that last moment as he stepped forward and looked down, and everybody fell back for him, and only the sea's boom was audible as it beat on the cliffs below, somebody (he did not turn to look, for he knew who it was) coming up to his side, and putting her arm through his, said in a tremulous voice,

" He is better there. In their death they are not divided."

It was Fenella.

At the next moment, something he could not resist, something unconquerable and overwhelming, made him put his arms about her and kiss her.

CHAPTER THIRTEEN

THE SAVING OF KATE KINRADE

THE Governor was waiting for Stowell at the side gate to Ballamoar.

" You look ill, my boy, and no wonder," he said. " Fenella and I are to take a short cruise in the yacht before the autumn ends. You must come along with us."

For the farmers and fishermen who had travelled long distances a meal had been provided in the barn—a kind of robustious after-wake for the Deemster, presided over by the elder and younger Robbie Creers.

Alick Gell alone returned with Stowell to the house. In his black frock coat and tall silk hat he had walked back from the Church by Stowell's side, snuffling audibly but saying nothing. To Stowell's relief he was still silent through luncheon and for several

hours afterwards. It was not until they were in the porch, and
Gell was on the point of going, that anything of consequence
was said.

"What about Bessie?" asked Stowell.

"Oh, Bessie?" said Gell (he looked a little confused)
"Bessie's all right, I think. But there's trouble coming in that
quarter, I'm afraid."

"What trouble?"

"As we were walking along Langness yesterday—I went
down to tell her about the Deemster—we met Cæsar Qualtrough
coming from the farm."

"Qualtrough?"

"You know—father of the young scoundrel who got us into
that scrape at King William's."

"I remember."

"He's a friend of Dan Baldromma's, and Dan is a tenant of
my father's and . . . . But good Lord, what matter! I've worse
things than that to worry about."

As Gell was going out of the gate, the night was falling and
the stars were out, and he was saying to himself, "Does he really
care for the girl, or is it only a sense of duty?"

And Stowell, as he closed the door and went back into the house
(empty and vault-like now, as a house is on the first night after
the being who has been the soul of it has been left outside) was
thinking, "I can't allow Alick to be my scapegoat any longer."

But at the next moment he was thinking of Fenella. With
mingled shame and joy he was asking himself what was being
thought of the incident in the churchyard—by Fenella herself, by
the Governor, by everybody.

Next day the Attorney-General came with the will. Except
for a few legacies to servants, the Deemster had left everything
to his son.

"So, with your mother's fortune, you are one of the rich men
of the island, now, Victor. A great responsibility, my boy! I
pray God you may choose the right partner. But " (with a meaning smile) "that will be all right, I think."

During the next days Stowell occupied himself with Joshua
Scarff, the Deemster's clerk (a tall, thin, elderly man wearing
dark spectacles) in paying-off the legacies. Only one of these
gave him any anxiety. This was Janet's, and it was accompanied
by a pension, in case Victor should decide to superannuate her.
Against doing so all his heart cried out, but something whispered
that if Janet were gone it might be the easier for Bessie.

Janet was in floods of tears at the possibility.

" I couldn't have believed it of the Deemster! " she said. " I really couldn't! You can keep the legacy, dear. I have no use for it except to give it back to you. But I won't leave Ballamoar. 'Deed, I won't! Not until another woman comes to be mistress in it, and wants me to go. And she never will, the darling—I'll trust her for that, anyway."

A day or two later Stowell was in his father's room, when he came upon an envelope inscribed: " *To be opened by my son.* " It contained a ring, a beautiful and valuable gem, with a note saying:

" *This was your mother's engagement ring. I wish you to give it to Fenella Stanley. Take it yourself.* "

Stowell was stupefied. Struggling with a sense of his duty to the girl whom he had sent to Derby Haven he had been telling himself that he must never see Fenella again. But here was a sacred command from the dead.

For three days he thought he could not possibly go to Government House. On the fourth day he went.

The beauty and charm of the atmosphere of Fenella's home were heart-breaking. And Fenella herself, in a soft tea-gown, was almost more than he could bear to look upon.

She, too, seemed embarrassed, and when Miss Green (an English counterpart of Janet) left them alone with each other, and he gave her the ring, saying what his father had told him to do with it, her embarrassment increased.

She held it in her fingers, turned it over and looked at it, and said, " How lovely! How good of him! " And then, trembling and tingling, and with a slightly heightened colour, she looked at Stowell.

Suddenly a thought flashed upon him. Why had his father told him to take the ring to her himself? The answer was speaking in Fenella's eyes—that, at the topmost moment of their love, he should put it on.

At the next instant the Governor entered the drawing-room, and Fenella, holding up her hand (she had put the ring on for herself by this time) cried:

" See what the Deemster has left to me! "

" Beautiful! " said the Governor, and then he looked from Stowell to his daughter.

Stowell rose to go. He had the sense of flying from the house. Fenella must have thought him a fool. The Governor must have thought him a fool. But better be a fool than a traitor!

A week passed and then an idea came to him. He would tell

the truth to Bessie's people—the whole truth if necessary. That would commit him once for all to the line of honour. Having taken that public plunge there could be no looking back, and the bitter struggle between his passion and his duty would then be over.

With a certain pride at the thought of being about to do an heroic thing he set out one day for Ramsey, intending to return by Baldromma. But on entering his outer office his young clerk told him that Mr. Daniel Collister was in his private room, that he had been waiting there for two hours, and refusing to go away.

Dan, with his short, gross figure, was standing astride on the hearthrug, and without so much as a bow he plunged into his business.

A respectable man's house was in disgrace. His step-daughter had run away. Been carried off by a scoundrel—there couldn't be a doubt of it. A month gone and not the whisper of a word from her. The mother was broken-hearted, so he had been traipsing the island over to find the girl.

"I belave I'm on the track of her at last though. She's down Castletown way, and the man that's been the cause of her trouble isn't far off, I'm thinking."

"And whom do you say it is, Mr. Collister?"

"Somebody that's middling close to yourself, sir—Mr. Alick Gell, the son of the Spaker."

"No, no, no!"

"Who else then?"

Stowell tried to speak but could not.

"Wasn't he the cause of her disgrace at the High Bailiff's? And hasn't he been keeping up his bad character ever since— standing by the side of disorderly walkers in the Douglas Coorts, they're saying?"

He must have promised to marry the girl. But he hadn't. He (Dan) had been to the Registrar's at Douglas and found that out.

"The toot! The boght! The booby! I was warning her enough. The man that takes advantage of a dacent girl isn't much for marrying her afterwards."

Remembering Dan's share in the catastrophe, Stowell was feeling the vertigo of a temptation to take the gross creature by the neck and fling him through the window.

"Why do you come to me?" he asked.

"To ask you to tell your friend that he's got to make an honest woman of the girl."

"Is that all you are thinking about?"

Dan drew a quick breath, then dug both hands into the upright pockets of his trousers, thrust forward his thick neck, with a gesture peculiar to the bull, and answered:

"No, I'm thinking of myself as well, and what for shouldn't I? I'm going to stand up for my own rights, too. The man that treats my girl like that has got to marry her, and I'm not going to be satisfied with nothing less."

Then picking up his billycock hat and making for the door he said:

"I lave it with you, Mr. Stowell, Sir. If the Dempster was the grand gentleman people are saying, his son will be seeing justice done to me and mine. If not, the island will be too hot for the guilty man, I'm thinking."

When Dan had gone Stowell felt sick and dizzy, and as if he were drawing back from the edge of a precipice. His heroic act of self-sacrifice had dwindled to a ridiculous weakness.

This man, with his blatant vulgarity of mind and soul, at Ballamoar! His father-in-law! A member of his family! Riding over him with a degrading tyranny! In the dining-room, with his broad buttocks to the fire—never, never, never!

Hardly had Dan's footsteps ceased on the stair when the young clerk came from the outer office in great excitement.

"His Excellency is here. He's coming upstairs, Sir."

II

"Helloa, I've found you."

The Governor was in yachting costume.

"Well, the yacht is lying outside, and Fenella and I are doing a little circumnavigating of the island, so come along."

Stowell tried to excuse himself, but the Governor would listen to no excuses.

"Everybody says you are looking like a ghost these days, and so you are. Therefore come, let's get a breath of sea-air into you."

"But your Excellency. . . ."

"I've brought one of the ship's boys ashore for your bag, so pack it quick. . . ."

"But really. . . ."

"Where's your bedroom and I'll pack it myself."

"No, no! But if I must. . . ."

"That's better! I'll smoke a pipe and wait for you."

"After all, why not?" thought Stowell, as he packed his bag and put on flannels and a blue jacket. This flying away from Fenella was unworthy of a man. It was cowardly, contemptible. He must learn to resist temptation.

Half an hour later he was riding with the Governor in a dinghy over the fresh waters of the bay towards a large white yacht, "The Fenella," with the red ensign fluttering over her. The gangway was open and as Stowell stepped on to the spotless deck of the ship, her namesake, also in yachting costume, was waiting to receive him.

The mainsail, mizzen and jib being set, the grey-bearded captain, in blue with brass buttons, called on his boys to swing the dinghy up to the davits and haul in the anchor. In a few minutes more, to the hiss and simmer of the sea, the yacht was running free before the wind, leaving the town to the south behind it.

The bell rang for luncheon, and with the Governor and Fenella, Stowell crossed to the companion and went down to the saloon. Books and field-glasses were lying about the sofas and the table was glistening with silver and glass. Blue silk curtains, with the sunlight shining through them, were fluttering over the skylight and the port-holes. How fresh! How charming!

When they came up on deck an hour afterwards they were doubling the Point of Ayre, and the lighthouse at the northernmost end of it was looking like a marble column with a glittering eye. Towards six o'clock they cast anchor for the night off Peel.

The sun was then setting, and the herring fleet (a hundred boats) going out for the night were passing in front of the red sky like a flight of black birds. By the time dinner was over the drowsy spirit of the sunset had died over the waters behind them, the twilight had deepened to a ghostly grey, and the moon had risen over the little fishing town in front and the gaunt walls of the ruined Peel Castle which stands on an island rock.

The Governor, who had sent ashore for the day's newspapers, remained in the cabin to read them. But Stowell and Fenella sat on deck under the moon and the stars. The air had become very quiet. There was no sound anywhere except the tranquil wash of the waves against the yacht and the whispering of the sea outside.

Fenella talked and laughed. Stowell laughed and talked. They found it so easy to talk to each other.

The night wore on. The moon going westward made the broken walls of the Castle stand up black above the shore, with its empty window-sockets like eyes looking from the lighter sky.

Stowell talked of the old ruin and its legendary and historical associations—St. Patrick, the spectre hound (*the Mauthe Doo*), the ecclesiastical prison and the graves in the roofless Cathedral.

" But I'll tell you a story that beats all that," he said.

" About a woman of course? " said Fenella.

" Yes—a fallen woman."

" Ah! "

" Her name was Kate Kinrade. She gave birth to an illegitimate child, and the Bishop—he was a saint—thinking that her
conduct tended to the dishonour of the Christian name, ordered
that, for the saving of her soul, she should be dragged after a
boat across the bay of Peel on the fair of St. Patrick at the height
of the market."

" And was she? "

" The fishermen refused at first to carry out the censure, and
then excused themselves on the ground that St. Patrick's day was
too tempestuous. But being threatened with fines, they did it at
last—in the depth of winter."

Fenella's gaiety had gone. Stowell gazed at her face in the
moonlight. It was quivering and her bosom was heaving.

" And the Bishop was a saint, you say? "

" If ever there was one."

" He ordered the woman to be dragged through the sea at the
tail of a boat? "

" Yes."

" And what did he do to *the man?* "

Stowell gasped. There was silence for a moment, and then the
Governor's voice came from the skylight of the cabin:

" Are you people never going to turn in? "

" Presently."

" I am, anyway."

It was late. The lights of the little town had blinked out one
by one. Only the red light on the stone pier was burning.

Fenella recovered her gaiety after a while, shouted for echoes
to the Castle rock, and then took Stowell's arm to go down the
companion.

On reaching the darkened saloon she stepped on tiptoe and
dropped her voice under pretence of not disturbing her father, who
would be asleep. At the door of her cabin she ceased laughing
and said,

" Hush! I'm going to say something."

" What? "

" I don't know if you're aware of it, but ever since I came home
you've been calling me ' Miss Stanley,' and I've been calling
you—anything."

" Well? "

" We used to call each other by our Christian names before.
Couldn't we go back to that? "

" Would you like to? "

There was a pause, and then, in a whisper,

9

" Victor ! "

" Fenella ! "

" Good-night ! "

It had been like a kiss.

Stowell went to his cabin in rapture, in pain, with a delicious thrill and a sense of stifling hypocrisy. What a hypocrite he had been! It was not to resist temptation but to dally with it that he had come on this cruise.

He was there under false pretences. He had pledged himself to the girl at Derby Haven, and yet . . . .

Thank God, he had gone no farther! There was only one way of escape from the perpetual fire of temptation—to hasten his marriage with Bessie Collister. He must see her as soon as possible and suggest that they should marry immediately. It was heart-breaking, but there was no help for it, if he was to stand upright as an honourable man.

Dan Baldromma? Well, what of him? He could shut the door on Dan—of course he could!

Next morning Stowell was the first on deck. The air was salt and chill; the day had not yet opened its eyes; there was a whir-ring of wings and a calling of sea-birds; and through a sleepy white mist, that might have been the smoke of the moon, the herring fleet were coming like pale ghosts back to harbour.

A fresh breeze sprang up with the sunrise and the Captain lifted anchor and stood out towards the south. Sheep were bleat-ing on the head-land of Contrary, and as they opened the broad bay of the Niarbyl the thatched cottages under the cliffs were smoking for breakfast.

When they reached Port Erin the Governor came up and ordered anchor to be cast again, saying they would lie there and go out with the herring fleet in the evening.

Seeing his opportunity, Stowell said he would like to go ashore for a few hours—a little business.

" Mind you're back by four o'clock then—we'll sail at high-water."

As Stowell was being sculled ashore in the dinghy he was say-ing to himself:

" No Kate Kinrade for me—never, never ! "

III

An hour later Stowell was in Derby Haven, a little fish-ing village, smelling of sea-wrack and echoing with the cry of gulls.

The Misses Brown, in their oiled ringlets and faded satin dresses, received him, in their old maids' sitting-room, with much ceremony, and he speedily realised that Gell, in trying to shield him, had gone farther than he expected.

"You wish to see Miss Collister? Well, since you are such a close friend of Mr. Gell there can be no objection. . . . Bessie! A gentleman to see you."

Stowell heard Bessie coming downstairs with great alacrity, but on seeing him she drew up with a certain embarrassment.

"Oh, it's you?"

She was shorter than he had thought, and the impression made by her photograph of something common in her beauty was deepened by the reality.

"Should we take a walk?" he said.

She hesitated for a moment, then went upstairs and returned presently in a round hat and a close-fitting costume which sat awkwardly upon her. What a change! Where was the free, warm, natural, full-bosomed girl with bare neck and sunburnt arms who had fascinated him in the glen?

They took the unfrequented path on the western side of Langness—a long serpentine tongue of land which protruded from the open mouth of the sea. He tried to begin upon the subject of his errand but found it impossible to do so.

"Bye and bye," he thought, "bye and bye."

Bessie kept step with him, but was almost silent. He asked if she was comfortable in her new quarters, and she said they were lonesome after the farm, but old Miss Brown was a dear and Miss Ethel a "dozey duck."

The common expression humiliated him. He inquired if she had been able to relieve her mother's anxiety, and she answered no, how could she, without letting her stepfather know where she was?

"They're telling me he's travelling the island over looking for me, but I don't know why. He was always dead nuts on me when I was at home."

Again he felt ashamed. He found it impossible to keep up a conversation with the girl. To attempt to do so was like throwing a stone into the sand—no echo, no response.

Only once did Bessie say anything for herself. She was walking on the landward side of the path, and seeing an old man, with a pair of horses, grubbing a hungry-looking field, with a cloud of sea-gulls swirling behind him, she said it was dirty land, full of scutch, and the farmer was laying it open to the frosts of winter.

Stowell was feeling the sweat on his forehead. How was it

posible to lift up a girl like this? She would be the farm girl to
the last. Good Lord, what magic was there in marriage to change
people and ensure their happiness?

Ballamoar? That lonesome place inside the tall trees! He
might shut out her family, but would not she—illiterate, uninter-
esting, inadequate—shut out his friends? And then, he and she
together there, with nothing in common, alone, in the long nights
of winter . . . . Oh God!

Ashamed of thinking like that of the girl, and having reached
the lighthouse by this time, he drew her arm through his and
turned to go back. The warmth of the contact revived a little of
the former thrill, and he laughed and talked.

The voice of the sea was low that day, and across the bay came
shouts and cheers in fresh young voices—the boys of King
William's were playing football. That brought memories to both
of them and he began to talk about Gell.

" Dear old Alick, he's such a good fellow, isn't he? "

" 'Deed he is," said Bessie.

" By the way, he's a sort of old flame of yours, I believe," said
Stowell, looking sideways at the girl, and Bessie blushed and
laughed, but made no answer.

Those black eyes, those full red lips. Yes, this was the
girl who . . . .

But the idea of a marriage founded on the passion which had
brought them together revolted him now, and he let Bessie's arm
fall to his side.

When they got back to the old maid's cottage he had still said
nothing of what he had come to say. " Later on," he was telling
himself, but a secret voice inside was whispering, " Never! It
is impossible! "

The elder of the Miss Browns followed him to the gate to ask
if he did not see a great improvement in her charge, and when he
said that Bessie seemed to be a little subdued, she cried:

" Bessie? Oh dear no, not generally! Ask Mr. Gell."

Perhaps the girl was not well to-day—they had thought she
had not been very well lately.

" And how is she getting on with . . . . " (the word stuck in
his throat) " with her lessons? "

" Wonderfully! Of course she has long arrears to make up,
but the way she works to fit herself for her new station . . . .
well, it's enough to make a person cry, really."

Stowell felt as if something were taking him by the throat.

" In fact my sister and I used to wonder and wonder what she
did with her bedroom candles until we found out she was sitting

up after everybody had gone to sleep to learn her grammar and spelling."

Stowell felt as if something had struck him in the face. Every hard thought about Bessie seemed to be wiped out of his mind in a moment.

Going back to Port Erin (he walked all the way) he could think of nothing but that girl sitting up in her bedroom to educate herself, in her poor little way, that she might become worthy to be his wife.

If he disappointed her now what would become of her? Would she kill herself? Would the world kill her? Kate Kinrade? The days of the Bishop and the woman were not over yet.

No, he must keep his pledge, and make no more wry faces about it. If it had been his duty before it was more than ever his duty now.

But Fenella?

He must put her out of his mind for ever. He would be the most unhappy man alive, but then his own happiness was not the only thing he had to think about. He could not live any longer under false pretences. He must find some way of telling Fenella that he had engaged himself while she was away—that he was a pledged man.

But what then? There would be nothing more between them as long as they lived—not a smile or the clasp of a hand! She whom he had loved so long, never having loved anybody else! It would be like signing his death-warrant.

The dead leaves from the roadside were driving over his feet; his eyes ached and his throat throbbed, but he gulped down his emotion. After all he would be the only sufferer! Thank God for that anyway!

As he reached Port Erin, he saw the white sails of the yacht against the blue sea and sky.

"Yes, I must tell Fenella—I must tell her to-night," he thought.

CHAPTER FOURTEEN

THE EVERLASTING SONG OF THE SEA

"Ah, here you are at last! Just in time! A breeze sprang up an hour ago, and the Captain would have gone without you but for me. The herring fleet have gone already. Look, there they are, sailing into the sunset."

Fenella was in high spirits. Having prevailed upon the Governor to let them have a real night with the herrings (turning the

yacht into a fishing boat) she had borrowed a net and hired fishermen's clothes—oilskins and a sou'-wester for herself and a
" ganzy " and big boots for Stowell.

It was impossible to resist the contagion of Fenella's gaiety.
" Why try? " thought Stowell. It would be his last night of
happiness. To-morrow he would have to bury it for ever.

In a few minutes, having cleared the harbour, they had opened
the land on either side and were standing out for the fishing
ground. Within two hours, in the midst of the fleet, they were sailing over the Carlingford sands, midway between the island and
Ireland, and the sea-birds skimming above the water were showing
them the shoal.

Dinner was over, and Stowell, in jersey and big boots up to his
thighs, saw Fenella come on deck in her oilskin coat and sou'-
wester—with the new and surprising beauty which fresh garments,
whatever they are, give to every woman in the eyes of the man who
loves her.

What shouts! What laughter! Stowell kept saying to himself:
" Why not? It will soon be over."

They slackened sail and waited for the sun to go down before
shooting their nets. Presently the great ball of flame descended
into the sea, the admiral of the fleet ran his flag to his masthead,
and the Captain cried, " Shoot! "

Then the brown net, with its floats, was dropped over the stern
(Fenella taking a hand and shouting with the men), the foresail
was hauled down, and the mizzen set to keep the ship head to the
wind. And then, all being snug for the night, came the fisherman's prayer:

" *Dy hannie Patrick Noo shin as nyn maaty* " (May St.
Patrick bless us and our boat) with something about the living and
the dead—the crew and the fish.

After that came the throwing of the salt, a more robustious and
less religious ceremony, which threw Fenella into fits of laughter.

" What does it mean? " she asked.

" Goodness knows! "

" How delightful! "

The grey twilight came down from the northern heavens, and
then night fell—a dark night without moon but with a world of
stars. Stowell and Fenella were leaning over the side to watch the
phosphorescent gleams which, like flashes of light under the surface, came from the fish that were darting away from the prow.

" Isn't it wonderful—the fish going on and on to the goal of
their perpetual travels? " said Fenella.

" They always come back to the place they were spawned, though," said Stowell.

" Like humans, are they? You remember—' Back to the heart's place here I keep for thee.' "

Stowell felt as if a hand were at his throat again. " Bye and bye," he thought. Before they turned in for the night he would tell her everything.

Suddenly there was a crash at the stern—the anchor had been lifted up and then banged down on the deck.

" What's that? " cried Fenella.

" They're proving the nets to see if the fish are coming," said Stowell, and hurrying aft together they found the water milky white and full of irridescent rays.

A couple of warps of the net were hauled aboard, and twelve or fifteen herring fell on to the deck. Fenella picked them up, wriggling, cheeping and twisting in her hands and threw them into a basket—she was in a fever of excitement.

After that several of the boats that were fishing alongside called across to know the result of the proving, and the Captain answered them in Manx, with the crude symbolism of the sea.

" Let me do it next time," said Fenella.

" Do you think you can, miss? " asked the Captain.

" She can do anything," said Stowell, and when the next boat called, Fenella (with Stowell to prompt her) stood ready to reply.

" *R'ou prowal, bhoy?* " cried the voice out of the darkness.

" What's he saying? Quick! "

" He's asking were you proving, boy. Say ' *Va*—I was.' "

Fenella put her open palms at each side of her mouth, under her sou'-wester, and cried, " *Va!* "

" *Quoid oo er y piyr?* "

" He asks what you found in your net. Say ' *Pohnnar*—a child.' "

" Oh my goodness! *Pohnnar*," cried Fenella.

" *Cre'n eash dy pohnnar?* "

" He asks what is the age of your child. Say ' *Dussan ny quieg-yeig*—twelve to fifteen.' "

" My goodness gracious! *Dussan ny quieg-yeig*," cried Fenella.

By this time everybody was in convulsions of laughter, and Stowell could scarcely resist the impulse to throw his arms about Fenella and kiss her. " Soon! Soon! I must tell her soon! " he thought.

The wind had dropped and a great stillness had fallen on the sea. The glow from the lights of the Dublin was in the western sky; the revolving light of the Chicken Rock (the most southerly point of Man) was in the east; and for two miles round lay the herring boats, with their watch-lights burning on the roofs of their net houses, and looking like stars which had fallen from the darkening sky on to the bosom of the sea.

Fenella began to sing, and before Stowell knew what he was doing he was singing with her:

> She: *Oh Molla-caraine, where got you your gold?*
> He: *Lone, lone, you have left me here.*

It was entrancing—the hour, the surroundings, the charm and sonority of the sea! "But this is madness," thought Stowell. It would only make it the harder to do—what he had to do.

Nevertheless he went on, and when they came to the end of another Manx ballad *Kiree fo naightey* (the sheep under the snow) he said:

"Would you like to know where that old song was written?"

"Where?"

"In Castle Rushen—by a poor wretch whose life had been sworn away by a vindictive woman."

"And what had he done to her? Betrayed her, and then deserted her for another woman, I suppose. That's the one thing a woman can never forgive—never should, perhaps."

"I must tell her soon," thought Stowell. But he could think of no way to begin—no natural way to lead up to what he had to say.

The night was now very dark and silent. The majesty and solemnity around were grand and moving. Fenella, who had been laughing all the evening, was serious enough at last.

"It's almost as if the sea, grown old, had gone to sleep with the going down of the sun, isn't it?" she said.

"The sea isn't always like this, though," said Stowell.

"No, it can be very cruel, can't it? Rolling on and on, with its incessant, monotonous roar through the ages! What heartless things it has done! Millions and millions of women have prayed and it has no heed to them."

"How can I do it? How can I do it?" Stowell was asking himself.

"Oh, what a thing it is to be a sailor's wife!" said Fenella. "Only think of her with her little brood, in her cottage at Peel, perhaps, when a sudden storm comes on! Giving the children their supper and washing them and undressing them, and hearing them say their prayers and hushing them to sleep, and then going downstairs to the kitchen, and listening to the roar of the sea on the castle rocks, and thinking of her man out here in the darkness, struggling between life and death."

Stowell knew, though he dare not look, that she was brushing her handkerchief over her eyes.

" Victor," she said, " don't you think women are rather brave creatures? "

" The bravest creatures in the world! " he answered.

" I knew you would say that," said Fenella, in a low voice. " And that's why I always think of you as their champion, fighting their battles for them when they are wronged and helpless."

Stowell felt as if he were choking. He could not go on with this hypocrisy any longer. He must tell her now. It would be like committing suicide, but what must be, must be.

" Fenella. . . ."

But just then the loud voice of the Captain cried " Strike! " and at the next moment Fenella was flying aft, to tug at the net and shake out the herrings that came up with it.

What shouts! What screams! What peals of laughter!

It was midnight before the joy and bustle of the catch were over, and the net was shot again. The Governor was then smoking his last pipe in the Captain's cabin, and Stowell, with Fenella on his arm, was walking to and fro on the deck.

" Need I tell her at all? " he was thinking.

He felt as if he were being swept along by an irresistible flood. He could not doom himself to death. With Fenella by his side he could think of nobody and nothing but her. Sometimes, when they crossed the light from the skylight, they turned their faces towards each other and smiled.

After a while Stowell found himself bantering Fenella. Catching a flash of her ring (his mother's ring) on the hand that was on his arm, he pretended it was gone and asked if it had fallen off while she was pulling at the net.

" Gone! The ring you ga— . . . . I mean the Deemster gave me! No, here it is! What a shock! I should have died if I had lost it."

She was radiant; he was reckless; the little trick had uncovered their hearts to each other.

They heard a step on the other side of the deck.

" Fenella! "

It was the Governor going down the companion. " Time to turn in, girl! We are to breakfast at Port St. Mary at nine in the morning, you know."

" I'm coming, father."

" Good-night, Stowell! "

" Good-night, Sir! "

But he could not let Fenella go. It was a sin to go to bed at all on such a heavenly night.   At last, at the top of the companion, he loosed her arm, with a slow asundering, and said,

"The Governor says we are to breakfast at Port St. Mary— do you think we shall if this calm continues?"

She laughed (her laugh seemed to come up from her heart) and said, "I'm not worrying about that."

"No?"

"When a woman has all she wants in the world in one place why should she wish to go to another?"

"And have *you*?"

"Good-night!" she said, holding out both hands.

He caught them, and the touch communicated fire. At the next moment he had lifted her hands to his lips.

She drew them down, and his hands with them, pressed them to her breast and then broke away, and was gone in an instant.

Stowell gasped. "She loves me! She loves me! She loves me!"

Nothing else mattered! Let the world rip!

II

Stowell did not go below that night. For two hours he tramped the deck, laughing to himself like a lunatic.

"She loves me! She loves me! She loves me!"

When the watch had to be changed at two o'clock he sent the man to his berth and took his place. And when the dawn broke and the lamps of the fishing fleet blinked out, and the boats showed grey, like ghosts, on the colourless waste around, and the monotonous chanting of the crews far and near told him the nets were being hauled in, he shouted down the fo'c'sle for the men. And when they came on deck he helped them to haul in their own net and to empty their catch (it was the Governor's order) into the first "Nickey" that came along.

The grey sky in the east had reddened to a flame by this time. Then up from the round rim of the sea rose the everlasting sun, and lo, it was day! God, what an enchanted world it was! All the glory and majesty of the sea seemed to be singing hymns to the same tune as that of his own heart:

"She loves me! She loves me! She loves me!"

A light wind sprang up, a cool blowing from the south, just enough to ripple the surface of the water. Already some of the fishing boats had swung about and were standing off for home. Stowell helped to haul the mainsail, and shouted with the men as they pulled at the ropes and the white canvas rose above them.

"She loves me! She loves me! She loves me!"

Within half an hour the wind had freshened to a summer gale and they were running before a roaring sea. The sails bellied out, the yacht listed over, the scuppers were half full of water, but Stowell would not go below. For a long hour more he held on and looked around at the fishing boats as they flew together in the brilliant sunshine between the two immensities of sky and sea.

" She loves me! She loves me! She loves me! "

Helloa! Here was his own little island with the sun riding over the mountain-tops! The plunging and rearing of the yacht gave the notion that the mountains were nodding to him. " Good morning, son." What nonsense came into a man's head when his heart was glad!

" She loves me! She loves me! She loves me! "

Ah, here were the cliffs of the Calf, with their hoary heads in the flying sky and their feet in the thunder of the sea! And here was the brown-belted lighthouse of the Chicken Rock, which Fenella and he had picked up last night! And here was the shoulder of Spanish Head, and here was the belly of the Chasms, ringing with the cry of ten thousand sea fowl!

" She loves me! She loves me! She loves me! "

Suddenly there came a shock. They were opening the bay of Port St. Mary, with the little fishing town lying asleep along its sheltered arm, when he saw across the Poolvaish (the pool of death) the grey walls of Castle Rushen, and the long reach of Langness. And then memory flowed back on him like a tidal wave.

Derby Haven! The old maids' house! The girl burning her candle in her bedroom to educate herself that she might become worthy to be his wife!

" Oh God! Oh God! "

If Fenella loved him he had stolen her love. He had no right to it, being married already, virtually married—bound by every tie that could hold an honourable man.

He felt like a traitor—a traitor to Fenella now. He recalled what he had said last night. One step more and——

Thank God, he had gone no farther! If he had allowed Fenella to engage herself to him, and then the facts about Bessie Collister had become known, as they might have done through Dan Baldromma——

He must go. He must go immediately. His miserable mistake must not bring disgrace on Fenella also.

The yacht was sliding into the slack water of the bay, and the row-boats of the fish-buyers, each flying its little flag, were coming out to meet the fishing boats, when Stowell went down to the saloon—still dark with its blue silk curtains over skylight and portholes.

He took off his fisherman's clothes, put on his own, and sat down at the table to scribble a note to the Governor:

> "Excuse me! I must go up to Douglas by the first train. Have just remembered an important engagement.
>
> Hope to call at Government Office to-morrow."

As he was leaving the saloon he looked back towards the cabin in which Fenella lay asleep. His eyes were wet, his heart throbbed painfully, he felt as if he were being banished from her presence as by a curse. Renunciation—life-long renunciation—that was all that was left to him now.

The fleet were in harbour when he went on deck, a hundred boats huddled together. And when he stepped ashore the fish salesmen were selling the night's catch by auction, and the bronze-faced and heavy-bearded fishermen, in their big boots, were counting their herrings in mixed English and Manx:

"Nane, jeer, three, kiare, quieg . . . . warp, tally!"

CHAPTER FIFTEEN

THE WOMAN'S SECRET

WHEN Stowell awoke next morning at Ballamoar a flock of sheep, liberated from a barn, were bleating before a barking dog. He had passed a restless night. All his soul revolted against the renunciation he had imposed upon himself. It was like life-long imprisonment. Yet what was he to do? He must decide and decide quickly.

Suddenly he thought of the Governor. The strong sense and practical wisdom of the Governor might help him to a decision. But Fenella's father! How could he tell his story to Fenella's father?

At last an idea came to him whereby he could obtain the Governor's counsel without betraying his secret. He was at the crisis. On what he did now the future of his life depended. And not his own life, only, but Fenella's also, perhaps, and . . . . Bessie Collister's.

At three o'clock he was at the Government offices in Douglas. Police inspectors were at the door and moving about in the corridors. One of them took him up to the Governor's room—a large chamber overlooking the street and noisy from the tram-cars that ran under the windows. The Governor's iron-grey head was bent over a desk-table.

"Sit down—I shall not be long."

Stowell felt his heart sink in advance. Never would he be able to say what he had come to say.

"Well, you gave us the slip nicely, didn't you?" said the Governor, raising his head from his papers.

"I'm sorry, Sir," said Stowell (he felt his lip trembling). "It was an important matter, and I've come to town to-day to ask your advice on it."

"Something you've been consulted about?"

"Well . . . . yes."

"I'm no authority on law, you know."

"It's not so much a matter of law, Sir, as of morality—what an honourable man ought to do under difficult circumstances."

The Governor looked up sharply. Stowell struggled on.

"A client . . . . I should say a friend . . . . engaged himself to a young woman awhile ago, and now, owing to circumstances which have arisen since, he finds it difficult to decide whether it is his duty to marry her."

"Manxman?"

"Yes."

"What class?"

Stowell felt his voice as well as his lips trembling. "Oh, good enough class, I think."

The Governor picked up his pipe from the table, charged it, lighted it, turned his chair towards the fireplace, threw his leg over the rail-fender and said:

"Fire away."

Then trembling and ashamed, but making a strong call on his resolution, Stowell told his own story—as if it had been that of another man.

When he had come to an end there was a long silence. The Governor pulled hard at his pipe and there was no other sound in the room except the rattle of the tram-cars in the street.

Stowell felt hot, his lips felt dry, and pushing back his black hair, he found sweat on his forehead.

"It was a shocking blunder, of course," he said. "My man doesn't defend himself. Still he thinks the circumstances . . . ."

"You mean it wasn't deliberate?"

"Good Lord, no!"

"In fact a kind of accident?"

"One might say so."

"Any harm done?"

" Harm? " Stowell turned white and began to stammer. " I
. . . . no, that is to say . . . . no, I've never heard . . . . "

" And yet he promised to marry the girl? "

" He felt responsible for her. He couldn't be a scoundrel."

" Did he care for her—love her? "

" I can't say that, Sir. He might have thought he did."

" And now he loves another woman? "

" With all his heart and soul, Sir."

" But " (the Governor was puffing placidly) " he has promised
to marry the little farm girl, and she's away somewhere educating
herself to become his wife? "

" That's it, Sir," said Stowell (his head was down), " and now
he is asking himself what it is his duty to do. I have told him it is
his duty as a man of honour to carry out his promise—to marry the
girl, whatever the consequences to himself. Am I right, Sir? "

There was another moment of silence, and then the Governor,
taking his pipe out of his mouth, and bringing his open palm down
on the table, said:

" No! "

" No? "

" It would be marrying the wrong woman, wouldn't it? "

" Well . . . . yes, one might say that, Sir."

" Then it would be a crime."

" A crime? "

" A three-fold crime."

The Governor rose, crossed the floor, then drew up in front of
Stowell and spoke with sudden energy.

" First, against the girl herself. She's an attractive young
person, I suppose, eh? "

Stowell nodded.

" But uneducated, illiterate, out of another world, as they say?"

Stowell nodded again.

" Then does your man suppose that by sending her to school
for a few months he will bridge the gulf between them? Is that
how he expects to make her happy? Ten to one the girl will be
a miserable outsider in her husband's house to the last day of her
life. But that's not the worst, by a long way."

" No? "

" If he marries her it will out of a sense of duty, will it not? "

" Ye-es."

" Well, what woman on God's earth wants to be married out
of a sense of duty? And if he loves another woman do you think
his wife will not find it out some day? Of course she will! And
when she does what do you think will happen? I'll tell you what

will happen. If she's one of the sensitive kind she'll feel herself crushed, superfluous, and pine away and die of grief and shame, or perhaps take a dose of something . . . . we've heard of such happenings, haven't we? And if she's a woman of the other sort she'll go farther."

" You mean . . . ."

" Suspicion, jealousy, envy! She may not care a brass farthing about her husband, but her pride as a wife will be wounded. She won't give him a day's peace, or herself either. He'll never be an hour out of her sight but she'll think he's with the other woman. And then—what's sauce for the goose is sauce for the gander! If he has another woman as likely as not she'll have another man—we've heard of that, too, haven't we? "

Stowell dropped his head. His heart was beating high, and he was afraid his face was betraying it. The Governor touched him on the shoulder, and continued,

" In the next place, it would be a crime against the man himself. He's a young fellow of some prospects, I suppose? "

" I . . . . I think so."

" And the girl has some family, hasn't she? "

" Yes."

" They may be good and worthy folk of whom he would have no reason to be ashamed. But isn't it just as likely that they are people of quite another kidney? Sisters and brothers and cousins to the tenth degree? Some vulgar and rapacious old father, perhaps, who hasn't taken too much trouble to keep the girl out of temptation while she has been at home, but freezes on to her fast enough after she has made a good marriage. Possible, isn't it? "

" Quite possible, sir."

" Well, what are your man's own friends going to do with him with a menagerie like that at his heels? No, he has fettered himself for life to failure as well as misery, and while his wife is railing at him about the other woman he is reproaching her with standing in his light. So the end of his noble endeavour is that he has set up a little private hell for himself in the house he calls his home."

Stowell was wincing at every word, but all the same he knew that his eyes were shining. The Governor looked sharply up at him for a moment, lit his pipe afresh and said,

" Then there's the other woman. I suppose her case is worthy of some consideration? "

" Indeed, yes."

" If she cares for the man . . . . "

" I can't say that, Sir."

" Well, *if* she does, she too will suffer, will she not? And what has she done to deserve suffering? Nothing at all! She's the innocent scapegoat, isn't she? "

" That's true."

" Fine woman, I suppose? "

" The finest woman in the world, Sir."

" Just so! But your man would doom her to renunciation—a solitary life of sorrow and regret. And so the only result of his praiseworthy principles, his sense of duty, as you say, and all the rest of it, is that he will have ruined three lives—the life of the woman he marries and does not love, the life of the woman he loves and does not marry, and his own life also."

" Then you think, Sir . . . . you think he should stop even yet? "

" Even at the church door, at the altar-steps—if there's no harm done, and he is sure she is the wrong woman."

Stowell felt as if the vapours which had clouded his brain so long had been swept away as by a mountain breeze, but he thought it necessary to keep up the disguise.

" I feel you must be right, sir," rising to go. " At all events I cannot argue against you. But I think you'll agree that . . . . that if my man can wipe out this bad passage in his life without injury to anybody and without scandal . . . . I think you will agree that his first duty is to tell the woman he loves . . . . "

" Eh? What the deuce . . . . Good heavens, no! "

" But surely he couldn't ask a pure-minded girl . . . . "

" To take the other woman's leavings? Certainly he couldn't if she knew anything about it. But why should she? Why should a pure-minded girl, as you say, be told about something that happened before she came on to the scene? "

Stowell's scruples were overcome. He had argued against himself, but he knew well that he had wished to be beaten. He was going off when the Governor, following him to the door, laid a hand on his shoulder and said,

" When a man has done wrong the thing he has got to do next is to say nothing about it. That's what your man has got to do now. It's the woman secret, isn't it? Very well, he must never reveal it to anybody—never, under any circumstances—never in this world! "

II

Next day, at Ballamoar, after many fruitless efforts to begin, Stowell was writing to Bessie Collister.

" Dear Bessie,—I am sorry to send you this letter and it is very painful for me to write it.   But I cannot allow you to look forward any longer to something which can never happen.

" The truth is—I must tell you the truth, Bessie—since you went to Derby Haven I have found that I do not love you as I ought, to become your husband.   That being so, I cannot do you the great wrong of marrying you.   It would not be either for your good or for mine.   And since I cannot marry you I feel that we must part.   I am miserable when I say this, but I see that in justice to you, as well as to myself, nothing else can be . . . . "

He could go no further.   A wave of tenderness towards Bessie came over him.   He had visions of the girl receiving and reading his letter.   It would be at night in her little bedroom, perhaps— the room in which she burnt her candle to learn her lessons.

No, it would be too cruel, too cowardly.   He would not write —he would go to Derby Haven and break the news to the girl himself.

But that evoked other and more fearful visions.   They would be walking along the sandy path at Langness with the stark white lighthouse at the end of it.   " Bessie," he would be saying, " We must part; it will be better for both of us.   It has all been my fault.   You have nothing to reproach yourself with.   But you must try to forget me, and if there is anything else I can do . . . . " And then the reproaches, the recriminations, the tears, the supplications, the appeals: " Don't throw me over!   You promised to stand up for me, you know.   I will be good."

It would be terrible.   It would make his heart bleed.   Nevertheless he must bear it.   It was a part of his punishment.

He had torn up his letter and was putting his hand on the bell to order the dog-cart to be brought round to take him to the railway station, when a servant came into the room and said,

" Mr. Alick Gell to see you, sir."

Gell came in with a gloomy and half-shamefaced look.   His tall figure was bent, his fair hair was disordered, and his voice trembled as he said,

" Can't we take a walk in the wood, old fellow?   I have something to say."

" I don't know how to tell you," he began.   They were crossing the lawn towards the plantation.   " Its about Bessie."

" Bessie? "

" I . . . .   I'm madly in love with her."

10

Stowell stopped and looked without speaking into Gell's twitching face.

"I knew you wouldn't be able to believe it, but don't look at me like that."

"Tell me," said Stowell.

And then, stammering and trembling, Gell told his story. He didn't know how it began. Perhaps it was pity. He had been sorry for the girl, over there in that lonely place, so he went down at first just to cheer her up. Then he had found himself going frequently, buying her presents and taking her out for walks. When he had realised how things were he had tried to pull up, but it was too late. He had struggled to be loyal—to strengthen himself by talking of Stowell—praising him to the girl, excusing him for not coming to see her—but it was useless. His pity had developed into love, and before he had known what he was doing Bessie was in his arms. At the next instant he had felt like a traitor. He was frantically happy and yet he wanted to kill himself.

"It was terrible," he said. "I couldn't sleep at night for thinking of it. Bessie wanted you to be told. In fact she wrote you a letter, saying we couldn't help loving each other, and asking you to release her. But I couldn't let her go that far. 'Then go to Ballamoar and tell him yourself,' she said. And at last I've come. And now . . . . now you know."

Stowell listened in silence. His first feeling was one of wounded pride. He had really been a great fool about the girl! What fathomless depths of conceit had led him to think she would break her heart if he gave her up? And then the long struggle between his love and his duty—what a mountebank Fate seemed to have made of him! But his next feeling was one of relief—boundless, inexpressible relief. The iron chain he had been dragging after him had been broken. He was free!

Gell, who was breathing hard, was watching Stowell from under his cap, which was pulled down over his forehead. They were walking in a path that was thick with fallen leaves, and there was no sound for some moments but that of the rustling under their feet.

"Why don't you speak, old fellow? I've behaved like a cad, I know. But for God's sake, don't torture me. Strike me in the face with your fist. I would rather that—upon my soul, I would."

"Alick," said Stowell, putting his arm through Gell's. "I'm going to tell you something."

"What?"

" Do you know what I was on the point of doing when you came? Going down to Derby Haven to ask Bessie to let me off."

" Is that true? You're not saying it merely to . . . . But why? "

" Because what's happened to her has happened to me also—I love somebody else."

" No? Really? . . . . But who . . . . who is the other girl? . . . . Is it . . . . It's Fenella, isn't it? "

" Yes."

" How splendid! I'm glad! And of course I congratulate you . . . . No? . . . . You've not asked her yet? But that will be all right—of course it will! "

Taking off his cap to fan himself with, Gell broke into fits of half hysterical laughter. Then he said:

" You don't mind my saying something now that it's all over? No? Well, to tell you the truth I could never believe you really cared for Bessie. I thought you were only marrying her as a sort of duty, having got her into trouble with Dan Baldromma. And it was so—partly so—wasn't it? That didn't excuse me, though, did it? Lord, what a relief! I feel as if you had lifted ten tons off my head."

A dark memory came to Stowell. " Has she told him? "

" Bessie will be relieved, too, and just as glad as I am. Do you know, there's a heart of gold in that girl. She's never had a dog's chance yet. Not much education, I admit, but such spirit, such character! Such a woman too—you said so yourself, remember."

A still darker memory of something the Governor had said came to Stowell. " Didn't you say Bessie had written to me? " he asked.

" Yes, she did, yesterday; but I destroyed her letter."

" Do you know, I wrote to Bessie to-day, and I destroyed my letter also."

" No? What fun if your letters had crossed in the post," said Gell, and tossing his cap into the air, he broke into still louder peals of laughter.

Again Stowell felt immense relief. It was impossible that Bessie could have told him. And if she hadn't, why should he? Why injure the girl in Gell's eyes? Why tarnish his faith in her? It was the woman's secret, therefore he must never reveal it— never in this world.

They were walking on. Gell with a high step was kicking up the withered leaves.

" What about your people? " asked Stowell.

"Ah, that's what I've got to find out. I'm going home now to tell them. My mother is always advising me to marry and settle down, but of course she'll jib at Bessie, and the sisters will follow suit. As for my father, he has only one son, as he says, and I must have a better allowance. He cut it down after that affair in the Courts, you know."

They were at the gate to the road, and pulling it open, Gell said:

"Phew! How different I feel from what I did when I was coming in here half an hour ago! I thought you would kick me out the minute I had told you. But now we're going to be better friends than ever, aren't we?"

"Good-bye and good luck, old fellow," said Stowell.

"Good-bye, and God bless you, old chap," said Gell.

Stowell stood at the gate and watched him going off with long strides, his shoulders working vigorously.

"Never again! We can never be the same friends again," thought Stowell, as he turned back to the house.

He was feeling like a man who in a moment of passion has secretly wronged his life-long friend and can never look straight into his eyes again.

But the sense of a barrier between Gell and himself was soon wiped out by the memory of Fenella. He was free to love her at last! No more hypocrisy! No more self-denial! No more struggles between passion and duty! The past was dead. Life from that day forward was beginning again for all of them.

"Was that Alick Gell in the wood with you?" asked Janet, who had come to the door to call Stowell in to tea.

"Yes."

"Goodness me! He must be a happy boy. He was laughing enough, anyway."

III

Stowell went to bed early that night, slept soundly and was up with the coming of light in the morning.

The farm lads were not yet astir, but going round to the stable he saddled a horse for himself (a young chestnut mare that had been born on one of his own birthdays) and set off for a ride to relieve the intoxication of his spirits.

The air was keen, but both he and his horse sniffed it with delight. As they passed out of Ballamoar the sun rose and played among the red and yellow leaves of the plantation, for the summer was going out in a blaze of glory. They crossed the Curragh, dipped into the glen, and climbed the corkscrew path to the mountain.

Stowell thought he had never felt so well. And the little mare, catching the contagion of his high spirits, snorted and swung her head at every stride and dug her feet into the ringing ground.

" Helloa, Molly, here we are at the top! "

Looking back he saw the flat plain below, dotted over with farms, each with its little farmhouse surrounded by its clump of sheltering trees. God, how good to think that every one of them was a home of love! Love! That was the great uniter, the great comforter, the great liberator, the great redeemer!

And to think that all this had been going on since the beginning of the world! That generation after generation some boy had come up this lovely glen to court his girl! Lord, what a glorious place the world was, after all!

His eyes were beaming like the sunshine, and to make his joy complete he galloped over the mountain-tops until he came to a point at which he could look down on Douglas and catch a glimpse of Fenella's home in the midst of its trees.

> " *Peace in her chamber, wheresoe'er it be,*
> *A holy place . . . .* "

Then back to Ballamoar at a brisk canter, with the air musical with the calls of cattle, the bleating of sheep and the songs of birds. And then breakfast for a hungry man—cowrie and eggs and fresh butter and honey and junket, which the Manx called pinjean.

At three o'clock in the afternoon he was on his way to Government House, and by that time the intoxication of his high spirits had suffered a check.

What had Fenella thought of his flight from the yacht? Had she believed his excuse for it? What interpretation had she put upon his intention of calling at Government Offices the following day? And the Governor—had he seen through the thin disguise of that story?

But the cruellest question of all, and the hardest to answer, was whether after all, even now that he was free, he had any right to ask Fenella to become his wife? He, a sin-soiled man, and she a stainless woman!

He felt as if he ought to purge his soul by telling Fenella everything. Yet how could he do that without inflicting an incurable wound on her faith in him? And then what had the Governor said? " Never under any circumstances."

As he walked up the carriage drive to Government House he saw the Governor's tall figure, and the Attorney-General's short one, through the windows of the smoking-room. The Governor came to the door to meet him.

"The very man we were talking about. Come in! Sit down. We have something to propose to you."

The Governor was going up to London on urgent business at the Home Office and the Attorney had to go with him. In these circumstances it had been necessary to arrange that the Court of General Gaol Delivery (interrupted by the Deemster's death, but now summoned to resume) should sit without the Governor, and the Attorney had been suggesting that Stowell should represent him in an important case.

"What is it, Sir?" asked Stowell.

"Murder again, my boy; but of a different kind this time."

A Peel fisherman had killed his wife with shocking brutality, yet everybody seemed to sympathise with him, and there was a danger that a Manx jury might let him off.

"Splendid opportunity to uphold law and order! You'll take the case?"

"With pleasure!"

"Good! The Attorney will send you the papers. And now, I suppose, you would like to see Fenella?"

"May I?"

"Why not? You'll find her in the drawing-room."

On his way to the drawing-room Stowell met Miss Green coming out of it. She smiled at him, and said, in a half-whisper,

"I think you are expected."

When he opened the door he saw Fenella sitting with her back to him at a little desk on one side of the bay window, with a glint of its light on her bronze-brown hair.

"Who is it?" she said as he entered. But at the next moment she seemed to know, and, rising, she turned round to him and smiled.

He thought she had never looked so beautiful. He wanted to crush her in his arms, and at the same time to fall at her feet and kiss the hem of her dress.

There was a moment of passionate silence. He stepped towards her but stopped when two or three paces away. A riot of conflicting emotions were going on within him. He felt strong, he felt weak, he felt brave, he felt cowardly, he felt proud, he felt ashamed.

Still nothing was said by either of them. Her eyes were glistening, she was breathing quickly and her bosom was heaving. He saw her moving towards him. Her hand was trailing along the desk. He felt as if she were drawing him to her, and by a nervous, but irresistible impulse he held out his arms.

"Fenella," he said, hardly audibly.

At the next moment, as in a flash of light, she sprang upon his breast, and at the next her arms were about his neck, his own were around her waist, her mouth was to his mouth, and the world had melted away.

Ten minutes later, with faces aflame, they went, hand in hand, into the smoking-room. The Governor wheeled about on his revolving chair to look at them.

"Well," he said, "it's easy to see what you two have come about. But not for six months! I won't agree to a day less, remember."

CHAPTER SIXTEEN

AT THE SPEAKER'S

BEFORE Alick Gell reached his father's house another had been there on the same errand.

Earlier in the afternoon Dan Baldromma, while running his hands through the ground flour in the mill, with the wheel throbbing and the stones groaning about him, had been struck by a new idea.

"Liza," he said, returning to the dwelling house and standing with his back to the fire and his big hands behind him, "that young wastrel ought to be freckened into marrying the girl, and I'm thinking I know the way to do it, too."

"It's like thou do, Dan," said Mrs. Collister.

Dan's device was of the simplest. It was that of sending the mother of Bessie Collister to the mother of Alick Gell to threaten and intimidate her.

"But sakes alive, man, that's an ugly job, isn't it?"

"It's got to be done, woman, or there'll be worse to do next, I tell thee. Thou don't want to see thy daughter where her mother was before her."

"Well, well, if I must, I must," said Mrs. Collister. "But, aw dear, aw dear! If thou hadn't thrown the girl into the way of temptation by shutting the door on her . . . . "

"Hould thy whist, woman, and do as I tell thee, and that will be the best night's work I ever done for her."

Half an hour later, having swept the earthen floor, hung the kettle on its sooty chain, and laid the table for Dan's tea, Mrs. Collister toiled upstairs to dress for her journey, and came down in the poke bonnet and satin mantle which she wore to chapel on Sunday.

Meantime Dan had harnessed the old mare to the stiff cart and brought it round to the door. Having helped his wife over the wheel and put the rope reins in her hands, he gave her his parting instructions.

"See thou stand up for thy rights, now! This is thy chance and thou's got to make the best of it!"

"Aw well, we'll see," said the old woman, and then the stiff cart rattled over the cobbled "street" on its way to the Speaker's.

In her comfortable sitting-room, thickly carpeted and plentifully cushioned, Mrs. Gell was awakened from her afternoon nap by the scream of the peacocks.

"It's Mistress Daniel Collister of Baldromma to see you, ma'am," said the maid.

At the next moment, Mrs. Collister, with a timid air, hobbled into the room on her stick, and the two mothers came face to face.

"You wish to speak to me," said Mrs. Gell.

"If you plaze, ma'am," said Mrs. Collister, huskily.

Isabella Gell, a sour-faced young woman, came into the room and stood behind her mother's chair. Mrs. Collister took the seat that was assigned to her, and fumbled the ribbons of her bonnet to loosen them.

"It's about my daughter, ma'am."

"Well?"

"My daughter and your son, ma'am."

"Eh?"

"Cæsar Qualtrough of the Kays has seen them together. They're living down Castletown way, they're saying."

"Living . . . . my son and your daughter?"

"So they're saying, ma'am."

"I don't believe it! I don't believe a word of it!"

"I wish in my heart I could say the same, ma'am. But it's truth enough, I'm fearing."

"And if it is—I don't say it is, but *if* it is—why have you come to me?"

Then trembling all over, Mrs. Collister continued her story. Her poor girl was in trouble. When a girl was in trouble the world could be cruel hard on her. Nobody would think the cruel hard it could be. If a girl did wrong it was because somebody she was fond of had promised to marry her. What else would she do it for? When a young man had behaved like that to a poor girl he ought to keep his word to her. And if he had a mother, and she was a good Christian woman . . . .

Mrs. Gell, who was beating her foot on the carpet, broke in impatiently.

" In short, you think my son ought to marry your daughter? "

" It's nothing but right, ma'am."

" And you've come here to ask me to tell him to do so? "

" If you plaze, ma'am."

" Well, I never! " said Isabella.

" She's a mother herself, I was thinking, and if one of her own girls was in the same position . . . . "

" The idea! " said Isabella.

" Mrs. Collister," said Mrs. Gell, with a proud lift of her head, " I was sorry when I heard of the trouble your daughter had brought on you, but what you are doing now is a piece of great assurance."

" But Bessie is a good girl, ma'am. And if she married your son you would never have raison to be ashamed of her."

" Good indeed! If a girl isn't ashamed to be living with a young man the less said about her goodness the better."

" Aw well, ma'am," said Mrs. Collister (her faltering tongue had become firmer and her timid eyes had begun to flash), " if she's living with the young man, he's living with her, and the shame is the same for both, I'm thinking."

Mrs. Gell drew herself up in her chair.

" I'm astonished at you, Mrs. Collister! A woman yourself, and not seeing the difference."

" Aw yes, difference enough, ma'am! And when a young man doesn't keep his word it's the woman that's knowing it best by the trouble that's coming on her."

Mrs. Gell, whose anger was rising, lifted her chin again and said, " If your daughter is in trouble, Mrs. Collister, how are we to know that she had not brought it on her own head, just to get Alick to marry her? "

" The creature! " said Isabella.

" And how are we to know that you and your husband have not encouraged the girl in her wickedness just to get our son for your son-in-law? "

" Aw well, ma'am," said Mrs. Collister (she was fumbling at the strings of her bonnet to tighten them), " if you are thinking as bad of me as that . . . . "

" You talk of the danger to your daughter if my son doesn't marry her," said Mrs. Gell. " But what of the danger to my son if he does? His life will be ruined. He will never be able to raise his head in the island again. His father will disown him. Marry your daughter indeed! Not only will I not ask him to marry her, but if I see the slightest danger of his doing anything so foolish I will do everything I can to prevent it."

" Aw well, we'll say no more, ma'am," said Mrs. Collister, and she shuffled to her feet.

But Mrs. Gell was up before her.

" Alexander Gell, son of the Speaker and grandson of Archdeacon Mylechreest, married to the step-daughter of Dan Baldromma and the nameless offspring of Liza Collister . . . . "

" Ma'am ! "

Mrs. Collister had hobbled to the door, and was going out, humbled and beaten, when Mrs. Gell's last words cut her to the quick. For more than twenty years she had taken the punishment of her own sin and bowed her head to the lash of it, but at this insult to her child the weak and timid creature turned about, as brave as a lion and as fierce as a fury.

" I'm not your quality, I know that, ma'am," she said, breathing quickly, " but a day is coming, and maybe it's near, when we'll be standing together where we'll both be equal. Just two old mothers, and nothing else between us. If you've loved your son, I've loved my daughter, whatever she is, ma'am. And when the One who reads all hearts is after asking me what I did for my child in the day of her trouble, I'll be telling Him I came here to beg you on my knees to save her from a life of sin and shame, and you wouldn't, because your worldly pride prevented. And then it's Himself, ma'am, will be judging between us ! "

II

There had been a sitting of the Keys that day, and when the Speaker returned home he found his wife on the sofa with a damp handkerchief over her forehead and a bottle of smelling-salts in her hand. She told him what had happened.

" Well, well," he said, " so that's what it means. But there's no knowing what hedge the hare will jump from."

His figure was less burly than before, his head was more bald and his full beard was whiter, but his eyes flashed with the same ungovernable fire.

" That girl must be a thoroughly bad one," said Mrs. Gell. " It's not the first time she has got our Alick into trouble, remember. We must save our son from the designing young huzzy."

" Tut ! It's not the girl I'm troubling about."

" Who else, then ? "

" The man ! I might have expected as much, though ! "

Coming home in the train he had had some talk with Kerruish, his advocate and agent. Dan Baldromma, who was back with his rent, was refusing to pay, and saying " Let the Spaker fetch me to Coort, and I'll tell him the raison."

" Then can't you settle with the man, Archie? "

" Settle with Dan? I'll settle with Alick first, Bella, and if he has given that scoundrel the whip hand of me I'll break every bone in his body."

" But it may not be true. It cannot be true. Unless Alick tells me so himself I'll never believe a word of it."

They were at tea in the dining-room, country fashion, the Speaker at the head of the table with a plate of fish before him, and his wife and daughters at either side, when Alick entered.

" Helloa! " he cried, with a forced gaiety. But only his mother responded to his greeting and made room for him by her side. She saw that he was paler and thinner, and that his hand trembled when he took his cup.

The Speaker, who had turned his rough shoulder to his son, tried to restrain himself from breaking out on him until the meal would be over and he could take him into his own room, but before long his impatience overcame him.

" What's this we're hearing about you—that you are carrying on with a girl? "

" Do you mean Bessie Collister, Sir? " said Alick.

" Certainly I mean Bessie Collister. And I thought you gave me your word that you would see no more of her."

" But that was the promise of a boy, Sir. Did you expect it to bind the man also? "

" The man? The man! " said the Speaker, mimicking his son's voice in a mincing treble. " Do you call yourself a man, bringing disgrace on your name and family."

" What disgrace, Sir? "

" What disgrace? All the island seems to have heard of it. Is it necessary to tell you? Living secret, so they say, with a woman who isn't fit company for your mother and sisters."

" If anybody told you that, Sir," said Alick (his lower lip was trembling), " he told you a lie—a damned lie, Sir! "

" There! " cried Mrs. Gell, turning to her husband. " What did I say? It isn't true, you see."

" Of course it isn't true, mother; and the best proof that I'm not behaving dishonourably to Bessie Collister is that I intend to marry her."

It was a sickening moment for Mrs. Gell, and the Speaker, for an instant, was dumbfounded.

" Eh? What? You intend to marry . . . . "

" Yes, Sir; and that's why I'm here to-day—to bring you the

news, and to ask you to restore the allowance you cut down in the spring, you know."

" That . . . . that . . . . that bast— . . . . "

" Archie! " cried Mrs. Gell, indicating their daughters.

" Bessie is a good girl, father," said Alick. " What happened before she was born wasn't her fault, Sir."

" So you've come to bring us the news and to ask me to double your allowance? "

" If you please, Sir. You couldn't wish your son and his wife . . . . "

" His wife! There you are, Bella! That's what I've been working day and night thirty years for—to see my son throw half my earnings—all that I can't will away from him—into the hands of a man like Dan Baldromma! "

" But Alick will be reasonable," said Mrs. Gell. " He'll give the girl up."

" He'll have to do that, and quick too, or I'll cut off his allowance altogether."

" Do you mean it, Sir? " said Alick—he was pushing his chair back.

" Do I mean it? Certainly I mean it. You'll give the girl up or never another penny of mine shall you see as long as I live! "

" All right," said Alick, rising from the table, " I'll earn my own living."

The Speaker broke into a peal of scornful laughter. " *You* earn your living! That's rich! "

" Give her up? " cried Alick. " I'll break stones on the highway or porter on the pier before I'll give up her little finger! "

" You fool! You confounded fool! But no fear! She'll give *you* up when she finds you've lost your income."

" Will she? I'll trust her for that, Sir."

" Then get away back to her—you'll not be the first by a long way."

Alick, who had been trying to laugh, stopped his laughter suddenly, and said, " What do you mean by that, Sir? "

" Mean? Do you want me to tell you what I mean? "

" Archie," cried Mrs. Gell, and again she indicated their daughters.

" Get out of this, will you? " cried the Speaker to the girls, who had been sitting with their noses in their teacups.

The girls fled from the room, but stood outside to listen.

" Father," said Alick, " you must tell me what you mean."

" Mean! Mean! Don't stand there cross-examining your own

father. You know what I mean! If half they say about the young b— . . . . is true she's fit enough for it, anyway."

"If any other man had said that," said Alick, quivering, "I should have knocked him down, Sir."

"What's that? You threaten me?" cried the Speaker. His voice was like the scream of a sea-gull, and making a step towards Alick he lifted his clenched fist to him.

Mrs. Gell intervened, and Alick retreated a pace or two.

"Take care, Sir," he said. "You can't treat me like that now. I'm not a child any longer."

"Then get away to your woman . . . . and to hell, if you want to."

"There was no need to tell me twice, Sir. I'm going. And as God is my witness, I'll never set foot in this house again."

At the next moment the peacocks were screaming outside, and the Speaker, who had thrown up the window, was shouting through it in a broken roar,

"Alick! Alick Gell! Come back, you damned scoundrel! Alick! Alexander . . . . "

They had to carry him upstairs and send for Dr. Clucas. It had been another of his paralysing brain-storms. It was not to be expected that he could bear many more of them.

CHAPTER SEVENTEEN

THE BURNING BOAT

Two days later, Gell was stepping into the train for Castletown on his way to Derby Haven.

"Give me up because my income is gone? Not Bessie! Not Bessie Collister!"

But Bessie had gone through deep waters since he had seen her last.

From the first Victor Stowell had disappointed her. To live in the dark—hidden away, unrecognised, suppressed—it had not been according to her expectations. Her pride, too, had been wounded by being sent back to school. It was true that without being asked, Mr. Stowell had promised to marry her at some future time, but perhaps that was only because he was the son of the Deemster and therefore afraid of her step-father and of the cry there would be all over the island if anything became known.

If it had only been Alick! Alick would not have been ashamed of her. He would have taken her just as she was and never seen any shortcomings.

After the first days at Derby Haven she had found herself looking forward to Alick's visits. When she knew he was coming everything brightened up in her eyes and even her tiresome lessons became delightful. Before long she felt her heart leap up whenever the Misses Brown called, " Bessie, a gentleman to see you! "

It is easy to kindle a fire on a warm hearth. Alick had been Bessie's first sweetheart, perhaps her only one. Suddenly a wonderful thing happened to her. She found herself in love. She had thought she had always been in love with somebody, but now she realized that she had never been in love before. She was in love with Alick Gell. And she wished to become his wife.

That altered everything. She began to see how ignorant she was compared with Alick and how much she was beneath him. She remembered his three tall sisters who held their heads so high at anniversaries and bazaars, and thought what a shocking thing it would be if they were able to look down on her. How she worked to be worthy of him!

She had no qualms about Stowell. Her only anxiety was about Alick. She was certain that he loved her, yet what a fight she had for him! He was always talking about Stowell, and praising him up to her. When he excused his friend for not coming to see her she was quite sure it was all nonsense. And when he gave her presents and said they were from Stowell she knew where they came from.

One day he brought a wrist-watch with the usual message, and after he had put it on (how his hands were trembling!) she tried to thank him, but didn't know how to do so.

At last an idea occurred to her. They were walking on the Langness, just by the ruin of a windmill, whose walls and roof had been carried away by a gale.

" Alick," she said, " I wonder if my new watch is right by the clock at Castle Rushen? "

Alick put his hands to his eyes like blinkers (for the sun was setting) and looked across the bay. While he did so, Bessie slipped off on tiptoe and hid behind the walls of the windmill. As soon as she was missed there was a laugh and a shout and then a chase. Bessie dodged and Alick doubled, Bessie dodged again, but at length she slipped into a hole, and at the next moment Alick caught her up and kissed her.

" Now, what have you done? " she said, and her face was suffused with blushes.

After that there could be no disguise between them. Bessie felt no shame, and it never occurred to her that she had been guilty of treason. But Gell talked about disloyalty and said he would never be at ease until she had made a clean breast of it to Stowell.

" Then go and tell him we couldn't help loving each other," she said.

When he was gone she was very happy. Mr. Stowell would give her up. Of course he would. What had happened between them was dead and buried. Whatever else he was Victor Stowell was a gentleman. He would say nothing to Alick.

Then came a shock. On the following morning she felt unwell. She had often felt unwell since she came to Derby Haven, and the Misses Brown, simple old maids, seeing no cause except the change in the girl's way of life, wanted to send for a doctor. But doctors were associated in Bessie's mind with death. If you saw a doctor going into a farmhouse one day you saw a coffin going in the next.

Chemists were not open to the same objection. Often on market days, after she had sold out her basket of butter and eggs, she had called at the chemist's at Ramsey for medicine for her mother. So, saying nothing to her housemates, she slipped round to the chemist's at Castletown and asked for a bottle of mixture.

The chemist, an elderly man with a fatherly face, smiled at her, and said:

" But what is it for, miss? "

Bessie described her symptoms, and then the smiling face was grave.

" Are you a married woman, ma'am? " asked the chemist.

Bessie caught her breath, stared at the man for a moment with eyes full of fear, and then turned and fled out of the shop.

All that day she felt dizzy and deaf. The earth seemed to be slipping from under her. Memories of what she had heard from older women came springing to the surface of her mind, and she asked herself why she had not thought of this before. For a long time she struggled to persuade herself that the chemist was wrong, but conviction forced itself upon her at last.

Then she asked herself what she was to do, and remembering what she had learned as a child at home of her mother's miserable life before her marriage, she found only one answer to that question. She must ask Mr. Stowell to marry her. The thought of parting from Alick was heart-breaking. But the most terrible thing was that she found herself hoping that Stowell would refuse to release her.

It had been a wretched day, dark and cheerless, with driving mist and drizzling rain. Towards nightfall the old maids lighted a fire for her in the sitting-room, which was full of quaint nick-nacks and old glass and china. The tide, which was at the bottom of the ebb, was sobbing against the unseen breakwater, and the gulls on the cobbles of the shore were calling continually.

Bessie was crouching over the fire with her chin in her hand when she heard the sneck of the garden gate, a quick step on the gravel, a light knock at the front door, a familiar voice in the lobby, and then old Miss Ethel saying behind her:

"A gentleman to see you, Bessie."

Her heart did not leap up as before, and she did not rise with her former alacrity, but Alick Gell came into the room like a rush of wind.

"What's this—unwell?" he cried.

"It's nothing! I shall be better in the morning," she said.

"Of course you will."

And then, after a kiss, Gell sat on a low stool at Bessie's feet, stretched his long legs towards the fire, and began to pour out his story.

He had seen Stowell and the matter had turned out just as she had expected. Splendid fellow! Best chap in the world, bar none!

"But what do you think, Bess? The most extraordinary coincidence! Dear old Vic, he has been busy falling in love, too! Fact! Fenella Stanley, daughter of the Governor! Magnificent girl, and Vic is madly in love with her! So there's to be no heart-breaking on either side, and that's the best of it. Makes one think there must be something in Providence, doesn't it?"

He was laughing so loud that the china in the room rang, but Bessie was turning cold with terror.

"And . . . . what about your father?" she faltered.

"My father?"

"Well . . . . to tell you the truth there was a bit of a breeze there," he said, and then followed the story of the scene at the Speaker's.

"But no matter! I'm not without money, so we can be married at once, and the sooner the better."

"But Alick," she said (he was stroking her hand and she was trying to draw it away), "do you think it's best?"

"Best? Why, of course I think it's best. Don't you?"

She did not reply.

"Don't you?" he said again, and then, getting no answer, he became aware that she, who had been so eager for their marriage before he went to Ballamoar, was now holding back.

"Bessie," he said, "has anything happened while I've been away?"

"No! Oh no!"

" You're . . . . you're not thinking of the loss of the income, are you? "

" No, no; 'deed, no! "

" I knew you wouldn't. When my father taunted me with that, saying you would give me up as soon as you knew my allowance was gone, I said, ' Not Bessie! I'll trust her for that, Sir.' "

Bessie began to cry. Alick was bewildered.

" What is it, then? Tell me! Are you . . . . are you thinking of Stowell? "

At that name she was seized by the mad impulse which comes to people on dizzy heights when they wish to throw themselves over—she wanted to blurt out the truth, to confess everything. But before she could speak Alick was saying,

" I shouldn't blame you if you were. I'm not his equal—I know that, Bessie. But even if he were free I shouldn't give you up to him now. No, by God, not to him or to anyone.

His voice was breaking. She looked at him. There were tears in his eyes. She could bear up no longer. With the cry of a drowning soul she flung her arms about him and sobbed on his breast.

An hour later, having comforted and quietened her, Gell was going off with swinging strides through the mist to catch the last train back to Douglas.

" She was thinking of me—that was it," he was telling himself. " Thought I would come to regret the sacrifice and wanted to save me from being cut off by my family. So unselfish! Never thinking of herself, bless her! "

And Bessie, in her bedroom was saying to herself, " He's that fond of me that he'll forgive me, whatever happens."

She lay a long time awake, with her arms under her head, looking up at the ceiling.

" Yes, Alick will forgive me, whatever happens," she thought.

And then she blew out her candle, buried her head in her pillow, and fell asleep.

II

When Gell reached the railway-station he found the carriages waiting at the platform, half-full of impatient passengers. A trial, which was going on in the Castle, was nearing its close, and the station-master had received orders that the last train to town was to be kept back for the Judges and advocates.

" The Peel fisherman," thought Gell. And, remembering that this was the case in which Stowell was to represent the Attorney-

11

General, he walked over to the Court-house, whose lantern-light was showing like a hazy white cloud above the Castle walls.

The little place was thick with sea mist, hot with the acid odour of perspiration, and densely crowded but breathlessly silent. The trial was over, the prisoner had been found guilty, and the Deemster (it was Deemster Taubman, sitting with the Clerk of the Rolls as Acting Governor) was beginning to pronounce sentence:

" Prisoner at the bar, it will be my duty to communicate to the proper quarter the Jury's recommendation to mercy, but I can hold out no hope that it will be of any avail. You have been found guilty of the wilful murder of your wife, therefore I bid you prepare . . . . "

And then followed those dread words in that dead stillness, which bring thoughts of the day of doom.

Gell caught one glimpse of the prisoner, as he stood in the dock, in his fisherman's guernsey, looking steadfastly into the face of his Judge, and another glimpse as a way was cleared through the spectators and he walked with a strong step to the door leading to the cells.

Then the court-house cleared to a low rumble that was like the muffled murmuring that is heard after a funeral.

Gell asked for Stowell, and was told that his friend had gone down to the Deemster's room with one of the advocates for the defence to draw up the terms of the recommendation. Therefore he returned to the station with a group of his fellow advocates, and on the way back he heard the story of the trial—little knowing ing how close it was to come to him.

The prisoner (his name was Morrison) had married the murdered woman in the winter. She had been a comely girl who had always borne a good character. On their wedding morning they had received many presents, one of them being a fishing-boat. This had been the gift of a distant relation of the bride's, a middle-aged man who had since married a rich widow.

At Easter, Morrison had gone off with the fleet to the mackerel fishing at Kinsale, and while there he had received an anonymous letter. It told him that his young wife had given birth, less than six months after their marriage, to a still-born child.

Morrison had said nothing about the letter, but he had made inquiries about the man who had given him the boat, and been told that he had borne a bad reputation.

At the end of the mackerel season Morrison had returned to the island with the rest of the fleet, and for everybody else there had been the usual joyful homecoming.

It had been late at night on the first of June, when the stars were out and the moon was in its first quarter. As soon as the boats had been sighted outside the Castle Rock the sound signal had gone up from the Rocket House, and within five minutes the fishermen's wives had come flying down to the quay, with their little shawls thrown over their heads and pinned under their chins.

Then, as the boats had come gliding into harbour, there had been the shrill questions of the women ashore and the deep-toned answers of the man afloat:

" Are you there, Bill? " " Is it yourself, Nancy? "

Some of the younger women, who had had babies born while their husbands had been away, had brought them down with them, and one young wife, holding up her little one for her man to see, by the light of the moon and the harbour-master's lantern, had cried:

" Here he is, boy! What do you think of him? "

Almost before the boats could be brought to their moorings the fishermen had leapt ashore in their long boots and gone off home with their wives, laughing and talking.

Morrison had not gone. His wife had not been down to meet him. Somebody had shouted from the quay that she was still keeping her bed and was waiting at home for him. But he had been in no hurry to go to her. When everything was quiet he had shouldered his boat to the top of the harbour, unstepped her mast, and run her ashore on the dry bank above the bridge.

Then going back to the quay, which was now deserted, he had broken the padlock of an open yard for ship's stores, taken possession of a barrel of pitch, rolled it down to the bank by the bridge, fixed it under his boat, pulled out its plug, applied a match to it, and then waited until both barrel and boat were afire and burning fiercely.

After that he had walked home through the little sleeping town to his house in the middle of a cobweb of streets at the back of the beach. Opening the door (it had been left on the latch for him) he had bolted it on the inside, and then going to the bedroom and finding his young wife in bed, with a frightened look under a timid smile, he had charged her with her unchastity, compelled her to confess to it, and then strangled her to death with his big hands —the marks of his broad thumbs, black with tar, being on her throat and bosom.

In the middle of the night the fishermen who lived in the streets nearest to the harbour, awakened by a red glow in their bedrooms, had said to their wives:

" What for are they burning the gorse on Peel hill at this time of the year? "

But others, who were neighbours of Morrison's, having heard cries from his house in the night, had gathered in front of his door in the morning, and, getting no answer to their knocking, had burst it open and found the woman lying dead on the bed and the man huddled up on the floor at the foot of it. And when they had pushed him and roused him he had lifted his haggard face and said,

" I've killed my sweetheart."

Such was the fisherman's story, and when the defence had concluded their case, asking for an acquittal on the ground of unbearable moral provocation, and saying that never could there have been better grounds for the application of the unwritten law, the Jury was obviously impressed, and somebody at the back of the court was saying,

" If they hang him for that they'll hang a man for anything."

Against this sympathy for the accused, Stowell had risen to make his reply for the Crown.

He did not deny the dead woman's transgression. It was true that she must have known when she married the prisoner that she was about to become the mother of a child by another man. But if that moral fact could be urged against the wife, was there nothing of the same kind that could be advanced in her favour?

She had been cruelly betrayed and abandoned. Looking to the future she had seen the contempt of her little world before her. What had happened? In the dark hour of her desertion the prisoner had come with the offer of his love and protection. It was in evidence that for a time she had held back and that he had pressed himself upon her. None could know the secret of the dead woman's soul, but was it unreasonable to think that standing between the two fires of public scorn and the prisoner's affection she had said to herself, as poor misguided women in like cases did every day: " He loves me so much that he will forgive me whatever happens."

But had he forgiven her? No, he had killed her, wilfully, cruelly, brutally, not in the heat of blood, but after long deliberation—he, the big powerful brute and she the weak, helpless, half-naked woman—the woman who had been faithful to him since the day he married her, the woman he had sworn to love and cherish until death parted them.

No, the plea of moral justification was rotten to the heart's core, and had nothing to say for itself in a Court of Law. The defence had urged that it was founded on the laws of nature—that marriage implied chastity on the woman's part, and this woman had come to her husband unchaste. On the contrary, it was founded on the barbarous law of man—the infamous theory that a wife was the property of her husband and he was at liberty to do as he liked with her.

A wife was not the property of her husband. He was not at liberty to do as he liked with her. There was no such thing as the unwritten law. What was not written was not law. And if, as the result of the verdict in that court, it should go forth that any man had a right to kill his wife in any circumstances—to be judge and jury and accuser and executioner over her—the reign of law and order in this island would be at an end, no woman's life would be secure, the daughter of no member of that jury would any longer be safe, and human society would dissolve into a welter of civilised savagery—the worst savagery of all.

The effect of Stowell's reply had been overwhelming. The jury had either been frightened or convinced, and even the prisoner himself, during the more intimate passages, had held down his head as if he felt himself to be the vilest scoundrel on earth.

Among the advocates (they had reached the station by this time, got into their carriages, and lit up their pipes) opinion was more divided. The younger men were enthusiastic, but some of the older ones thought the closing speech for the Crown had been false in logic and bad in law.

One of the latter, with a special cock of the hat, (it was old Hudgeon, the young men called him " Fanny " now), sat with his shaven chin on the top of his stick and said:

" Well, it's a big gospel the young man has got to live up to, with all his tall talk about women. But we'll see! We'll see! "

Gell, who was wildly excited by his friend's success, was walking to and fro on the platform waiting for Stowell's arrival. When he came (he was the last to come) he had a graver look on his face than Gell had ever seen there before, except once, and he seemed to be painfully preoccupied.

" Ah, is it you? " he had said, when Gell laid hold of him—he had started as if he had seen a ghost.

They got into the train together and had a carriage to themselves. Gell began with his congratulations, but Stowell brushed them aside, and said:

" What happened with your father? "

Gell told his story as he had told it at Derby Haven—that the Speaker had cut up badly and turned him out of the house.

" But what do I care? Not a ha'porth! Best thing that ever happened to me, perhaps."

" And Bessie? "

" Oh, Bessie? Well, that's all right now. A bit troubled

at first about my being cut off by the family and losing my income. Just like a woman! So unselfish!"

There was silence for some time after that save for the rumble of the carriage wheels. Then Gell said he was sorry he had told Bessie about the loss of the income. She would always be thinking he would regret the sacrifice he had made for her. If he could only find some way of showing her it didn't matter, because he could always get plenty of money . . . .

"And why can't you?" said Stowell.

"How?"

"It's two pounds a week you draw on me for Miss Brown, isn't it?"

"Yes."

"Then I'll make it ten on condition that you don't pay me back a penny until I ask for it."

"What a good chap . . . . " But Gell could get no farther —his eyes were full and his throat was hurting him.

On arriving at Douglas he saw Stowell across the platform to the northern train, and just as it was about to start, he said:

"By the way, old man, you don't mind my saying something?"

"Not a bit! What is it?"

"You've hanged that poor devil of a Peel fisherman, and I suppose he deserved it. But I caught a glimpse of him as he was going down to the cells, and I thought he looked a fine fellow."

"He *is* a fine fellow."

"Do *you* say that? He made a big mistake in killing the wife, though, didn't he? If I had been in his place do you know what *I* should have done?"

"What?"

"*Killed the other man.*"

Stowell drew back in his seat and at the next moment the train started.

As it ran into the country a black thought, a vague shadow of something, was swirling like a bat in the darkness of Stowell's brain. That was not the first time it had come to him. It had come to him in Court, while he was speaking, startling him, stifling him, almost compelling him to sit down.

"But Bessie's case was different," he thought. "She was not deserted. She sent Alick to me herself. Therefore it's impossible, quite impossible."

Nevertheless, he slept badly that night, and as often as he awoke he had the sense of a red glow in his bedroom and of being blinded by the fierce glare from a burning boat.

CHAPTER EIGHTEEN

THE GREAT WINTER

" COME in, my boy. Sit down. Take a cigarette. I have important news for you."

The Governor had returned from London and was calling Stowell into his smoking-room.

" First, about that recommendation to mercy. It has gone through. The death sentence has been commuted to ten years' imprisonment."

" I am glad, Sir—very glad."

" Next, your speech, deputizing for the Attorney, was reported —part of it—in the London newspapers and made a good impression."

" I'm very proud, Sir."

" I dined with the Home Secretary the following night, and the Lord Chief Justice, who was among the guests, was warm in his approval. Acid old fellow with noisy false teeth, but quite enthusiastic about your defence of law and order. Crime was contagious like disease, and there was an epidemic of violence in the world now. If society was to be saved from anarchy then law alone could save it. Some of their English courts—judges as well as juries—had been criminally indulgent to crimes of passion. Our little Manx court had shown them a good example."

" That is very encouraging, Sir."

" Very! And now the last thing I have to tell you is that Tynwald Court this morning voted a sum for a memorial to your father, leaving the form of it to me. I've decided on a portrait by Mylechreest, your Manx artist, to be hung in the Court-house at Castle Rushen. Mylechreest knew the Deemster (saw him at his last Court, in fact) and thinks he can paint the portrait from memory. But if you have any photographs let him have them without delay. And now off you go! Somebody's waiting for you in the drawing-room."

During the next six months Stowell worked as he had never worked before. Four hours a day at his office or in the Courts, and uncounted hours at home. Janet used to say she could never look out of her bedroom window at night without seeing his light from the library on the lawn.

Nevertheless he was at Government House every day, and Fenella and he had their cheerful hours together.

Winter came on. It was such a winter as nobody in the island could remember to have seen before. First wind that lashed the sea into loud cries about the coast, blew over the Curraghs with a perpetual wailing, ran up the glen with a roar, and brought the "boys" out of their beds to hold the roofs on their houses by throwing ropes over the thatch and fastening them down with stones.

Then rain that deluged the low-lying lands, so that women had to go to market in boats; and then mist that hid the island for a week and brought more ships ashore than anybody had seen since the days of the ten black brothers of Jurby who (long suspected of wrecking) were caught stuffing the box tombs in the churchyard with rolls of Irish cloth.

But neither wind, nor rain, nor mist, kept Stowell from Fenella.

Clad in boots up to his thighs, with an oilskin coat tightly belted about the waist and a sou'wester strapped down from crown to chin, he would cross the mountains on his young chestnut mare, with the island roaring about him like a living thing, and arrive at Fenella's door with his horse's flanks steaming and his own face ablaze.

After the wind and the rain came a long frost, which laid its unseen hand on the rivers and waterfalls, making a deep hush that was like a great peace after a great war. In the middle of the island (the valley of Baldwin) there was a tarn into which the mountains drained, and as soon as this was frozen over Stowell and Fenella skated on it.

What a delight! The ice humming under their feet like a muffled drum; the air ringing to their voices like a cup; the sun sparkling in the hoar frost on the bare boughs of the trees; the blue sky sailing over the hilltops, capped with white clouds that looked like soft lamb's wool.

God, how good it was to be alive!

Then came a great snow that brought a still deeper silence, broken at Ballamoar only by the skid of the steel runners of the stiff carts, whose wheels had been removed, and the smothered calling of the cattle which had been shut up in the houses.

But what rapture! Every morning the farmers looked out of their windows, thick with ice, to see if the snow had gone, but as Stowell drew his blind and the snow light of the winter's sun came pouring in upon him, he thought only of another joyous day with Fenella.

Then up to Injebreck in white sweaters and woollen helmets to fly down the long slopes on ski, with all the world around them robed and veiled like a bride.

There was a broad ridge on the top, a great divide, separating the north of the island from the south, and as they skimmed across it from sight of eastern to sight of western sea, it was just as if they were sailing through the sky with the white round hills for clouds and the earth lying somewhere far below.

They were doing this one day when Stowell came upon a place where the snow was honeycombed with holes.

" Helloa ! There's something here ! " he cried.

Digging into the snow he found a buried sheep, still alive but unable to stand. So, taking it by its front and back legs he swung it over his head on to his shoulders and carried it to a shepherd's hut a mile away, where a turf fire was burning, and dogs, with snow on their snouts, were barking about a pen of bleating sheep that had been similarly recovered.

His delight at this rescue was so boisterous that he went back and back for hours and brought in other and other sheep.

Fenella, who followed him with his ski staffs, was in raptures. This was a new side of Victor Stowell, and she had a woman's joy in it. He was not only clever, he was strong. He could not only make speeches (as nobody else in the world could), he could ride and skate and ski, and (if he liked) he could lift a woman in his arms and throw her over his shoulder. Something would come of this some day—she was sure it would.

They were at the top of the pass, stamping the snow off their ski, and shaking it out of their gloves, before going down to the Governor's carriage which (also on runners) was waiting for them at the inn at the bottom of the hill. The sun was setting and the red light of it was flushing Fenella's face. She looked sideways at Stowell with a mischievous light in her eyes and said,

" Now I know what you are, Sir."

" Yes ? "

" You are not a lawyer, really."

" No ? "

" You're an old Viking, born a thousand years after your time."

" You don't say."

" Yes," she said, making ready for flight, " one of those sea robbers you told me of, who came to take posession of the island and capture its women."

" Really ? "

" I dare say you're sorry you're not back with your ridiculous old ancestors, catching a woman for your wife."

" Not a bit ! I've caught one aready."

" Eh ? What ? If you mean . . . . Don't be too sure, Sir ! You've not caught *me* yet ! "

" Haven't I ? Look out then—I'm going to catch you now."

" Catch me ! " she cried, and away she flew down the slopes, laughing, screaming, rocking, reeling, and leaping over the drifts, until at length she tumbled into a deep one, with head down and ski in air, and came up half blind, with Stowell's arms about her and his lips kissing the snow off her chin and nose.

What a winter! Could there be any sorrow or sin or crime in the world at all? And what did it want its prisons and courts for?

But the thaw came at length, and then the noises of the garrulous old island began again with the rattle of the cart wheels, the rumble of the rivers running to the sea, and the mooing and bleating of the liberated cattle and sheep, coming out of their Ark and going back to the discoloured grass of the fields.

Stowell and Fenella felt as if they were descending to a world of reality from a world of dreams.

" Good-night! "

They were in the porch at Government House after the last of their winter expeditions. He was crushing her in his arms again, to the ruin of her beautiful hair, and whispering of the time that was coming when there would be no need for such partings.

" Three months yet, Sir! "

" Heavens, what an age! "

And then home to Ballamoar, with his young chestnut under him sniffing the night air, and over his head a paradise of stars.

II

" *Come immediately. Important news for you.*"

It was a telegram from the Governor, who had been in London again. Stowell went up to Douglas by the first train.

" It's about the Deemstership."

" Ah! "

" Old Taubman, as you know, has been complaining of overwork ever since your father died. The winter had crippled him and he is down with rheumatism. Fortnightly courts being postponed, cases in arrears—it was necessary to do something. So I went up to Whitehall last week and told them a successor would have to be appointed. They asked me to recommend a name and I recommended yours."

" Mine, Sir? "

" Yours! It was all right, too, until I had to tell them your age, and then—phew! A judge and not yet thirty! I stood to my ground, said this was the age of youth, quoted the classical examples. Anyhow, there was my recommendation—take it or leave it."

" And what was the result, Sir? "

" The result was that the Lord Chief was consulted, and then our insignificance saved us. Yes, there was precedent enough for young judges in colonies and dependencies. And this being a case of a worthy son succeeding a worthy father . . . . and so on and so forth."

" Well? "

" Well, the end of it is that you are to go up to see the Home Secretary after the House has risen at Easter."

Stowell's heart was beating high, yet he hardly knew whether he was more proud than afraid. He mumbled something about the claims of his seniors at the bar.

" Oh yes, I know! All the old stick-in-the-muds! But keep your end up in London and I'll keep mine up here."

" You are very good, Sir. You have always been good to me."

The Governor, who had been rattling on, in a rush of high spirits, suddenly became grave and spoke slowly.

" Not at all," he said. " And I'm not thinking of you as . . . . what you are going to be. I'm thinking of you as your father's son, and expecting you to live up to your traditions. We want the spirit of the great Deemster in the island these days. Violence! Violence! Violence! I agree with the Lord Chief. It seems as if the world is getting out of hand. Justice is the only thing that can save it from anarchy—utter anarchy and ruin. Let's have no more recommendations to mercy! When people commit crime let them suffer. When they take life—no matter who or what they are—let them die for it."

" And by the way " (Stowell was leaving the room), " your father's portrait is finished. We must unveil it before you go up to London."

Trembling all over, Stowell went into the library to tell Fenella.

" How splendid! " she said. She was glowing with excitement. " You've done magnificent work for women as an advocate, but only think what you will be able to do as a judge! There isn't a poor, wronged girl in the island who won't know that she has a friend on the Bench! "

END OF SECOND BOOK

THIRD BOOK
THE CONSEQUENCE

CHAPTER NINETEEN

THE EVE OF MARY

BESSIE COLLISTER had passed through a very different winter. When she read in the insular newspaper the long report of the trial of the Peel fisherman she was terrified. Men did not forgive their wives, then, in such cases? On the contrary the more they loved them the less they forgave them.

Gell came bounding into the sitting-room while she had the newspaper in her hand and before she had time to hide it away he saw what she had been reading.

" Terrible, isn't it? " he said. " Poor devil, I was sorry for him. When a woman deceives a man like that the law ought to allow him to put her away. He did wrong, of course, but he had no legal remedy—not an atom. Old Vic made out a magnificent case for the woman, but she deserved all she got, I'm afraid."

Bessie gave a frightened cry, and then Gell said, as if to conciliate her.

" I'll tell you what, though. If the woman was guilty there was somebody else who was ten times guiltier, and that was the other man. The scoundrel! The treacherous, deceitful scoundrel, skulking away in the dark! I should like to choke the life out of him. That's what I said to Stowell going up in the train. ' If I had been in the husband's place do you know what I should have done?' I said. ' I should have killed the other man.' "

Bessie's terror increased ten-fold. Dread of what Gell might do sat on her like a nightmare. To marry him seemed to be impossible, yet not to marry him, now that she loved him so much, seemed to be impossible also.

A secret hope came to her. It was early days yet. Perhaps something would happen to her bye-and-bye, which, being over and done with, would leave her free to marry Alick with a clean heart and conscience.

To help it to come to pass, she stayed indoors, took no exercise, and ate as little as possible. Her health declined, and her face in the glass began to look peaky. She took a fierce joy in these signs of increasing weakness. The Miss Browns kept a few chickens in their back garden, and one morning, after the snow had begun to fall, they found Bessie in bare feet going out to feed them.

"Bessie, what *are* you doing?" they cried.

"It's nothing," she said. "I'm used of it, you know. I was eight years old before I wore shoe or stocking."

Meantime she was putting Gell off and off. "Time enough yet, boy," she would say as often as he asked her.

"She's thinking of me again," thought Gell, and he began on a long series of fictions to account for his new-found prosperity. He was getting along wonderfully in his profession, and was better off now than he had been before he lost his allowance. But still it was "Bye-and-bye! Time enough yet, boy!"

One day Gell came with an almost irresistible story. He had bespoken a house in Athol Street. It was just what they wanted. Close to the Law Library and nearly opposite the new Court House. Two rooms on the ground floor for his offices, two on the first floor for their living apartments, and two on the top for the kitchen and for the maid.

It is the temptation that no woman can resist—the desire to have a home that shall be all her own—and for a few weeks Bessie fell to it. Evening after evening, she and Alick sat side by side in the sitting-room making catalogues of all they would require to set up a household. Gell took charge of the tables and chairs and side-boards. Bessie was the authority on the blankets and linen. It was such a delight to construct a home from memory! And then what laughs and thrills and shamefaced looks when, in spite of all their thinking, they remembered some intimate and essential thing which they had hitherto forgotten.

"Sakes alive, boy, you've forgotten the bedstead."

"Lord, so I have. We shall want a bedstead, shan't we?"

But even this fierce gambling with her fate broke down at last with Bessie. The certainty had fallen on her. The natural strength of her constitution had withstood all the attacks she had made upon it. Whether she married Gell, or did not marry him, there was nothing before her except suffering and disgrace. How could she keep his love against the shame that was striding down on her?

Christmas had come. It was Christmas Eve. The Manx people call it Oie'l Verry (the Eve of Mary), and during the last hour before midnight they take possession of their parish churches, over the heads of their clergy, for the singing of their ancient Manx carvals (carols). The old Miss Browns were to keep Oie'l

Verry at their church in Castletown. They had always done so, and this time Bessie was to go with them.

It was a clear cold winter's night with crisp snow underfoot, and overhead a world of piercing stars.

As the two old maids in their long black boas, and Bessie in a fur-lined coat which Gell had sent as a Christmas present, crossed the foot-bridge over the harbour and walked under the blind walls of the dark castle, the great clock in the square tower was striking eleven. But it was bright enough in the market place, with the light from the church windows on the white ground, and people hurrying to church at a quick trot and stamping the snow off their boots at the door.

It was brighter still inside, for the altar and pulpit had been decorated with ivy and holly, and, though the church was lit by gas, most of the worshippers, according to ancient custom, had brought candles also.

The church was very full, but the old Miss Browns, with Bessie behind them, walked up the aisle to the pew under the reading-desk which they had always rented. The congregation about them was a strangely mixed one, and the atmosphere was half solemn and half hilarious.

The gallery was occupied by farm lads and fisher-lads chiefly, and they were craning their necks to catch glimpses of the girls in the pews below, while the girls themselves (as often as they could do so without being observed by their elders) were glancing up with gleaming eyes. In the body of the church there were middle-aged folks with soberer faces, and in the front seats sat old people, with slower and duller eyes and cheeks scored deep with wrinkles—the mysterious hieroglyphics of life's troubled story, sickness and death, husbands lost at half-tide and children gone before them.

An opening hymn had just been sung, the last notes of the organ were dying down, the clergyman, in his surplice, was sitting by the side of the altar, and the first of the carol singers had risen in his pew, candle in hand, to sing his carval.

He was a rugged old man from the mountains of Rushen, half landsman and half seaman, and his carol (which he sang in the Manx, while the tallow guttered down on his discoloured fingers) was a catalogue of all the bad women mentioned in the Bible, from Eve, the mother of mankind, who brought evil into the world, to " that graceless wench, Salome."

After that came similar carols, sung by similar carol-singers and received by the boys in the gallery with gusts of laughter which the Clerk tried in vain to suppress. But at last there came a carval sung in chorus by twelve young girls with sweet young voices and faces that were chaste and pure and full of joy—all carrying their candles as they walked slowly up the aisle from the western end of the church to the altar steps.

Their carol was an account of the Nativity, scarcely less crude than the carols that had gone before it, though the singers seemed to know nothing of that—how Joseph, being a just man, had espoused a virgin, and finding she was with child before he married her, he had wished to put her away, but the angel of the Lord had appeared to him and told him not to, and how at last he had carried his wife and child away into the land of Egypt, out of reach of the wrath of Herod the King, who was trying to disgrace and destroy them.

A little before midnight the clergyman rose and asked for silence. And then, while all heads were bowed and there was a solemn hush within, the great clock of the Castle struck twelve in the darkness outside. After that the organ pealed out " Hark, the herald angels sing," and everybody who had a candle extinguished it, and all stood up and sang.

The bells were ringing joyfully as the congregation trooped out of the church, but for some while longer they moved about on the crinkling snow in front of it, saluting and shaking hands, everybody with everybody.

" A Merry Christmas and a Happy New Year to you."

" Same to you, and many of them."

They saluted and shook hands with Bessie also.

Then the Verger put out the lights in the church behind them, and in the sudden darkness the crowd broke up, one more Oie'l Verry over, and under the slow descent of the starlight the cheerful voices and crinkling footsteps went their various ways home.

Back at Derby Haven, Bessie, who had been on the point of crying during the latter part of the service, ran up to her room, flung herself face down on her bed and burst into a flood of tears.

If she, too, could only fly away, and stay away, until her trouble was over! But how could she do that? And where could she go to?

II

Two months passed. Bessie's time was fast approaching, and the nearer it came the more she was terrified by the signs of it. The symptoms of coming maternity which are a joy and a pride to married mothers were a dread and a terror to her. Had she brought herself so low that she could not live through the time that was before her? At one moment she thought of going to Fenella.

Everybody said how good Miss Stanley was to girls in trouble. But when she remembered Fenella's relation to Stowell, and Stowell's to Gell, and her own to all three, she told herself that Fenella Stanley was the one woman in the world whom she must never come face to face with.

At length, thinking death was certain, she saw only one thing left to do—to go back to her mother. It was not thus that she had expected to return, but nothing else was possible now. In her helplessness and ignorance, having no one to reassure her, the high-spirited girl became a child again. Twenty years of her life slipped back at a stride, and she felt as she used to do when she ran bare-foot on the roads and fell and bruised her knees, or tore her little hairy legs in the gorse and then went home to lie on her mother's lap and be rocked before the fire and comforted.

But going home had its terrors also. There was Dan Baldromma! What could she do? Was there no way out for her?

One day the elder of the Miss Browns (she gave music lessons to old pupils at their own homes) came back from Castletown with a " shocking story." It was about a witch-doctor at Cregnaish—a remote village at the southernmost extremity of the island, where the inhabitants were supposed to be descended from a crew of Spanish sailors who had been wrecked on the rocky coast below.

The witch-doctor was a woman, seventy years of age, and commonly called Nan. Hitherto she had lived by curing ringworms on children and blood-letting in strong men by means of charms that were half in Latin and half in Manx. But now young wives were going to her to be cured of barrenness, or for mixtures to make their husbands love them; and worst of all, the young girls from all parts of the island were flocking to her to be told their fortunes—whether their boys at the mackerel fishing were true to them, or going astray with the Irish girls of Kinsale and Cork.

" It's shocking, this witchcraft," said old Miss Brown. " In my young days it was given for law that the women who practised such arts should stand in a white sheet on a platform in the market-place with the words *For Charming and Sorcery* in capital letters on their breasts."

Bessie said nothing, but next day, after breakfast, making excuse of her need of a walk, she hurried out, took train to Port Erin, and climbed, with many pauses, the zigzag path up the Mull Hills to where a Druids' circle sits on the brow, and Cregnaish (like a gipsy encampment of mud huts thatched with straw) sprawls over the breast of them.

It was a fine spring morning, with the sea lying still on either side of the uplands, and the sun, through clouds of broken crimson, peering over the shoulder of the Calf like a blood-shot eye.

Bessie had no need to ask her way to the witch-doctor's house, for troops of young girls were coming down from it, generally in pairs, whispering and laughing merrily. At length she came upon it—a one-storey thatched cottage with a queue of girls outside.

When the last of the girls had gone, and Bessie still stood waiting on the opposite side of the rutted space which served for a road, a wisp of a woman, with hair and eyebrows as black as a shoe, but a face as wrinkled as the trunk of the trammon tree, came to the door and said,

"Come in, my fine young woman. There's nothing to be freckened of."

It was Nan, the witch-doctor, and Bessie followed her into the house.

The inside was a single room with a fire at one end and a bed at the other. The floor was of hardened clay and the scraas of the roof were so low overhead that a tall man could scarcely have stood erect under them. Bundles of herbs hung from nails in the sooty rafters and when the old woman closed the door, Bessie saw that the *Crosh cuirn* (the cross of mountain ash) was standing at the back of it.

"I'm in trouble, ma'am," said Bessie, who was on the verge of tears, "and I'm wanting to know what to do and what is to happen to me."

The witch-doctor, whose quick eyes had taken in the situation at a glance, said,

"Aw yes, bogh, trouble enough. But knock that cat off the cheer in the choillagh and sit down and make yourself comfortable."

Bessie loosened her fur-lined cloak and sat in the ingle, with the fire at her feet and a peep of the blue sky coming down on her from the wide chimney.

"They were telling me a fine young woman was coming," said the witch-doctor (she meant the invisible powers), "and it was wondering and wondering I was would she have strength to climb the brews. But here you are, my chree, and now a cup o' tay will do no harm at all."

Bessie tried to refuse, but the old woman said,

"Chut! A cup o' tay is nothing and here's my taypot on the warm turf and the tay at the best, too."

While Bessie sipped at her cup the witch-doctor went on talking, but she took quick glances at the girl from time to time and sometimes asked a question.

12

At length she bolted the door, drew a thick blind over the window, knelt before the hearth, and called on Bessie to do the same, so that they were kneeling side by side, with no light in the darkened room except the red glow fom the fire on their faces and the blue streak from the sky behind the smoke from the chimney.

After that the witch-doctor mumbled some rhymes about St. Patrick and the blessed St. Bridget, then put her ear to the ground, saying she was listening to the *Sheean ny Feaynid*, the invisible beings who were always wandering over the world. And then she began on the fortune, which Bessie, who was trembling, interrupted with involuntary cries.

"There's a fair young man in your life, my chree (*Yes*) and if you're not his equal you're the apple of his eye. There's a poor ould woman, too, and she praying and praying for her bogh-millish to come home to her (*Oh!*) and the longing that's taking the woman at times is pitiful to see. 'Where is my wandering girl to-night,' she's singing when she's sitting by her fireside; and when she's going to bed she's saying, 'In Jesu's keeping nought can harm my erring child.'"

At this Bessie broke down utterly, and the witch-doctor had to stop for a moment. Then she began again in a different strain,

"There's an ould man too . . . . yes . . . . no . . . . (*Yes, yes!*) as imperent as sin and as bould as a white stone, and with a vice at him as loud as a trambone. Aw, yes, woman-bogh, yes, there's trouble coming on you, but take heart, gel, for things will come out right before long and it's a proud woman you're going to be some day. But you must go home to the mother, my chree, and never take rest till you're laying your head under the same roof with her."

"And will the young man be true to me whatever happens?"

"True as true, my chree, and his heart that warm to you at last that it will be like gorse and ling burning on the mountains."

"And will the old man be able to do him any injury?"

"Lough bless me, no! Neither to him nor you, gel. Roaring and tearing and mad as a wasp, maybe, but nothing to do no harm at all."

Bessie had crossed the old woman's palm with sixpence as she came into the house, but she emptied her purse into it going out, and then went down the hill with a light step and a lighter heart.

Alick Gell was at Derby Haven when she got back, having been waiting for more than an hour. Seeing her coming down the road with her face aglow, he dashed off to meet her, and broke into a flood of joyous words.

"Helloa! Here you are at last! Looking as fresh as a

flower, too? What did I say? Didn't I tell you that you had only to get about and take exercise and you would be as right as rain in no time? But, look here, Bess " (he had drawn her arm through his), " you've kept me waiting all winter and now that you're getting better I'm going to stand no more nonsense."

Bessie was laughing.

" I'm not! Upon my soul, I'm not! You wouldn't let me put up the banns at Malew, thinking Dan Baldromma would hear of them through Cæsar Qualtrough, and come here making a noise at Miss Brown's, though he has no more right over you than the Coroner, and no more power over me than a tomtit. But there are other ways of marrying besides being called in church, and one of them is by Bishop's licence."

" Bishop's licence? "

" Certainly! You just go up to the Registrar's in Douglas, sign your names in a book, pay a few pounds, get the Bishop's certificate, and then you can be married wherever you like and as quietly as you please. And that's what we're going to do now."

" Now? You mean to-day? "

" Well, no, not to-day. I have to go to the Castle this afternoon. They're unveiling a portrait of the old Deemster. And what do you think, Bess? "

" What? "

" There's a whisper that Stowell is to be made Deemster in succession to his father. Glorious, isn't it? Splendid chap! Straight as a die! Rather young, certainly, but there's not one of the old gang fit to hold a candle to him. He's to go up to London to-morrow, so I want to see the last of him. But I'll be down by the first train after the boat sails in the morning, and then we'll go back to Douglas together."

They had reached the gate of the old maid's house by this time and Gell was looking at his watch.

" Pshew! I must be off! Ceremony begins at three and it's that already. Wouldn't miss it for worlds. By-bye! . . . Another one! . . . . Oh, but you must, though."

Bessie looked after him as he hurried down the road, swinging his arms and pitching his shoulders, as he always did when his heart was glad. Then she went indoors, ran upstairs and set herself to think things out.

She must go before Alick could get back. When he arrived to-morrow she must be on her way to her mother's. It was earlier than she had intended, but there was no help for that now. And then it would be all right in the end—the *Sheean ny Feaynid* (the Voices of Infinity) had said so.

After her child had been born her mother would take it and bring it up as her own—she had heard of such things happening in Manx houses, hadn't she? And when all was over and everything was covered up, she would come back, and then . . . . then Alick and she would be married.

In the light of what the witch-doctor had said it seemed to her so natural, so simple, so sure. But later in the evening, it tore her heart woefully to think of Alick coming from Douglas on the following day and finding her gone. So she wrote this note and stole out and posted it:

" Don't come to-morrow. I'll be writing again in the morning, telling you the reason why."

CHAPTER TWENTY

VICTOR STOWELL'S VOW

THE old Court-house at Castle Rushen was full to overflowing. Nearly all the great people of the island were there—the Legislative Council, the Keys, the leaders of the Bar, the more prominent members of the clergy, the long line of insular officials, with their wives and daughters.

A pale shaft of spring sunshine from the lantern light was on the new portrait of the Deemster, which had been hung on the eastern wall and was still covered by a white sheet.

The time of waiting for the proceedings to begin was passed in a low buzz of conversation, chiefly on one subject. " Is it true that he is to follow his father? " " So they say." " So young and with so many before him—I call it shocking." " So do I, but then he's the son of the old Deemster, and is to marry the daughter of the Governor."

At the last moment Stowell and Fenella arrived and were shown into seats reserved for them at the end of the Jury-box. Then the conversation (among the women at least) took another turn. " Well, they're a lovely pair—I will say that for them."

The Governor, accompanied by the Bishop and the Attorney-General, stepped on to the crimson-covered dais, and the proceedings commenced.

The Governor's own speech was a short one. They had gathered to do honour to the memory of one of the most honoured of their countrymen. The memory of its great men was a nation's greatest inheritance. If that was true of the larger communities it was no less true of the little realm of Man.

" Hence the island," said the Governor, " is doing a service to itself in setting up in this Court-house, the scene of his principal activities, the memorial to its great Deemster which I have now the honour to unveil."

When the Governor pulled a cord and the white sheet fell from the face of the picture there was a gasp of astonishment. The impression of reality was startling. The Deemster had been painted in wig and gown and as if sitting on the bench in that very Court-house. The powerful yet melancholy eyes, the drawn yet firm-set mouth, the suggestion of suffering yet strength—it was just as he had been seen there last, summing up after the trial of the woman who had killed her husband.

As soon as the spectators, who had risen, had resumed their seats, the Governor called on the Attorney-General.

The old man was deeply moved. The Deemster had been his oldest and dearest friend. It was difficult for him to remember a time when they had not been friends and impossible to recall an hour in which their friendship had been darkened by so much as a cloud. If it was true that the memory of its great men was a nation's greatest inheritance, the island had a great heritage in the memory of Deemster Stowell. He had been great as a lawyer, great as a judge, great as a gentleman, as a friend, as a lover, as a husband, and (with a glance in the direction of the jury-box) as a father also.

" I pray and believe," said the Attorney, " that this memorial to our great Deemster may be a stimulus and an inspiration to all our young men whatsoever, particularly to such as are in the profession of the Bar, and especially to one who bears his name, has inherited many of his splendid talents, and may yet be called, please God, to fill his place and follow in his footsteps."

When the old man sat down there was general applause, a little damped, perhaps, by the last of his references, and then followed the event of the afternoon.

By the blind instinct that animates a crowd, all eyes turned in the direction of Victor Stowell. He sat by Fenella's side, breathing audibly with head down and hands clasped tightly about one of his knees.

There was a pause and then a low stamping of feet and Fenella whispered,

" They want you to speak, dear."

But Stowell did not seem to hear, and at length the Governor called on him by name.

When he rose he looked pale and much older, and bore a resemblance to the picture of his father on the opposite wall which few had observed before.

He began in a low tense voice, thanking His Excellency for asking him to speak, but saying he would have given a great deal not to do so.

" The only excuse I can have for standing here to-day," he said, " is that I may thank you, Sir, and this company, and my countrymen and countrywomen generally, in the name of one whose voice, so often heard within these walls, must now be silent."

After that he paused, as if not quite sure that he ought to go further, and then continued,

" If my father was a great Judge, it was chiefly because he was a great lover of Justice. Justice was the most sacred thing on earth to him, and no man ever held higher the dignity and duty of a Judge. Woe to the Judge who permitted personal motives to pervert his judgment, and thrice woe to him who committed a crime against justice. Therefore, if I know my father's heart and have any right to speak for him, I will say that what you have done this afternoon is not so much to perpetuate the memory of Douglas Stowell, Deemster of Man, as to set up in this old Court-house, which has witnessed so many tragic scenes, an altar to the spirit of Justice, so that no Judge, following him in his place, may ever forget that his first and last and only duty is to be just and fear not."

He paused again and seemed to be about to stop, but, in a voice so low as to be scarcely audible, he said,

" As for myself I hardly dare to speak at all. What my dear master has said of me makes it difficult to say anything. Some people seem to think it is a great advantage to a young man to be the son of a great father. But if it is a great help it is also a great responsibility and may sometimes be the source of a great sorrow. I never knew what my father had been to me until I lost him. I had always been proud of him, but I had rarely or never given him reason to be proud of me. That is a fault I cannot repair now. But there is one thing I can do and one thing only. I can take my solemn vow—and here and now I do so—that whatever the capacity in which my duty calls me to this place, I will never wilfully do anything in the future, with my father's face on the wall in front of me, that shall be unworthy of my father's son."

There were husky cheers and some clapping of hands when Stowell sat down, but most of the men were clearing their throats and wiping the mist off their spectacles, and nearly all of the women were coughing and drying their eyes.

Others were to have spoken but the Governor closed up the proceedings quickly, and then there was a general conversazione.

The officials were talking in groups:—" Wonderful! The Governor and the old Attorney were grand, but the young man was wonderful!" "We might go farther and fare worse." "Like his father, you say?" (it was the Attorney-General) "so like what his father was at his age that sometimes when I look at him I think I'm a young man myself again, and then it's a shock to go home and see an old man's face in the glass."

A group of old ladies had gathered about Fenella, whose great eyes were ablaze.

"It was beautiful, my dear, but there was just one other person who ought to have been here to hear it."

"Who?"

"The old Deemster himself, dear."

"But he was," said Fenella.

The Governor drew Stowell aside. "Its all right, my boy! Must have been instinct, but you touched your people on their tenderest place. Pretty hard on you, perhaps, but I knew what I was doing. The opposition in the island is as dead as a door nail already. Get into the saddle in London and you'll never hear another word about it."

There were only two dissentients.

"Aw well, we'll see, we'll see," said the Speaker—he was going out of the Castle (head down and his big beard on his breast), with old Hudgeon the advocate.

As he passed through the outer gate his son Alick came running hotfoot up to it.

It was a cruel moment.

II

Victor Stowell left the island for London at nine o'clock next morning. The first bell of the steamer had been rung, the mails were aboard, and the more tardy of the passengers were hurrying to the gangway, with their porters behind them, when the Governor's carriage drew up and Stowell leapt out of it.

A large company of the younger advocates (all former members of the "Ellan Vannin") were waiting for him.

"Come to see me off? Yes? Jolly good of you," said Stowell, and he stood talking to them at the top of the pier steps till the second bell had been rung.

Down to that moment nobody had said a word about the object of his journey, although every eye betrayed knowledge of it. But just as he was crossing the gangway to the steamer one of the advocates (a little fat man with the reputation of a wag) cried, with a broad smatch of the Anglo-Manx,

" Bring it back in your bres' pockat, boy "—meaning the King's commission for the Deemstership.

" You go bail," said Stowell, and there was general laughter.

He was settling himself with his portmanteau in the deck cabin that had been reserved for him when somebody darkened the doorway.

" Helloa ! "

It was Gell. His cheeks were white, his face looked troubled, and he was breathing rapidly as if he had been running.

" What's amiss? " said Stowell. " Something has happened to you. What is it? "

Gell stepped into the cabin, and with a suspicion of tears both in his eyes and voice, told his story.

It was Bessie again. He didn't know what had come over the girl. She had been holding off all winter. First one excuse, then another.

" I've done all I can think of. Taken a house in Athol Street and furnished it beautifully (thanks to you, old fellow), but it's no use, seemingly."

" When did you see her last? "

" Yesterday, and I thought I had settled everything at last. She wouldn't be called in church, so I arranged that I was to go down to Derby Haven this morning, as soon as your boat sailed, and we were to come up to the Registrar's to sign for a Bishop's license. And now, by the first post . . . . this."

With a trembling hand Gell took out of his pocket the letter which Bessie had written the night before and handed it to Stowell.

With a momentary uneasiness Stowell read the letter.

" Reason? What is it likely to be, think you? "

" I don't know. I can't say. It's a mystery. I've racked my brains and can only think of one thing now."

" And what's that? "

" That she finds out at last that she doesn't care enough for me to marry me."

" Nonsense, old fellow."

" What else can it be? There can be nothing else, can there? "

Stowell's uneasiness increased. " What do you intend to do? "

" Go down just the same. I've been telegraphing saying I'm coming. That's why I'm late getting down to the boat."

" And if she persists? "

" Give her up and clear out, I suppose."

" You mean leave the island? "

" Why shouldn't I? I've only been a stick-in-the-mud here and couldn't do much worse anywhere else, could I? Besides " (his voice was breaking) "there's my father. You remember what he said. I couldn't face it out if the girl threw me over."

"She's not well, is she?"

"Not very."

"Nothing serious?"

"No—nothing, the Miss Browns think, that we might not expect after such a change in her life and condition."

"Then that's it! Cheer up, old man! It will all come right yet. Women suffer from so many things that we men know nothing about."

"If I could only think that . . . ."

"You may—of course you may."

"Victor," said Gell, taking Stowell's hand, "will you do one thing more for me?"

"Certainly—what is it?"

"Nobody can read a woman as you can—everybody says that. If Bessie gives me the same answer to-day will you go down to Derby Haven with me when you come back, and find out what's amiss with her?"

"Assuredly I will . . . . that is to say . . . . if you think . . . ."

"Is it a promise?"

"Undoubtedly. It shall be the first thing I do when I return to the island."

"All ashore! All ashore!"

A sailor was shouting on the deck outside the cabin door, and the third bell was ringing.

Gell was the last to cross the gangway.

"Good-bye and God bless you, and good luck in London! You deserve every bit of it!"

At the next moment the gangway was pulled in, the ropes were thrown aboard, and the steamer was gliding away.

The young advocates on the pier-head were beginning to make a demonstration. One of them (the wag of course) was singing a sentimental farewell in a doleful voice and the others were join-ing in the chorus:

> " *Better lo'ed ye canna be,*
> *Will ye no come back again?* "

Some of the other passengers (English commercial travellers apparently) were looking on, so to turn the edge of the joke Stowell sang also, and when his deep baritone was heard above the rest there was a burst of laughter.

"Good-bye! Good-luck! Bring it back, boy!"

Gell was standing at the sea-end of the pier, waving his cap and struggling to smile. At sight of his face Stowell felt ashamed of his own happiness. A vague shadow of something that had come to him before came again, with a shudder such as one feels when a bat strikes one in the dusk.

At the next moment it was gone. The steamer was swinging round the breakwater and opening the bay, and he was looking for a long white house (Government House) which stood on the heights above the town. He had slept there last night, and this morning Fenella, parting from him in the porch, while the Governor's high-stepping horses were champing on the gravel outside, had promised to signal to him when she saw the steamer clearing the harbour.

Ah, there she was, waving a white scarf from an upper window. Stowell stood by the rail at the stern and waved back his handkerchief. Fenella! He could see nothing but her dark eyes and beaming smile, and Gell's sad face was forgotten.

It was a fine fresh morning, with the sun filtering through a veil of haze and the world answering to the call of Spring. As the boat sailed on, the island seemed to recede and shrink and then sink into the sea until only the tops of the mountains were visible—looking like a dim grey ghost that was lying at full stretch in the sky.

At length it was gone; the sea-gulls which had followed the steamer out had made their last swirl round and turned towards the land, but Stowell was still looking back from the rail at the stern.

The dear little island! How good it had been to him! How eager he would be to return to it!

The sun broke clear, the waters widened and widened, the glistening blue waves rolled on and on, the ship rose and fell to the rhythm of the flowing tide, the throb of the engines beat time to the deep surge of the sea, and the still deeper surge of youth and love and health and hope within him.

Dear God, how happy he was! What had he done to deserve such happiness?

CHAPTER TWENTY-ONE

MOTHER'S LAW OR JUDGE'S LAW?

BESSIE had passed a miserable night. Having been awake until after five in the morning she was asleep at nine when somebody knocked at her bedroom door. It was old Miss Ethel with a telegram. Bessie opened it with trembling fingers.

" *Nonsense dear am coming up as arranged Alick.*"

With fingers that trembled still more noticeably Bessie returned the telegram to its envelope and slid it under her pillow, saying (with a twitching of the mouth which always came when she was telling an untruth),

"It's from Mr. Gell. He wants me to meet him in Douglas. I am to go up immediately."

"That's nice," said Miss Ethel. "The change will do you a world of good, dear. I'll run down and hurry your breakfast, so that you can catch the ten-thirty."

Bessie dressed hastily, put a few things into a little handbag, and then sat down to write her promised letter. It was a terrible ordeal. What could she say that would not betray her secret? At length she wrote:

> "DEAR ALICK,—Do forgive me. I must go away for a little while. It is all my health. I have been ill all winter and suffered more than anybody can know. But God is good, and I will get my health and strength back soon, and then I will return and we can be married and everything will be alright. Do not think I do not love you because I am leaving you like this. I have never loved you so dear as now. But I am depressed, and I cannot get away from my thoughts. And please, Alick dear, don't try to find me. I shall be quite alright, and I shall think of you every night before I go to sleep, and every morning when I awake. So now I must close with all my love and kisses.
>
> —BESSIE. xxxxx"

Having written her letter, and blotted it with many tears, she pinned it to the top of her pillow, without remembering that the telegram lay underneath. Then she hurried downstairs, swallowed a mouthful of breakfast standing, said good-bye to her old housemates with an effort at gaiety, and set off as for the railway station.

She had no intention of going there. The morning haze was thick on the edge of the sea, and as soon as she was out of sight of the house she slipped across the fields to a winding lane which led to the open country.

During the night, crying a good deal and stifling her sobs under the bed-clothes, she had thought out all her plans. It was still two months before her time, and to be separated from Alick as long as that was too painful to think about. It was also too dangerous. Long before the end of that time he would search for her and find her, and then her secret would become known, and that would be the end of everything.

She had been to blame, but what had she done to be so unhappy? Why should Nature be so cruel to a girl? Was there no
way of escape from it?

At length a light had dawned on her.   Remembering what she
had heard of women doing (wives as well as unmarried girls) to
get rid of children who were not wanted, she determined that her
own child should be still-born.   Why not?   It threatened to
separate her from Alick—to turn his love for her into hatred.   Why
should it come into the world to ruin her life, and his also?

Yes, she would tire herself out, expose herself to some great
strain, some fearful exhaustion, and thereby bring on a sudden
and serious illness.   Instead of taking the train she would walk
all the way home to her mother's house—twenty odd miles, fifteen
of them over a steep and rugged mountain road.   It would be
dangerous to a girl in her condition, but not half so dangerous
as marrying Alick now, and running the risk of an end like that
of the poor young wife of the Peel fisherman.

And then it would be so much fairer.   If her fault, her misfortune, could be wiped out before she married Alick, nobody
could say she had deceived her husband.

Such was the wild gamble with life and death which Bessie had
decided upon at the prompting of love and shame and fear.   The
consequences were not long in coming.

The winding lane had to cross the railway line near to a village station before it reached the open country, and coming
sharply upon the level-crossing at a quick turning she found the
gates closed and a train drawing up at the platform.

She knew at once that this must be the train from Douglas
which Alick Gell was to travel by, and in a moment she saw him.
He was sitting alone in a first-class carriage, looking pale and
troubled.   In the next compartment were four or five young advocates from the south side of the island, who had been up to see
Stowell off by the steamer.   They were smoking and laughing,
and one of them, who appeared to have been drinking also, seeing
Bessie coming up to the gate, dropped his window and swung off
his hat to her.

Bessie dropped back to the partial cover of the fence.   Only
her fear of attracting attention restrained her from flying off
altogether.   Alick had not yet seen her.   It tore her terribly to see
how ill he looked.   He was only three or four yards away from
her.   His head was down.   At one moment he took off his cap
and ran his fingers through his fair hair as if his head were
aching.   She could scarcely resist an impulse to pass through the

turnstile and hurry up to him. One look, one smile, one word, and she would have thrown everything to the winds even yet.

But no, the guard waved his flag, the engine whistled, the train jerked backward, then forward, and at the next instant it had slid out of the station. Alick had not seen her. He was gone. It had been like a stab at her heart to see him go.

II

Half an hour later she was on the rugged mountain road that led to her mother's house in the north of the island. Her first fear was the fear of being overtaken and carried back. At Silverburn, where a deep river gurgles under the shadow of a dark bridge, she heard the crack of whips, the clatter of horses' hoofs and the whoop of loud voices.

It was nothing. Only two farm shandries, the first containing a couple of full-blooded farm girls, and the second a couple of lusty farm lads, racing home after market, laughing wildly and shouting to each in the free language of the countryside. It was like something out of her former life—one of the outbreaks of animal instinct that had brought her to where she was.

But no matter! She would be a proud and happy woman yet —the *Sheean ny Feaynid* had said so.

After the fear of being pursued came the fear of being lost— becoming an outcast and a wanderer. She had toiled up to the Black Fort on the breast of the hill. The morning haze had vanished by this time, the sun had come out, the larks were singing in the cloudless sky, the smell of spring was rising from the young grass in the fields, the roadsides were yellow with primroses and daffodils, and the whole world was looking glad with the promise of the beautiful new year that was already on the wing. It was heart-breaking.

Feeling hot and tired after her climb, she sat on a stone. The sea was open from that point, and on the farthest rim of it she could see a red-funnelled steamer and two black shafts of smoke. Stowell! Never before had she thought bitterly of him. But he was there, going up to London in comfort, in luxury, while she . . . .

It was cruel. But crueller than her bitter thoughts of Stowell were her tender thoughts of Gell. He would be at Derby Haven now, reading (with that twitching of the lower lip which she knew so well) the letter she had left behind for him, while she was here, running away from the arms of the man who loved her. But no matter about that, either! One day, two days, three days, a week perhaps, and she would return to him. She was to be a proud and happy woman yet—the *Sheean ny Feaynid* had said so.

Hours passed. The road stretched out and out, became steeper and steeper. Bessie felt more and more tired. She was often compelled to sit by the wayside, and sometimes, being worn out by the want of sleep, she fell into a dose. The sky darkened and dropped; the sun went down behind the mountains to the west with a straight black bar across its face that was like a heavy lid over a sullen eye. Would she be able to reach home that night? She would! She must! Alick was waiting for her to come back. She dare not keep him long.

Evening had closed in before she reached the top of the hill. It was a long waste of bracken and black rock, with no farms anywhere, and only a few thatched cottages that crouched in the sheltered places like frightened cattle in a storm. Feeling weak and faint from long climbing and want of food, she was about to sit down again and cry, having lost hope of reaching her mother's house that night, when she came upon a little lamb, scarcely a month old, which had strayed away from the flock and was too tired to go farther.

The poor creature bleated piteously into her face, and she lifted it up in her arms and carried it a long half mile (the lost carrying the lost, the desolate comforting the desolate) until she came to a high gate at which a mother sheep was plunging furiously in her efforts to get out to them. Bessie put the lamb to its feet, and it clambered through the bars, plucked at the teat, and then there was peace and silence.

This strengthened her and she went on for some time longer with a cheerful heart. Yes, she must reach home that night. And if it was as late as midnight before she got there, so much the better! Nobody must see her come, and then her mother would be able to conceal everything.

Night fell. It began to rain and the wind to rise. She had never been afraid of darkness or bad weather, but now she took a wild delight in them. Remembering what other women had done, she took off her shoes and walked on the wet roads in her stockings. It was risky but she cared nothing about that. It might bring on a fever, but she was strong—she would soon get over it.

Farmers returning empty from market offered her a lift, but she declined and toiled on. The lighted windows of the farmhouses, gleaming through the darkness, called her into warmth and shelter, but she struggled along. The soles of her stockings were soon worn to shreds and the stones of the roads were beginning to cut her feet, but she would not put on her shoes. In her frenzy she hardly felt the pain. And besides, what she was suffering for Alick was as nothing compared to what Alick had suffered for her. Only one night! It would soon be over.

She had walked at her slow pace down a deep descent and through a long valley when she came upon an inn and a big barn that was a scene of great festivity. She knew what it was. It was one of the " Bachelors' Balls " which, beginning with *Oiel Thomase Dhoo* (the Eve of Black Thomas) and going on through the spring of the year, the unmarried men in remote places gave to the unmarried girls of the parish.

The rain was now falling in torrents and the wind had risen to the strength of a gale, but it must have been close and hot inside the barn, for as Bessie passed on the other side of the way, the doors were thrown open. The rude place was densely crowded. Stable lamps hung from the rough-hewn rafters. At one end the musicians sat on a platform raised on barrels; at the other end girls in white blouses were serving tea from a long plank covered with a table-cloth and resting on trestles. In the space between, a dense group of young men and women were dancing with furious energy.

This, too, was like something out of her own life. Ah, if somebody had only told her . . . .

But what matter! She would be a proud and happy woman yet—the *Sheean ny Feaynid* had said so.

It was now midnight by the wrist-watch that Alick had given her, and she had still another hill to climb, steeper than the last if shorter. While she was going up the rain flogged her face as with whipcord, and, when she reached the top, the wind, sweeping across the low-lying lands from the sea, tore at her skirts as if it were trying to strip her naked. At one moment it brought her to her knees, and she thought she would never be able to rise to her feet again. It was very dark. She was feeling weak and helpless.

Once more she remembered Stowell. He would be on his way to London now. She could see him (Alick had often painted such pictures) sitting in a brightly-lit first-class railway carriage, smoking cigarettes and sipping coffee.

At this thought her whole soul rose in revolt. Why was he there while she was here? She had never loved him; he had never loved her; they had both done wrong. But why for the same fault should there be such different punishment?

People who went to churches and chapels talked of nature and God. They said God was good and He was the God of nature. It was a lie—a deception! If God was good He was not the

God of nature. If He was the God of nature He was not good. Nature was cruel and pitiless. Only to a man was it kind. If you were a woman it had no mercy on you. It never forgot you; it never forgave you. Therefore a woman had a right to fight it, and when it threatened to destroy her happiness, and the happiness of those who loved her, she had a right to kill it.

That was what she was doing now. Perhaps she had done it already. The heavy burden that had been lying so long under her heart had given no sign of life for hours. So much the better! That passage in her life must be dead and buried. Victor Stowell must be wiped out for ever. Then she could marry Alick Gell with a clean heart and conscience.

Therefore, courage, courage! She would be a proud and happy woman yet—the *Sheean ny Feaynid* had said so.

Only the great thing was to get home before daybreak, so that nobody might see her until all was over.

Somewhere in the dead and vacant dawn a pale, forlorn-looking woman, whom nobody could have known for Bessie Collister, was approaching the village of the glen. She had been eighteen hours on her journey, most of the time on her feet. Her fur-lined cloak was sodden and heavy. Her black hair had been torn from its knot and was hanging dank over her neck and shoulders. Her feet, in her dry boots, were cold and bleeding. A silk scarf which had been tied over her closely-fitting fur cap was dripping, and a little bag on her arms was wet through with all that was contained in it.

She had expected to arrive before break of day, but nobody in the village was yet stirring. In the long street of whitewashed houses all the window blinds were still down and looking like closed eye-lids.

She tied up her hair, removed the scarf and put on a veil from her handbag, drew it closely over her face, and then walked with head down and a step as light as she could make it, through the sleeping village.

She met nobody. Not a door was opened; not a blind was drawn aside; she had not been seen. She drew a long breath of relief. But suddenly, with the first sight of the mill, came a stab of memory,

Dan Baldromma!

Since the witch-doctor had told her that though Dan might rage and tear he could do no harm to her or to Alick she had ceased to think of him. But why had she not thought of the harm he might do to her mother? All the way up since she was a child she had seen the tyrannies he had inflicted upon her mother through her. What fresh tyranny would he inflict on her now?—now that she was coming home like this to be a burden to . . . .

For a moment Bessie told herself she must go back even yet. But she was too weak and too ill to go one step farther. All the same she could not face her step-father in her present condition. If she could only get upstairs to her bedroom and sleep—sleep, sleep!

She listened for the mill-wheel—it was not working. She looked at the mill-door—it had not yet been opened. It was impossible that Dan could be in bed—he was such an early riser. He must have gone up the brews to look at the heifers in the top fields.

With a slow step she went over to the dwelling-house. The door was shut, but she could hear sounds from the kitchen. There was the shuffling of slow feet, accompanied by the tap of a walking-stick; then the blowing and coughing of bellows and the crackling of burning gorse; and then the measured beating of a foot on the hearthstone, keeping time to a husky and tremulous voice that was singing—

> " *Safe in the arms of Jesus,*
> *Safe in His tender care.*"

With a palpitating heart Bessie lifted the latch, pushed the door open and took one step into the kitchen. Her mother, who was still wearing her night-cap, was sitting on the three-legged stool in the choillagh, stirring porridge in the oven-pot that hung from the slowrie. She had heard the click of the latch and was looking round.

There was silence for a moment. Bessie tried to speak and could not. The old woman rose on rigid limbs and her hand on the handle of her stick was trembling. It was just as if the spirit of someone she had been thinking about had suddenly appeared before her.

" Is it thyself, girl? " she said, in a breathless whisper.

" Mother! " cried Bessie, and she took another step forward.

Again there was a moment of silence. With her heart at her lips Bessie saw that her mother's eyes were wandering over her figure. Then the stick dropped from the old woman's hand to the floor and she stretched out her arms, and her thin hands shook like withered leaves.

" Bolla veen! bolla veen! " she cried, in a low voice that was a sob. " It's my own case over again."

And then the girl fell into her mother's arms and buried her head in her breast and cried, as only a suffering child can cry, helplessly, piteously.

13

A moment later, there was a heavy footstep outside, and the ring of an iron tool thrown down on the " street." The old woman raised her face with a look of fear.

" It's thy father," she whispered.

III

Dan Baldromma had risen earlier than usual that morning. For more than a week there had not been water enough to his mill-wheel for his liking, and suspecting the cause of the shortage he had put a pick over his shoulder and walked up the glen.

There was a little croft on the top of the brews half a mile nearer to the mountain. It was called Baldromma-beg (the little Baldromma) and its occupants (sub-tenants of Dan Baldromma) were a quaint old couple—Will Skillicorne, a long, slow-eyed, slow-legged person who was a class-leader among the " Primitives," and his wife, Bridget, a typical little Manxwoman of her class, keen-eyed, quick-tongued, illiterate and superstitious.

Their croft was thirsty land, though water in abundance was so near, and to every request that it should be laid on in pipes from the glen, Dan had said, " Let your wife carry it—what else is the woman there for ? "

Bridget had carried it for ten years. Then her anger getting the better of her, she put on a pair of her husband's big boots and rolled two great boulders into a neck of the river, with the result that a deep stream of sweet water came flowing down to her house and fields.

This was just what Dan had suspected, and coming upon the new-made dam, he stretched his legs across it, swung his pick and sent the boulders tumbling down the glen, with a torrent of water from Baldromma-beg at the back of them.

But Bridget, also, had risen earlier than usual that morning, and, hearing the sound of Dan's pick, she went out to him at his bad work and fell on him with hot reproaches.

" Was there nothing doing down at the mill, Dan Collister," she cried, " that thou must be coming up here to put thy evil eye on other people's places ? "

" Get thee indoors, woman," growled Dan, " and put thy house in order."

" *My* house in order ? Mine ? And what about thine ? Thine that is a disgrace to the parish and the talk of the island."

" Keep a civil tongue in thy head, Mrs. Skillicorne, or maybe I'll be showing thee the road at Hollantide."

" Turn me out of the croft, will thou ? Do it and welcome !

I give thee lave. It would be middling aisy to find a better farm, and Satan himself couldn't find a worse landlord. But set thou one foot on this land until my year is over and if there's a bucket of dirty water on the cowhouse floor I'll throw it over thee. Put my house in order indeed! Where's thy daughter, eh? Where's thy daughter, I say?"

"I've got no daughter, woman, and well thou knows it," said Dan.

"'Deed I do. No wonder the Lord wouldn't trust thee with a daughter of thy own, the way thou's brought up this one. The slut! The strumpet! Away with thee and look for her—it will become thee better."

But Dan having finished his work was now plunging down the glen and old Will Skillicorne had come out of his house half dressed, with his braces hanging behind him.

"Come in, woman—lave the man to God," said Will.

"God indeed! The dirt! The ugly black toad! God wouldn't bemane Himself talking to the like."

"Thou's done it this time, though, I'm thinking. Thou heard what he said about Hollantide?"

"Chut! Get thee back to bed. What's thou putting thy mouth in for? Who knows where the man himself will be by that time?"

With a face like a black cloud after this encounter, Dan threw down his pick on the cobbles of the street and went into the kitchen to work off his anger on his wife.

"That's what thou's done for me, ma'am! There's not a trollop in the parish that isn't throwing thy daughter's bad doings in my face."

The kitchen was full of smoke, for the porridge in the oven-pot had been allowed to burn, and it was not until he was standing back to the fire, putting his pipe in the pocket of his open waist-coat, that Dan saw Bessie where she had seated herself, after breaking out of her mother's arms, by the table and in the darkest corner.

He took in the girl's situation at a glance, but after the manner of the man he pretended not to do so.

"God bless my soul," he cried. "Back, is she? Well, well! But what did I say, mother? ' No need to send the Cross Vustha (the fiery cross) after her, she'll come home.' And my goodness the grand woman's she's grown! Fur caps and fur-lined cloaks and I don't know the what! Just come to put a sight on the mother and the ould man, I suppose. No pride at all at all! I wouldn't trust but there's a grand carriage waiting for her at the corner of the road."

"Aisy, man, aisy," said Mrs. Collister, picking up her stick, "don't thou see the girl has walked?"

"Walked, has she?" said Dan, raising his thick eyebrows in pretended astonishment. "You don't say! All the way from Castletown? Well, well! So that's how it is, is it? The young waistrel has thrown her over, has he?"

Bessie had to put her hand to her throat to keep back the cry that was bubbling up.

"Aisy, man, aisy with the like," said the old woman. But Dan was for showing no mercy.

"Goodness me, the airs she gave herself going away! I might shut my door on her, but there would be others to open theirs. And now they *have* opened them, and shut them too, I'm thinking."

Bessie, crushed and silent, was clutching the end of the table. Dan stepped over to her, laid hold of her left hand, lifted it up, as if looking for her wedding ring, and then flung it away.

"Nothing!" he said. "She's got nothing for it neither. I might have followed her to Castletown, but I didn't. 'I'll lave her to it,' I thought. 'Maybe the girl's cleverer than we thought, and will come home mistress of Baldromma and a thousand good acres besides.' But no, not a ha'porth! And now she has come back to ate us up for the rest of our lives! The toot! The boght! The booby!"

"Dan Collister," said the old woman, "don't thou see the girl is ill?"

"Ill, is she?" said Dan. "I wouldn't trust but she is, ma'am. So it's worse than I thought, and maybe before long there'll be another mouth to feed."

Bessie dropped her head on the table.

"But not in this house, if you plaze, miss. It happened here once before, and the island would be having a fine laugh at me if it happened again."

Once more Dan stepped over to Bessie and touched her arm.

"You're like a dead letter, you've come to the wrong address, mistress. It wasn't Dan Baldromma's thatched cottage you were wanting, but the big slate house down the road where the paycocks are scraming. I'll trouble you to go there."

"Sakes alive, man," cried the old woman, "thou'rt not for turning the girl out of doors?"

"I am that, ma'am," said Dan, going over to the door. "No trollop shall be telling me again that my house is the disgrace of the parish and the talk of the island."

Then throwing the door wide and rattling the catch of it, he said,

"Out of my house, miss! Out of it! Out of it!"

Bessie, who had been sitting motionless, raised her head and rose to go, although scarcely able to take a step forward, when she felt a hand that was trembling like a leaf laid on her shoulder.

"Stay thou there, and leave this to me."

It was the old woman who had been crouching over the fire on the three-legged stool and had now risen, thrown her stick away as if she had no longer any need of it, and was facing her husband with blazing eyes.

"Thou talks and talks of this house as thine and thine," she said. "What made it thine?"

"The law, if thou wants to know, woman," said Dan.

"Then the law is a robber and a thief."

Dan looked at his wife in astonishment, and then burst into a fit of forced laughter.

"Well, that's good! That's rich! That's wonderful! What next, I wonder?"

"Do you want me to tell thee the truth, Dan Collister? Before the girl, too? Then there's not a stick or a stone in the place that in the eyes of heaven does not belong to me."

"What?"

"Not a stick or a stone, except the landlord's, that wasn't bought with my father's money—John Corteen, a man of God, if ever there was one."

"Pity his daughter didn't take after him, then."

"Pity enough, Dan Collister. But when I brought shame into his house he forgave me. And when the finger of death was on the man the only trouble he had in life was what was to become of his girl when he was gone."

"Truth enough, ma'am, he had to find thee a husband, hadn't he?"

"He hadn't far to look, though. And if thou had nothing in thy pocket and not much on thy back thou had plenty in thy mouth to make up for it. Thou were not afraid of scandal! Thou didn't mind marrying a girl who had been talked of with another man!"

"And I did, didn't I?"

"Thou did, God forgive thee! But not till the man's trembling hand had reached up to the hole in the thatch over his bed for his stocking purse and counted the money out to thee. Three hundred good Manx pounds he had worked thirty years for and saved up for his daughter. And then thou swore on the Holy Book to be good to his girl and her baby, and the man's dying eyes on thee. And now—now thou talks of turning my girl out of the house—this house that would have been her house some day if thou had not come between us. But no! Thou shan't do that."

"Shan't I?"

" 'Deed thou shan't! She may have done wrong, but if she has it's no more than her mother did before her, and if *I* daren't turn her out for it *thou* shalt not."

"We'll see, ma'am, we'll see," said Dan. He was buttoning up his waistcoat and putting on his coat.

"It's no use talking to a woman. There's not much sense to be got out of the like anyway. But when a man marries, the property of the wife becomes the property of the husband—that's Dempster's law, isn't it? And standing up for your legal rights, and not being forced by your wife, or anybody else, to find maintenance for another man's offspring when it comes—that's Dempster's law too, I belave."

"Yes," said the old woman, " and standing up for your own flesh and blood when she's sick and weak and the world is going cold on her and she has nowhere else to lay her head in her trouble—that's Mother's law, Dan Collister, and it's older than the Dempster's, I'm thinking."

"Do as you plaze, ma'am," said Dan. "If you want more noising about the bad doings of your daughter it's all as one to me."

He took his billycock hat down from the "lath" under the ceiling and continued,

"I'll hear what the Speaker has to say about this, though. His wife wasn't for doing much for thee when the honour of this house was in question, but maybe she'll alter her tune now that it's the honour of her own."

He drew his whip from its nail over the fireplace and stepped to the door.

"And if this matter ends as I expect I'll be hearing what the Coorts have to say about it, too. Young Mr. Sto'll is to be made Dempster they're telling me. They're putting him in for it, anyway, and he is bosom friend to the Spaker's son. But friend or no friend," he said, with his hand on the hasp, and ready to go, "maybe his first job when he comes back to the island will be to send his Coroner to this house to turn the man's mistress and her by-child into the road."

"Tell him to send her coffin at the same time, then," cried the old woman, almost screaming. "Mine too, Dan Collister. That's the only way he'll turn my daughter out of this house, I promise thee."

But the old woman collapsed the moment her husband had gone, and staggering to the rocking-chair she dropped into it and cried. Then Bessie, who had not yet spoken, rose and said, crying herself,

"Don't cry, I'll go away myself, mother."

But the old woman was up again in a moment.

"No, thou'll not," she said. "Thou'll go up to thy bedroom in the dairy loft—the one thou had in the innocent old times gone by. Come, take my arm—my good arm, girl. Lean on me, woman-bogh."

CHAPTER TWENTY-TWO

THE SOUL OF HAGAR

Two hours had passed. Bessie was in her bedroom—the little one-eyed chamber (entered from the first landing on the stairs) in which she had dressed for Douglas. But the sheet of silvered glass on the whitewashed wall which had shone then with the light of her beaming eyes was now reflecting her broken, tear-stained, woebegone face.

She knew that her journey had been in vain, that her sufferings had been wasted. Her child was not to be stillborn. Through the closed door she heard Dan Baldromma going off in the stiff cart. He was going to the Speaker, to threaten him with the shame of her unborn child, and to call upon him to compel his son to marry her.

Wild, blind error! But what would be the result? Alick would hear of her whereabouts and learn of her condition and that would be the end of everything between them. All her secret scheme to wipe out her fault, to keep her name clean for Alick, to preserve his beautiful faith in her, would be destroyed, and he would be dead to her for ever.

But no, come what would that should not be! And if the only way to prevent it was to make away with her child when it came she must do so. Only nobody must know—not even her mother.

Time and again the old woman came hobbling upstairs, bringing food and trying to comfort her.

"Will I send for Doctor Clucas, Bessie?"

"No, no. I shall be better in the morning."

The day passed heavily. She could not lie down. Sometimes she sat on the edge of the bed; sometimes stood and held on to the end of it; and sometimes walked to and fro in the narrow space of her bedroom floor. Having no window in her room her only sight of the world without was through the skylight in the thatch, which showed nothing but the sky. The only sound that reached her was the squealing of a pig that was being killed at a neighbouring farm.

At length darkness fell. Hitherto she had been thinking of
her unborn child with a certain tenderness, even a certain pity.
But now, in the wild disorder of her senses, she began to hate it.
It seemed to be some evil spirit that was coming into the world to
destroy everybody. Why shouldn't she kill it? She would! Only
she must be alone—quite alone.

Shivering, perspiring, weak, dizzy, she was sitting in the darkness when her mother came to say good-night.

" Here are a few broth. Take them. They'll warm thee."

" No, no."

" Come, let me coax thee, bogh."

Bessie refused again, and the old woman's eyes began to fill.

" Will I stay up the night with thee, Bessie? "

" Oh, no, no ! "

" I'll leave my door open then, and if thou art wanting anything thou'll call."

" Yes, yes."

" Thy father isn't home yet, and if thou'rt no better when he
goes by thy door thou must tell him and he'll let me know."

Bessie raised her eyes in astonishment, and the old woman, with
a shamefaced look, began to apologize for her husband. He was
not so bad after all, and when a woman had taken a man for better
or worse . . . .

" Do *you* say that, mother? "

Something quivered in the old woman's wrinkled throat.

" Well, we women are all alike, thou knows."

" Good-night and go to sleep, mother."

Bessie hustled her mother out of the room, but hardly had she
gone than she wanted to call her back.

" Mother! Mother! " she cried in the sudden access of her
pain, but though her door was ajar her mother, who was going
deaf, did not hear her.

At the next moment she was glad. Her mother believed in
God and religion. To burden her conscience with any knowledge
of what she meant to do would be too cruel.

But Bessie's terror increased at every moment. The night outside was quiet, yet the air seemed to be full of fearful cries. At the
bidding of some instinctive impulse she blew out the candle, and
then, in the darkness and solitude, a great terror took hold of her.

" Alick! Alick! " she cried, but only the deep night heard
her. At last, in the paroxysm of her pain, she fell back on the
bed—she was unconscious.

When she came to herself again she had a sense of blessed
ease, like that of sailing into a quiet harbour out of a tempestuous

sea. Before she opened her eyes she heard a faint cry. She
thought at first it was only a memory of the bleating of the lost
lamb on the mountains. But the cry came again and then she knew
what had happened—her child had been born!

Time passed—how long or what she did in it, she never afterwards knew. Her weakness seemed to have gone and she had a
feeling of surprising strength. The bitterness of her heart had
gone too, and a flood of happiness was sweeping over her.

It was motherhood! To Bessie too, in her misery and shame,
the merciful angel of mother-love had come. Her child! Hers!
Hers! Make away with it? Kill it? No, not for worlds of worlds!

It was a boy too! Thank God it was a boy! A woman was so
weak; she had so much to suffer, so many things to think about.
But a man was strong and free. He could fight his own way in
life. And her boy would fight for her also, and make amends for
all she had gone through.

It was the middle of the night. The glimmering and guttering
candle on the wash-table (she had been up and had lit it afresh)
was casting dark shadows in the room. Only a little dairy loft
with the turfy thatch overhead, and the sheepskin rugs underfoot,
but oh, how it shone with glory!

Bessie was singing to her baby (words and tune springing to
her mind in a moment) when suddenly she heard sounds from outside. They were the rattle of cart wheels and the clatter of horse's
hoofs on the cobbles of the " street."

Dan Baldromma had come home!

Her heart seemed to stop its beating. She blew out her candle
and listened, scarcely drawing breath. She heard her step-father
tipping up his stiff-cart and then shouting at his horse as he
dragged off its harness in the stable. After that she heard him
coming into the house and throwing his heavy boots on to the
hearthstone. Then she heard the thud, thud, thud of the old man's
stockinged feet on the kitchen floor—he was about to come upstairs.

At that moment the child, who had been asleep on her arm,
awoke and cried. Only a feeble cry, half-smothered by the close-
ness of the little mouth to her breast, but in Bessie's ears it sounded
like thunder. If her step-father heard it, what would he do?
Involuntarily, and before she knew what she was doing, she put
her hand over the child's mouth.

Then thud, thud, thud! Dan Baldromma was coming upstairs.
Bessie could hear his thick breathing. He had reached the landing. He seemed to stop for a moment outside her door. But he
passed on, went up the second short flight, pushed open the door
of her mother's room and clashed it noisily behind him.

Then Bessie drew breath and turned back to her child. She was shocked to find that in her terror she had been holding her trembling hand tightly down on the child's mouth. It had only been for a moment (what had seemed like a moment), but when she took her hand away and listened, in the throbbing darkness, for the child's soft breathing, no sound seemed to come.

With shaking fingers she lit her candle again, and then held the light to the baby's face.

The little, helpless, innocent face lay still.

" Can it be possible . . . . no, no, God forbid it! "

But at length the awful truth came surging down on her. She had killed her child.

II

When Bessie awoke the next day the sun was shining on her eye-lids from the skylight in the thatch. She had some difficulty in realising where she was. Before opening her eyes she heard the muffled lowing of the cows in the closed-up cow-house, and had an impulse to do as she had done in earlier days—get up and milk them. At the next moment she heard her mother's shuffling step on the kitchen floor, and then the tide of memory swept back on her.

But she was a different woman this morning. She had no remorse now, no qualm, no compunction. What she had done, she had done, and after all it was the best thing that could have happened—best for her, best for Alick, best for everybody.

Her child being dead she no longer loved it. All she had to do was to bury it away somewhere, and then everything would go on as she had intended. Meantime (before going to sleep) she had taken her precautions. Nobody must know. If there had been reasons why she should not take her mother into her confidence last night they were now increased tenfold.

After a while her mother came up with her breakfast. A veil seemed to dim the old woman's eyes—she looked as if she had been crying.

" How are thou now, bogh? "

" Better! Much better! I told you I should be better in the morning."

The old woman was silent for a moment and then said,

" Thou were not up and downstairs in the night, Bessie? "

" 'Deed no! Why should you think so? "

" Because I shut the wash-house door when I went to bed and it was open when I came down in the morning."

Bessie's lips trembled, but she made no answer.

A little later she heard her step-father talking loudly in the kitchen. He had seen the Speaker, having waited all day for him. There had been a stormy scene. The big man had foamed at the mouth, talked about blackmail, threatened to turn him out of the farm at Hollantide, and finally shouted for Tom Kermode, his steward, to fling him into the road.

" I lave it with you, Sir," Dan had answered. " If you prefer the new Dempster, when he comes, to see justice done to the girl, it's all as one to me."

Bessie could have laughed. Wicked, selfish, scheming—how she was going to defeat it!

All morning she lay quiet; thinking out her plans. Half a mile up the glen there was a large stone of irregular shape, surrounded by a wild tangle of briar and gorse. The Manx called it the *Claghny-Dooiney-marroo*—the dead man's stone, the body of a murdered man having been found on it. By reason of this gruesome association of the bloody hand upon it, few approached the stone by day and the bravest man (unless he were in drink) would hesitate to go near it by night.

Bessie decided to bury her child under the *Clagh-ny-Dooiney*. It would lie hidden for ever there; nobody would find it.

The day was long in passing, for Bessie was waiting for the night. She heard the young lambs bleating in the fields and the cocks crowing in the haggard. A linnet perched on the ledge of her skylight (her mother had opened it) and looked in on her and sang.

At length the sky darkened and night fell. The moon (it was in its first quarter) sailed across her patch of sky and disappeared. Once or twice the skylight was aglow with a palpitating red light —someone was burning gorse on the mountains. But the fires died down and then there was nothing save the sky with its stars.

Her mother came again to say good-night. She had the pitiful look of a woman who was struggling to keep back her tears.

" Wilt thou not sit up, Bessie, while I make thy bed for thee? "

Bessie started and then stammered: " Oh, no! I mean . . . . it will do in the morning."

The old woman looked down at her with eyes which seemed to say, " Can thou not trust thy mother, girl? " But she only sighed and went off to bed.

Somewhere in the early morning (Dan having gone to bed also) Bessie got up to make ready. She found herself very weak, and it took her a long time to dress. When she was about to put on her shoes she remembered that they were new and told herself they would creak as she went downstairs, so she decided to go barefoot again.

Having finished her dressing she took from under the bed-clothes what she had hidden there, and began to wrap it in a large silk scarf. It was the scarf she had worn in the storm—a present from Alick, with "Bessie" stamped on one corner.

Seeing her name at the last moment, she tore a strip of the scarf away, and threw it aside (intending to destroy it in the morning), opened her door, listened for an instant and then crept downstairs and out of the house.

The night was chill and the ground struck cold into her body. It was very dark, for the moon and stars had gone out, and there was no light anywhere except the dull red of the gorse fires on the mountains, which had sunk so low as to look like a dying eye. But Bessie could have found her way blindfolded.

Carrying her burden she crossed the wooden bridge and reached the path that went up the glen. Just as she did so she heard the sound of singing, of laughter and of carriage-wheels on the high road. A company of jolly girls and boys were driving home after one of their Bachelor Balls in a neighbouring parish. That cut deep, but Bessie thought of Alick and the wound passed away. She would return to him in a few days; they would be married soon, and then she, too, would be glad and happy.

How dark it was under the trees, though! She had left it late. The dawn was near, for the first birds were beginning to call.

"It must be here," she thought, and she slipped down from the path to the bed of the glen.

But the trees were thicker there, and, being already in early leaf, they obscured the little light that was left in the sky. Where could the stone be? The briars were tearing at her dress and the tall nettles were stinging her hands. She was feeling weak and lost and had begun to cry. How the dogs howled at her step-father's farm!

Suddenly a breeze rose and fanned the gorse fires on the mountains to a crackling glow. And then a red flame rent the darkness and lighted up the valley from end to end, making it for a few moments almost as clear as day.

Bessie was terrified. Here was the *Clagh-ny-Dooiney* almost at her feet, but this bright light was like an accusing eye from heaven looking down on her and pointing her out.

For a moment she wanted to drop down among the briars and hide herself. But making a call on her resolution she crept up to the big stone, stooped, pushed her burden under the overlapping lip of it, and then rose, turned about and ran.

Trembling and weeping she stumbled her way home. It was lighter now. The day was coming rapidly and the small spring leaves were shivering in the cold wind that runs over the earth before the dawn. The lambs were bleating in the unseen fields, and the newly-born ones were making their first pitiful cry. It sounded like the cry of her child as she had heard it last night, and it tore her terribly.

The little face, the little hands, the little feet she had left behind—why had she not been brave and strong and faced the world with them?

Should she stop and go back! She tried to do so but could not. The more she wanted to return the faster she ran away.

Her strength was failing her, and she was scarcely able to put one foot before another. Often she stumbled and fell and got up again. Was she going the right way home?

" Alick! Alick! " she cried, and the hot tears fell over her cold cheeks.

At last she saw the dark roof of the mill-house against the leaden grey of the sky. She had reached the bridge over the mill-race when she felt a light on her face and saw a figure approaching her. Somebody was coming up the glen and the lantern he carried was swinging by his side as he walked.

Then the instinct of self-preservation took possession of her. Dizzy, dazed, breathing rapidly and trembling in every limb, she crossed the bridge quickly, crept up to the door of the dwelling house, stumbled upstairs to her room, tore off her outer garments, dropped back on to her bed, and then fell (almost in a moment) into the sleep of utter exhaustion.

III

Bridget Skillicorne had had a cow sick that night. It had been suffering from a colic, probably due to grazing among the rank grass which had been lying under the water that had been drained away. But Bridget was sure that " that dirt Baldromma " had " wutched " it (bewitched it) just to spite her for what she had said.

She had tried a hot bran mash in vain. The cow still writhed and roared, so nothing remained, if they were not to lose their creature, but that Will should go to the Ballawhaine (a witch-doctor who lived nine or ten miles away on the seaward side of the Curragh) and get a charm to take off the witching.

Old Will, being a class-leader, was well aware that such sorcery was the arts of Satan. But if the cow died it would make a big hole in their stocking-purse to buy another, so his conscience compounded with his pocket, and he agreed to go.

"Aw well, a few good words will do no harm at all," he said, and carrying his stable lantern he set out towards nine o'clock on his long journey.

Then Bridget, taking another lantern, a half-knitted stocking and a three-legged stool, went into the cow-house to sit up with her cow and watch the progress of its malady.

Towards midnight the creature became easier, and, gathering her legs under her, lay down to sleep. But Bridget remained three hours longer in the close atmosphere of the cow-house, waiting for old Will but thinking of Dan, and making her needles go with a furious click at the thought of his threat to evict her.

The upper half of the cow-house door stood open, and somewhere in the dark hours towards dawn she was startled by a bright light and the hissing and crackling of a sudden fire outside. She knew what it was (such fires on the mountains were not uncommon), but nevertheless she stepped out to see.

She saw more than she had expected. In the glen below her brew, where every bush and tree stood out for a moment in the flare of the burning gorse, she saw the figure of a woman. The woman was standing by the *Clagh-ny-Dooiney*. She had something white under her arm. After a moment she knelt, put her parcel under the lip of the stone and then hurried away.

Who was she? In her present mood, with her mind running on one subject, Bridget could have no uncertainty. It was the Collister girl! It must be! What had she been doing down there? In her own walk through life Bridget had never stepped aside, therefore she was severe on those who had. There was only one thing that could bring a girl out of bed in the middle of the night to a place like that. The slut! The strumpet!

When Will Skillicorne reached home half-an-hour afterwards he was carrying a wisp of straw. With this he was to make the sign of the cross on the back of the sick cow, and say some good words about St. Patrick and St. Bridget, giving it at the same time a hot drink of meal and water.

"But the craythur is better these three hours," said Bridget.

"Praise the Lord!" said Will. "That must have been the very minute the good man came down from his bed to me in his flannel drawers!"

"But did thou meet anybody as thou was coming up the glen?"

"Maybe I did."

"Was it a woman?"

"It's like it was, now."

"Did she go into the mill-house?"

" I believe in my heart she did, though."

Bridget was triumphant.

It was the Collister girl! There could not be a doubt about it. And at break of day she would go down to the glen and see what she had left under the *Clagh-ny-Dooiney.*

" Show me the road at Hollantide, will he? The dirt! The dirty black toad! We'll see! We'll see! "

IV

Bessie's sleep of exhaustion deepened to delirium and for a long day she lay in the grip of it. When she floated out of her unconsciousness, she had a sense of confusion. A babel of meaningless voices, like the many sounds of a wild night, were clashing in her brain. A man and a woman were in her bedroom, talking like somnambulists.

" Her feet have been bleeding. Where has she been, think you? "

The man's voice must be that of Doctor Clucas, and then came some vague answer in the woman's voice, with a thick snuffle and a suppressed sob—her mother's.

Bessie heard no more. A cloud passed over her brain that was like the rolling mist that alternately reveals and conceals a bell-buoy at sea. When it cleared she heard a strange woman's voice outside the house—her bedroom door had been left open that her mother might hear her if she called.

" I didn't know thy daughter had come home, Liza Collister."

" And how dost thou know now, Bridget Skillicorne? "

" How? There's someones coming will tell thee how, woman."

Bessie felt as if somebody had struck her in the face. Had anything become known? Later she heard her step-father speaking in the kitchen.

" Is she herself yet."

" Not yet."

" Better she never should be."

" Sakes alive, man, what art thou saying? "

" I'm saying that old trollop on the brews is after finding something under the *Clagh-ny-Dooiney* and sending her man to the police to fetch it."

" Fetch what? "

" Just a parcel in a silk scarf with a lil arm sticking out— that's all, ma'am."

The doctor at the hospital had been holding a post-mortem, and

now Cain, the constable, was to make a house to house visitation
of the parish to find the mother of the child.

Bessie covered her mouth to suppress a scream. But something whispered, " Hush! Keep still! They know nothing! "

Early next day she was awakened by the sound of many men's
voices downstairs, and her mother's voice in angry protestation.

" I tell thee, I know nothing about it. The girl came home to
me three days ago, and I put her to bed, and she has never since
been out of it."

" They all say that, ma'am," said one of the men. It was
Cain, the constable.

A little later, while Bessie lay with closed eyes and her face to
the wall, she became aware of several persons in her bedroom, and
one of them leaning over her. She knew it was Cain—she could
hear his asthmatical breathing.

" Is she really unconscious, doctor? "

" Undoubtedly she is. You can leave her for a few days anyway. She'll not run away, you see."

After that, listening intently, Bessie heard the constable ranging the room as if examining everything.

" What's this? " he asked.

Bessie drew a quick breath, but dared not look around.

" Only a remnant seemingly," said the doctor.

" We'll be taking it with us, though," said the constable, and
then the rolling mist of unconsciousness covered everything again.

When it passed Bessie knew that the police were suspecting
her. They thought they had found her out, and they were going
to bring the whole machinery of the law to punish her. What a
wicked thing the law was! She had injured nobody—nobody that
anybody had ever seen in this world. She had only tried to save
somebody she loved from shame and pain. And yet the constables, the courts and the coroners were all in a conspiracy to
crush one poor girl! No matter! She would deny everything.

Next day was Sunday. Bessie heard the church bells ringing
across the Curragh, and, before they stopped, the singing of a
hymn. The Primitives were holding a service at the corner of
the high road before going into their chapel. After the hymn
somebody prayed. It was Will Skillicorne. Bessie (listening
through her open skylight) recognised the high pitch of his preaching voice. He would be standing on the chapel steps.

There was a great deal about " carnal transgression," about
" brands plucked from the burning," about " the judgments of the
Lord," and finally about the " conscious sinner," throwing herself
upon her Saviour and repenting of " the sin she had committed

against God." At the close of his prayer Will gave out the first
two lines of another hymn—

> " *I was a wandering sheep,*
> *I did not love the fold.*"

Bessie knew whom all this was meant for. The Primitives
were torturing her. But they were torturing somebody else as well.
Through the singing and praying she heard her mother's sighs
downstairs, and the beating of her foot on the hearthstone, as she
sat by the fire and listened to the service for her guilty child.

What a cowardly thing religion was! Sin? What sin had she
committed? She had never intended to do wrong, and only those
who had gone through it could know what she had suffered. Anyway, such as she was God had made her. She would admit nothing. Nothing whatever.

Two days passed. Bessie's heart softened and became calm.
The police were leaving her alone—they must have given up that
nonsense about punishing her. Everything was going to turn out
as she had expected.

On the third day, her mother, coming into her bedroom, found
her with widely-opened eyes and all her face a smile. Yes, she
was herself once more. In fact there had not been much amiss
with her. Only, never having been ill before, she had been frightened and had come home to be nursed by her mother. But now she
was better and must soon go back . . . . back to where she
came from.

She told her mother about Alick and how fond he was of her—
parting from his father and sisters and even his mother for her
sake. It was quite a mistake to suppose that Alick had refused to
marry her. He would have married her long ago, and it was she
who had been holding back. Why? She wished to be strong
and well first. It wasn't fair to a man to let him marry a sick
wife—was it?

The old woman, with a broken face, looking sadly down at the
girl, said, " Yes, bogh! It's like it isn't, bogh," and turned her
eyes away.

On the fourth day Bessie got out of bed and moved about the
room just to show how strong she was.

" See what a step I have now. I could walk miles and
miles, mother."

The moral of that was that she must go back to Derby Haven
without more delay. Alick was waiting for her and he would be
growing anxious. She must take the first train in the morning.

"It's rather early, but never mind about breakfast. A cup of tea and a piece of barley bonnag—that will do."

Late that night, when Mrs. Collister, going to bed with a heavy heart, looked in to say good-night, Bessie asked to be called in good time in the morning.

"Don't forget to waken me. I used to be the first up, you know, but now I'm a sleepy-head."

And then she kissed her mother (never having kissed her since she was a child) and the old woman's eyes overflowed.

Left alone, in the dark, she began to think how good God had been to her after all. Only those who had sinned and suffered knew how good He could be. She remembered the text about the friend who, when all earthly friends forsake you, sticketh closer than a brother. Also, with a certain shame, she recalled the hymn the Primitives had sung on Sunday morning, and, covering her head in the bedclothes, she sang two lines of it—

> "But now I love my Father's voice,
> I love my Father's home."

How happy she was! At that time to-morrow she would be in bed at Derby Haven, having seen Alick and arranged everything.

Next morning, when she awoke, she was startled to find the sun pouring into the room. She knew by the line it made on the wall that the first train must have gone. The chickens, too, were clucking at the kitchen door, and they never came round before breakfast.

She had risen on her elbow intending to call, when she heard the roll of a van-like vehicle drawing up in front of the house, and immediately afterwards, a man's husky, asthmatical voice in the kitchen, mingling with her mother's shrill treble.

"Go upstairs and tell her to make ready, ma'am."

"No, no; the girl's not fit for it, I tell thee."

"She's fit enough for the prison hospital, anyway."

"She has never been out of my door since she came into it."

"We'll lave that to the High Bailiff and the Dempster, if you plaze."

Bessie, supporting herself on her trembling arm, could scarcely restrain herself from screaming. One moment she sat and gasped, and then, grasping her head with both hands, she turned about and fell forward and buried her face in her pillow.

At the next moment she was conscious of somebody coming into her room, and at the next, from somewhere at the foot of the bed, she heard her mother say, in a strange voice she had never known before—throbbing, choking, scarcely audible—

" They have come for thee, Bessie."

CHAPTER TWENTY-THREE

STOWELL IN LONDON

VICTOR STOWELL had been more than a week in London. For-tune had favoured him from the first. The Home Secretary (a tall, spare, elderly man, with a clean-shaven face of rather severe expression) rose when Stowell entered his room as if a spirit had appeared before him. " My youth again," the young man thought, but it was a different matter this time.

" Has anybody ever told you that you resemble your father, Mr. Stowell ? "

It turned out that the old Deemster and the Home Secretary (a barrister before he became a statesman) had been in chambers together in the Middle Temple while reading for the bar, and that the politician had never lost respect for the man who, in spite of brilliant promise of success in England (he might have become an English High Court Judge with six times his Manx salary), had returned to the obscurity of his little island and the service of his own people.

" You have high traditions to live up to, young man. Sit down."

Then came the subject of the interview. The authorities had satisfied themselves that on the score of legal capacity the Gover-nor's recommendation was not unjustified. The only serious diffi-culty was Stowell's youth. The principles on which the Crown selected elderly and even old (sometimes very old) men for the positions of Judges were simple and sound. First, seniority of service, and next, maturity of character, so as to avoid the dangers that come from the temptations, the trials, even the turbulent emotions of early life, which might easily conflict with the calm of the judicial office. Still, these principles could be too rigidly followed—particularly in remote colonies and small dependencies where the range of suitable selection was limited.

After this came a personal catechism, the old man looking at the young one over the rims of his tortoise-shell spectacles. Mar-ried? Not yet. Expect to be? Yes, Sir. Soon? Not, not for a long time. How long? Six weeks at least, Sir.

The ends of the severe mouth rose perceptibly, and in any other face they might have broken into a smile.

Daughter of the Governor, isn't she? Yes, but that isn't her chief characteristic, Sir. What is? That she is the loveliest and noblest woman in the world.

" Oh! "

Again the severe mouth relaxed, and the Home Secretary asked Stowell where he was staying. Stowell told him (the Inns of Court Hotel, Holborn) and he made a note of it.

" Remain there until you hear from me again, Mr. Stowell, and meantime say nothing about this interview to anybody."

" Not anybody whatever, Sir ? "

The Home Secretary's stern old face became genial and charming as he rose and held out his hand.

" Well, that supreme being, perhaps . . . . Good day! "

" So here I am, my dear Fenella," wrote Stowell, " back in the bedroom of my hotel, telling you all about it. How long I may have to remain in London, goodness knows, therefore I propose to tell you something about my ways of life while I wait.

" Such a change in me! When I was in London last (with Alick Gell, you remember) I spent my days and nights in the hotels, restaurants, theatres and music-halls that are the lovely and beloved world of woman. It is the world of woman still, but quite another realm of it.

" Two nights ago I strolled westward along Oxford Street, and thought (with a lump in my throat) about De Quincey and his Ann. Then, cutting through Clare Market to the Temple and finding the gate closed, I tipped the porter to let me walk through the Brick Court, and stood a long half hour before a house in the silent little square, thinking of the day when the women of the town sat on the stairs while poor Noll (Oliver Goldsmith) lay dead in his rooms above. And then, coming out into Fleet-street (midnight now) where the big printing presses were throbbing behind dark buildings, I tried to think I saw the great old Johnson, God bless him, picking up the prostitute from the pavement, carrying her home on his back and laying her on his bed.

" Last night I strolled eastward to look at the outside of the Settlement in which you used to be Lady Warden (in the unbelievable days before you came back to Man), and returning by a dark side street, I came upon a queue of women crouching in the cold before the doors of a Salvation Shelter. They were waiting for four in the morning when they would have a fighting chance of one of the beds (i.e., boxes like open coffins lying cheek by jowl on the floor of a big hall) after the washerwomen who were then asleep in them would get up and go to work.

" But the climax came this morning (Sunday morning) when I went to service at the Foundling Hospital. Such a sweet scene—at first sight at all events. The little women, like little nuns, in their linen caps and aprons, singing like little angels in their sweet young voices. But my God, what tragedy lurked behind that picture also !

" I did not hear much of the sermon for thinking of the mothers of these ' children of shame ' and the conditions under which they must have given birth to them—sometimes in a garret, in secret, alone, driven to dementia by a sense of impending shame. How often a poor miserable girl in the degradation of childbirth (which should be the crown of a woman's glory) must have been tempted to kill her child in fear of the fate that awaited both it and her ! And to think of the giant arm of the mighty law coming down on a creature like that to punish her ! Lord, what crimes are committed in the name of Justice !

" There you are now ! That's what you've done for me. 'Deed you have though. It's truth enough, girl. You've opened my ears to the cry of the voice of suffering woman, and that is the saddest sound, perhaps, that breaks on the shores of life. And the moral of it all is that if I do become a Judge (God knows I'm almost afraid to hope for it) you must be my helper, my inspirer, the tower of my strength.

" Oh, my darling, how much I love you ! It seems to me that I lost all my life until I came to love you. How well I recall the blessed day when I loved you first ! It was the first time I saw you—the first time really. Don't you remember? In the glen, that glorious autumn afternoon. The vision has followed me ever since and I wish I could blot out every day of my life when I have not thought of you.

" There you are again ! You see what you've done, ma'am. But I'm not always on the heights. What do you think? I've bought a motor car, and every morning I go up to Hampstead with a teacher to learn to drive.

" It is for our honeymoon. You called me a Viking once, and I'm not going to be a Viking for nothing. As soon as you are mine, mine wholly, I am going to pick you up and carry you off to all the inaccessible places in the island—the bent-strewn plains of Ayre, where a lighthouse-man lives alone with his wife and nothing else save the sea for company; the shepherd's hut on Snae-fell, where there is nothing but the sky, and the sandy headlands of the Calf with the mists of the Atlantic sweeping over them.

" Meantime, think of me in a box of a bedroom five storeys up, with the roaring tide of London traffic running, like a Canadian river, sixty feet below, and write—write, write! Tell me what is happening in the 'lil islan'' which is lying asleep to-night in the Irish Sea. God bless it, and all the kind and cheery souls in it! God bless it for evermore!

"STOWELL."

II

"My dear Victor,—You cannot imagine what a joy your letter was. Do you know it was my first love-letter? Of course I behaved like a dairymaid—took it up to bed, put it on my pillow and said, 'You are Victor, you know,' and laid my cheek on it.

"Whatever have you done to make me so foolish? Was it only half of you (the physical half) that went away, leaving the spirit half with me? I want the other half, though, the substantial half, so tell your Home Secretary (I like him) to hurry up and send you home.

"You do wrong not to see the beautiful women, dear. The woman who is afraid of her husband looking at other women is building her house on the sand. I should like to say to myself, 'He has seen the loveliest women in the world, yet he comes back to *me*.'

"All the same I love you for looking at the darker side of woman's life. It is more apparent in the greater communities, but it is here, too, and that is why I am looking eagerly forward to your appointment as Deemster, which will make you a creator of the law as well as an administrator of it. You must have no misgivings, though. Why should you? A man who has a stainless scutcheon is just what women want for their champion. And if I may help you how happy I shall be!

"You ask what is happening in the island. Well, apart from politics (of which I know nothing except that they seem to be always the same story) the only thing of consequence is the case of a young woman charged with the murder of her illegitimate child.

"She is a country girl who, having run away from home some months ago, returned recently very ill and was put to bed, and remained there until arrested. But in the meantime the body of a new-born infant was found under a large stone half a mile away, and it is said to have been hers.

"She denies all knowledge of the child, but the medical testimony seems to be sadly against her, and there is some direct evidence also, though it is not above the suspicion of being tainted by malice.

"She has been up before the High Bailiff and committed to the next sitting of the General Gaol Delivery, so you are likely to hear more of the case. Poor thing, whatever her sin, she has already had a fearful punishment, for she is very ill, having apparently exposed herself to dreadful sufferings in the hope of preventing her baby from being born alive.

" She is now in the prison hospital, and this morning I drove over to see her. A good-looking girl, almost beautiful (with the sort of beauty which attracts the less worthy side of a certain type of man), but her cheeks are now terribly thin and pale, and her big black eyes (her finest feature) have that wild look which one sees in a captured animal that gazes and gazes.

" I liked the girl, but she did not seem to like me. In fact she shrank from me (the only girl who ever did so) and when I tried to be nice to her, and asked her to trust me, and to tell me who was responsible for her condition, so that I might find him and fetch him to her, she broke into a flood of fierce denial.

" Either the girl is a great story-teller or she is a great heroine, and I am half inclined to think she may be both. My guess would be that she is trying to shield the guilty man. The clothes she had worn were better than a farm girl could afford to buy, and that suggests that her fellow-sinner belongs to a class above her.

" Isn't it shocking that the law provides no punishment for the man who ruins a girl's life—ruining her soul at the same time, for that is what it often comes to. But, please God, *you* will be on the bench, so she is sure to have justice.

" Our Society has decided to undertake her defence, but we are at a loss whom to employ. We cannot afford a high fee either— ten or fifteen guineas at the outside. Can you suggest anybody?

" I intend to be present at the trial, and to stand by the girl's side, for she will have nobody else, poor creature. But oh, how I wish I might plead for her! Although her fellow-sinner will not stand for judgment, how I should like to tear the mask from his face and cry in open court, ' Thou art the man!'

" Good-night, dear! It's 10 p.m., and such delicious dreams are waiting for me upstairs. Bring your motor-car back, and when the time comes (I shall not keep you long) you may carry me off to wherever you please.

" Listen, I am going to say something. There is not much in the heart of a woman that you don't know already, but I am about to let you into a secret. The woman who does not want her husband (if only he loves her) to control her, command her, and do anything and everything he likes with her, isn't really a woman at all—*she's only a mistake for a man!*

" Victor, after that burst of nonsense I cannot conclude without telling you again how much I love you. I love you for your-

self, just yourself alone, quite apart from anything you may do or
have done, whether good or bad, right or wrong, and I shall go
on loving you whatever may happen to you in the future, whether
you become Deemster or not, go up or go down.

" But when I think of the life that is so surely before you, and
that I shall walk through it by your side, perfectly united with
you, sharing the same hopes and aims and desires, enjoying the
same sunshine and weathering the same storms, I have a vision of
happiness that makes me cry for joy.

" Come back to me soon, dearest. The spring is here in all her
youthful beauty; the daffodils are nodding; the gorse on the hedges
is a blaze of gold; the sky is blue; the sea is lying asleep under a
divine shimmer of sunshine, and your island—your island that is
going to be so proud of you—is waiting to clasp you to her heart.

" And so am I, my Victor!

" FENELLA."

III

" MY OWN DEAR FENELLA,—I am so troubled about the young
woman who is to be charged with the murder of her child that
(time being short) I must write at once on the subject. It looks
like a case of the temporary mania which so often prompts women
to take life (their own or their children's) in the hope of avoid-
ing shame.

" God, when I think of it, that in all ages of the world tens of
thousands of women have gone through that fiery furnace and that
never one man since the days of Adam has come within sight of it,
I want to go down on my knees to the meanest and lowest of them
as the martyrs of humanity.

" Infanticide is of course a serious crime in any country, and
especially serious in the Isle of Man now, when the Governor has
made up his mind to show no mercy to persons guilty of fatal
violence. But the killing of a new-born child is usually treated as
felonious homicide. Therefore, if you carry out your intention of
standing by the girl's side, you may safely tell her (in order to
save her from possible shock) that even a verdict of guilty will
not mean death.

" How I wish you could plead for the poor thing! But instruct
counsel for the defence and you will really be pleading, and I,
for one, if I am present, will hear your quivering voice in every
word he says.

" As for the choice of an Advocate—why not Alick Gell? He
has not had too many chances, poor chap, and it will hearten him

(he was rather down when I saw him last) to be entrusted with a serious case like this.

" Tell him to look up Galabin and Murrell on Forensic Medicine—he'll find both in the Law Library. The first step is to make sure that the poor creature (I assume she is not too well educated) has not mistaken infanticide for concealment; and the next, to insist on proof of ' a live birth,' which it is practically impossible to establish (except on the girl's confession) in a case of solitary delivery.

" Yes, you are almost certainly right in thinking she is trying to shield the guilty man, and, criminal though she is, she may be (as you say) an absolute heroine. In that event I trust it may not fall to my lot to try her. God save me from sitting in judgment on a woman who stands silent in her shame to shield the honour of the man she loves!

" But as for hunting down the guilty man, that (don't you think so?) is perhaps another matter. If it has to be done at all it is only a woman—a pure and stainless woman—who has a right to do it. No man who knows himself, and how near every mother's son of us has been to the verge of the pit, will be the first to throw a stone. You remember—' But for the grace of God there goes John Wesley.' Oh, my darling, how can I ever be grateful enough for what you have done for me . . . .

*　　　*　　　*　　　*　　　*　　　*　　　*

" Helloa! The page boy has just been up with a letter from the Home Secretary. ' I have the pleasure to inform you that the King has been pleased to approve of your appointment to the position of the Deemster of the Isle of Man . . . . '

" How glorious! Here I have been all day saying to myself, ' Who, in God's name, are you that you should be Judge over anybody?' and now I'm glad—damned glad, there is no other word for it.

" I shall telegraph the news to you in a few minutes, but I feel as if I want to take the first boat home and become my own messenger. That is impossible, for I have to call on the Lord Chancellor to-morrow about my Commission. And then I have to see to the transport of my car, and the purchase of my Judge's wig and gown. But wait, only wait! Three days more I shall have you in my arms.

" My respectful greetings to the Governor. Say I know how much I owe to him for this unprecedented appointment. Say, too, I shall hold myself in readiness for the ceremony of the swearing-in, whenever he desires it to take place; also for the next Court of General Gaol Delivery if Deemster Taubman is still down with his rheumatism.

" And now bless you again, dearest, for all your beautiful faith in me. God helping me, I'll do my best to deserve it. But you must be my guardian watcher, my sentinel, my star.

" What a dear old world it is, darling! It seems as if there ought to be no suffering of any kind in it now—now that the sky is so bright for you and me.

" VICTOR."

" P.S. *Important.* Don't forget to employ Gell in that case of the girl who killed her baby. Alick's her man. *Mind you, though—he must compel her to tell him everything.*"

CHAPTER TWENTY-FOUR

ALICK GELL

FOR ten days Alick Gell had been searching for Bessie Collister. When he first read her letter on reaching Derby Haven (he read it a hundred times afterwards) he remembered something his father had said in taunting him—" You'll not be the first by a long way! " Then he recalled the case of the Peel fisherman and a black thought came hurtling down on him. At the next moment he hated himself for it.

" What devil out of hell made me think of that? " he asked himself.

But why had Bessie run away from him? The only explanation he could find was the one Stowell had given on the steamboat—women had illnesses which men knew nothing about, and in the throes of their mania they sometimes hid themselves, like sick animals, from their friends—most of all from those they loved. Were not the newspapers full of such cases?

" That's it! That's it! My poor girl! "

Having arrived at this explanation of Bessie's flight, he had no compunction about going in search of her. Her malady might be only temporary, but, while it lasted, Heaven alone knew what dangers she might expose herself to.

At first it occurred to him to call in the assistance of the police. But no, that would lead to publicity, and publicity to misunderstanding. Bessie would get better; he must keep her name clear of scandal. His voice shook and his lip trembled as he told the Misses Brown to say nothing to anybody. His warning was unnecessary. The terrified old maids, who had at length begun to scent the truth, had decided to keep their own counsel.

Within half an hour Alick was on the road. He had no doubt of overtaking Bessie—she was only half an hour gone. But which way would she go? It was easier to say which way she would not go. She would not go to the north of the island where she would be known to nearly everybody. Above all, she would not go home—the home of Dan Baldromma.

All that day he wandered through Castletown—every street and alley. At nightfall he was back at Derby Haven. Had Bessie returned? No! Had anything been heard of her? Nothing!

Next day he set out on a wider journey—all the towns and villages of the south, Port St. Mary, Port Erin, Fleswick, Ballasalla, Colby, Ballabeg and Cregneash. He walked from daylight to dark, and asked no questions, but at every open door he paused and listened. When he saw a farm-house that stood back from the high road he made excuse to go up to it—a drink of milk or water.

Day followed day without result. His heart was sinking. More than once he met somebody whom he knew and had to make excuse for his rambling. Wonderful what a walking tour did to blow the cobwebs from a fellow's brain after he had been shut up too long in an office! His friends looked after him with a strange expression. He had been something of a dandy, but his hair was uncombed and his linen was becoming soiled and even dirty.

At length he became a prey to illusions. He always slept in the last house he came to, and one night, in a fisherman's cottage near Fleswick, he was awakened by the wind blowing over the thatch. He thought it sounded like the voice of Bessie, and that she was wandering over the highway in the darkness, alone and distraught.

Next day he began to inquire if anything had been seen of such a person. He was told of a young woman who, found walking barefoot on the lonely road to Dreamlang, had been taken to the asylum, and he hurried there to inquire. No, it was not Bessie. Some poor young wife who (only six months married and beginning to be happy in the prospect of a child) had lost her husband in an accident at the mines at Foxdale.

The dread of suicide took hold of him. One day a fish-cadger on the road told him that a young woman's body had been washed ashore at Peel. Again it was nothing—nothing to him. The wife of the captain of a Norwegian schooner which had been wrecked off Contrary—with her eyes open and her baby locked in her rigid arms.

Alick's heart was failing him. Do what he would to keep down evil thoughts they were getting the better of him. Sometimes he rested on the seat that usually stands outside the white-washed porch of a Manx cottage, and although he thought he said so little he found that the women especially such of them as were mothers of grown-up girls) seemed to divine the object of his journey.

" Aw, yes, that's the way with them, the boghs, especially when there's a man bothering them. Was there any man, now . . . . "

But Alick was up and gone before they could finish their question.

Thus ten days passed. Absorbed in his search, perplexed and tortured, he had seen no newspaper and heard nothing of what was happening in the island. Suddenly it occurred to him that Bessie could not have left him so long without news of her. She could not be so cruel; she must have written, and her letter must be lying at his office.

People who knew him, and saw him return to Douglas, could scarcely recognise him in the pale, unwashed, unshaven man who climbed the steps from the station, looking like a drunkard who had been sleeping out in the fields.

His chambers, when he turned the key (he had no clerk now), were stuffy and cheerless. The ashes of his last fire were on the hearth, and his desk was covered with dust. Behind the door (he had no letter-box) a number of circulars and bills lay on the ground, but, running his trembling fingers through them, he found no letter from Bessie.

There was a large and bulky envelope, though, with the seal of Government House, and marked " Immediate." What could it be? On the top of a thick body of folio paper he found a letter. It was from Fenella Stanley.

> " DEAR MR. GELL,—At the suggestion of Mr. Stowell, who is still in London, I am writing on behalf of the Women's Protection League, to ask you if you can undertake the defence of the young woman in the north of the island who is to be charged with the murder of her new-born child."

Alick paused a moment to draw breath.

> " You will see by the report of the High Bailiff's inquiry and the copy of the Depositions which I enclose that the girl denies everything, and that her mother supports her, but the evidence is only too sadly against her—particularly that of the doctors and of two neighbours who live higher up the glen."

Alick felt his heart stop and his whole body grew cold.

" Her step-father . . . . "

The letter almost dropped from his fingers.

" Her step-father has not been asked by the prosecution
to depose, and it is doubtful if the defence ought to call him."

He was becoming dizzy. The lines of the letter were running
into each other.

" Innocent or guilty, the girl has suffered terribly. She
has been several days in hospital at Ramsey, but she was
to be removed to Castle Rushen this morning. Her case is
to come on next week at the Court of General Gaol Delivery,
so perhaps you will send me a telegram immediately saying
if you can take up the defence.

" As you see the poor creature is herself an illegitimate
child—the name by which she is commonly known being
Bessie Collister."

Alick shrieked. He had seen the blow coming, but when it
came it fell on him like a thunderbolt.

It was all a lie—a damned lie! Nobody would make him believe it. Bessie arrested for the murder of her child! She had
never had a child.

He leapt to his feet and tramped the room on stiffened limbs
and with a heart throbbing with anger. Then, half afraid, but
doing his best to compose himself, he took the report and the
Depositions out of the big envelope, and, sitting before the dead
hearth with his shaking feet on the fender, and holding the folio
pages in his dead-cold hands, he read the evidence.

As he did so he shrieked again, but this time with laughter.
What a tissue of manifest lies! The Skillicornes and their quarrel
with Dan Baldromma—what a malicious conspiracy! Lord, what
blind fools the police could be! And the Attorney, had he come to
his second childhood?

Again and again Alick thumped the desk with his fist and filled
the air of the room with the dust that rose in the sunshine which
was now pouring through the windows.

There was a photograph of Bessie on the mantelpiece—a copy
of the same that she had sent to Stowell. He snatched it up and
kissed it. Never had Bessie been so dear to him as now—now
when she was in prison under a false accusation. And the best
of it was that *he* was to get her off. He must see her at
once, though.

"My poor girl! In Castle Rushen!"

The first thing to do was to wash and change (he cut himself badly in shaving), but in less than half-an-hour he was at the Post-office telegraphing to Fenella.

"Gladly."

Brief as the message was, the clerk at the counter could hardly decipher the agitated handwriting.

A few minutes later he was at the Police-office, asking the Chief Constable for an order to allow him, as Bessie's advocate, to see her alone in her cell.

At two o'clock he was back at the railway-station, taking the train for Castletown. As he stepped into his carriage the newsboys were calling the contents of the evening paper:

Victor Stowell appointed Deemster.

Glorious! Bessie would have a human being on the bench. Thank God for that anyway!

II

"I don't know what you are talking about—I really don't. You make me laugh. Whatever will you say next! I was ill and I came home to have my mother nurse me, and that was all I knew until Cain, the constable, came to bring me here."

It was Bessie before the High Bailiff. Her face was thin and pale, and she was clutching the rail of the dock in an effort to keep herself erect, while her shrill voice echoed to the roof.

The magistrate was about to commit her to prison when Dr. Clucas rose in the body of the Court-house.

"Your worship," he said (his voice was husky and his eyes had a look of tears), "the defendant is suffering from the temporary mania which is not unusual in such cases. I suggest that she should be sent to the hospital."

Bessie fainted. The next thing she knew was that she was in bed in a hospital ward, and that another doctor (a younger man with thin hair and a large pugnacious mouth) was leaning over her, and laying his hand on her breast. She pushed it off, and then he said, in an authoritative tone,

"My good woman, if you are innocent, as you say, the best proof you can give is that of a medical examination."

At this Bessie broke into fierce wrath.

"If you touch me again," she cried, "I'll tear your eyes out!"

Then she fainted once more, and for two days lay in a strong delirium. When she came to herself a nurse with a kind face was by her side, saying " Hush! " and doing something at her breast with a glass instrument.

She knew she had been delirious (having a vague memory of crying " Alick! Alick! " as she returned to consciousness) and was in fear of what she might have said.

" Is it morning? " she asked.

" Yes, dear."

" Then it's the next day? "

" The next but one."

" Have I been wandering? "

" A little."

" Did I call for anybody? "

" Yes."

She dare not ask whom, but lay wondering if Alick knew where she was and what had happened to her. After a while she said,

" Is it in the papers? "

The nurse nodded, and after a moment, with her eyes down, Bessie said,

" Has anybody been here to ask for me? "

" Yes, your mother—she comes night and morning."

" Nobody else? "

" Nobody."

Bessie broke into sobs and turned her face to the wall. Alick knew! He had given her up! She had lost him!

When she recovered from an agony of tears her eyes were glittering and her heart was bitter. What did she care what became of her now? They might do what they liked with her. Deny? What was the good? She would deny no longer. She would tell the truth about everything.

Then Fenella Stanley came. Bessie thought she liked Miss Stanley better than any woman, except her mother, she had ever known. But that only made it the harder to hold to her resolution, for if she told the truth she would surely hurt Fenella. " Oh, why do you come to torture me? " she cried, when Fenella asked who was her " friend." And not another word would she say.

Two days later, before breakfast, Cain, the constable, came with a sergeant of police to take her to Castle Rushen. She did not care! Why should she? But as she was leaving the hospital the nurse with the kind face whispered,

" Good-bye, dear. You're all right now. I'm going away and will say nothing."

It was a cruelly beautiful morning, with a golden shimmer from the rising sun upon a tranquil sea. The railway station was full of townspeople going up to Douglas (it was market day there), so Bessie was hurried into the last compartment.

When the train ran into the country a flood of memories swept over her and she found it hard to keep back her tears. The young lambs were skipping on the hill-sides; the sheep were bleating; girls in sun bonnets were coming from the whitewashed outhouses to drive the cattle into the fields.

When they drew up at the station for the glen the shingly platform was crowded with passengers waiting for the train—rosy-faced women with broad open baskets of butter and eggs, and elderly farmers smoking their strong thick twist and surrounded by their panting dogs. Bessie knew them all. At the last moment a young woman in a low cut blouse ran up—it was Susie Stephen.

Bessie crept into a corner of the carriage and closed her eyes. But she could not shut out everything. Over the rumble of the wheels, when the train started again, she heard shrieks of laughter from the compartment in front. The elderly men were jesting in their free way with the girls, and the girls, nothing loth, were answering them back.

At the junction of St. John's, the train had to stop for carriages from Peel to be linked on to it, and while the coupling was going on one of the passengers strolled along the platform. It was Willie Teare, who had wanted to marry Bessie, and he saw her behind the constables. At the next moment a throng of girls gathered outside her window, but the constables pulled down the blinds.

"Take your seats! Take your seats!"

The train went on. There was no more laughter from the passengers in the compartment in front. Bessie understood—they were whispering about her.

Her heart was becoming hard. Sitting in the darkened carriage, with spears of sunlight flashing from the flapping blinds, she heard the constables talking about Mr. Stowell. It was reported that he had been made Deemster. He would make a good Deemster, too.

"A taste young, maybe, but clever—clever uncommon."

On reaching Douglas, where they had to change into the train for Castletown, Bessie was being hustled across the platform, between the constables, when she became aware of a crowd of women and girls who were crushing up to stare at her. There was a whispering and muttering.

"There she is!"   "Serve her right, *I* say!"

Half-an-hour later she was in Castle Rushen. The darkness within was blinding after the sunshine without. A woman with short and difficult breathing was moving about her. It was Mrs. Mylrea, the female warder. She took off Bessie's cloak and hat, and, leaving her a brown blanket and a hard pillow, went away without speaking a word.

But then came Vondy, the head jailer, with words enough for both of them. Bessie did not know she was crying until the old man, in his blundering way, began to comfort her.

" Tut, tut, gel! They're not for hanging you yet at all. While there's life there's hope! "

Left alone at last, and her eyes accustomed to the darkness, she saw where she was—in a stone vault that had a small grill in the door (behind which a candle was burning) and a barred and deeply-recessed window, near the ceiling, through which a dull ray of borrowed light was coming, for the prison overlooked the harbour on the west of the Castle.

By this time her tears were turned to gall. A frightful revulsion had come over her soul. What had she done to deserve all this? The injustice of it, the cruelty, the barbarity, the hypocrisy!

Men were all alike. Go on, *she* knew what men were! A man only wanted one thing of a girl, and when he got that he forgot all about her. Alick Gell was the best of them, yet even he had forsaken her now that she was in trouble.

She had never intended to do harm to anybody, and yet there she was, and would remain, until they came to take her to the Court-house on the other side of the Castle-yard. Then hundreds of eyes would be on her (women's eyes too) and when she raised her own she would see Mr. Stowell on the bench.

What a mockery! Mr. Stowell her judge! What would he do? His " duty " of course. All right, let him do it! Only *she*, too, would do something. After he had tried her and sentenced her and finished with her, she would tell him something. Why shouldn't she? And what did she care what happened to anybody else? Fenella Stanley was nothing to her.

Suddenly she thought again about Alick Gell. If she did what she intended to do (tell everything) Alick also would be disgraced. The shame of her misfortune would follow him to the last day of his life. Even his own father would cast it up to him. Hadn't she done enough harm to Alick already? If he had deserted her, she had deceived him. And yet she had deceived him only because she loved him.

" Alick! Alick! Alick! "

Her heart was crying. She was wishing she were dead.

She had flung herself down on her plank bed, with her face to

15

the blank wall, when she heard the dead beating of footsteps in the corridor outside. At the next moment the door of her cell was opened and Tommy Vondy, the jailer, was saying,

"Mr. Alexander Gell, the advocate, to see you alone."

III

"Bessie!"

The jailer had gone. Alick was breathing quickly in the darkness by the door, and Bessie was huddled up on the bed, with the dull ray of reflected light upon her from the wall above.

"Bessie!"

His voice was low and full of tears. At first she did not answer.

"It's Alick. Won't you speak to me?"

"Go away!"

He could hear that she was crying.

"You won't send me away, Bessie. I have been looking for you all over the island. It was only to-day I heard where you were and what had happened. I have come to help you—to save you."

He saw the dark form rising on the bed.

"Do you know what they say I did?"

"Yes, I know everything."

"And you don't believe it?"

"Not one word of it."

"You think I am innocent?"

"I am sure you are."

"Alick!"

With a great sob that shook her whole body she rose to her feet and flung herself upon him. For a long time they stood clasped in each other's arms, and crying like children. Then they sat down side by side on the plank bed. His arm was about her, and her head was on his shoulder.

He was trying to make his voice cheerful, though it cracked sorely, while he reproved her for her tears. She would soon be free to leave that place. There was really nothing against her. Never had there been such a trumped-up case. The police must be crazy.

She clung to him with a frightened tenderness while he told her of the letter from Fenella Stanley asking him to take up the defence on behalf of the Society.

"Of course I should have taken it up in any case, you know. And now you must authorise me to defend you."

She was startled. In the half darkness he saw her pale face (so pale and so thin) raised to his with a frightened look.

" You? "

" Why not, dear? I'm an advocate. You don't suppose I'm going to leave your defence to anybody else, do you? "

" No, no! You must not! "

" But why? Can't you trust me, Bess? "

" It isn't that."

" What then? "

Bessie did not answer him, and he went on talking, though his voice was breaking again. He knew he was not a born lawyer and a great speaker like Stowell, but the facts were so clear that he had only to state them and they would speak for themselves.

A fierce struggle was going on in Bessie's soul. He whom she had wronged (never having wronged anybody else), he for whom she had committed her crime, wanted her to authorise him to stand up in Court and say she had not committed it. She had deceived him once—could she deceive him again?

" No, no, no! I cannot! "

Alick was puzzled. " What do you mean, Bessie? Why shouldn't I be your advocate? "

" I don't want any advocate."

" But you must have one. It isn't enough to be not guilty—we must *prove* you're not. Why shouldn't I do so? "

At length she was forced to make some explanation. The police were determined to have her condemned; therefore he would lose his case and that would go against him.

" Good gracious, girl, what nonsense! Anybody may lose a case. The greatest lawyers have lost cases. But it's impossible that I should lose this one. And even if I lose it—do you know what I shall do? "

" What? "

" Wait outside the prison door until you come out and marry you the same day to show that I believe in you still."

At that Bessie was in floods of tears again. And again they cried in each other's arms like children.

Then Alick, after drying his eyes in the darkness, put on a brave air, and told her what she had to do.

" Listen to me now. This is a low conspiracy, but if we are to defeat it, you must stick to your story. I shall have to put you in the box, for you must leave the Court without a stain on your character. First of all you must say . . . . "

And then sitting by Bessie's side in the dark cell, with only the candle looking in on them from the outside ledge of the grill, he rehearsed the facts as they were to be given in Court—how by the cruelty of her step-father she had been shut out of the house late at night and had had to go elsewhere; how she had returned, being unwell, and wishing her mother to nurse her, and how she had been put to bed and had never left it until the constables came to take her away.

Bessie listened in silence, gazing before her like a captured sheep, and answering only by a nodding of her head.

"If the Attorney asks you anything else—no matter what— you must say you know nothing about it—do you understand?"

"Yes."

"Say it after me then—' I know nothing about it.'"

Bessie repeated the words like a woman talking in her sleep— "' I know nothing about it.'"

"That's all right. Leave the rest to me."

"You think I shall get off?"

"I'm sure of it. If the General Gaol is held next week, we'll be married the week after."

"But, Alick?"

"Yes."

"Your father and sisters, will they not always cast it up at you that your wife has been tried for . . . ."

"Let them! If they do the Isle of Man will be dead to me for ever. We'll go abroad—to America perhaps—and leave everything and everybody behind us."

Bessie was crying once more, and Alick, to conceal his own tears, was going off with great bustle.

"Good-bye! I'll be here again to-morrow. And oh, what do you think, Bess? Great news! Stowell has been made Deemster. So if the good Lord in Heaven will only keep that damned old Taubman in bed a little longer with his rheumatism, Stowell will be on the bench and you'll have a fair trial at all events. Good-bye!"

For the next half-hour Bessie sobbed with joy. Tell the truth and destroy Alick's faith in her? Never! Never in this world!

CHAPTER TWENTY-FIVE

THE DEEMSTER'S OATH

It was the morning of the day of the swearing-in of the new Deemster at Castle Rushen. The Bishop had asked permission to solemnise the ceremony with a religious service—a custom long unobserved.

The service was held in a groined chamber of moderate size

within walls thirty feet thick, once the banqueting-hall of the Kings of Man, now the jail chapel, with an atmosphere that seemed to be compounded equally of the intoxicated laughter of the old revellers and the moans of the condemned prisoners.

For the event of the day the chill place had been suitably decorated. Flags hung on the tarred walls, red cushions from the neighbouring church had been laid on the bare benches; a carpet had been stretched down the aisle of the flagged floor; a white embroidered altar-cloth covered the plain communion table, from which the light of four candles in silver candlesticks flickered on the faces of the small congregation—chiefly officials, with their wives and daughters.

Shortly before eleven, the hour fixed for the service, Stowell entered, wearing for the first time the wig and gown of a judge, and he was led to one of three arm-chairs at the front. A little later there came through the thick walls the sound of soldiery clashing arms outside the Castle, and at the next moment the Governor arrived in General's uniform of red and gold, with Fenella behind him in a large spring hat (her face glowing with animation), and they took the two remaining chairs. Then the Bishop in his scarlet robes came in, preceded by his crozier, and the service began.

It was short but solemn. First a psalm of David ("He shall judge thy people with righteousness and thy poor with judgment"); then an epistle to the Romans ("Owe no man anything"); and then an improvised prayer by the Bishop, asking the Almighty to grant His strength and wisdom to His servant who was shortly to take the solemn oath of his great office, that he might deliver the poor and needy, deal faithfully with all men, and show mercy to such as had erred and sinned. Then came the hymn "Thou Judge of quick and dead," and finally the Benediction.

Stowell was strongly affected. He knelt at the prayer, and when the service was at an end and it was time to go, Fenella had to touch his shoulder.

The sun was bright outside, and they blinked their eyes as they crossed the courtyard to the Court-house.

The stately little chamber was full, save for the seats that had been reserved for the officials. There was a flash of faces, a waft of perfume, a flutter of handkerchiefs and a hum of whispering as the Governor stepped up to the scarlet dais, with Stowell following him and taking for the first time the seat of the Judge.

People who had been talking of the youth of the new Deemster were heard to say that in his judge's wig he seemed older than they had expected and so like the portrait on the wall that one could almost fancy that his father was looking through the windows of his eyes.

The proceedings began with the Governor calling upon Stowell for his Commission, and then reading it aloud—" Our trusty and well-beloved Victor Stowell to be Deemster of this isle."

After that everybody stood while the new Judge took the oath of fealty to the King. Then the Deemster's clerk, Joshua Scarff, in his coloured spectacles, handed up a quarto copy of the Bible and a deep hush fell on the assembly, for the time had come for the Deemster's oath.

The Governor and Stowell rose again, but all others remained seated. Each laid one hand on the open Book, and the Governor read the oath, clause by clause in loud, strong tones that seemed to smite the walls as with blows. And, clause by clause, Stowell repeated it after him in a lower voice that was sometimes barely audible:

" *By this Book and the holy contents thereof* . . . . "

" *By this Book and the holy contents thereof* . . . . "

" *And by all the wonderful works which God hath miraculously wrought in heaven and on the earth beneath in six days and seven nights, I, Victor Christian Stowell* . . . . "

" *I, Victor Christian Stowell, do swear that I will, without respect or fear or friendship, love or gain, consanguinity or affinity, envy or malice, execute the laws of this isle justly betwixt our Sovereign Lord the King and his subjects within the isle, and betwixt party and party, man and man, man and woman* . . . . "

" *. . . . man and woman.* . . . . "

" *. . . . as indifferently as the herring bone doth lie down the middle of the fish.*"

There was a deep silence until the oath was ended and then a general drawing of breath.

The Governor and the new Deemster sat and the Clerk of the Rolls handed up the *Liber Juramentorum*, the Book of Oaths, a large volume in faded leather with leaves of discoloured parchment.

It was observed, and afterwards remarked upon, that when Stowell took up the pen to sign he hesitated for a moment, and then wrote his name rapidly and nervously, and that, in the silence, a diamond ring which he wore on his right hand (it was a present from Fenella) clashed with a discordant sound against the glass tray as he threw the pen back.

The business being over, the Bishop gave out the hymn that is sung at the close of nearly all Manx festivals, " O God, our help," and all rose and sang.

Stowell rose with the rest, but he did not sing. He was no longer conscious of the eyes that were on him. The emotion which he had been struggling to repress had at length conquered his self-control. While the Court-house throbbed with the singing he was thinking of the Judges who had stood in the same place and taken that oath before him. There had been a thousand years of them.

He turned to the eastern wall and his father's melancholy eyes seemed to look at him. " Yes, you too," they seemed to say, " must now do the right, whatever it may cost you. You are no longer yourself only. The souls of all your predecessors have this day entered into your soul. You must consider yourself no more. You must be just—or perish."

The hymn came to an end and there was a shuffling of feet like the pattering of water in the harbour at the top of the tide. The next thing Stowell knew was that he was unrobed and going down the Deemster's private staircase to the Court-yard of the Castle.

A large company was there waiting to congratulate him. Janet (he had ordered that a front seat should be reserved for her) was holding a little court of elderly ladies, to whom she was relating wonderful stories of his childhood. She broke away from them to kiss him. And then she kissed Fenella also and whispered,

" Don't forget to send him home in time, dear."

" I'll not forget," said Fenella.

And then she, on her part, with a face aflame, whispered something to the Governor, who, shaking hands all round, was making ready to go.

" What? You want to return in the automobile? Very well, off you go! The Attorney will take pity on your forsaken father."

Outside the gate there was a great crowd, behind a regiment of red-coated soldiers, and when the Governor and the Attorney-General drove off they broke into a cheer which drowned the clash of steel and the first bars of the National Anthem.

But that was as nothing compared with the demonstration when Stowell went off in his car, sitting at the wheel, with Fenella beside him.

" Long live the new Deemster—hip, hip—hip ! "

The great shout, the mighty roar of voices, brought a surging to Stowell's throat and a tightening to his breast. It followed his car, going off in the sunshine, until it shot over the bridge that crossed the harbour, and there Fenella turned back her glistening wet eyes and bowed.

*　　*　　*　　*　　*　　*　　*

Others heard it. The prisoners in their dark cells, rising from their plank beds and hunching their shoulders in the chill air, listened to the joyous sounds from without, which broke the usual silence of their gloomy walls, and said to themselves,

" What are they doing now, I wonder? "

There were seven prisoners in the Castle that day. One of them was Bessie Collister.

II

" Addio! See you at supper! "

Fenella was waving to the Governor and the Attorney, and laughing at their slow speed, as she and Stowell shot past them before they had left the town.

The morning was beautiful, the sky blue, the sea glistening under a fresh breeze. They were running, bounding, leaping along the roads, and talking loudly above the hum of the car. Stowell had caught the contagion of Fenella's high spirits and awakened from his long trance.

" Well, what did you think of it? "

" The ceremony? Lovely! "

" But you were crying all the time! "

" It must have been through looking at you, then. There was everybody doing you honour, and you looked like a man going to execution."

He laughed; she laughed; they laughed together, but they had their serious moments for all that. One of them came when she spoke of the Oath, saying how quaint and amusing it was.

" A little frightening, though," said Stowell.

" Frightening? "

" Well, yes, I thought so. Made one feel as if old Job had had something to say for himself. Who was I to judge others, having done wrong myself? "

" Really! You wicked fellow! I wasn't aware you had so many sins to answer for. But *I* know! "

And then, in flash after flash, each sparkling like a diamond, came pictures of his predecessors. The solemn judge; the jesting judge; the judge who suspected all men of lying; the judge who believed everybody told the truth; the sour, dour, swearing and hanging judge, who served Justice as if she had been a Juggernaut, and the gay Judge who bought and sold her as he did his mistresses.

" What a procession! And the question was, which kind were you going to belong to—eh? "

Again he laughed; they both laughed; and the car flew on. Another serious moment came. He mentioned the Book of Oaths, saying that while turning over its leaves with their faded ink he had been seized with a sudden fear of writing his name, whereupon Fenella, with a mischievous look of gravity, cried again,

" *I* know. You thought you were signing your death-warrant."

Yet another serious moment came when she asked him if he had not been proud of the send-off his countrymen had given him at the Castle gate. He replied that he would have been so but for the wretched thought that if anything happened to him their love would as suddenly turn to hate, and they would howl as loudly as they had cheered.

" But what nonsense! " cried Fenella. " Love—what I call love—is not like that. It never dies and never changes."

" Never? "

" Never! If I loved anybody and anything happened, I should fight the world for him."

" Even if he were in the wrong? "

" Goodness yes! Where would be the merit of fighting for him if he were in the right? "

" Darling! " cried Stowell, and, the road being clear, and nobody in sight, he had to slow down the car to kiss her.

After that he threw off the solemnity of the ceremony and gave himself up to the intoxication of love. With Fenella by his side, looking up at him with her beaming eyes, and laughing with her gay raillery, what else could he think about? A few miles out of Castletown he said,

" Let us take the old road back—it's longer."

" Yes, it's longer."

Every fresh mile was a fresh delight. How the Spring was coming on! Look at the gorse, already in its glory! And the lambs just born and still trembling on their doddering limbs! And the tragic old hens with their fluffy yellow broods! And then the cottages, half buried in their big fuchsias! And the farmers whitewashing their farmhouses to wipe out the stains of winter!

" What a jolly old world it is, isn't it? " he cried.

" Isn't it? " she answered, and without looking to see if the way was clear, he had to slow down the car and kiss her again.

A few miles south of Douglas they turned into a road that ran like a shelf along the edge of the cliffs, with the sea surging on the grey rocks below, and nothing but its round rim against the sky. The breeze was stronger out there, but every gust was a joy. Stowell took off his hat and threw it to the bottom of the car. Fenella unpinned hers and held it on her knee. His black hair tumbled over his forehead, and her bronze-brown hair, loosened from its knot, flew about her head like a flag.

More than ever now they had the sense of flying. The sun danced on the breakers; the foam floated in trembling flakes into the blue sky; the sea-fowl screamed about them. With the taste of the brine on their lips, and the sting of it in their blood, they shouted at every sight and sound.

" Look at that white horse down there! See how he rears his head and plunges forward. Ah, he has had enough! No, he's coming on again with a roar! "

" But look at the sea-holly and the wild thyme! And the rabbits scuttling into their holes! And the goats on the peaks of the cliffs! "

" Lord! What a jolly old world it is, though! "

" Didn't you say that before, Victor? "

" Did I? Well, I'm going to say it every blessed day of my life to come."

" No, no! Take care! We're on the edge of the cliff. We'll be over! "

" No matter—another kiss! "

The wind was from the south, and the sea, breaking along the broken line of the coast, was making a sound like that of the ringing of bells. It was the phenomenon of nature which gave rise to the tradition that a town lies buried under the sea at that point, so that Manx fishermen, coming back from their fishing-ground at sunrise, will sometimes say, " The wedding bells are ringing! "

Stowell heard them now, over the roar of the waves in their mad welter, and he cried,

" Listen to the bells! "

" What bells? "

" *Our* bells! " he cried.

And then at the full power of their lungs, over the hum of the engine and the boom of the breakers, they sang a verse of the song of the submerged city:

> " *Here where the ocean is whitened with foam,*
> *Here stood a city, an altar, a home.*
> *Hark to the bells that ring under the sea,*
> *Salve Regina! Salve Regina!*
> *Love is the Queen for you and for me,*
> *Salve, Salve Regina!* "

After that they laughed again, and in sheer gaiety of heart, sang every nonsensical thing they could think about, until, being breathless and hoarse and compelled to stop, Fenella said,

" I wonder what those people in the Court-house would think if they could see their great man now! But I suppose there has never been a great man since the beginning of the world but some woman has known him for what he really is—just a big boy! "

At three o'clock in the afternoon luncheon was over at Government House; the Governor and the Attorney-General had gone off to smoke; Miss Green, like a wise woman, had betaken herself to her room, and Fenella and Stowell were alone.

" Now you must get away to Ballamoar. I promised Janet to send you back in time. Some kind of welcome home, you know."

But Stowell stood over her (she was at the piano) and whispered,

" When? "

She pretended not to understand him, and again, and in a more emphatic voice, he demanded,

" When? "

She was compelled to comprehend at last, and said that if all went well, and he behaved himself, and her father approved, a month that day, perhaps . . . . no, two months . . . .

" Done! "

A few minutes later they were in the porch for their last parting. He was holding her in a long embrace. He felt like Jacob who had waited so long for Rachel. He would never be entirely happy until she was wholly his.

She laughed—a nervous and palpitating laugh.

" Rachel indeed? Take care it isn't Leah in the morning, Sir."

But seeing the cloud that crossed his face at that word, she kissed him of herself, saying they belonged to each other already and nothing could ever separate them.

" Nothing? "

" Nothing! "

And then a long tremulous kiss and he was gone.

III

Home!

He had reached the top of the mountain road, and the setting sun was striking him full in the face. To right and left, before and behind, across the broad waters, stood the dim ghosts of England, Scotland, Ireland and Wales. But what did he care for these greater scenes? Down yonder was Ballamoar, and to him, as to his father, it was enough to be Deemster of Man and Judge of his own people.

News of his home-coming had been telegraphed from Douglas,

and when his car shot out of the glen the church bells were ringing all over the Curagh. People working in the fields climbed the hedges to wave as he went by, and feeble old men came to the doors of the cottages to lift up the hooked handles of their sticks to him.

On reaching the entrance to Ballamoar he found a crowd waiting at the gate, and a streamer from post to post, saying—

WELCOME TO

HIS FATHER'S SON.

The hum of the automobile awakened the colony of rooks in the tall trees, and, swirling above the lawn, they raised a deafening clamour. This brought from the porch Janet (back from Castletown) with a flutter of black frocks and white aprons behind her.

A great company of the people of the parish were at tea in the hall, chiefly women, but of all classes, from the nervous wife of the Vicar to the widow of the cowman.

" Don't get up," cried Stowell.

He had entered with a shout, tossing his hat on to the settle and saluting everybody by name, just as he used to do when he was a boy and annexed them all for relations.

" Sit here, Auntie Kitty. This is your seat, Alice. Parson, wont you take the bottom of the table? And, Dad " (this to Robbie Creer in his Sunday homespun), " take my place by Mrs. Creer while I help Jane with the teacups."

" Did thou hear that, mistress? " said Robbie behind his hand to Janet, who was turning the tap of the tea urn. " They may make him Dempster, but he doesn't forget his old friends for all."

In a moment everybody was talking and laughing. It was just as if a fresh breeze had come down from the mountains on a hot day in harvest.

During tea Joshua Scarff arrived with a green portfolio under his arm.

" I've brought some documents you'll wish to look at before the Court sits, your Honour."

" Good! Put them on the desk in the library and then come back and have some tea."

The twilight deepened and the company prepared to go. Stowell stood at the door, with Janet beside him, while the young girls of the choir of the Methodist chapel ranged themselves in front of the house and sang in their sweet young voices, which floated through the gathering gloom, " God be with you till we meet again."

" Good-night, all! "

" Good-night, your Honour ! "

Night! The great day had dropped asleep; the clock on the landing was striking nine; dinner was over; Janet (she had " a head ") had gone to her room, and Stowell was stepping on to the piazza.

The wind had fallen and the night was silent, almost breathless. The revolving light on the Point of Ayre was answering to the gleam on Galloway; and the moon, which was almost at the full, was glistening on the waters that rolled between.

How beautiful, how limpid! It was just such a night as that on which Fenella and he had sat out there together. He could still see her as she was then—the slim young girl in a white dress and satin slippers, with her intoxicating f ace in the frame of the silk handkerchief which she had bound about her head. And now she was to become his wife!

A great new vista was opening out to him. Life was about to begin in earnest. With that splendid woman by his side he was going to rise (if God would be so good to him) out of the muddy imperfections of his lower nature. His breast swelled; his throat tightened; his heart sang; he was entirely happy.

Suddenly he remembered Alick Gell. He had not seen him at Castletown that day, or at all since he returned from London. Why was that? Could it be possible that the matter they had spoken about on the steamer . . . .

No, no! Still he must fulfil his promise. He would step into the library and write a line saying he was ready to go down to Derby Haven if necessary.

As he passed through the dining-room he framed the words of his letter: " Where were you, you old scoundrel, that you were not at the Swearing-in? I suppose the matter you mentioned has righted itself since I went away, but if not and you still want me . . . . "

IV

The house was very quiet. He felt an unaccountable chill coming over him. On the threshold of the library he paused. He had the sense of a mysterious presence in the room. The log fire had burnt low; the lamp on the desk, under his mother's portrait, had been turned down; deep shadows lay around.

Making an effort he entered, stepping softly, yet hardly knowing why he did so. On reaching the desk he turned up the light and then his eye fell on the green portfolio which he had last seen under Joshua Scarff's arm. It bore a label on which was written:

" *Calendar of Cases to be tried at the Spring Session of the Court of General Gaol Delivery. Presiding Deemster—* DEEMSTER VICTOR STOWELL."

Then came a moral thunderclap. Opening the Calendar he read these words on the first page of it:

REX v. CORTEEN
FOR MURDER
DEPOSITIONS.

That Elizabeth Corteen, commonly called Bessie Collister, on or about the fifth day of April—in the parish of Ballaugh, in the Isle of Man, feloniously, wilfully, and of her malice aforethought, did kill and murder a certain male child, contrary to the form of the Statute in such cases made and provided, and against the peace of our Sovereign Lord the King, his Crown and dignity.

A mist rose before Stowell's eyes. He could not read any more, but stood for a moment looking down at the writing. Life seemed to run out of him in a pounding rush. The walls of the room, and particularly the picture of his mother, began to reel about in a rapidly increasing vertigo. He put his hand on a chair but felt nothing. At the next moment darkness came and he knew no more.

END OF THIRD BOOK

FOURTH BOOK
THE RETRIBUTION

CHAPTER TWENTY-SIX
THE WIND AND THE WHIRLWIND

NEXT day the insular newspapers announced that the new Deemster, on his return home from Castletown, after the ceremony of his swearing-in, had had a sudden seizure. A heavy fall had been heard by the servants, and they had found their master lying on the floor of the library, unconscious.

Early in the morning Robbie Creer had driven into town for Dr. Clucas, who had ordered rest—absolute rest.

" We must have three full days in bed, Mr. Stowell, Sir. And if it is necessary to postpone the Court of General Gaol Delivery, I think . . . . I really think we must ask his Excellency to do so."

Stowell drew a deep breath and fell asleep. When he awoke it was mid-day. He was in bed in his father's bedroom and Fenella was sitting by his side, holding his hand. After he had opened his eyes she leaned over him and kissed him, saying in a soft voice that he would soon be better.

" It was that oath-taking, dear. I could see you were taking it too seriously."

His heart was still warm with the embraces of yesterday, yet he tried in vain to kiss her back. But he laughed a little and made light of his seizure. It was nothing, but a little dizziness; he would be about again in a day or two.

" Would you like me to stay and nurse you? "

" No, no! . . . . I mean you needn't . . . . "

His stammering broke down and his face gloomed, but with a quick smile she said,

" Oh, very well, Sir, if you won't have me, Janet will take care of you, and send me a telegram night and morning to say how you are. Won't you, Janet? "

From some unseen place behind the curtains of the four-poster, Janet, snuffling and blowing her nose, answered that she would.

" And now I'll be wishing you good-morning, Sir," said

Fenella, making (after another kiss) a stately curtsey to him as he lay in bed.

The sounds of the wheels of the Governor's carriage having died off on the drive, Stowell found himself alone and face to face with a tragic problem—what was he to do about the trial of Bessie Collister?

This, then, was the case Fenella had written about while he was in London. Why had he not thought of it before? He could not pretend that he had never had misgivings. Again and again the evil shadow of a dread possibility had crossed his mind like a vanishing dream at the moment of awakening.

He had put it aside, banished it, explained it away to himself. In the fullness of his happiness he had even forgotten it altogether. But Nature did not forget. And now his sin had fallen on him like an avalanche—fallen as only an avalanche falls, when the sky is blue, the air is warm and the sun is shining.

He had no doubt about Bessie's guilt. But what about his own? And if he were guilty (in the second degree), being the first cause of the girl's crime, how could he sit in judgment upon her?

To try his own victim, to question her, to go through the mockery of weighing the evidence against her, to condemn her, to sentence her—it would be impossible, utterly impossible, contrary to all legal usage, a violation of the spirit if not the letter of his oath in his first hour as a Judge.

And then the human side of it—the terror, the peril! That poor girl in the dock, in the depths of her shame and the throes of her temptation, while he, her fellow sinner . . . .

No, no, no! It would not only be a crime against Justice; it would be a sin against God.

Joshua Scarff came in the afternoon. Standing by the bed, and looking down through his dark spectacles, he said,

"This is a pity, your Honour! A great pity! Such interesting cases! Your Honour must have wished to study them before sitting in Court."

"Joshua," said Stowell (he was breathing hard and speaking with difficulty), "go to Deemster Taubman, tell him what has happened, and say that if, as a great favour, he can take the Court next week, I shall be eternally grateful."

The Deemster's clerk was almost speechless with dismay. His Honour's first Court! Pity! Great pity!

But Stowell felt an immense relief. Thank God, there was another Deemster to fall back upon. He need not break the spirit of his oath. Bad as the event was at the best, at least there need be no conflict between his private interests and his public duty.

II

Stowell, in spite of Dr. Clucas, got up next morning. He was sitting before the fire in the library when Janet came in to say that Mrs. Collister of Baldromma was asking to see the Deemster. She had come to plead for her daughter—that girl who was to be tried for killing her baby.

"I told her she shouldn't have come here and that the old Deemster would never have seen her. But it's pitiful to see the poor thing. She is lame, too, and has walked all the way. What am I to say to her?"

Stowell struggled with himself for a moment, and then, with an embarrassed utterance said,

"Let her come in."

"This is very wrong of you, Mrs. Collister" (he was trying to keep a firm lip and to speak severely); "you know it is against all rule."

The old woman, trembling and wiping her eyes, said she knew it was, but she had known his father. There had been none like him—no, not the whole island over. He had been every poor person's friend. If anybody had been injured she had only to draw to him for refuge and he had protected her. And if any poor girl had gone wrong, and broken the law, perhaps, it was the big man himself who was always there to show her mercy.

"That's why I thought maybe his son, if he had his father's heart . . . . and people are saying he has too . . . . maybe his son wouldn't send a poor mother away when she's in trouble and has nobody else to go to."

"Sit down, Mrs. Collister."

The old woman sat in the chair which Janet turned for her, and began on her story.

"Its about Bessie."

She had always been a good girl. No mother ever had a better. And if people were saying she had been in trouble before, might the Lord forgive them when their own time came, for it was lies they were putting on the girl.

"And if she's in trouble now, your Honour, it's like it's not all her own fault neither."

First there was her father. He had been shocking hard on the girl, shutting her out of the house in the dark of night and so throwing her into the way of temptation.

"Until they lay me under the sod I'll never get it out of my ears, Sir—the sound of her foot going off on the street."

16

And when the girl came home again, looking that weak that it seemed as if the world wasn't willing to stand under her, the father had taunted her with coming back to eat them up, and maybe bringing another mouth to feed.

" So if she did the terrible shocking thing they're saying . . . . I don't know if she did, your Honour . . . . I don't know if she ever left the dairy loft from the minute I took her up to it until Cain the constable (may the Lord forgive him!) came dragging her down . . . . but if she did, it's like it was because the poor child was alone in the dark midnight, and out of herself entirely, and not knowing what she was doing, and perhaps freckened of what the old man would be saying in the morning."

Stowell was silent. The old woman cried softly to herself for a moment and then said,

" Nobody knows what that is, your Honour, except them that has gone through it."

Then she wiped her eyes, one after another, and said she could not sleep " a wink on the night," lying in her white bed and thinking of Bessie where she was now. And having read " in class " last evening how the Lord heard the cry of Hagar for her son in the wilderness she had thought his Honour might hear her cry for her daughter.

Stowell knew that his feelings as a man were getting the better of his duty as a Judge, so he tried to be severe with the old woman, telling her she had no right to come to him, and that he had done wrong to listen to her.

" In fact I could not have received you at all but for one thing —I am not going to try your daughter's case."

The old woman was appalled.

" Do you mean, Sir, that you'll not be trying Bessie? "

" No, Deemster Taubman will probably do so."

At that the old woman broke into a flood of tears.

" Aw dear! Aw dear! And me praying on my knees on the kitchen floor that the Lord would bring you back in time from London—someones being so hard on poor girls in trouble! "

Again Stowell was silent, and for some moments nothing was heard but the woman's broken sobs. At length, unable to bear any longer the sight of the old mother's disappointment, he said he would do what he could for her. If he could not sit on her daughter's case he would write to Deemster Taubman, explaining her condition and describing her temptations.

" God bless you for that," cried the old woman. And then Janet said it was time to go, his Honour being unwell.

" May the Lord give him health and strength and long life, ma'am ! "

People were right when they were telling her he had his father's heart. He had too. She was going out of the room with hope kindled, when she said,

" You must excuse a poor woman if she did wrong in coming to you, Sir."

" We'll say no more about that now," said Stowell. " Go home and rest, mother."

At that word the old woman broke down utterly. But after a moment her weak eyes shone and she said,

" Bessie is not your quality, Sir, but if she gets off she'll write to thank you."

" No, no ! She must never do that," said Stowell.

" Come now, Mrs. Collister," said Janet.

But having reached the door, the old woman turned her wet face, and seeing the portrait of Stowell's mother on the wall, and mistaking it for that of Fenella, she said,

" They're telling me you're to be married soon, your Honour. May the Lord give you peace and love in your own home, and that's better than gold or lands, Sir."

Stowell tried to reply, but he could only wave his hand and turn to the window as the old woman left the room.

Why not? What sin against God would it be to unite this suffering woman to her suffering daughter, if he could do so without wronging Justice?

A moment afterwards Janet came back wiping her eyes.

" Oh, these mothers ! They're fit enough to break one's heart, Victor."

III

Stowell was in the dining-room next day when he heard the clatter of a horse's hoofs on the drive, and, a moment later, a voice in the hall, saying,

" The Deemster will see *me*, Jane."

It was Alick Gell. His tall figure was more bent than usual; his hair was disordered; his eyes glittered; he was deeply agitated.

" Excuse me, old fellow. You know why I've not been here before. It's Bessie. I'm busy every hour, getting up her case. Awful, isn't it? I can't make myself believe it even yet. Sometimes in the middle of the night I hear myself crying ' Good God, it can't be true ! ' "

Stowell could scarcely find voice to reply. He remembered

what he had advised Fenella to get Gell to do. Had Bessie
told him?"

"I received Fenella's letter and of course I am taking up the
defence. I've seen Bessie, too, and arranged everything. She's
innocent and I'll fight for her to the last breath in my body.
But look here—read this," he said, dragging a crumbled newspaper from his pocket, and handing it to Stowell with a trembling hand.

It was a copy of the day's insular paper containing a para-
graph which said that the continued illness of the new Deemster
would probably prevent him from presiding at the forthcoming
sitting of the Court of General Gaol Delivery.

"That's the first edition. When it was published at twelve
o'clock I couldn't wait until the afternoon train, so I hired a horse
from Fargher, the jobmaster, and I've galloped all the way.
Don't tell me it's true."

Stowell answered in a low tone that perhaps it might have to
be, whereupon Gell made a cry of dismay.

"Then God help my poor girl! It will be Taubman, and
she'll not have a dog's chance with him."

Taubman was a brute—especially in cases of this kind. What
did people say about him—that when he saw a woman in the dock
he was like a cat who had seen a rat? It was true. He was always
bullying the juries who showed humanity to girls in trouble.

"The infernal old blockhead! He has rheumatism in the legs,
they say. I wish to heaven he had it in his throat, and it would
choke him."

And then the barbarous old Statute! Practically repealed in
every other country, but still capable of operation in the Isle of
Man. Think of it! Five years, ten years, fifteen years—even
death itself, perhaps!

"Stowell, we are old chums . . . . it's not right of me, I know
that . . . . but for the sake of our old friendship, sit on Bessie's
case yourself."

Stowell felt as if he were on the edge of a precipice. Abysmal
depths lay before him at the next step. With an awful secret in
his heart he felt that it was almost impossible to speak one word
more without betraying himself. He was silent for a moment
while Gell stood over him with wild eyes which he had never seen
before. At length he said,

"Bessie is to plead Not Guilty?"

"Certainly."

"Will she stick to that?"

"Undoubtedly. Why shouldn't she? Besides, she has given me her promise."

Again Stowell was silent for a moment; then he said,

"I cannot promise to conduct the Court, but if Taubman will do so, and I'm fit to sit with him, I'll . . . . I'll see she has a fair trial."

Gell made a shout of joy.

"That's good enough for me. Just like you, old fellow."

He snatched up his cap—a different man in a moment.

"I must get back to town now. I have the witnesses to arrange for. Not too many of them unfortunately. There's the mother, she's all right, but not likely to be good in the box. I'm not calling the step-father. It seems he's giving the case away in the glen. The damned old blackguard! I should like to break his ugly neck. I jolly well will, too, one of these days. But Bessie will clear herself. Since she's going to be my wife she must leave the Court without a stain. Good-bye and God bless you, old chap! . . . . No, no, don't come to the door." (Stowell was for seeing him out.) "Take care of yourself. Good men are scarce. And then you've got to be fit for the Court, you know. By-bye!"

Stowell watched him from the window as he rode down the drive on his tired horse, patting its neck and encouraging it with cheery cries.

Now he understood why Bessie had held off while Gell had wished to marry her. It had been a case of the wife of the Peel fisherman over again, with the difference that Bessie (to avoid the danger of deceiving her husband) had made away with her child before marriage instead of after it. Wild, foolish, frantic scheme! Yet what courage! What strength! What affection!

But if, under Taubman's searching questions, the conspiracy of love should fail, and Bessie's defence should collapse, and Gell should see that she had deceived him, and that *he* too . . . .

No, no, that must not be! After all, what outrage on Justice would it be to keep a case like this out of the hands of a cold-blooded inhuman legal machine who would commit more crime than he punished?

Still standing by the window, Stowell heard the clatter of a horse's hoofs on the high road. Gell, in high spirits, was galloping home.

IV

Later in the day Stowell was alone in the library reading the Depositions. In his secret heart he knew that a wicked temptation had come to him—the temptation to get Bessie off, and to stop the flood of evil which would surely follow if Deemster Taubman tried her and she were condemned. But all the same he was struggling to drown his qualms in contempt of the case against her.

How little there was to it! The direct evidence was almost childish. The medical testimony was the only thing of consequence, but how sloppy, how inconclusive! Was there anything against Bessie which he, if he had been the advocate for the defence, could not have riddled with as many holes as there were in a cullender? Then why shouldn't he sit on her case?

Guilty? Perhaps she was; but, even so, was it not the theory of the law that she had to be *proved* guilty—that a prisoner should have a fair legal trial and be convicted or acquitted according to the evidence before the Court? Why shouldn't he?

Suddenly he became aware of a tumult at the front door. Somebody was bawling in a loud voice,

"I'll see the Dempster if I have to shout the house down."

It was Dan Baldromma. Stowell stepped into the hall and said to the housemaid, who was barring the door against the intruder,

"Let him come in, Jane."

Dan, with his short, gross figure, rolled into the house without remembering to take his hat off.

"Well, what do you want?" said Stowell—he was quivering with anger.

"I want to know what is to be done for me?" said Dan.

"For you?"

"For my daughter then—my step-daughter, I mane."

When he had seen Mr. Sto'll last—it was at his office in Ramsey—he had warned him that the man who had got his daughter into disgrace had got to marry her. But had he? No! He had refused—he must have done. And that was the reason why she did what they say. But, behold you, who was being blamed for it? Himself! Yes, people were looking black at him and saying he had thrown the girl into the way of temptation.

That was not the worst of it either. He had expected dacent tratement about the farm when he became father-in-law to the man who would come into it by heirship. But now the girl was in Castle Rushen, and if they sent her over the water the Spaker would be turning him out of house and home.

"He's after threatening it already—to show me the road at Hollantide . . . . What's that you say, Sir? Thinking of myself, am I? Maybe I am, then, and what for shouldn't I? Near is my shirt but nearer is my skin, they're saying."

Stowell, swept by gusts of passion, was doing his best to control himself.

" Well, what have you come to me for? " he asked.

Dan thrust forward his thick neck with his bull-like gesture, and said,

" To tell you to get her off."

" Even if she is guilty? "

" Chut! Who's to know that if the Coorts acquit her? They are wayses and wayses. Lawyers are mortal clever at twisting the law when they're wanting to. You're Dempster now; and the bosom friend of the man that got my girl into this trouble has got to get her out of it."

" So," said Stowell, breathing hard, " you have come to ask me to degrade Justice " (Dan made a grunt of contempt), " not to save the girl but to protect you—you and your rag of a character?"

Dan drew himself up with a short laugh, half bitter and half triumphant.

" Rag, is it? Take care what you're saying, Mr. Sto'll, Sir. You may be a big man in the island now, but there's them that's bigger and that's the people."

Stowell pointed with a quivering hand to the clock on the landing, and said,

" Look at that clock. If you're not out of this house in one minute . . . . "

Dan's laugh rose to a cry of derision.

" So that's it, is it? That's what the first Justice of the Peace in the Isle of Man is, eh? Son of the ould Dempster too! The grand ould holy saint as they're . . . . "

But before he could finish, Stowell, with a shout that drowned Dan's laugh as if it had been the whimper of a baby girl, laid hold of the man by the collar of his coat and the slack of his trousers and flung him out of the open door and clashed it after him.

Dan, who had rolled and tossed and bumped on the path like a fat hogshead kecked from the tail of a cart, picked himself up and went staggering down the drive, shaking his first at the house and pouring his maledictions upon it in a voice that was like the broken howl of a limping dog.

Janet came running from her room, and seeing Stowell with his eyes aflame and panting for breath, said,

" Oh dear! Oh dear! Now you'll be worse."

" On the contrary, I'll be better—better in every way," he said.

His resolution was taken. Never would he sit on Bessie's case. Nothing should tempt him to do so.

But Fate had not yet done with him.

V

On the afternoon of the following day Stowell walked for a long hour on the shore, trying to deaden the tumult in his brain in the loud surge of the sea. Returning to Ballamoar he found the Governor's carriage outside the house. Had the Governor come to see him? It was Fenella. She was at tea with Janet in the library.

Although she rose to greet him with all the sunshine of her smile he could see that her face was feverish.

" Ive come to the north on three errands," she said.

" So? "

" First to see yourself, of course, and I find that, in spite of doctor's orders, you have already resumed your gypsy habits."

" He *would* go out, dear," said Janet.

" Next, to deliver a message from the Governor."

" Yes? "

" He has postponed the Court for three days in the hope that you may be able to sit then."

" Ah ! "

" My last errand was to see the mother of that poor girl who is to be charged with the murder of her child."

" The mother? "

" Yes, I've just left her. She still says she knows nothing. It's pitiful ! A simple, sincere, religious old soul, who has seen trouble of her own apparently. I don't think for a moment she would tell an untruth, yet it is easy to see that in her heart she believes her daughter to be guilty."

" Guilty? "

" Yes, but there's somebody guiltier than the girl—the man."

Stowell was silent; but he felt his face twitching.

" That's why I am so anxious that you should sit on this case if you can, Victor, not leave it to Deemster Taubman. Old Judges often refuse to investigate collateral facts, and so the woman is punished and the man goes free."

" They can't do otherwise, dear. They can't try the man."

" Not if he has been a party to the crime? "

" A party . . . . "

" Yes ! I'm satisfied that in this case he is, too."

The girl might be guilty, but she could not have done all she was charged with. It was physically impossible. Somebody must have helped her. And that somebody (the old mother having to be ruled out) must be the man who had it to his interest to save his miserable character by concealing the fact that the girl had given birth to a child at all.

Stowell had as much as he could do to cover his embarrassment. He lowered his voice and said,

" That's a blind alley. I've read the Depositions. I'm sure it is, dear."

" Perhaps it is, perhaps it isn't," said Fenella. " I intend to follow it up anyway."

" How? " said Stowell, but rather with his mouth than his voice.

" I'm already on the track of something."

" On the track . . . . "

" Yes. It seems that somebody has been telling the mother that on the night when the girl left home (shut out by her abominable step-father, you know) she went to the house of a Mrs. Quayle, living on the south shore in Ramsey."

Stowell's heart thumped and his lips quivered.

" Mrs. Quayle? "

" Why, that must be the housekeeper at your chambers, dear," said Janet, busy with her teacups.

" You know her? . . . . But then everybody knows everybody in the Isle of Man," said Fenella.

" With a sense of duplicity, Stowell found himself saying, " Well? "

" Well, I'm going to see this Mrs. Quayle on my way home to Government House. She'll be able to tell me how long the girl stayed with her, who took her away, and where she went to."

Stowell dropped his head, feeling that he wanted to escape from the room, and Fenella (indignantly, passionately, vehemently) went on to denounce the guilty man.

" Of course the girl is shielding him. A woman always does that. I should do it myself if I were in the same position. But oh, how I should like to find him out! Even if he has taken no part in the actual crime, how I should like to punish him—to expose him! You *must* sit on this case—you really must, dear."

When the time came for Fenella to go Janet took her upstairs to look at some new decorations that had been made in the room that was to be her boudoir. Stowell remained in the library, and the sound of Fenella's step on the floor above beat on his stunned brain with the drumming noise of a train in a tunnel.

He had a sense of cowardice which he had never felt before,

At one moment he wanted to tell Fenella everything, thinking that would be the end of his tortures. But at the next he reflected that it would be the beginning of hers—inflicting an incurable wound upon her affection. And then if Bessie were going to be acquitted, as seemed possible (the evidence being so unconvincing), why should he enlarge the area of the shameful secret?

When Fenella returned (saying, as she came downstairs, how beautiful her room was and how proud she would be of it) he took her out to the carriage.

"Do you remember," she whispered (she had recovered her gay spirits, the coachman was on the box), "do you remember the first time you saw me off from here?"

He nodded and tried to smile.

"I was too bashful to shake hands and you were too shy to look at me."

And being seated in the carriage and the door closed on her, she said,

"By the way, wouldn't you like to drive over with me to Mrs. Quayle if I brought you home again?"

"No, no . . . . I mean . . . ."

She laughed merrily. "Oh, very well! You've refused me again! I'll remember it, Sir."

After the carriage had disappeared at the turn of the drive, Stowell went up to his room, shut the door behind him and covered his face in his hands.

Fenella hunting him down! Blindly, unconsciously, innocently, while urging him, entreating him, almost compelling him to sit on the case. The woman he loved and who loved him was trying to destroy him. Was this to be his punishment?

Mrs. Quayle? No, she would say nothing. If she thought it would injure his mother's son no power on earth would prevail upon her to speak. But sooner or later, by one means or other, Fenella would find out, and then . . . .

"God be merciful to me, a sinner!" he moaned, smothering the sound of the words behind his hands.

Could he sit in judgment on Bessie Collister's case with all the forces of the defence (inspired by Fenella) directed towards branding the Judge as the real criminal Impossible! Yet what could he do?

At length an idea occurred to him. He would go up to Government House, tell the whole truth to the Governor and ask to be relieved of his duty. It would be a terrible ordeal, but there was no escape from it.

"Yes, I will go up to the Governor in the morning."

CHAPTER TWENTY-SEVEN

THE JUDGE AND THE MAN

"HELLOA! Glad to see you about again. Fenella has gone off to the south of the island somewhere, but she'll be home for luncheon. Take a cigar? No? Not smoking yet? I must anyway."

"I've come to see you on a serious matter, Sir," said Stowell—he felt his lips trembling.

"So?"

The Governor glanced up quickly, charged his pipe and then settled himself to listen.

"You will remember the story I told you—about the man who had promised to marry a girl and then fallen in love with somebody else?"

"Perfectly."

Stowell paused a moment. His lips became pale and his hands contracted.

"Well?"

"That was my own story, Sir."

There was another moment of silence. Stowell had expected an exclamation of surprise, a clang of astonishment, but the Governor's face was still to the fire and the only sound he made was the swivelling of the pipe between his teeth.

"You advised me to break off the engagement and I did so."

"What was the result?"

"The girl was relieved."

"Relieved?"

"Yes, because she, too, had in the meantime fallen in love with somebody else—my friend Gell."

"How fortunate!"

"It seemed so at first. I thought Providence had stepped in to help her out. But Fate has kept a terrible reckoning, Sir."

"What has happened?"

"The girl has committed a crime. She is in Castle Rushen awaiting her trial for the murder of her new-born child."

"The woman Collister?"

"Yes. And now I'm a Judge and in ordinary course it is my duty to try her."

There was another period of silence, broken only by the rapid puffing of the Governor's pipe.

"But that's not all, Sir. Being in this frightful position everything is tempting me to corrupt Justice. First, my natural

desire to influence the trial in favour of the girl—perhaps to get
her off altogether. Next, pity for her poor mother who has been
pleading for mercy. Then, friendship for Gell who has been
begging me to try the case because the old Statute is severe and
my colleague cruel. And last of all the step-father of the girl who
has been trying to intimidate me."

"Well?"

"I think you will see it is impossible for me to sit on a case in
which my private interest and my public duty conflict—utterly
impossible. It would be against all usage, all justice."

The Governor removed his pipe. His face had become cold
and hard. "You speak of your colleague—have you done anything with him?"

"Yes. I've asked him to sit instead of me."

"What if he cannot?"

"Then I will ask you, Sir, to send for another Judge from
across the water."

Stowell had struggled through to the end, although perspiration had been breaking out on his forehead. When he had finished
the Governor sat for some time without speaking.

Obscure motives were operating within him. In the depths of
his mind (scarcely known to himself) he was asking himself,
"How will all this, if I allow it to go farther, affect Fenella?
Will it stop her marriage, disturb her happiness, destroy her life?"
But on the surface of his mind he was only aware of considerations
of public welfare. He was irritated by what had occurred. It
was an impediment in his path which he wished to kick out of
the way.

He rose, laid his pipe on the mantelpiece, and standing with
his back to the fire and his hands behind him, his chin firm and his
mouth set hard, he said, with sudden energy,

"Now listen to me. I always knew that was your own story."

"Yes?"

"What I did not know was that any harm had been done.
Did you?"

"Indeed no."

"Did the girl?"

"It is incredible."

"Do you know that she has killed her child?"

"Not certainly. She denies it, and the evidence is not too
convincing."

"Do you know that she ever had a child?"

"No . . . . I can't say . . . . She denies that also, and
the medical testimony is far from conclusive."

" Do you know—are you satisfied—that if she had a child, and killed it, the child was yours? "

Stowell, with a gulp, stammered something about Bessie having been a good girl before he met her.

" But do you know *anything?* "

" Well, no . . . . I can't say . . . . "

" Then, good heavens, what are you thinking about? Knowing nothing, nothing really, you are acting, and asking me to act, on a cloud of conjectures. I'll not do it."

Stowell drew his breath with a gasp of relief. It was just as if he had been living for days in the stuffy atmosphere of a sealed room and somebody had broken open a window. His head was down; the Governor touched his shoulder.

" My friend, you are doing that poor girl a cruel injustice."

Stowell was startled and looked up.

" In your own mind you are finding her guilty before she has been tried."

" Ah ! "

" You are doing yourself an injustice, too. Even if the girl committed this crime—I say *if*—*you* are not responsible for it."

Stowell began to stammer again. " I . . . . I did wrong in the first instance, Sir, and nothing but wrong . . . . "

But the Governor said sharply, " Of course you did wrong in the first instance. But that has nothing to do with the wrong which she (if she is guilty) has done since. It can't be supposed that you had any sympathy with her act, can it? "

" God forbid ! "

" Did you desert her? Did you leave her to the mercy of the world? Has she ever been in want? Was she in any danger of being unable to provide for her offspring when it came? "

" No . . . . I cannot say . . . . "

" Then what folly to think you are responsible for what she did in taking the life of her child—if she did take it. No, other facts and motives operated with the girl. And whatever those facts and motives were, you, so far as I can see, had nothing to do with them —nothing whatever."

Stowell's pulse was beating high. He tried to say something about his moral responsibility, but again the Governor cut him short.

" Your moral responsibility ! " he said, with a ring of sarcasm. " I'm sick of this sentimental talk about moral responsibility— man's responsibility for the conduct of woman, and all the rest of it. The person who commits the crime is the criminal—that's the only foundation of law and order."

"Then you think, Sir," said Stowell, "that since I . . . . "

"I think," said the Governor, "that the whole thing is unfortunate, damnably unfortunate, but since you are not responsible for the girl's crime, if she committed a crime at all, and knew nothing about it, and have no sympathy with it, you ought to go on doing your duty. Why shouldn't you? . . . . Interested? Of course you are interested. In a little community like this a Judge is nearly always interested. Isn't that what your Deemster's oath is intended to provide for?"

Stowell muttered something about being afraid, and again the Governor caught him up.

"Afraid? What are you afraid of? The public? Doesn't it occur to you that the only risk you run in that direction is not the risk of sitting on this case but of *not* sitting on it? There must be people who have seen you coming here this morning, and if you are not in Court on the appointed day, aren't they likely to ask why?"

"There's Gell . . . . "

"Certainly there's Gell . . . . When the marriage was broken off you didn't tell him anything, did you?"

Stowell shook his head. "How could I?"

"Yes, how could you? And now he wishes you to sit, and, if you don't, isn't he likely to suspect the reason?"

"There . . . . there's Baldromma."

"That wind-bag! Likely to make a cry against the administration of justice, is he? Well, the surest way to squelch such people is to walk over them."

"There's the girl herself."

"Of course, there's the girl herself. But if she is guilty and has held her tongue thus far, she'll probably continue to do so."

The Governor made a turn across the room and then drew up sharply.

"There's myself, too. I suppose I deserve some consideration?"

"Indeed yes."

"Then go on with your duty—that's all I ask of you."

With a thrill of relief Stowell rose to go. But oh, misery of the heart, he had kept his most searching objection to the last.

"There is somebody else, your Excellency."

"Who else?" asked the Governor, laying down the pipe he had taken up.

"I hate to mention her in this connection—Fenella."

"Fenella? Why, what on earth has Fenella . . . . "

And then Stowell told him.

Having interested herself in this case, Fenella was hunting down the guilty man that he might be exposed and punished—punished by public obloquy if he could not be punished by law.

"If she finds him before the trial how can I possibly sit? Whatever happens it will be coloured by her knowledge of the truth. If the girl is acquitted she will think I have helped her to escape punishment in order to salve my conscience or cover my share in her crime. And if she is condemned what happiness can there be for either of us after that?"

He had spoken with emotion, but the Governor, who had recovered from his surprise, replied impatiently,

"Aren't you crossing the bridge before you come to the river?"

Stowell made no answer, and at the next moment there was the sound of carriage wheels coming up the drive.

"It's Fenella," said the Governor, looking out of the window. "I'll ask you to say nothing to her about the subject of our conversation. And listen " (he was re-lighting his pipe and puffing at it with lips that smacked angrily; Stowell's hand was on the door), " don't let my girl make a damned fool of you."

II

"Victor, I have something to tell you," said Fenella.

"Yes?"

They were in the library. She was looking feverish; he was feeling ashamed, embarrassed and afraid.

"I have found out who was the friend of that poor girl."

He gazed at her without speaking.

"It will be a great shock to you—it was Alick Gell."

"No, no!"

"I'm sorry, dear. I knew you would be unable to believe it. But it's true—terribly true."

Mrs. Quayle, the evening before, had said very little. Nobody had called to see the girl while she stayed at her house, and nobody had come to take her away. She, herself, had seen her off by the train, and all the girl had told her was that she was going to a school at Derby-Haven.

"But that was enough for me," said Fenella. " This morning I went down to Derby-Haven and found there was only one school there. It is kept by two maiden ladies named Brown. Simple old things, very timid and old-fashioned. They were thrown into terrible commotion by my call, and having read the reports in the newspapers they were at first afraid to say anything. But after I had promised that they should not be mixed up in the matter in any way, I got them to speak. Mr. Alick Gell had brought the girl to their house. He had paid for her, and they had always looked upon him as her intended husband. So it's a certainty, you see—a shocking certainty."

Stowell was breathless.

"But my dear Fenella," he said, "this is a mistake. You are drawing a false inference . . . ."

But Fenella only shook her head.

"Yes. I knew your loyalty to your friend would compel you to say so. But what do you think? I have since found that the fact is common knowledge."

Returning in the train she had occupied a compartment with two men—the strangest looking creatures she had ever seen in a first-class carriage. One of them turned out to be the girl's step-father and the other a member of the House of Keys.

"Cæsar Qualtrough?"

"Cæsar? Yes, that was the name. They talked about the forthcoming trial and didn't seem to mind my hearing them—perhaps wished me to. The step-father (he spoke as if the whole case had been got up to disgrace *him*) was complaining that he had not been called by either side. But no matter, he would force himself upon the Court and expose the real criminal—the Speaker's son. It was all a trick. But it should not succeed. He would put the saddle on the right horse, he would. And then they talked about you."

"What . . . . what about me?"

"That the report of your being too ill to sit was a lie. You were not ill at all and never had been—the step-father knew better. You were merely shirking your duty to save your friend in some way. But that trick shouldn't succeed either, or the people should know what Judges in the Isle of Man were. So you see you *must* sit on this case, dear—if you are fit for it. You can't afford to have it said that you have sacrificed your duty as a Judge to your personal interests. At your first Court, too."

Stowell was in torture. In spite of the Governor's warning, an almost overpowering impulse came to him to confess, to make a clean breast of everything, there and then, and once for all.

"Fenella," he began (his breath was coming and going in gusts), "who knows if the guilty man is Gell? It may be some-body else."

"Who else can it be?"

He tried to say "It is I," but hesitated—he could not shatter in a word the whole world he lived in. At the next moment she was praising his fidelity, which would not allow him to think ill of his life-long friend.

"But *he* has no such delicacy," she said. "Knowing what he knows he is still going to defend the girl, and that's equal to defending himself, isn't it? How shocking!"

Stowell's shame at his moral cowardice reached the point of abasement, and he dropped his head. Then, carried away by her own pleading, Fenella put her arms about his neck, tenderly and caressingly, and told him she knew well what a hard thing she was asking him to do—to sit in judgment on his friend also, for that was what it would come to. But she would love him for ever if he would do it. It would be like the crown of all her hopes, the fulfilment of all she had worked for, if in some way (*he* would know best how) a poor girl who had sinned and suffered should have mercy shown to her, and not be left alone in her shame, but have the partner of her sin (no matter who he was or how near he came) standing side by side with her.

There was a moment of silence. Stowell was like a man groping in the dark of a black midnight. At length a light seemed to dawn on him. If he sat on this case he could save an innocent man at all events.

"You *will* sit, will you not?"

"Yes."

And then she kissed him.

III

Back at Ballamoar, Stowell found the Deemster's clerk waiting for him.

It had taken Joshua three days to see Deemster Taubman, and when at length he was admitted to the big man's presence he had found him in bed, with his shaggy head and unshaven face on the pillow and his lower extremities through the legs of a cane-bottomed chair which supported his bed-clothes.

"What? What's that?" he had roared. "Sit at the General Gaol? Go back to your master and tell him I'm lying here in the tortures of the damned, not able to put a foot to the ground."

Stowell drew a long breath. Fate had spoken its last word! It was now certain that he must sit on the case of Bessie Collister.

His spirits rose and he began to see things more clearly. Had he not exaggerated his own importance in this affair? He had been thinking of his part in the forthcoming trial as if the issue of Bessie's fate depended upon him. But not so. It depended upon the Jury. Guilty or not Guilty,—he had nothing to do with that.

17

Therefore, in the deeper sense, Bessie would not be tried by him at all. Why had he been frightening himself?

Had a Judge, then, no power, no voice, no influence? Thank God, yes! It was for the Judge to direct the jury on questions of law, to see that they had a right understanding of it and that their verdict corresponded with the evidence. What an important function—especially in a case like this! What a mercy old Taubman was unable to sit on it!

He thought again of Bessie's position. Pitiful, most pitiful! But the law was no Juggernaut, intended to crush the life out of a poor unfortunate girl. Mercifully administered it was rather her Sanctuary to which she might fly for refuge. And it *should* be mercifully administered.

Why not? Good heavens, why not? What wrong would it be to temper Justice with mercy—even to strain the law a little in the prisoner's favour? No one but himself would know. And if it were suspected that he was showing favour to the prisoner, people would consider him deserving of praise rather than censure for trying to snatch a young and helpless creature from the clutches of a cruel old Statute.

Besides, was it not one of the higher traditions of the bench that the Judge was first Counsel for the accused? Judges had not always acted on that principle. Some of them, in times past, had hunted their wretched prisoners gallowswards with gibes. Taubman was still like that. He thought sympathy with such women as Bessie Collister was sentimental weakness, that to deal mercifully with them was to encourage them, and thereby do a wrong to public morality.

" God bless me, yes! *I* know Taubman," he told himself.

Then he thought of Gell. Whatever Bessie might be, Gell was innocent, and after the girl herself the greatest sufferer. Should he suffer further from an unfounded suspicion? God forbid! It would be his duty as Judge to see that no blustering person in Court bellowed accusations which, once out, might stick to an innocent man for the rest of his natural life.

After that he thought of himself. The only risk he ran was from Bessie's despair. If Gell were falsely accused she might break silence and tell the truth to save him. What a vista! Bessie, Gell, himself, Fenella! But no, that should not be! The law was no thumb-screw; a law-court was no torture-chamber. It would be his duty as Judge to protect the girl against any form of legal provocation.

Last of all, with a thrill of the heart, he thought of Fenella. She had drawn him on, constrained and compelled him to promise

to sit on Bessie's case. But she had only wished, out of the greatness of her pity, to see that the poor girl should have a just trial.
She should too! It would be his duty as Judge to see to that.

"Good Lord, yes! And what a mercy the case is not coming
before Taubman."

Thus in the scorching fire of his temptation he tried to stand
erect in the belief that he had sunk himself in his high office—
that he was about to become the champion and first servant of
Justice. But well he knew in his secret heart that in the fierce
struggle which had been going on within him between the Judge
and the Man, the Man had conquered.

During the next two days he worked day and night in the
library, looking up authorities and verifying references. On the
third day he set out in his car for Castletown. Janet saw him off
in the mist of early morning. He was very pale; he had eaten
scarcely any breakfast. She looked anxiously after him until he
disappeared behind the trees. There was the odour of fresh earth
in the air and the rooks were calling. It was like an echo from
the past.

When he arrived at Castle Rushen there was a crowd at the
gate, and all hats were off to him, as they had been to his father,
when he passed through the Judge's private entrance.

Inside the courtyard, where the steps go up to the public part
of the Court-house, there was another crowd and a certain commotion. The police were pushing back a tumultuous person who
in a raucous voice was demanding to be admitted although the
place was full.

It was Dan Baldromma.

CHAPTER TWENTY-EIGHT

THE TRIAL

For a good hour before the arrival of the Deemster, Castle
Rushen had been full of activity. In the Court-house itself, warm
with sunshine from the lantern light, Robbie Stephen, the chief
Coroner of the island, who looked like a shaggy old sheep-dog,
had been selecting candidates for the Jury-box.

Seventy-two of them had been summoned, six from each of
twelve parishes, and now he was reducing the number to thirty-
two, twelve for the Jury and twenty more to meet the contingency
of arbitrary challenging.

Everybody claimed exemption, but the Coroner listened to
none. Standing back to the empty bench, swelling with impor-

tance and with his seventy-two men huddled together like sheep
at one side of the chamber, he called them out at his discretion and
with a wave of the hand passed them over to the other side to wait
for the trial.

"Now, then, Willie Kinnish, thou'rt a good man; over with
thee." "No, no, Mr. Stephen, you must excuse me to-day, Sir."
"Tut, tut! You Maughold men haven't served on a jury these
seven years." "But I have fifty head of sheep going to Ramsey
mart this morning, and what's to pay my half year's rent if I'm
not there to sell them?" "Chut, man! Lave that to herself.
She's thy better half, isn't she?"

Meantime, in the chill corridors underground the jailer and his
turnkey were rattling their keys, opening the doors of the cells
and shouting to the prisoners to make ready for the Court.

"Patrick Kelly! Charles Quiggin! Nancy Kegeen! John
Corlett! Cæsar Crow! Robert Quine! Elizabeth Corteen!"

Hearing her name called, Bessie, having no fear, got up from
her plank bed, and when Mrs. Mylrea, the woman warder, with her
short, loud, difficult breathing, brought back her cloak and fur hat,
she put them on leisurely.

"Quick, girl!" said the warder. "You don't want to keep the
Dempster waiting, do you?"

Bessie laughed, but made no answer. At the next moment she
was in the darkness of the corridor, walking at the end of a short
procession of other prisoners, and at the next she was drawn up,
with her prison companions, into the blinding sunlight of a little
paved quadrangle which was surrounded by high walls and had the
sound of the sea coming down into it from the free world outside.

By this time the Court-house upstairs was in a state of yet
greater activity. The thirty-two possible jurymen, having reconciled themselves to being "trapped," were standing under the
jury-box, talking of the weather which was bringing the crops on
rapidly and would increase the price of early potatoes. Inspectors of police were bustling about; Joshua Scarff was laying a
green portfolio with paper, pens and ink, on the bench in front of
the Deemster's scarlet armchair, and a number of advocates were
coming in laughing by a door which communicated with their
room off the ramparts.

The last of the advocates to enter was Alick Gell. He took a
seat immediately in front of the empty dock, looking pale and
worn and scarcely able to hold the papers which he carried in his
nervous hands. A little later the Attorney-General, who was to
prosecute for the Crown, came in with a grave face, followed by
old Hudgeon, his junior, with a sour one. And shortly before

eleven (the hour appointed for the beginning of the trial) a lady was brought by an Inspector from the door to the Judge's room and seated beside Gell in front of the dock. It was Fenella.

Then the outer doors to the court-yard were thrown open and the public admitted. They rushed and tore their way into the Court-house, men and women together, talking and laughing loudly. The big clock in the Castle tower was heard to strike, and the Inspector, standing near the dais, cried in a loud voice,

"Silence in Court!"

The babel of voice subsided and everybody rose who had been seated. Then the Court came in and took their seats on the bench of judgment—the Governor in his soldier's uniform, and Stowell and the Clerk of the Rolls in their Judges' wigs and gowns.

It was remarked that the new Deemster looked ill and almost old. A wave of sympathy went out to him from the first. It was whispered among the spectators that he had come straight from a sick-bed, and that the Governor insisted on his presence, saying he must have him "dead or alive."

"Coroner, fence the Court," said the Governor, and then old Stephen, who had already taken his place in the Coroner's box, raising the pitch of his voice, recited the ancient formula:

"*I do hereby fence this Court in the name of our Sovereign Lord the King. I charge that no person shall quarrel, bawl or molest the audience, that all persons shall answer to their names when called. I charge this audience to witness that this Court is fenced; I charge this audience to witness that this Court is fenced; I charge this whole audience to witness that this Court is fenced.*"

Everybody knew that it was for the Deemster to speak next, but for a sensible moment he did not do so. Then he said, almost beneath his breath,

"Let the prisoners be brought in."

In the continued silence there came the sound of bustle outside, with the patter of feet on the pavement below, and then a shuffling of steps on the stairs. The prisoners were coming up, but the police had difficulty in clearing a passage for them. The voice of the jailer, Tommy Vondy, was heard to cry, "Make way!" There was a period of waiting. At one moment the people in court caught the sound from the staircase of a scarcely believable thing —the laugh of a woman? Who could she be?

At length the prisoners were brought in, pushed through the throng that stood thick at the back, and hurried into the dock, which was like a long pew behind the circular seats of the advocates and directly in front of the bench.

There were seven of them, a sorry company, two women and five men, with nothing in common save the pallid, almost pasty complexions which had come of the dank air they had been living in.

There was another moment of silence. It was time for the Deemster to take the pleas, but again he did not speak immediately. He had the look of a man who was struggling against physical weakness. The blood rushed to his pale face and as quickly disappeared. "He's not fit for it to-day," people whispered.

But at the next moment, in a low voice, and with the appearance of one who was making an effort to command his strength, the Deemster was reading the indictments.

He took the prisoners in the order in which they stood before him, beginning with the one on the extreme left. He was a very young man, almost a boy, with a face that might have been that of his mother when she was a girl. His name was Quiggin; he had been a bank clerk and was charged with embezzlement. He pleaded Guilty and looked down as if he expected the earth to open under his feet.

The next was a gross, fat, middle-aged woman with red cheeks and many heavy gold rings on her stubby fingers. Her name was Kegeen, and she was charged with robbing drunken sailors in a house she had kept in an alley off the south quay. In a torrent of words she denied everything and accused the police of blackmailing her.

The last was Bessie Collister and the Deemster paused preceptibly when he came to her.

She had carried herself straight when she entered the Court and was now sitting with her head thrown back. But, seeing that of all the prisoners she was the one on whom the eyes of the spectators were fastened, she had reached up her hands to a veil which was wrapped about her fur hat and drawn it down over her face. Observing this at the last moment, and thinking it the cause of the Deemster's silence, the jailer said in an audible whisper,

"Put up your fall, Bessie."

She did so, disclosing her thin white face and large eyes. And then in a voice so low that it would have been scarcely audible but for the strained silence in the court-house, the Deemster said,

"Elizabeth Corteen, stand up."

Bessie rose without embarrassment and fixed her eyes on the Deemster. And then he charged her.

"It is charged against you that on or about the fifth day of April—in the parish of Ballaugh, in the Isle of Man, feloniously, wilfully and of your malice aforethought, you did kill and murder a certain male child, contrary to the form of the Statute in such case made and provided, and against the peace of our Sovereign Lord the King, his Crown and dignity. How say you, are you guilty or not guilty? "

Without hesitation or halting, looking straight into the eyes of the Judge and speaking in a voice so clear that it resounded through the silent Court-house, Bessie answered,

" Not Guilty."

Her tone and bearing had gone against her. " The huzzy! " whispered one of the female spectators. " She might have more shame for her position, anyway. And did you see the way the forward piece looked up at the Deemster? "

II

It was not until Stowell had stepped on to the bench that he had realized what he had done for himself.

When he had asked for the prisoners to be brought in, and Bessie had come at the end of the short line and taken her place in the dock with the constable behind her, he had been seized with a feeling of choking shame.

That woman, looking so much older, with pallid cheeks sucked in by suffering, could she be the same? All the barrage he had built up for the protection of his position as Judge seemed to have gone down at the first sight of the girl's face. What a scoundrel he had been!

From that moment a whirl of confused emotions had held possession of him. When the time came to charge the prisoner he had felt as if he were reading out his own indictment. And when she had looked up fearlessly into his face and pleaded Not Guilty it was the same as if she were accusing himself.

After that he had a sense of acting as a detached person. In a strange voice, which did not seem to be his own, he heard himself asking the Attorney-General which case he wished to take first. The Attorney answered, " The murder case," and after the Clerk of the Rolls had read out the names of the jurymen, and they had taken their places in the jury-box, he heard himself, in the same strange voice, swearing them on the holy evangelists to " a true verdict give, according to the evidence and the laws of this isle."

When he turned his eyes back, Bessie was alone in the dock, save for the woman warder (with blue lips and a look of suffering) who sat at the farther end of it. She was still looking fearlessly up at him, and in front of her sat two others whose eyes were also fixed on his face—Alick Gell and Fenella. At that sight a terrible feeling took hold of him—that these three were the real judges in this trial and he was the prisoner at the bar.

He did not recover from the shock of this feeling until the Attorney-General began on the prosecution.

The Attorney, usually so kindly, was bitterly severe. The time had gone by when it could be said with truth that crime was practically unknown in the Isle of Man. Here, as elsewhere, crimes of all kinds were only too common, and not least common was the crime of infanticide.

The present case was one of peculiar atrocity. The prisoner was a young woman who might be said, not uncharitably, to have inherited a lawless disposition. After a reckless girlhood she had disappeared from her home, for no apparent reason, rather less than a year ago and remained away (nobody knew where or in what company) until a few weeks ago. She had then been ill and was put to bed in a condition which gave only too much reason for the belief that she was about to become a mother. That was on the fifth of April and two days later the body of a new-born infant had been found in a remote place, wrapped up and hidden away.

It would be established by witnesses that the infant had been born alive, that it had died by suffocation, and that the prisoner (incredible as it might appear) had been seen to bury it.

" Such," said the Attorney-General, " are the facts of this most unhappy case, and though the prisoner pleads Not Guilty, the evidence which I shall now call will leave no doubt that the child was her child and that it died by her hands. Therefore I ask (as well for the sake of humanity as for the good name of this island) that the Jury shall give such a verdict against the prisoner as will act as a deterrent on the heartless women, unworthy of the name of mothers, who, to save themselves from the just consequences of their evil conduct, are taking the innocent lives which under God they gave."

There had been a tense atmosphere in the Court-house during the Attorney-General's speech, and when it was over there were half-suppressed murmurs, hostile to the prisoner.

Looking towards the dock Stowell saw that Bessie was quite unmoved, but that Fenella, in front of her, was flushed and hot, and Gell's lower lip was trembling. Stowell was conscious of a complicated struggle going on within him and then of a blind and headlong resolution. He was going to save that girl—he was going to save her at all costs!

The first witness was the constable, a middle-aged man with a sour expression. After he had been sworn by the Deemster, the Attorney-General examined him.

His name was Cain and he was constable for the parish in which the crime had been committed. On the morning of April the seventh he received an information from Old Will Skillicorne of Baldromma-beg that something had been seen under the *Claghny-Dooiney*. He had gone there and found the body of a newborn child, and had taken it to Dr. Clucas, who had made an examination. Later the same day he had taken statements from Old Will and his wife, relating to the prisoner, and had sent them up to the Chief Constable of the island at Douglas. The Chief Constable had ordered him to make a house-to-house visitation through the parish to see if any other woman might have been the mother of the child. He had done so with the result that the prisoner was the only person who had come under suspicion. She was then ill in bed, but in due course he had arrested her, and charged her before the High Bailiff, who had committed her for trial at that court—sending her to the hospital in the meantime.

With obvious nervousness Gell rose to cross-examine the witness.

"How far is it from the prisoner's home to the *Clagh-ny-Dooiney?*"

"Half a mile, maybe."

"What kind of road would you call it?"

"Rough and thorny, most of it."

Gell sat with a look of satisfaction, and the Deemster leaned forward.

"Constable," he said, "when you made your house-to-house visitation did you go beyond the boundary of your parish?"

"No, your Honour."

"Where *is* the boundary?"

"The glen is the boundary—the western side of it, Sir."

"How near to the western boundary are the nearest houses in the next parish?"

"Four hundred yards, perhaps."

"How many of them are there?"

"Fifteen or twenty, your Honour."

"Yet, though you visited the prisoner's home, which was half-a-mile from the *Clagh-ny-Dooiney*, you did not visit—you were not told to visit—the fifteen or twenty houses which were only four hundred yards away?"

"They were not in my parish, your Honour."

There was audible drawing of breath in court. Fenella, who

had been reaching forward, dropped back, and Gell's pale face
was smiling.

The next to be called was Dr. Clucas. His hands were twitching and his rubicund face was moist with perspiration—he was
obviously an unwilling witness.

Yes, when the constable brought the body of the child he made
a post-mortem examination. Applying the usual medical tests he
came to the conclusion that the child had been born alive and had
died of suffocation. On the morning of the following day he
had been called in to see the prisoner. She was suffering from
extreme exhaustion—a condition not inconsistent with the idea of
recent confinement.

Gell, gathering strength but still agitated, rose again.

" How long had the child lived? "

" An hour or two, probably."

" And how long had it been dead? "

" Twenty-four to thirty hours at the outside."

" Is it your experience that within twenty-four to thirty hours
after confinement a woman can walk half-a-mile along a rough
and thorny road and carry a burden? "

" It certainly is not, Sir."

Gell sat with a piteous smile of triumph on his pale face, and
the Deemster leaned forward again.

" Doctor," he said, " you speak of applying the usual medical
tests—are they entirely reliable? "

" They are not infallible, your Honour. They have been
known to fail."

" Then this child may have breathed and yet not had a
separate existence? "

" It may—it is just possible, Sir."

" And the unhappy mother, whoever she may be, though obviously guilty of concealing its birth, may not have been guilty
of the much greater crime of killing it? "

" That's so . . . . she may not, your Honour."

There was a still more audible drawing of breath in court when
the doctor stood down. Fenella's eyes were shining and Gell's
were sparkling with excitement.

The next witness was Bridget Skillicorne. She wore a big
poke bonnet and a Paisley shawl which smelt strongly of lavender.
She was very voluble (provoking ripples of laughter by her broad
Manx tongue) and the Attorney-General had more than he could
do to restrain her.

Aw, 'deed yes, she remembered the night of the sixth-seventh
April, for wasn't it the night she had a cow down with the gripes?

Colic they were calling it, but wutching it was, and she believed in her heart she knew who had wutched the craythur. So she sent her ould man over to the Ballawhaine for a taste of something to take off the evil eye. And while she was sitting in the cowhouse itself, waiting for the man to come home (it was terr'ble slow the men were, both in their heads and their legs), she saw the light of a fire that had blown up on the mountains. " Will it reach the hay in my haggard? " she thought, and out she went to look. And, behold ye, what did she see but the glen as light as day and a woman on her knees putting something under the *Clagh-ny-Dooiney*. Who was she? The Collister girl of course. Sure? Sarten sure! And as soon as it was day she went down to the stone to see what the girl had left there. What was it? A baby—what else? Lying there in a scarf, poor bogh, like a little white mollag.

" What's mollag? " (Bridget's Manx had gone beyond the Attorney, but the jurymen were smiling.) " Ask them ones—*they* know."

Gell, with a newspaper-cutting in his hand, rose to cross-examine the old woman.

" You and your husband are sub-tenants of the prisoner's step-father, isn't that so? "

" Certainly we are—you ought to know that much yourself, Sir."

" I see you told the High Bailiff you were on bad terms with your landlord."

" Bad terms, is it? I wouldn't bemane myself with being on any terms at all with the like."

" He threatened to turn you out of your croft at Hollantide, didn't he? "

" He did, the dirt! "

" And you said you'd see him thrown out before you? "

" It's like I did, and it's like I will, too, for if your father, the Spaker . . . . "

The Attorney-General rose in alarm. " Is it suggested by these questions that the witness has an animus against the prisoner's family and is conspiring to convict her? "

" That," said Gell, in a ringing voice, " is precisely what *is* suggested."

" What? " cried Bridget, bobbing her poke bonnet across at Gell. " Is it a liar you're making me out? Me, that has known you since you were a loblolly-boy in a jacket? "

The Deemster intervened to pacify the old woman, and then took her in hand himself.

"Bridget," he said, "how far is it from your house on the brews down to the *Clagh-ny-Dooiney*? Is it three or four hundred yards, think you?"

"Maybe it is. But it's yourself knows as well as I do, your Honour."

"Is your sight still so good that you can see a woman to know her at that distance?"

"Aw, well, not so bad anyway. And then wasn't it as bright as day, Sir?"

"Listen. This court-house is not more than fifteen yards across, and less than ten to any point from the box in which you stand. Do you think you could recognise anybody you know in this audience?"

"Anybody I know? Recognise? Why not, your Honour?"

"You know Cain the constable?"

"'Deed I do, and his mother before him. A dacent man enough, but stupid for all . . . . "

"Well, he is one of the three constables who are now standing at this end of the jury-box—which of them is he?"

"Which? Do you say which, your Honour?" said Bridget, screwing up her wrinkled face. "Why, the off-one, surely."

There was a burst of irrepressible laughter in court—Bridget had chosen wrongly.

The next witness was old Will Skillicorne. He was wearing his chapel clothes, with black kid gloves, large and baggy, and was carrying a silk hat that was as straight and long and almost as brown as a length of stove-pipe. When called upon to swear he said he believed the old Book said "Swear not at all," and when asked what he was he answered that he believed he was "a man of God."

Aw, yes, he believed he remembered the night of the six-seventh of April, and he was returning home from an errand into Andreas when the prisoner passed him coming down the glen.

"At what time would that be?" asked Gell.

"Two or three in the morning, I belave."

"Then it would be still quite dark?"

"I was carrying my lantern, I belave."

"What was the prisoner doing when she passed you?"

"Covering her eyes with shame, I belave, as well she might be."

"Then you did not see her face?"

"I belave I did, though."

"Believe! Believe! Did you or did you not—yes or no?"

"I belave I did, Sir."

" Mr. Skillicorne," said the Deemster, " you attach importance to your belief, I see."

The old man drew himself up, and answered in his preaching tone,

" It's the rock of my salvation, Sir."

" Your wife told us that your errand into Andreas was to see the Ballawhaine about your sick cow. Is that the well-known witch-doctor? "

" I . . . . I . . . . I belave it is, Sir."

" And what did he give you? "

" A . . . . a wisp of straw and a few good words, Sir."

" Then you believe in that too—that a wisp of straw and a few good words . . . . "

But the Deemster could not finish—a ripple of laughter that had been running through the Court having risen to a roar which he did not attempt to repress. " He has made up his mind about this case," said someone.

The Attorney-General, who was looking hot and embarrassed, called the last of his witnesses. This was the house-doctor at the hospital, the young man with the thin hair and pugnacious mouth.

Asked if he remembered the prisoner being brought into hospital he said " Perfectly." Had he formed any opinion of her condition? He had. What was it? That she had been confined less than five days before. What made him think so? First her unwillingness to be examined and then . . . .

" She refused? "

" She did, your Honour, and threatened violence, but she became unconscious soon afterwards and then . . . . "

" Stop! " said the Deemster, and looking down at the Attorney he asked if the High Bailiff, in committing the prisoner, had ordered that she should be examined.

The Attorney-General shook his head helplessly, whereupon the Deemster, with a severe face, turned back to the witness.

" You are a qualified medical practitioner? "

" I am," said the witness, straightening himself.

" Then of course you know that for a doctor to examine a woman against her will and without a magistrate's order is to commit an offence for which he may be severely punished? "

The pugnacious mouth opened like a dying oyster.

" Y-es, your Honour."

" Therefore you did not examine her? "

" N-o, your Honour."

" And you know nothing of her condition? "

" No——"

" Stand down, Sir."

There was a commotion in the court-house. The prisoner's face was still calm, but Fenella's was aglow and Gell's was ablaze.

" Mr. Attorney," said the Deemster quietly, " have you any further evidence? "

The Attorney, who had been whispering hotly to Hudgeon, said,

" No, there was a nurse who might have given conclusive evidence, but, thinking the doctor's would be sufficient, my colleague has allowed her to leave the island. No, that is my case your Honour."

Stowell, secretly glad at the turn things had taken, was about to put an end to the trial, when Gell, intoxicated by his success, leapt up and said,

" I might ask the Court to dismiss this case immediately on the ground that there is nothing to put before the jury. But the wicked and cruel charge may follow the accused all her life, therefore I propose, with the Court's permission, to waive my right of reply and call such positive evidence of her innocence as will enable her to leave this court without a stain on her character."

" The fool! " thought Stowell. But just at that moment the clock of the Castle struck one, and the Governor said,

" The Court will adjourn for luncheon and resume at two."

As Stowell stepped off the bench his eye caught a glimpse of the inscription on a brass plate which had lately been affixed to the wall under his father's portrait—

" *Justice is the most sacred thing on earth.*"

His head dropped; he felt like a traitor.

III

When the trial was resumed the Attorney-General had not returned to court, so Hudgeon represented the Crown. He was offensive from the first, but Gell, whose spirits had risen preceptibly, was not to be put out.

The witness he called first was Mrs. Collister. The old mother had to be helped into the witness-box. Her poor face was wet with recent tears, and in administering the oath Stowell hardly dared to look at her. Remembering the admissions she had made to him at Ballamoar he knew that she had come to give false evidence in her daughter's cause.

She made a timid, reluctant and sometimes inaudible witness. More than once Hudgeon complained that he could not hear, and Gell, with great tenderness, asked her to speak louder.

"Speak up, Mrs. Collister. There's nothing to fear. The Court will protect you," he said. But Stowell, who saw what was hidden behind the veil of the old woman's soul, knew it was another and higher audience she was afraid of.

With many pauses she repeated, in answer to Gell's questions, the story she had told before—that her daughter had returned home ill on the fifth of April, that she had put her to bed in the dairy-loft and that the girl had never left it until Cain the constable came to arrest her.

"You saw her day and night while she was at your house?"

"Aw, yes, Sir, last thing at night and first thing in the morning."

"And you know nothing that conflicts with what she says—that she never had a child and therefore could not have killed it?"

"'Deed no, Sir, nothing whatever."

She had answered in a tremulous voice which the Deemster found deeply affecting. Once or twice she had lifted her weak eyes to his with a pitiful look of supplication, and he had had to turn his own eyes away. "I should do it myself," he thought.

"And now, Mrs. Collister," said Gell, "if you were here this morning you heard what the Attorney-General said—that your daughter had been of a lawless disposition and had run away from home without apparent reason. Is there any truth in that?"

"Bessie was always a good girl, Sir. It was lies the gentleman was putting on her."

"Is the prisoner your husband's daughter?"

"No, Sir," the old woman faltered, "his step-daughter."

"Is it true that her step-father has always been hard on her?"

The old woman hesitated, then faltered again, "Middling hard anyway."

"Don't be afraid. Remember, your daughter's liberty, perhaps her life, are in peril. Tell the Jury what happened on the day she left home."

Then nervously, fearfully, looking round the Court-house as if in terror of being seen or heard, the old woman told the story of the first Saturday in August.

"So your husband deliberately shut the girl out of the house in the middle of the night, knowing well she had nowhere else to go to?"

"Yes, if you plaze, Sir."

"It's a lie—a scandalous lie!" cried somebody at the back of the court.

"Who's that?" asked the Governor, and he was told by the

Inspector of Police (who was already laying hold of the inter-rupter) that it was the husband of the witness.

"A respectable man's character is being sworn away," cried Dan. "Put me in the box and I'll swear it's a lie."

In the tumult that followed the Deemster raised his hand.

"This Court has been fenced," he said severely, "and if any-body attempts to brawl here . . . . "

"Then let me be sworn. I'm only a plain Manxman, blood and bone, but I can tell the truth as well as some that make a bigger mouth."

"Behave yourself!"

"Give me a chance to save my character and fix the disgrace of these bad doings where it belongs."

"I give you fair warning . . . . "

"Put the saddle on the right horse, Dempster. He's near enough to yourself, anyway."

"Silence!"

"Why doesn't he come out into the open, not hide behind the skirts of a girl with a by-child?"

"Remove that man to the cells, and keep him there until the trial is over."

"What?" cried Dan, in a loud voice.

"Remove him!" cried the Deemster, in a voice still louder, and at the next moment, Dan, shaking his fist at the prisoner and cursing her, was hustled out of Court.

When the tempestuous scene was over and silence had been restored, the witness was trembling and covering her face in her hands and Hudgeon was on his feet to cross-examine her.

"I think your father was the late John Corteen, the Methodist?"

"Yes, sir."

"He was a good man, wasn't he?"

"As good a man as ever walked the world, Sir."

"He had a reputation for strict truthfulness—isn't that so?"

"'Deed it is, Sir. The old Dempster would take his word without asking him to swear to it."

"You were much attached to him, were you not?"

The old woman wiped her eyes, which were wet but shining.

"That's truth enough, Sir."

"And now he's dead and I daresay you sometimes pray for the time when you'll see him again?"

"Morning and night, every day of my life since I closed the man's dying eyes for him."

The advocate turned his gleaming eyes to the Jury and the side of his powerful face to the witness.

" You are a Methodist yourself, aren't you? "

" Such as I am, Sir."

" And as a Methodist you are taught to believe that truth is sacred and that a lie (no matter under what temptation told) is a thing of the devil and no good can come of it? "

The old woman faltered something that was barely heard, and then the big advocate turned quickly round on her, and said in a stern voice, looking full into her timid eyes,

" Mrs. Collister, as you are a Christian woman and expect to meet your father some day, will you swear that when your daughter returned home on the fifth of April you did not see at a glance that she was about to become a mother of a child? "

The old woman shuddered as if she had been smitten by an invisible hand, breathed audibly, tried to speak, stopped, then closed her eyes, swayed a little and laid hold of the bar in front of her.

" Inspector, see to the witness quickly," cried the Deemster.

At the next moment the old woman was being helped out of the witness-box and borne towards the door, where, realising what she had done for her daughter, she broke into a fit of weeping, which rent the silence of the Court until the door had closed behind her.

" In that cry," said the advocate, " the Jury has heard the answer to my question. It is proof enough that the prisoner had a child, and that her mother knew it."

" If so, it is proof of something else," cried Gell (he had leapt to his feet and was speaking in a thrilling voice), " that a strong man can find it in his heart to use his great forensic skill to crush a poor weak woman who is fighting for the life of her child. All his life through he has been doing the same thing—driving people into prison and dragging them to the gallows. He has made his name and grown rich and fat on it. God save me from a life like that! I am only a young lawyer and he is an old one, but may I live in poverty and die in the streets rather than outrage my humanity and degrade my profession by using the lures of the procurator and the arts of the hangman."

There was a sensation in Court. One of the younger advocates was heard to say, " My God, who thought Alick Gell was a fool? " And another who remembered the " Fanny " case in the Douglas police-courts, said, " He's got a bit of his own back, anyway."

When the commotion subsided, Hudgeon, with a face of scarlet, appealed to the Court:

18

"Your Honour, I ask your protection against this out-
rageous slander."

"Since you appeal to me," said the Deemster (whose own face
was aflame), "I can only say that you deserved every word of it."

Hudgeon tried to speak, but could not, his voice being choked
in his throat. And seeing that the Attorney-General had come
back to Court (he had just returned with Cain the constable, who
was carrying a parcel) he picked up his bag and fled.

Gell's time had come at last—the great moment he had been
waiting for so long. Although he had been shaken for an instant
by Mrs. Collister's silence he was not afraid now. He was going
to play his last and greatest card—put the prisoner in the box to
demolish for ever the monstrous accusation that had been intended
to ruin the life of an innocent woman. The Deemster trembled
as he saw Gell look round the Court with a confident smile before
he called his witness.

Bessie, whose big eyes had flamed with fury during her
mother's cross-examination, passed with a firm step from the dock
to the witness-box. In answer to Gell's questions she repeated
the evidence she had given before the High Bailiff, only more
emphatically and with a certain note of defiance.

When the Attorney-General rose to cross-examine her, it was
observed that he, too, had an air of confidence, as if something
had become known to him since morning.

"Do you adhere to your plea?" he asked.

"Indeed I do. Why shouldn't I?" said Bessie.

"Think again before it is too late. Do you still say that you
have never had a child, and therefore never killed and never
buried one?"

"Certainly I say so," said Bessie. "I don't know what you
are talking of."

"Constable," said the Attorney, turning to Cain, "open
your parcel."

There was a whispering among the spectators in Court, while
the constable was cutting the string and opening the brown-paper
parcel. The Deemster was shuddering, Gell's lower lip was
trembling, and Fenella (who was sitting, as before, in front of the
dock) was breathing deeply. The prisoner alone was unmoved.
The sun (it was now going round to the West) was shining down
on her from the lantern light. It lit up with pitiful vividness her
thin white face with its look of confidence and contempt.

"Do you know what this is?" asked the Attorney, holding
up a portion of a white silk scarf.

Bessie started as if she had seen a ghost. Then, recovering herself and turning her eyes away, she said, remembering what Gell had told her,

" I know nothing about it."

" You have never seen it before? "

" I know nothing about it."

The Attorney-General put the scarf outstretched on the table in front of him, and held up a narrower strip of the same material.

" Do you know anything about this, then? "

Bessie gasped and was silent for a moment. Then she said again, but with a stammer,

" I know nothing about it."

" Will you swear that it never belonged to you? "

A stabbing memory came back to Bessie. She remembered what she had heard about " a remnant " when the constables were ranging her room, and seeing no way of escape by further denial she said,

" Oh yes, I remember it now. I found it on the road when I was on my way home and bound it about my hat to keep it from blowing off in the wind."

The silence which had fallen upon the Court was broken by an audible drawing of breath. Gell, who had risen and leaned forward, dropped back.

" But if you found it on the road, how do you account for the fact that it has your name stamped on the corner of it? See—*Bessie.*"

Bessie was speechless for another moment. Then she said,

" Bessie is a common name, isn't it? "

" But how do you account for the further fact that these two pieces fit each other exactly? " asked the Attorney—laying the narrow strip by the broader portion.

Bessie became dizzy and confused.

" I can't account for it. I know nothing about it," she said.

The Deemster, who was breathing with difficulty, asked the Attorney what he suggested by the exhibits. The Attornew answered,

" The larger piece, your Honour, is the scarf which the body of the child was found in, while the narrower one was discovered in the prisoner's room, and the suggestion is that, taken together, they form a chain of convincing evidence that she is guilty of the crime with which she is charged."

Gell leapt to his feet. He had recognised the scarf as a

present of his own on Bessie's last birthday, and his great faith in the girl was breaking down, yet in a husky voice he said,

"Give her time, your Honour. She may have some explanation."

The Deemster signified assent, and then Gell, stepping closer to the witness-box, said,

"Be calm and think again. Don't answer hastily. Everything depends on your reply. Are you sure the scarf was not yours and that you lost the larger piece of it? Think carefully, I beg, I pray."

The advocate was losing himself, yet nobody protested. At length Bessie, with the wild eyes of a captured animal, broke into violent cries.

"Oh, why are you all torturing me? Wasn't it enough to torture my mother? I know nothing about it."

Gell dropped back to his seat. There was a profound silence. The great clock of the Castle was heard to strike four. The Deemster felt as if every stroke were beating on his brain. At length he said,

"A new fact has been introduced by the prosecution and it is only right that the defence should have time to consider it. It is now four o'clock. The Court will adjourn until morning. It is not for me to anticipate the evidence which the accused may give when the Court resumes, but if in the interval she can remember anything which will put a new light on the serious fact the Attorney-General has just disclosed, nothing she has said in her agitation to-day shall prejudice what she may say to-morrow."

He paused for a moment and then (with difficulty maintaining an equal voice) he added,

"It sometimes happens that a young woman in the position of the accused mistakes concealment for the much more serious crime of murder."

He paused again and then said,

"Whatever the facts in this unhappy case may prove to be, if I may speak to that mystery of a woman's heart which is truly said to be sacred even in its shame, I will say, ' Tell the truth, the whole truth; it will be best for you, best for everybody.' "

"The Court stands adjourned until eleven in the morning," said the Governor. "Meantime, let the advocate for the defence see the accused and give her the benefit of his legal advice and assistance. Jailer, look to the Jury that they are properly lodged in the Castle, and see that they hold no communication with persons outside."

IV

The Judges, the advocates and the spectators were gone, and Gell was alone in the Court-house. He was like a drowning man in an empty sea, clinging to an upturned boat.

Time after time he gathered up his papers and put them in his bag, then took them out again and spread them before him. At length, rising with a haggard face, he went downstairs with a heavy step.

At the door to the private entrance he came upon Fenella, who was waiting for her father. Her eyes were red as if she had been weeping, but they were blazing with anger also.

" Are you going down to her as the Governor suggested? "

" I cannot! I dare not! " he replied. And then, as if struck by a sudden thought he said, " But won't *you* go? "

" You wish me to speak to her instead of you? "

" Won't you? If she has anything to say she'll say it more freely to a woman."

Fenella looked at him for a moment.

" Very well, I'll go if you are willing to take the consequences."

" The consequences? To me? That's nothing—nothing whatever. Go to her, for God's sake. I'll wait here for you."

In the Deemster's room the Governor was putting on his military overcoat. He was not too well satisfied with himself, and as the only means of self-justification he was nursing a dull anger against Stowell.

" Well, we can only go on with it. There's nothing else to do now. Unfortunate—damnably unfortunate! "

A few minutes later, Stowell, sitting at the table in wig and gown, heard the clash of steel outside (a company of the regiment quartered in the town were acting as a guard of honour) and saw through the window the Governor's big blue landau passing over the bridge that crossed the harbour.

Gell would be with Bessie in her cell by this time. She was guilty. He must see that she was guilty. What a shock! What a disillusionment! All his high-built faith in the girl wrecked and broken!

At last he unrobed and went down the empty staircase. On opening the door to the court-yard he was startled to see Gell pacing to and fro with downcast head among the remains of some tombs of old kings which lay about in the rank grass.

" Ah, is it you? " said Gell, looking up at the sound of Stowell's footsteps. " You were good to her, old fellow. I can't help thanking you."

Stowell mumbled some reply and then said he thought Gell would have been with Bessie.

" I daren't go," said Gell. " But Fenella has gone instead of me."

" Fenella ? "

Stowell felt as if something were creeping between his skin and his flesh. Fenella and Bessie—those two and the dread secret!

" My poor girl ! " said Gell. " If she has anything to say—to confess—it won't hurt so much to say it to somebody else. But of course she hasn't—she can't have."

Stowell felt as if he had been suddenly deprived of the power of speech. Yes, Bessie would confess everything to Fenella. Not merely the birth of her child but also the name of her fellow-sinner—Fenella's desire to punish the guilty man would drag that out of her. Perhaps the confession was going on at that very moment. What a shock for Fenella too! All her high-built faith in *him* wrecked and broken!

" Well, let us hope . . . . "

" Yes, that is all we can do."

And then the two men parted, Gell returning to his pacing among the tombs of the dead kings and Stowell going out by the Deemster's door.

A few of the spectators at the trial were waiting to see the Deemster off, but he scarcely saw their salutations and did not respond to them.

CHAPTER TWENTY-NINE

THE TWO WOMEN—THE TWO MEN

On being taken back to her cell Bessie had burst into a fit of hysteria.

" The brutes ! They're only trying to catch me out that they may kill me. Why don't they do it then? Why don't they finish me? This waiting is the worst."

Her face was blue with rage, her voice was coarse and husky, her mouth was full of ugly and vulgar words—all the traces of her common upbringing coming uppermost.

At length, out of breath and exhausted, she broke into sobs. This quietened her and after a while she asked what had become of her mother.

Fenella, who was alone with her (the woman warder having

gone home ill), answered that some good women had carried her mother away and were going to take care of her.

" And where is . . . . "

" Mr. Gell? Upstairs. He sent me down to speak to you."

" I won't speak to anyone. They're all alike. They're only torturing me."

Fenella reproved the girl tenderly. Could she not see that the Deemster himself was trying to help her? He had adjourned the Court to give her another chance, and if she could only explain away the evidence of the scarf . . . .

" I won't explain anything. Why can't you leave me be? "

" You heard what the Deemster said, Bessie? Tell the truth; the whole truth; it will be best for you; best for everybody."

After that Bessie became calmer, and then Fenella (little knowing what she was doing for herself) pleaded with the girl to confess.

" I think I understand," she said. " Sometimes a girl loves a man so much that she cannot deny him anything. Thousands and thousands of women have been like that. Not the worst women either. But the dark hour comes when the man does not marry her—perhaps cannot—and then she tries to cover up everything. And that's your case, isn't it? "

" Don't ask me. I can't tell you," cried Bessie.

Fenella tried again, still more tenderly.

" And sometimes a girl who has done wrong tries to shield somebody else—somebody who is as guilty as herself, perhaps guiltier. Thousands of women have done that too, ever since the world began. They shouldn't, though. A bad man counts on a woman's silence. She should speak out, no matter who may be shamed. And that's what you are going to do, aren't you? "

But still Bessie cried, " I can't! I can't! "

" Don't be afraid," said Fenella. " The Deemster is not like some other judges. He has such pity for a girl in your position that he will do what is right by her whoever the man may be."

" Oh, why do you torture me? " cried Bessie.

" I don't mean to do that," said Fenella. " But a girl has to think of her own position in the long run, and it's only right she should know what it is. If she is charged with a terrible crime, and there is evidence against her which she cannot gainsay, the law has the power to punish her—to inflict the most terrible punishment, perhaps. Have you thought of that, Bessie? "

Bessie shuddered and laid hold of Fenella by both hands.

" On the other hand if she can explain . . . . if she can say that her child was born dead and that she merely concealed the birth of it, or that she killed it by accident, perhaps, when she was alone and didn't know what she was doing . . . . "

Bessie was breathing rapidly, and Fenella (still unconscious of the fearful game the unseen powers were playing with her) followed up her advantage.

" You can trust the Deemster, Bessie. He will be merciful to a girl who has stood silent in her shame to save the honour of the man she loves—I'm sure he will. And the Jury too, when they see that you did not intend to kill your child, they may . . . . who knows? . . . . they may even acquit you altogether."

Bessie was silent now, and Fenella could see, in the half darkness of the cell, that the girl's big pathetic eyes were gazing up at her.

" And then the people who have been thinking hard of you, because you have deceived them, will soften to you when they see that what you did, however wrong it was and even criminal, was done perhaps for somebody you loved better than yourself."

Suddenly Bessie dropped to her knees at Fenella's feet and cried,

" Very well, I will confess. Yes, it's true. I had a child, and I . . . . I killed it. But I didn't mean to—God knows I didn't."

" Tell me everything," said Fenella. And then, burying her face in Fenella's lap and clinging to her, Bessie told her story, mentioning no names, but concealing and excusing nothing.

Before she had come to an end, Fenella, who had been saying " Yes " and " Yes," and asking short and eager questions (the two women speaking in whispers as if afraid that the dark walls would hear), felt herself seized by a great terror.

" Then it was not Mr. Gell who took you into his rooms when your father shut you out? "

" No, no! Would to God it had been! "

" Then who was it? "

" Don't ask me that. I cannot answer you."

" Who was it? Tell me, tell me."

" I can't! I can't! "

" Was it in Ramsey—his chambers? "

" Yes."

" Is he? . . . . is he anything to me? "

Bessie dropped her head still deeper into Fenella's lap and made no answer.

" Is he? " said Fenella, and in her gathering terror, getting no reply, she lifted Bessie's head and looked searchingly into her face, as if to probe her soul.

At the next moment the dreadful truth had fallen on her. The girl's fellow-sinner, the man she had been hunting down to punish him, to shame him, to expose him to public obloquy, was Victor Stowell himself!

At the first shock of the revelation the woman in Fenella asserted itself—the simple, natural, deceived and outraged woman. This girl had gone before her! This common, uneducated creature of the fields and the farmyard! For one cruel moment she had a vision of Bessie in Stowell's arms. This was the face he had loved! These were the lips he had kissed! And she had thought he had loved her only—never having loved anybody else!

A feeling of disgust came over her. The girl had not even had the excuse of caring for Stowell. She had been thinking merely of a way of escape from the tyrannies of her step-father. Or perhaps an admixture of sheer animal instinct had impelled her. How degrading it all was!

Bessie, who had begun to realise what she had done, tried to take her hand, but Fenella drew back and cried,

" Don't touch me! "

All the thoughts of years about woman as the victim seemed to be burnt up in an instant in the furnace of her outraged feelings. An almost unconquerable impulse came to leave Bessie to her fate. Let her pay the penalty of her crime! Why shouldn't she?

But after a while a great pity for the girl came over her. If she had sinned she had also suffered. If she was there, in prison, it was only because she had been trying in her ignorant way to wipe out her fault.

But she herself . . . . her hopes gone, her love wasted . . . .

Fenella bursted into a flood of tears. And then Bessie (the two women had changed places now) began to comfort her.

" I'm sorry. I didn't think what I was doing. Don't cry."

At the next moment they were in each other's arms, crying like children—two poor ship-broken women on the everlasting ocean of man's changeless lust.

Bessie was the first to recover. She was full of hope and expectation, and visions of the future. Now that she had confessed everything the Deemster would tell the Jury to let her off, and then Alick would forgive her also.

" He *will* forgive me, will he not? "

She was like a child again, and Fenella found a cruel relief in humouring her.

" Yes, yes," she answered.

" When I leave this place I'm going to be so good," said Bessie. " I will make him such a happy life. We'll be marrried immediately—by Bishop's licence, you know—and then leave the Isle of Man and go to America. He often spoke of that, and it will be best . . . . After all this trouble it will be best, don't you think so?"

"No doubt, no doubt," said Fenella.

At length she remembered that Gell would be waiting for her. She must go to him. When she reached the corridor she paused, wondering what she was to say and how she was to say it. While she stood there she heard sounds from the cell behind her. Bessie was singing.

Meantime Gell had been fighting his own battle. The black thought which had come hurtling down on him at Derby Haven, when he first read the letter which Bessie had left behind her, was torturing him again. It was about Stowell, and to crush it he had to call up the memory of the long line of good and generous things that Stowell had done for him all the way up since he was a boy.

When at last he saw Fenella approaching he searched her face for a ray of hope, but his heart sank at the sight of it.

"Well?"

"She has confessed."

"She had a child?"

"Yes."

"It was born dead?"

"No, she killed it."

"God in heaven!" said Gell, and it seemed to Fenella that at that moment the man's heart had broken.

She knew she ought to say more, but she could not do so—nothing being of consequence except the one terrible fact of the man's betrayal.

"God in heaven!" said Gell again, and he turned to leave her.

"What are you going to do in the morning?"

"I don't know . . . . yet."

"Where are you going to now?"

"To . . . . Ballamoar."

Again she knew that she ought to say more, but again she could not.

Gell was making for the gate, and Fenella, bankrupt in heart herself, wanted to comfort him.

"Mr. Gell," she said, "I have been doing you a great injustice. I ask you to forgive me."

With his hand on the bolt he turned his broken face to her.

"That's nothing—nothing now," he said.

And again she heard "God in heaven!" as the gate closed behind him.

II

" Ah, here you are, dear ! "

It was Janet who had heard the hum of Stowell's car on the drive and had come hurrying out to meet him.

" You've had a tiring day—I can see that," she said, as she poured out a cup of tea for him. " Ah, these high positions ! ' There's nothing to be got without being paid for,' as your father used to say."

To escape from Janet's solicitude and to tire himself out so that he might have a chance of sleeping that night, he walked down to the shore.

A storm was rising. The gulls were flying inland and their white wings were mingling with the black ones of the rooks. The fierce sky to the south, the cold grey of the sea to the north, the bleak church tower on the stark headland, looking like a blinded lighthouse—they suited better with his mood.

Fenella ! She must know everything by this time. How was he to meet her eyes in the morning?

Gell ! He, too, must know everything now. How every innocent thing he had done to help his friend would look like cunning bribery and cruel treachery !

It was a lie to say that a sin could be concealed. An evil act once done could never be undone; it could never be hidden away. A man might carry his sin out to sea, and bury it in the deepest part of the deep, but some day it would come scouring up before a storm as the broken seaweed came, to lie open and naked on the beach.

The sky darkened and he turned back. On the way home he met Robbie Creer, and they had to shout to each other above the fury of the wind. The farmer had been over to the Nappin (the fields above the Point) and found hidden fissures in the soil three feet deep. They would lose land before morning.

At dinner Janet did her best to make things cheerful. There was the sweet home atmosphere—the wood fire with its odour of resin and gorse, the snow-white table-cloth, the silver candlesticks, all the old-fashioned daintiness. But Stowell was preoccupied and hardly listened to Janet's chattering. So she went early to her room, saying she was sure he wished to be alone—his father always did, during the adjournment of a serious case. His father again ! How her devotion to his father drove the iron into his soul !

It was late and the rain had begun to slash the window-panes when he heard the front door bell ringing. After a few moments be heard it ringing again, more loudly and insistently. Nobody answered it. The household must be asleep.

Then came a hurried knocking at the window of the dining-room and a voice, which was like the wind itself become articulate, crying out of the darkness,

" Let me in ! "

It was Gell. For the first time in his life Stowell felt a spasm of physical fear. But he remembered something which Gell had said at the door of the railway carriage in Douglas on the day of the trial of the Peel fisherman (" *I should have killed the other man* "), and that strengthened him. Anything was better than the torture of a hidden sin—anything !

" Go back to the door—I'll open it," he called through the closed window, and then he walked to the porch.

His heart was beating hard. He thought he knew what was coming. But when Gell entered the house he was not the man Stowell had expected—with flaming eyes and passionate voice— but a poor, broken, irresolute creature. His hair was disordered, his step was weak and shuffling, and he was stretching out his nervous hands on coming into the light as if still walking in the darkness.

" I had to come and tell you. She's guilty. She has con-fessed," he said.

And then he collapsed into a chair and broke into pitiful moaning. It was too cruel. He could have taken the girl's word against the world, yet she had deceived him.

" Did she say . . . . who . . . . "

" No."

" No? "

" I didn't ask. Some miserable farm-hand, I suppose—some brute, some animal. Damn him, whoever he is ! Damn him ! Damn him to the devil and hell ! "

Stowell felt a boundless relief, yet a sense of sickening duplicity.

" But what matter about the man? " said Gell. " It's the girl who has deceived me. I daresay I'm not the first either. Perhaps her step-father didn't turn her out for nothing. There may have been something to say for the old scoundrel."

Choking with hypocrisy, Stowell found himself pleading for the girl. Perhaps . . . . who could say? . . . . perhaps she had been more sinned against than sinning.

" Then why didn't she tell me? " said Gell. His voice was like a wail.

" Who can say . . . . " (Stowell felt a throb in his throat and was speaking with difficulty), " who can say she wasn't trying to save you pain . . . . knowing how you believed in her and cared for her? "

" But if she had only told me," said Gell. " If she had only been straight with me! "

Stowell felt himself on the edge of terrible revelations. But he controlled himself. If Bessie had concealed part of the truth what right had he to reveal it? After a moment of silent terror he asked Gell what he meant to do in the morning.

" Advise her to amend her plea and cast herself on the mercy of the Court."

" Yes, that is the only proper course now," said Stowell, and then Gell rose to go.

It was a wild night. The wind was higher than ever by this time and the rain on the windows was rattling like hail. Stowell asked Gell to sleep the night at Ballamoar, secretly hoping he would refuse. He did. He had bespoken a bed at the Railway Inn near to the station—he must go up by the first train in the morning.

Stowell saw him to the door, and held it open with his shoulder against the wind, which swirled through the hall, making the flame of the lamp on the landing to flame up in its funnel. Outside there was the slashing of leaves and the crackling of boughs among the elms around the lawn.

" Well, good-night," said Gell, and turning up the collar of his coat, he went off in the darkness and the rain.

Stowell turned back into the house with a sense of degradation he had never felt before. Oh, what a miserable coward a hidden sin made of a man! Sooner or later it would be revealed and then . . . . what then?

Suddenly he was startled by a new thought. Bessie's confession would give the trial an entirely different turn. If she pleaded guilty in the morning there would be nothing for the Jury to do. Either they would have to be dismissed or instructed to bring in a formal verdict. The verdict against the prisoner would depend upon the Judges. That is to say, Bessie's fate would depend upon him—upon him alone!

The first shock of this thought was terrible, but after a while he told himself that it came to the same thing in the end. The real responsibility was with the law. A judge was only the law's spokesman. For a given crime a given punishment. A judge did not make the sentence on a prisoner—he had only to pronounce it.

Strengthening himself so, he went to bed. For a long time he lay awake, listening to the many sounds of the storm. In the middle of the night he was startled out of his troubled sleep by a loud crash in the distance.

The morning broke fair, with a clear sky and the sea lying under the sunshine like a sleeping child. But as he drove off, after a scanty breakfast, he found the carriage-drive strewn with young leaves, the torn bough of an old elm stretching across his path, and a number of dead rooks lying about the lawn.

Outside the big gates he met Robbie Creer, who was riding barebacked on a farm horse. The farmer had been over to the Nappin and seen what he had expected. The headland was down; there was a Gob (a mouth) where the Point had been, and the sea was flowing between two cliffs that had been torn asunder.

Driving hard, Stowell arrived early at Castletown and found a crowd at the Castle gate, waiting for the trial as for a show. He was passing through the Deemster's private entrance when he had a vision of a scene which the spectators could not be counting upon. What if the prisoner, while making her confession, accused her Judge?

Joshua Scarff, in his coloured spectacles, was waiting at the door to the Deemster's room.

"I'm afraid your Honour is not well this morning," said Joshua.

"A little headache, that's all," said Stowell.

But he had stumbled on the threshold (a bad omen) and was wondering what would happen before he came out again.

CHAPTER THIRTY

THE VERDICT

WHEN the Court resumed Gell rose, with a haggard face, to make an announcement.

In accordance with the suggestion of his Excellency, the accused had been seen during the adjournment (though not by him), with the result that she had confessed to having given birth to a child and being the cause of its death.

"In these circumstances," he said, speaking in a husky voice, "I have taken the only course open to me—that of advising her to revise her plea, and with the permission of the Court she will now do so."

There was a moment of agitation in which the Court was understood to assent, and then Bessie was called upon to plead again. But hardly had she risen at the call of the Deemster when she broke down utterly and sob followed sob at every question that was put to her. At length she bowed her head and that was accepted as her plea of guilty.

Then Gell rose again and said,

" Although the prisoner pleads guilty to causing the death of her child, she says she did not so wilfully. Therefore I propose to put her back in the box to prove extenuating circumstances."

Once more the Court agreed, but when Bessie was removed from the dock to the witness-box she broke down again and not a word could be got out of her.

" It is only natural," said Gell, " that she should feel shame at having to take back what she said yesterday."

The Deemster bowed, and speaking with an obvious effort he appealed to the girl to answer the questions of her advocate. But still Bessie sobbed and made no answer.

" The Court has nothing left to it but to go on to judgment," said the Attorney-General.

At that moment, when the trial seemed to be brought to a stand-still, Fenella (sitting near to the witness-box) was seen to lean over and whisper to Gell, who rose and asked to be allowed to make a suggestion—that inasmuch as the accused was unable to answer for herself, somebody else, who knew what she wished to say, should be empowered to answer for her.

The Deemster, seeing what was coming, seemed to catch his breath, but after a moment he agreed. The course proposed, although unusual, was not contrary to the interests of justice or altogether without precedent—a deaf and dumb witness always giving evidence by a speaking proxy. Therefore if the Attorney-General did not object . . . .

" Not at all," said the Attorney.

" In that case," said Gell, " I will ask the lady who received the prisoner's confession to speak on her behalf—Miss Stanley."

It was said afterwards, when the events of that day had a fierce light cast back upon them, that when Fenella stepped up to the witness-box, and stood side by side with the prisoner, ready to take her oath, the Deemster seemed scarcely able to recite the familiar words to her.

" Please tell the Court, as nearly as possible in her own words, what the prisoner told you," said Gell.

There was a deep and concentrated silence. Never before had anybody witnessed so strange a scene. Speaking calmly and firmly, Fenella told Bessie's story as Bessie herself had told it—her journey from the south of the island, the birth and death of her child, and the burying of it under the *Clagh-ny-Dooiney*.

When she had finished, and Bessie, who was stifling her sobs,

had bowed her head in reply to a question from Gell that she
assented to what had been said on her behalf), the Attorney-
General rose to cross-examine.

" Does the prisoner deny," he said, " that when she returned
home she told her mother of her condition? "

" Yes, her mother knew nothing about it."

" Does she deny that by keeping her condition secret from the
person most proper to know of it, she deliberately intended to put
her child away by violence? "

" No, she does not deny that, but says that when her baby came
the instinct of motherhood came too, and from that moment onward
the idea of taking its life was far from her heart."

" Does the prisoner wish the Court to believe that—in spite of
her subsequent conduct in concealing the birth and death of her
child and in secretly burying it? "

" Yes, she does, and if a court of men cannot believe it, a
court of women would, because . . . . "

But the Attorney-General, with a look of triumph, sat down
quickly, and Fenella, flushing up to her flaming eyes, stopped
suddenly.

There was another moment of deep silence in Court, and then
Gell, who had to struggle with his emotion, rose to re-examine.

" Does the prisoner say that when she killed her child she did
so unconsciously and under the influence of fear? "

" Yes, under the influence of fear—fear of her step-father who
had behaved like a brute to her."

" Does she think that, however lamentable her act, she was
moved to it by pardonable motives? "

" Not pardonable motives merely," said Fenella, flaming up
again, " but nobly unselfish ones."

" Nobly unselfish motives! " said the Attorney-General, rising
again.   " Will the witness please tell the Court what she means
by nobly unselfish motives in a case like this? "

" I mean," said Fenella, hesitating for a moment, looking up at
the Deemster and then (before she could be stopped) speaking
with passion and rapidly, " I mean that this girl was betrayed at
the time of her sorest need by one who should have protected her,
not taken advantage of her. I mean that, falling in love afterwards with another man—a good man who was willing to make
her his wife—she committed the crime solely and only in an effort
to cover up her fault and to save her honour in the eyes of the man
who loved her. I mean, too, that the real guilt lies not so much
with this poor creature who sits here in her shame, as with the man
who used her, caring nothing for her, and then left her to bear the

consequences of their sin alone. Shame on him! Shame on him! May no good man own him for a friend! May no good woman take him for a husband! May he live to . . . . ''

The irregular outburst was interrupted by a cry from the advocates' benches. Gell had risen with wild eyes. He seemed to be trying to speak. His mouth opened but he said nothing, and after looking first at Fenella and then at the Deemster he sank back to his seat. And then Fenella, as if realising what she had done, sat also.

There were some moments of uneasy silence, and then the Attorney-General rose for the last time.

" It is impossible," he said, " not to be moved by what we have just heard, however improper on legal grounds it may have been. But the Court will not allow themselves to be carried away by their feelings. It is the natural consequence of great crimes that they should bring great suffering. The prisoner has confessed to a great crime. She has failed to establish proof of extenuating circumstances. Therefore, for the protection of human life, as well as the good name of this island, I ask for the utmost penalty of the law."

After that there was a long pause, broken only by some whispering on the bench. It was observed that the Deemster took no part in it, except to bend his head when the Governor and the Clerk of the Rolls leaned across and spoke to him. At length, with a manifest effort, and in a low voice (so low that the people in Court had to lean forward to hear him) he began to address the Jury.

II

" When a prisoner pleads Guilty," he said, " it is usual for the Court to proceed at once to the sentence. But in the present unhappy case it has been thought right that the Judge, in directing the Jury to find a formal verdict, should indicate the grounds on which the Court has based its judgment.

" The prisoner has pleaded guilty to taking the life of her new-born child. She has confessed that down to the hour of its birth she had the deliberate intention of making away with it, and the Court is unhappily compelled to find in her conduct only too many evidences of that design.

" But she has also said that after her child's birth, under the divine love and compassion of awakened motherhood, she repented of her intention of killing it, and that it came to its death by accident—the accident of semi-consciousness and the consequences of her fear. The Court would gladly accept this explanation if

19

it could be corroborated by the evidence. Unfortunately it cannot. On the contrary the prisoner's subsequent behaviour points to an entirely different conclusion. Therefore the Court has nothing before it but the prisoner's confession that she intended to take the life of her child, and the fact that she did indeed take it."

The Deemster paused (Gell had risen and was seen crushing his way out of Court); then he continued,

" How her child came by its death is between God and her conscience. It is not for me, or perhaps for any man, to read the secret of a woman's heart in the dark hour of the birth of her misbegotten child. Into the cloud of that mystery only the eye of Heaven can follow her. But I should fail in my duty as a Judge if I did not try to show that the Court is fully conscious of the physical weaknesses and spiritual temptations which lie in the way of a woman who is in the position of the accused."

Then followed, during some breathless moments, such speaking as nobody present had ever heard before except from Stowell himself, and only from him on the day when he snatched from the gallows the rag of a woman who had killed her husband.

It was a contrast of the conditions attending the birth of a child born in wedlock, and of a child born illegitimate. They all knew the first. The beloved young wife watching with a thrilling heart for the signs of that coming event which was to complete her joy; the happy months in which she is shielded from all harm; the tender solicitude of her husband; her own sweet and secret preparations for the little stranger who is to come; the guesses as to its sex; the discussions as to its name—until at length, in the fulness of its appointed time, the child born in wedlock comes, like an angel floating out of the sunrise, into a world that is waiting for it to take it into its arms.

But the child born out of wedlock—what of that? The poor mother, betrayed perhaps, abandoned perhaps, bereft of the love she counted upon, living for months in fear of every accusing eye, in dread of the being under her heart who is coming to shame her, to drive her from her home, to make her an outcast and a byword among women—until at last she creeps away to hide herself in some secret place, where, alone, in the darkness of night, distraught, amid the groans as of a thunderstorm, she faces death to bring her fatherless babe into a world that wants it not.

" What wonder if sometimes," said the Deemster, " in the pain of her body and the disorder of her soul, a woman (all the more if she has hitherto borne a good character) should be tempted to escape from her threatening disgrace by killing the child who is the innocent cause of it? "

But rightly or wrongly, the law could take no account of such temptations. In the great eye of Justice the issues of life and death were in God's hands only. Life was sacred, and not more sacred was the life that came in the palace, with statesmen waiting in the antechamber, the life of the heir to a throne, than the life that came in the hovel and under the thatch, the life of the bastard who was to run barefoot on the roads.

"It may be thought to be a hard law which takes no account of temptations to which women are exposed when nature demands that penalty from them which it never demands from men. But we who sit here have nothing to do with that. Judges are sworn to administer the law as they find it, whatever their own feelings may be. Therefore the Court has now no choice but to direct the Jury to find a verdict of guilty against the prisoner."

There was a deep drawing of breath in Court, and everybody thought the Deemster had finished, but after another short pause, in a tremulous voice which vibrated through all hearts, he continued,

"But the Jury has a right which the Judges cannot exercise— they can go beyond the law. And if, having heard the evidence in this case, and having God and a good conscience before them, the Jury, in finding their formal verdict, can come to a conclusion favourable to the prisoner's story, they may recommend her to the mercy of the Crown, and thereby lead, perhaps, to the lessening of her punishment, and even to the wiping of it out altogether. If not, the law must take its course, at the discretion of the Governor as the representative of the King."

When the Deemster's tremulous voice had ceased the jurymen put their heads together for a moment. Then one of them rose to ask if they might retire to their own room to consider the point left to them by His Honour.

"The Court agrees," said the Governor, and the jurymen trooped out.

The Judges and the advocates went out also, and the prisoner (who had been clinging to Fenella's hand) was removed. Only the spectators remained in their places. They were afraid to lose them for the concluding scene.

III

In a small unventilated room overlooking the Keep the Jury considered their share of the verdict.

"Gentlemen," said one (he was an auctioneer and a Town

Commissioner), " you heard what the Deemster said. We can't let her off but we can recommend her to mercy."

" Why should we? " said another, a tall landowner with a bad reputation about women. " She killed her child. Let her swing, I say."

" But she said she didn't intend to and that she was out of herself and frightened by her step-father," said a third—a fat butcher who was sitting astride on a chair and making it creak under him.

" Chut! That was only an after-thought," said a fourth—a little bald-headed English grocer.

" Still and for all we know what Dan Baldromma is," said the butcher, " an infidel who believes neither in God nor the devil."

" He's devil enough himself," said the grocer. " His father was the 'angman."

" That was his uncle," said the butcher.

" No, but his father. They called him Dan the Black, and after the 'anging of Patrick Kelly of Kentraugh . . . . "

" Question! Question! " cried the Town Commissioner. " Let's keep to the point, gentlemen."

" Let's get finished and away," said the grocer. " I've 'ad an addition to my family, I may tell you. A son at last after four daughters. My wife's getting up to-day and we're to 'ave a turkey for dinner. Let the woman off, I say."

" But we can't man. Didn't you hear what the Deemster said? "

" Then let the 'uzzy 'ang."

" Are we to recommend the girl to mercy—that's the question," said the Town Commissioner.

" Why shouldn't we? " said the butcher. " Hundreds and tons of girls have done as bad before now, and nobody a penny the wiser. Why make flesh of one and fowl of another? "

" If we show mercy to women of this sort we'll only encourage them in their bad conduct," said the landowner.

This led to a random discussion on the question of Women or Men, which were the worst? The landlord was loud in denunciation of women, the butcher was more indulgent.

" Look here," said the butcher, " this isn't a game a woman can go into a corner and play all by herself, you know. For every bad woman there's a bad man knocking about somewhere."

" A man isn't always filling his house with by-children anyway," said the landowner.

" No," said the butcher, " but he is sometimes filling other people's though."

" That's personal, and I won't stand it," cried the landowner, and then there were loud shouts with much smiting of the table.

In the midst of the tumult a quiet voice was heard to say,

" Hadn't we better lay this matter before the Lord, brothers? "

It was a northside farmer and local preacher, who (not always to his financial advantage) had made it the rule of his life, whether in the reaping of his corn or the sowing of his turnips, to wait for Divine guidance. In another moment he was on his knees, and one by one his fellow-jurymen, including the long landowner, had slithered down after him.

When they rose they were apparently of one opinion—that inasmuch as nobody except God knew why Bessie had killed her child (being alone and under the cloud of night) the only thing to do was to leave her to the Lord.

Meantime Gell, with restless and irregular footsteps, was striding about in the court-yard. Fenella's outburst had fallen on him like a flash of lightning in the darkness. Everything had suddenly become clear—all the vague fears that had haunted him so long, the suspicions he had thrust behind his back, the facts he had been unable to understand. What a blind fool he had been!

Stowell! His life-long friend, on whose word he would have staked his soul! There must have been a conspiracy to deceive him. Both Stowell and Bessie had been in it—Stowell to get rid of the girl he no longer wanted, and Bessie to cover up her disgrace by marrying him. What a plot! The woman he had loved and the man he had worshipped! He saw himself hoodwinked by both of them, lied to, perhaps laughed at. His life, his faith, his love had crashed down in a moment. It was too cruel, too damnable!

The air was chill, though the sun was shining, but Gell took off his wig and carried it in his hand, for his head seemed to be afire.

After a time the hatred he had felt for Bessie became centred, with a hundredfold intensity, upon Stowell. Even if Bessie had begun with an intention of betraying him, she must have repented of it afterwards, and committed her crime, poor girl, because (as Fenella had said) she had come to love him. But Stowell had carried on his deception to the last moment. He was carrying it on now, when he was sitting in judgment on his own victim. He meant to sentence her to death, too. Yes, under all his fine phrases it was easy to see that he meant to sentence her. But if he did so Gell would murder him.

" Yes, by God, I'll murder him," he thought.

In the darkness of her cell, with no light on her tortured face except that of the candle behind the grill, Bessie, breaking into another fit of hysteria, was reproaching Fenella with deceiving her.

"You told me that if I confessed the Deemster would let me off. But he is going to condemn me. Why couldn't you let me be What for did you come here at all? I didn't ask you, did I?"

"Be calm," said Fenella, "and I will explain everything."

After awhile Bessie regained her composure and then she asked for forgiveness.

"I beg your pardon. Sometimes I don't know what I am saying. It has been like that all through the time of my trouble. It was very wrong to forget how you spoke up for me in Court. You'll forgive me, won't you?"

And then Fenella, though sorely in need of comfort herself, comforted the girl and reassured her. The Court might be compelled to sentence her, as it had sentenced other girls for similar crimes, but the sentence would not be carried out. It never was in these days.

"Besides," she said, "the jury will recommend you to mercy, and then the Judges will exercise their discretionary power to reduce your punishment."

Bessie's eyes began to shine.

"You must really forgive me . . . . And Alick—do you think Alick will forgive me too?"

"Yes, when he sees that what you did was done out of your love for him."

"How good you are! . . . . And shall we be able to leave the Isle of Man and go away somewhere?"

"Perhaps . . . . some day."

"Oh, how good you are! I don't know what I've done for you to be so good to me. I didn't think anybody except a girl's mother could be so good to her."

She was like a child again. Her face, though still wet, was beaming. In the selfishness of her suffering it had not occurred to her before that her comforter had been suffering also, but now, in some vague way, she became aware of it.

"If they ask me who he was," she said, in a whisper (meaning who had been her fellow-sinner), "I'll never tell them—never!"

Fenella's humiliation was abject. "When we go back to Court," she said, "you must be brave, whatever happens."

"Will you let me hold your hand?" said Bessie.

And Fenella, scarcely able to speak, answered,

"Yes."

In the Deemster's room there was a painful silence. The Clerk of the Rolls was under the deeply-recessed window, turning over the crinkling folios of the Depositions in the case to be taken next. The Governor, stretched out in the leathern bound armchair before the empty fireplace, was smoking hard and trying to justify himself to his own conscience. Stowell was sitting at the end of the long table, with his head in his hands, gazing down at the red blotting-pad in front of him.

No one spoke. Occasionally there came from without the mournful cry of the gulls flying over the harbour, and, at one moment, the ululation of a crew of Irish sailors who were weighing anchor on a schooner in the bay.

The profound silence around only made louder the thunder in Stowell's soul. He knew he was at the crisis of his life. On what he did now the future of his life depended.

The address to the Jury had been a fearful ordeal, but the sentence would be terrible. To sentence Bessie Collister, having been the first cause of her crime—could he do it? It might only be a formal sentence (the Crown being certain to commute the punishment), but the awful words prescribed by the Statute—would they not choke in his very throat?

And then Fenella! Her voice was ringing in his ears still: " Shame on him! Let no good man own him for a friend! Let no good woman take him for a husband! "

" And what will be the end? " he asked himself.

He heard the door open behind him. A low hum of voices came down the staircase from the Court-house. There was a footstep on the carpeted floor. Somebody by his side was speaking. It was Joshua Scarff.

" The Jury are ready to return to Court, your Honour."

IV

When Stowell resumed his seat on the bench, and the buzz of conversation had subsided, he was conscious of the presence of only three persons besides himself—Bessie in the dock with Fenella by her side, and Alick Gell, with distorted face and wig a little awry, in the bench in front of them.

The Jurymen filed back. The Clerk of the Rolls read out their names and then asked for their formal verdict.

" You find the prisoner Guilty, according to the instructions of the Court? "

" Aw, yes, guilty enough, poor soul," said the foreman (it was the northside farmer), " but lave her to the Lord, we say."

There was a titter at this quaint finding, but it was quickly suppressed. Then the Clerk of the Rolls said,

"I assume that means that you recommend her to mercy?"

"Aw, yes, mercy enough too," said the foreman, "for when the sacrets of all hearts are revealed it's mercy we'll all be wanting."

After that Stowell was conscious of a still deeper hush in Court. He saw Bessie, in the full glare of her shame, standing in the dock, holding the rail with one hand and clinging to Fenella with the other.

He heard himself asking her if she had anything to say why judgment should not be pronounced upon her. She made no answer, but there was a strange expression of frightened hope in her face. He understood—she was expecting that he would save her even at the last moment.

At that sight there came to him one of those frightful impulses which tempt people on dizzy heights, from sheer fear of danger, to fling themselves into the abyss below.

"Prisoner at the bar," he said, "it has been said on your behalf that you were first led to do what you did by the act of one who remains unpunished while you have to bear the full weight of your fall. If you think it will lessen the burden of your crime to plead this as an extenuating circumstance speak—it is not too late to do so."

Bessie made no reply, and Stowell, who felt Fenella's eyes fixed on him, continued,

"Don't be afraid. If you think it will lighten your guilt in the eyes of the Court to mention that man's name, mention it."

Bessie swayed a little, as if dizzy, looked round at Fenella, and then turned back to the bench and shook her head.

The hush in Court was broken by a rustle of astonishment. Had the Deemster lost himself? Stowell was conscious of a movement by his side and of the Governor saying, in an angry whisper,

"Go on, for God's sake!"

At length, in a voice so low as to be only just heard even in the breathless silence, he said,

"Elizabeth Corteen, you have pleaded guilty to the charge of taking the life of your innocent child, the little helpless babe who had no other natural protector than the mother who bore it on her bosom. By this act you have brought yourself under the condemnation of the law, and it is for the law to punish you. But out of regard to your sufferings and the uncertainty as to your motives, the Jury have recommended you to mercy, and it will be my duty to see that their prayer is sent, through His Excellency the Governor, to the high and proper authority, in the hope that the measure of pardon which, in all but exceptional cases, is granted to persons in your position, may be extended to you also."

The tears were rolling down Bessie's cheeks, but Stowell saw that she was still looking up at him with the same expression.

"Meantime," he continued, "and however that may be, the Court has no choice but to condemn you to the punishment prescribed by law. We who sit here must act according to our oath and our duty. Justice" (he was pointing with a trembling hand to the motto under his father's picture) "is the most sacred thing on earth, and even . . . . even if your fellow-sinner himself sat on this bench, his first duty would be to Justice, for Justice is above all."

Then lowering his head and speaking rapidly, in a muffled and indistinguishable whisper, Stowell pronounced the sentence of death. None of it seemed to be clearly heard until he reached the last words (" and may God have mercy on your soul "), and then there came a loud scream from the dock.

Bessie, who had been leaning forward and listening intently (the look of hope and expectation on her face darkening to dismay and terror), had dropped back, and would have fallen but for Fenella, who had leapt up and caught her.

"Remove the prisoner," said the Governor sharply, and at the next moment the constables were carrying the girl out of Court screaming and sobbing.

But before she had gone there was a movement in the benches of the advocates. Alick Gell had risen again, with wild eyes, and he was shouting after her:

"Never mind, Bessie! I would rather be you than your Judge."

There was consternation in Court. Everybody was on his feet to look after the prisoner, and at Gell, who was being hustled out after her. But hardly had the door closed behind them, when there was another cry in Court:

" The Deemster! "

Stowell had risen also. He had stood looking after the prisoner until her last cry had died away in the corridor. Then he had turned about, as if intending to leave the bench, taken a step forward, stumbled, and dropped to one knee.

The Governor rose and reached forward to help him. But he recovered himself immediately. His face was very pale, but he smiled, a pitiful smile, as if saying, " A little dizziness, nothing more." and waved off assistance.

Bracing himself up, he stood aside for the Governor to go before him, and then walked out of Court with a firm step. The ring of his tread was plainly heard as he passed through the green baize door that led to the Deemster's room.

The spectators looked into each other's faces as if bewildered by what they had seen and heard. Although the business of the day was not yet over most of them trooped out, feeling that they had been witnessing a drama whereof only a part had been revealed to them—as by dark shadows on a white blind.

END OF FOURTH BOOK

FIFTH BOOK
THE REPARATION

CHAPTER THIRTY-ONE
" VICTOR! VICTOR! MY VICTOR! "

" GOOD heavens, how was I to know that things would turn out so badly? "

It was the Governor, alone with Stowell in the Deemster's room, at the end of the second day of the Court of General Gaol Delivery.

" As for you, what have you to reproach yourself with? So far as this case is concerned you have done nothing that is wrong or irregular. The girl was guilty. You gave her a fair trial. The law required that she should be condemned. You had to condemn her. Then why take things so tragically? "

" But Fenella? "

" She will get over it. Of course she will. What sensible woman is going to throw away the happiness of a life-time because of something that happened before she came on to the scene? "

" You heard what she said, Sir? "

" I did, and thought it nonsense. I heard what you said also, and thought it madness. What a providential escape! Thank God it is all over! The miserable case is at an end. Let us think no more about it."

An Inspector of Police came into the room to say that Miss Stanley had left the Castle at the close of the murder trial and asked him to tell her father that she was going home by train. The Governor, with knitted eyebrows and a frown, dismissed the Inspector, and then said to Stowell, as he turned to go,

" All the same I am bound to say the whole thing has been unfortunate—damnably unfortunate! "

Stowell continued to sit for some minutes in his robes after the Governor had left him. Joshua Scarff came with a glass of brandy.

" Take this, your Honour. It will strengthen your nerves for your drive home. I could see you were not well when you arrived this morning."

Stowell had drunk the brandy and was setting down the tumbler when the Inspector came back to say that after the murder trial he had liberated Dan Baldromma, but had just been compelled to arrest somebody else.

" Who else? "

" Mr. Gell.   The gentleman seems to have gone clean off it, Sir.   It's the loss of his case, I suppose."

Ever since the Court had risen he had been demanding to be allowed to see the Deemster and threatening what he would do to him.   So to prevent the Advocate from doing a mischief the police had put him in the cells.

" Set him at liberty at once," said Stowell.

" Before your Honour leaves the Castle? "

" Instantly."

The Inspector being gone (with the intention of disobeying the Deemster's command in order to ensure his safety), Joshua Scarff proceeded to read Gell's conduct by quite a different light. It was easy to see now that Mr. Gell had been the girl's fellow-sinner and therefore the cause of her crime.

" Pity!   Great pity! " said Joshua, as he helped Stowell to unrobe.   " But such connections always begin to end badly."

There were still a few of the spectators at the gate, waiting to see the Deemster away, and when he came out, with his white face, another wave of sympathy went out to him.

" They've been putting the young colt into the shafts too soon—that's what it is, I tell thee."

Driving over the harbour bridge in his automobile Stowell began to feel better.   The fresh air from the sea, after the close atmosphere of the Court-house, brought the blood back to his brain, and he thought he saw things more clearly.

The Governor had been right.   He could not have acted otherwise without being false to his oath as a Judge.   And if the miserable fact remained that he should never have been the Judge in this case at all, it was Fenella herself, above everybody else, who had thrust him into the furnace of that position.   Surely she would remember this, and it would plead in her heart for him?

Half-a-mile beyond the town he passed the Governor's big blue landau, and realised that by some half-conscious impulse he was taking the road to Government House instead of the direct way home.   So much the better!   He must see Fenella at the first possible moment, and find out what his fate was to be.

His spirits rose as he bounded along.   Granted he had done wrong in the first instance, terribly and cruelly wrong, hadn't he had many excuses? If Bessie Collister had told her everything, surely Fenella would see this, too, and seeing it, would understand?

But the great fact of all was that (except for the first catastrophe) his love of Fenella had been the root cause of all that had happened. If he had not loved Fenella with that deep, unconquerable, unquenchable love which had swept everything else away (all qualms and perhaps all conscience), nothing worse could have occurred. He would have married that poor girl now lying in prison. Yes, whatever the consequences to himself, he would have married her before Gell came back into her life, and further complications ensued. But after Fenella returned to the island no other woman had been possible to him. Surely she would see this also? And, if she did, nothing else would matter to either of them—nothing in this world.

Presently, driving at high speed, he realised that the half-conscious impulse which had carried him on to the road to Government House was sweeping him on to the rocky shelf on the coast along which he had driven with Fenella on the day he took his oath.

How fortunate! What was that she had said, then, as they sang together in the fulness of their joy over the hum of the engine and the boom of the sea?—that love, what she called love, never died and never changed, and if she loved anybody, and anything happened to him, she would fight the world for him, even though he were in the wrong!

Even though he were in the wrong!

She would do it now! He was sure she would! Yes, the first shock of the wretched revelation being over, she would see how he had suffered, and how he had striven to do the right, and then—then everything would be well.

Thus, as he flew over the roads, he built himself up in the hope of Fenella's forgiveness. But as he approached Government House his heart failed him again. Something whispered that the excuses he had been making for himself were no better than a pretence—that Fenella would see him now for the first time as the man he really was, not the man she had imagined him to be.

And then—what would happen then?

II

As soon as the trial was over and Bessie, weeping bitterly, was taken back to the cells, Fenella had left Castle Rushen. She was ashamed. Remembering her wild outburst under the Attorney-General's examination, she was reproaching herself bitterly.

Whatever Victor Stowell had done, what right had she to denounce him? She of all others! In open Court too!

And then Gell! Although nobody else had understood her, he had done so. He might have been living in a fool's paradise, but was it for her her to reveal the awful truth to him? In public, too, and at that harrowing moment?

To escape from the pain of self-reproach she kept on telling herself, as she went back in the train, that Stowell had deceived her. Oh, if he had only confessed, at any rate to her, she thought she could have forgiven him in spite of all. But no, he had hidden everything down to the last moment, and left her to find him out.

On reaching home she excused herself to old Miss Green and hurried up to her bedroom. Her head ached and her heart was sore—the young woman she had been working for had been found guilty and condemned. She told her maid she was tired, and if anybody asked for her she was not to be disturbed.

Two hours passed. Her heart was going through a wild riot of mingled anger and love. It was like madness. She loved Stowell; she hated him; she worshipped him; she despised him. At one moment she recalled with a bitter laugh the mockery of his questioning of Bessie Collister in the dock; at the next she remembered with scorching tears the pathos of his sentencing her.

Obscure motives were operating in her soul to intensify her pain. Jealous? She, jealous of that illiterate country girl who had murdered her illegitimate child—what nonsense! No, her idol was broken. She had set it so high and now it was in the dust.

She expected Stowell to come to her as soon as his Court was over. Again and again she raised her head from her wet pillow to listen for the sound of his car on the drive. Yet when a knock came at her door and her maid announced the arrival of the Deemster (never dreaming that the injunction against callers had been intended to apply to him) her first impulse was to send him away.

"Say I'm unwell and can't see him," she cried from her bed.

But at the next moment she was up and whispering at the door,

"Show Mr. Stowell into the library and tell him I shall be down presently."

Her voice was hoarse; her face was aflame; her eyes were red from persistent weeping. No water could sponge away those marks of her emotion. Never mind! He should see how he had made her suffer. She would go downstairs and charge him, face to face, with his deceit and hypocrisy, and then—then fling herself into his arms.

But when she opened the library door and saw him standing on the hearthrug, with head down and a look of utter abasement, her courage failed her. She dare not look twice at his ravaged face, so she sank on to the sofa and covered her eyes with her hands.

Several minutes passed in which neither of them spoke. There was no sound except that of his laboured breathing and of the ticking of the clock on the mantelpiece. "If he does not speak soon," she thought, "I shall break into tears and fly out of the room."

But she did not move, and at last came his voice, humble and broken, and thrilling through and through her:

"Fenella!"

She did not answer; she could not; and again, after another moment of silence, he said,

"Fenella, I have come to ask you to forgive me."

She wanted to burst out crying, and to prevent herself from doing so she broke into a flood of wrath.

"Forgive you?" she said. "Ask that poor creature in Castle Rushen to forgive you—that poor girl whom you have just condemned for a crime that is the consequence of your own sin."

He did not reply for a moment, and then came the same humble, unsteady voice, saying,

"No doubt you are quite right, quite justified, but if you knew everything—that I could not help myself—that it was the law . . . ."

"Oh, I know nothing about your laws," she cried, leaping up and crossing the room, "but they are unjust and barbarous and against reason and humanity if they allow a girl to be condemned to death for a crime like that while the Judge who was the first cause of it sits in judgment on his own victim."

"You are right there too," said Stowell, "but if you knew how I tried to avoid sitting on the case, and only allowed myself to do so at last in the hope of seeing justice done and thereby making some sort of amends . . . ."

"Amends!" cried Fenella. "What amends can there be for a wrong like that? Oh, I hate people who think they can make amends for one fault by committing another."

There was silence again for a moment and then Stowell said,

"You are right there also. There is a kind of wrongdoing that cannot be atoned for. I see that now. But if you knew how I have suffered for it and still suffer . . . ."

"Suffer? Why shouldn't you suffer? Isn't that poor girl suffering? Hasn't she suffered all along? And whatever you do for her now, won't she go on suffering to the last day and hour of her life?"

He dropped his head still lower under the lash of Fenella's scorn.

"That is not all either," she said in a broken voice, sitting on the sofa again and brushing her handkerchief over her eyes. "Perhaps that girl is not the only one who is suffering. I wanted to think so well of you, to be so proud of you. You were to be the defender of women, fighting their battle for them when they were wronged and helpless. And when you became a Judge . . . . Oh, I cannot bear to think of it. You have disappointed and deceived me. You are not the man I took you to be."

Outside the sun was setting. A dull ray from it was falling on his haggard face and brushing her bronze-brown hair.

"I thought you loved me too. It was so sweet to think you loved me—me only—never having loved anybody else. Every woman has felt like that, hasn't she? I have anyway. Other men might be faithless, but not you, not Victor Stowell. And yet, for the sake of your poor fancy for this country girl . . . ."

"Fenella!"

"Oh, what a fool I've been," she cried, leaping up again and dashing the tears from her eyes. "Forgive you? Never while that girl lies in prison as the consequence of your sin."

Stowell could bear no more. Stepping forward, he laid hold of Fenella by the shoulders, and approaching his face to her face he said,

"Listen to me, Fenella. I have done wrong—I know that. I am not here to excuse or defend myself, and if your heart does not plead for me I have nothing to say. But I swear before God that I have loved you with all my soul and strength, and if it hadn't been for that . . . ."

"Loved me!" cried Fenella, between a laugh and a sob. And then in the wild delirium of the sheer woman, she said,

"What proof of your love have you given to me compared to the proof you have given to that girl? Oh, when I think of it I could almost find it in my heart to envy her. I *do* envy her. Yes, degraded and shamed and condemned and in prison as she is, I envy her, and could change places with her this very minute. I would have given you anything in the world rather than this should be—anything, my honour, myself . . . ."

"Fenella!"

"Let me go! You are driving me mad. Leave me. I hate you. I despise you. You have broken my heart. I thought you were brave and true, but what are you but a common . . . ."

" Fenella ! "

" Coward! Hypocrite! Let me go! "

But she had no need to wrench herself away from him. His hands fell from her shoulders like lead, and at the next moment she was gone from the room.

He stood for a while where she had left him with the echo of her stinging words ringing in his ears. Bitter, unjust and cruel as they had been, he was struggling to excuse her. She did not understand. Bessie had not told her all. Presently she would come back and ask his pardon.

But she did not come, and after a while (it seemed like an eternity), feeling crushed, degraded, trampled upon, dragged in the dust and wounded in his tenderest affections, he left the room and the house.

Outside, where his automobile was standing, he still lingered, expecting to be called back. It was impossible that Fenella would let him part from her like this. He knew where she was—in the Governor's smoking-room which overlooked the drive. At the last moment she would knock at the window and cry, " Stay! "

Slowly he moved around his car, opening the bonnet, touching the engine, starting it, pulling on his long driving gloves. But still she gave no sign, and at length he prepared to step into his seat. Was this to be the end—the end of everything?

Meantime, Fenella, alone in her father's room and recovering from the storm of her anger, was beginning to be afraid. She wanted to go back to Stowell and say, " I was mad. I didn't know what I was saying. I love you so much."

But her pride would not permit her to do that, and she waited for Stowell to do something. Why didn't he burst through the door, throw his arms about her, and *compel* her to forgive him?

She listened intently for a long time, but there came no sound from the adjoining room. What was he doing? Presently she heard him coming out of the library, walking with a firm step down the corridor to the porch, opening the front door and closing it behind him.

Was he leaving her? Like this? Then he would never come back. She heard his footstep on the gravel and looking through the window she saw him, with his white face, raising his soft hat to wipe his perspiring forehead, and then climbing into the car. Could it be possible that he was going away without another word?

In spite of her jealousy and rage, she felt an immense admiration for the man who, loving her as she was sure he did, was yet so strong that he could leave her after she had insulted and

20

humiliated him. She wanted to throw up the window and cry, "Wait! I am coming out to you."

But no, her pride would not permit her to do that either, and at the next instant the car was moving away.

She watched it until it had disappeared behind the trees. Then she turned to go back to her bedroom. At the foot of the stairs she met Miss Green who, shocked at the sight of her disordered face, said,

"My goodness, Fenella! What has happened?"

In the plaintive voice of a crying child, Fenella answered,

"He has gone. I have driven him away."

Then she stumbled upstairs, locked the door of her room on the inside, threw herself face down on the bed, burst into a flood of tempestuous tears, and cried aloud to Stowell, now that he could no longer hear her—

"Victor! Victor! My Victor!"

CHAPTER THIRTY-TWO

THE VOICE OF THE SEA

"Forgive you? Never while that girl lies in prison as the consequence of your sin."

The words beat on Stowell's brain with the paralysing effect of a muffled drum. He was driving up the mountain road. Char-à-bancs, full of English visitors (who were laughing and singing in chorus), were coming down. The drivers shouted at him from time to time. This irritated him until he realised that his motor-car was oscillating from side to side of the road.

When he reached the top, where the road turns towards the glen, all the heart was gone out of him. The great scene no longer brought the old joyousness. With love lost and hope quenched the soul of the world was dead, and the heavens were dark above him.

At the bottom of the glen, where it dips into the Curragh, he came upon a group of bare-headed women, with their arms under their aprons, surrounding a little person with watery eyes, in a poke bonnet and a satin mantle. Mrs. Collister had returned from Castletown, and her neighbours were taking her home.

"Never mind, woman! It will be all set right at the judgment. And then the man will be found out and punished, too!"

At th coerner of the cross roads Dan Baldromma threw himself in front of the car, to draw it up, and in his raucous voice he fell on Stowell with a torrent of abuse.

" You've been locking up a respectable man, Dempster, but you can't lock up his tongue, and the island is going to know what justice in the Isle of Man can be."

Stowell made no answer. Any poor creature could insult him now.

Janet was waiting for him at Ballamoar, with a fire in the library, and the tea-tray ready. But the sweet home atmosphere only made him think of the happiness that had been so nearly within his reach.

Seeing that something was amiss, Janet assumed her cheeriest tone, brought out two patterns of damask, laid them over chairs, and asked which Fenella would like best for her boudoir.

" I don't know. I can't say. But . . . . it doesn't matter now."

Janet gathered up her patterns and went out of the room without a word.

" Forgive you? Never while that girl lies in prison." The stinging words followed him to his bedroom. They broke up his sleep. They rang like the screech of an owl through the darkness of the night.

Next day, not trusting himself to drive his car, he returned to Castletown by train. There were only two first-class compartments and both were full. He was about to step into a third-class carriage when a voice cried,

" This way, Deemster. Always room enough for you."

There was to be a sitting of the Keys that day and the compartment was full of northside members. The talk was about yesterday's trial, and Stowell realised that his management of the case had created a favourable impression. Merciful to the prisoner? Yes, until her guilt was established, but then just, even at the expense of friendship.

This led to talk about Gell as the girl's fellow-sinner.

" Shocking! But it's not the first time he has been mixed up with a woman."

Stowell felt an intolerable shame at Gell's undeserved obloquy and his own unmerited glory, but he could say nothing.

" It will kill the old man," said one of the Keys. The train had drawn up at a side station and his voice was loud in the vacant air.

" Hush! "

The Speaker was in the next compartment.

When the train started again a little man with the face of a ferret began to make facetious references to " Fanny." Stowell's hands were itching to take the ribald creature by the throat and fling him out of the window, but something whispered, " Who are you to be the champion of virtue ? "

At Court that day, and the day following, he found it hard to concentrate. At one moment an advocate said,

" Perhaps your Honour is not well this morning ? "

" Oh no! I heard you. You were saying . . . . "

The rapidity of his mind enabled him to make up for his lapses in attention, and when his time came to sum up he was always ready.

He was indulgent to the accused. All the other prisoners were acquitted—the fat woman for the reason that, bad as her character might be, the characters of her drunken sailors were yet worse (therefore no credit could be attached to their evidence), and the boy who had embezzled on the ground that his superiors at the bank had been guilty of almost criminal negligence, and the four months he had been in prison already were sufficient to satisfy the claims of justice.

The boy's mother, who was standing at the back, threw her arms about him and kissed him when he stepped out of the dock, and then, turning her streaming face up to the bench, she cried,

" God bless you, Deemster! May you live long and every day of your life be a happy one."

Back at home, Stowell plunged into the task of drawing up the report for the English authorities which was to accompany the recommendation to mercy. In two days (having his father's library to fall back upon) he knew more about the grounds upon which the prerogative of the Crown could properly be exercised than anybody in the island had ever before been required to learn, and when he had finished his task he had no misgivings.

Bessie's sentence would be commuted to imprisonment. And then (life for the poor soul being at an end in the Puritanical old island) he must find some secret means of sending her away.

" Never while that girl . . . . " But wait! Only wait!

Being legislator as well as Judge, he attended the first meeting of Tynwald Court after his appointment. The Governor administered the oath to him in a private room, and then, taking his arm, led the way to the legislative chamber.

" Do you know it's six days since you were at Government House, my boy? What is Fenella to think of you ? "

" Has she . . . . has she been asking for me, Sir ? "

" Well, no, not to say asking, but still . . . . six days, you know."

Stowell sat on a raised daïs between the Attorney-General and Deemster Taubman, who was sufficiently recovered to hobble in on two sticks. The proceedings were of the kind that is usual in such assemblies, the Manx people being the children of their mothers, loving to talk much and about many things.

He found it difficult to fix his attention, and was watching for an opportunity to slip away, when the vain repetitions which are called debate suddenly ceased and the Governor called on an Inspector by Police to carry round a Bill which had to be signed by all.

In the interval of general conversation that followed, Deemster Taubman, a gruff and grizzly person, leaned back in his seat, put his thumbs in the armholes of his soiled white waistcoat and talked to Stowell.

"You did quite right in that case of the girl Collister, Sir. In fact you were only too indulgent. I have no pity for the huzzies who run away from the consequences of their misconduct. Murder is murder, and there is no proper punishment for it but death."

"But the Jury recommended the girl to mercy, and her sentence will be commuted," said Stowell.

"Eh? Eh? Then you haven't heard what has happened?"

"What?"

"The Governor has reported against the recommendation."

"Reported against it?"

"Certainly. And as the authorities in London are not likely to read the report and are sure to act on the Governor's advice, the girl will go to the gallows."

Stowell felt as if he had been struck over the eyes by an unseen hand. As soon as he had signed the Bill (in a trembling scrawl) he whispered to the Attorney-General that he was unwell and fled from the chamber.

"Humph!" said Taubman, looking after him. "That young man is going to break down, and no wonder. His appointment as Deemster was the maddest thing I ever knew."

II

"No, Mr. Stowell, no! You must stay in bed for the next two days at least. I must really insist this time. No work, no excitement, no heart-strain. Remember your father, and take my advice, Sir."

It was Doctor Clucas, who, sent for by Janet, had arrived at Ballamoar before Stowell got out of bed in the morning.

With closed eyes Stowell reviewed the situation. It was shocking, horrible, intolerable. Not for fifty years had a woman suffered the full penalty of such a crime. He must find some way to prevent it.

But after a while a terrible temptation came to him. " Why can't I leave things alone? " he asked himself.

He had done all he could be expected to do. If the Crown, acting on the advice of the Governor, refused to exercise its prerogative of mercy, what right had he to interfere?

It might be best for himself, too, that the law should take its course—best in the long run. If Bessie's sentence were commuted to imprisonment what assurance had he that on coming out of prison she would allow him to send her away from the island? On the contrary she might refuse to be banished, and if she found that the blame of her misfortune had fallen on Gell she might tell the truth to free him.

What then? *He* would be a dishonoured man. His position as a Judge would be imperilled; his marriage with Fenella would be impossible, and his whole life would crash down to a welter of disgrace and ruin. But if Bessie were gone there would be no further danger. And after all, it would not be he but the law that had taken her life.

" Then why can't I leave things alone? " he thought.

He decided to do so, but his decision brought him no comfort. Towards evening he got up and went out to walk in the farmyard. There he met Robbie Creer, who was just home from the mill with his head full of a pitiful story.

It was about Mrs. Collister. Since her daughter's trial the old woman had fallen into the habit of walking barefoot in the glen, chiefly at midnight, and generally in the neighbourhood of the *Clagh-ny-Dooiney*. At first she had seen a light. Then she had heard a pitiful cry. She was certain it was the cry of a child, a spirit-child, unbaptised and therefore unnamed, and for that reason doomed to wander the world, because unable to enter Paradise. At length she had taken heart of God and going out in her nightdress she had called through the darkness of the trees, " If thou art a boy I call thee John. If thou art a girl I call thee Joney." After that she had heard the cry no more, and now she knew it had been Bessie's child, and the bogh-millish was at rest.

This story of the old mother's developing insanity rested heavily on Stowell's heart and went far to shake his resolution.

After a day or two he began to find his own house and grounds haunted. He could not go into the library without the kind eyes in his mother's picture following him about the room with a pleading look. He could not sit in the dining-room after dinner without remembering his week-ends as a student-at-law, when his father and he would draw up at opposite cheeks of the hearth, and the great Deemster would talk of the great crimes, the great trials and the great Judges.

But his worst ordeal was with Janet. Not a word of explanation had passed between them, yet he was sure she knew everything. One evening, going into her sitting-room, he found her with her knitting on her lap, and a copy of the insular newspaper on the floor, looking out on the lawn with a far-off expression. That brought memories of another evening when he had told her that no girl on the island had ever fallen into trouble through him, or ever should do.

"Ah! Is that you, Victor?" she cried, recovering herself and making her needles click, but he had gone, and her voice followed him from the room.

Still wrestling with his temptation to stand aside and let the law take its course, Ballamoar became intolerable to him. On the lame excuse of his fortnightly court in the northside town he decided to go to Ramsey, and wrote to Mrs. Quayle to get his old rooms ready.

But going from Ballamoar to his chambers was like leaping out of the fire into the furnace. When he opened a disordered drawer up came the Castletown portrait of Bessie Collister like a ghost out of the gloom. When he went for a walk to tire himself for the night his steps involuntarily turned towards the pier where the lighthouse had been shattered by lightning. When he returned and was putting the key in the lock of his outer door he had the tingling sense of a woman's warm presence behind him. When he pulled down his bedroom blind the broken cord brought a stabbing memory. And when he awoke in the morning he felt that he had only to open his eyes to see a girl's raven black hair on the pillow beside him.

But Mrs. Quayle's presence was the keenest torment of all. The good old Methodist moved about him at breakfast without speaking, but one morning, fumbling with her bonnet strings before going, she said,

"Deemster, have you remembered this case of Bessie Collister in your prayers?"

He removed to Douglas—the Fort Anne Hotel, a breezy place, which sits on the ledge of the headland and just over the harbour. At first the babble and movement of the hotel distracted him, but after a day or two he was drawn back into the mäelstrom of his own thoughts.

Having a private sitting-room he borrowed law books from the Law Library and sat far into the night to read them. He selected the treatises on Infanticide—those bitter records of the age-long strife between the laws of man and of God. Particularly he read the charges of the British Judges (Scottish too frequently), the bewigged ruffians who, in the abomination of their Puritanical tyranny, and the brutal lust of their judicial vengeance, had hounded poor women to the gallows in the very nakedness of shame.

"Damn them! Damn them!" he would cry, leaping up with a desire to trample on the dead Judges' graves. But then the same persistent voice within would say, "Wait awhile! Who are you to stand up for justice and mercy?"

Crushed and ashamed he would creep up to bed through the silent house, and thinking of the girl whose dark eyes had intoxicated him in the glen (the girl he had afterwards held in his arms) he would say,

"Is it possible that I can stand by and see her given over to the hangman?"

That terrified him. In the darkness he pictured to himself the scene of Bessie's death and burial, and thought of his after-life as a Judge, when he would have to go to Court to try other such cases —and Bessie lying out there in the prison-yard.

After Ballamoar, with its pastoral tranquillity, the twittering of birds and the sleepy singing of the streams, Fort Anne was sometimes a tempestuous place, with the wash of the waves in the harbour, the monotonous moan of the sea outside and the melancholy wail of the gulls. He thought he heard Bessie's cry in the voice of the sea—her piercing cry when she was being carried out of Court after he had sentenced her.

One night he thought Bessie was dead. He was dead too. They were standing side by side in an awful tribunal and she was accusing him before God.

"He let me die! He killed me! He is my assassin!"

The sound of his own voice awakened him. A dream! It was the grey of dawn; a storm had risen in the night; the white sea was rolling over the breakwater and the sea-fowl were screaming through the mist and roar.

No, by God! If it was a question of Bessie witnessing against him in this world or in the next, he had no longer any doubt which it should be. No more temptations! No more hypocrisy and self-doubt! No more wandering about like a lost soul!

He would go up to the Governor. He would call upon him to withdraw his objection to the Jury's recommendation. And if he refused . . . . he should see what he should see.

At eight o'clock in the morning he was walking down the quay in the calm sunshine, looking at the activities of the harbour, and nodding cheerfully to the fishermen as he passed. He was on his way to Government House, and his conscience, with which he had wrestled so long, was triumphant and erect.

Then came a shock.

He was crossing the stone bridge that leads up to the town when he saw the Governor's blue landau coming down in the direction of the railway station. It was open. Fenella was sitting in it.

Stowell was certain she saw him. But she only coloured up to the eyes and dropped her head. At the next instant her carriage had crossed in front of him and swept into the station-yard.

Something surged in his throat; something blinded his eyes. But after a moment he threw up his head and walked firmly forward.

"Wait! Only wait! We'll see!"

CHAPTER THIRTY-THREE

THE HEART OF A WOMAN

MEANWHILE Fenella had been going through her own temptation. On the night after the trial, having bathed her swollen eyes, she went down to dinner. Her father looked searchingly at her for a moment, and, as soon as they were alone, he said,

"Was it Stowell I saw driving towards the mountain road as I came up?"

"Perhaps it was," said Fenella.

"Then why didn't he stay to dinner?"

"Because . . . . I told him to go."

"Why?"

Fenella gulped down the lump that was rising in her throat and said,

"I have been deceived in him. He is not the man I supposed him to be."

"Don't be a fool, my dear. I understand what you mean. It is his conduct as a man, not as a Judge you are thinking of. But if every woman in the world thought she had a right to make a scrutiny into her husband's life before she married him there would be a fine lot of marriages, wouldn't there?"

Crude and even coarse as Fenella thought her father's moral philosophy, she found her self-righteousness shaken by it. Perhaps she had been unfair to Stowell. But why didn't he come and plead his own cause? She couldn't talk to her father, but if Victor came and told his own story . . . .

Victor did not come. For two days her pride fought with her love and she thought herself the unhappiest woman in the world. Then to escape from the pains of self-reproach she conceived the idea of a fierce revenge upon Stowell. She would devote herself to his victim! Yes, she would make it her duty to lighten the lot of the poor creature he had ruined and deserted.

After a struggle, and many shameful tears, she went back to Castle Rushen, little knowing what a scorching flame she was to pass through.

By this time Bessie was feeling no bitterness against Stowell. The jailer had told her that the Deemster could not have acted otherwise. The law compelled him to condemn her. But he had told the Jury to recommend her to mercy, and now he would be writing to the King to ask him to let her off.

" Aw, he's good, miss—he's real good for all."

" Do *you* say that, Bessie? After he has betrayed you? " said Fenella,

" Betrayed? I wouldn't say that, miss."

" But he . . . . he took you to his rooms? "

" What else could he do, miss? All the inns were shut and it was raining, and I had nothing in my pocket."

" But . . . . having taken advantage of your homelessness and poverty, he afterwards cast you off? "

A mysterious wave of injured vanity struggled with Bessie's shame and she said,

" 'Deed he didn't, then. He wanted to marry me."

" Marry you . . . . did you say marry . . . . "

" Yes, he did, and that was why he sent me to school."

" But afterwards . . . . afterwards he changed his mind and turned you off . . . . I mean turned you over to somebody else? "

" 'Deed no," said Bessie, with her chin raised. " It was me that gave him up after I found I was fonder of Alick."

Breathing hard, scarcely able to speak, with the hot blood rushing to her cheeks, Fenella compelled herself to go on.

" Did he know then that you . . . . "

" No, miss, and neither did I, nor Alick, nor anybody."

" And when . . . . when was it that you went . . . . "

" To his rooms in Ramsey? The first Saturday in August, miss."

Fenella went home, happy, miserable, tingling with shame and yet thrilling with love also. Stowell's victim had brought her heart back to him.

It was just because he had loved her more than he had loved that girl in prison that the worst had happened. It was just because she herself had persuaded, constrained and almost compelled him that he had sat on the case, not fully knowing what was to be revealed by it.

This lasted her half-way home in the train, and then her wounded pride rose again. After all Victor had been faithless to the love with which she had inspired him. If a man loved a woman it was his duty to keep himself pure for her. Victor had not done so, therefore she would never forgive him—never!

The Governor's carriage met her at the Douglas station, and when (wiping the scorching tears from her eyes) she reached Government House, she found another carriage standing by the porch.

" Miss Janet Curphey is here to see you, miss," said the maid.

II

From the day of the trial, when Victor had returned home with a white face and said, " It doesn't matter now," Janet had known what had occurred.

That Collister girl had corrupted Victor. She had always feared it would be so since " Auntie Kitty " had whispered over her counter that that " forward thing " of Liza Corteen's was boasting that Mr. Stowell had been " sooreying " with her in the glen. And now she had brought him under the very shadow of shame itself, just when life looked so bright and joyful.

Then came the insular newspaper with an account of Fenella's outburst at the trial. That was the cruellest blow of all. She had loved Fenella, and had always thought there would be nothing so sweet as to spread her wedding-bed for her, but now that she had taken sides against Victor and publicly denounced him, Janet's blood boiled. She would go up to Government House and give Fenella a piece of her mind. Why shouldn't she?

It was a dull afternoon when she set off for Douglas, and as she drove along the coast road she rehearsed to herself the sharp things she was going to say.

But when Fenella came into the drawing-room, looking so pale as to be scarcely recognisable as the radiant girl she used to be, and kissed her and sat by her side, Janet could scarcely say anything.

At length (Miss Green, who had been sitting at tea with her, having gone) Janet braced herself, and said, not without a tremor,

" I've come about Victor."

" Then he has told you? " said Fenella.

" 'Deed he hasn't, and you needn't either, because I know."

Fenella drew her hand away and dropped her head.

"I don't say he hasn't done wrong," said Janet, "but you seem to think he's the only one who is to blame."

"Oh no! I see now that the girl in Castle Rushen . . . . "

"The girl? I'm not thinking about the girl. Of course *she* is to blame. But is there nobody else to blame also? "

"Who else? "

"Yourself."

"Janet! "

"Oh, I'm telling you the truth, dear. That's what I've come for."

"But it all happened before I returned to the Island."

"That's why. If you hadn't stayed away so long it wouldn't have happened at all."

Then up from the sweet and sorrowful places of Janet's memory came the story of Stowell's love for Fenella—how he had worked for her and waited for her through all his long years as a student-at-law.

"It's me to know, my dear. He used to come home every week-end, and his poor father thought it was to see him, but I knew better. 'Any fresh news?' he would say, and I knew what news he wanted. When your photo came he held it under the lamp and said, 'Don't you think she's like my mother, Janet—just a little like?' And I told him yes, and that was to say you were like the loveliest woman that ever walked the world—in this island anyway."

Fenella was struggling to control herself.

"Poor boy, how he worked and worked for you! Jacob never worked harder or waited longer for Rachel. And what was his reward? You signed on at your ridiculous Settlement for seven years and sent word you would never marry. I had it from Catharine Green and it was a sorrowful woman I was to break the news to him. He looked at me with his mother's eyes, and it was fit enough to break my heart to see how he cried with his face on the pillow. But it was with his father's eyes he rose and said, 'It shall never happen again, mother.' He called me mother too, God bless him! "

Fenella was smothering her mouth in her handkerchief.

"If he went wrong after that, was it any wonder? Young men are young men, and the Lord won't be too hard on them for being what He has made them. Some people seem to think when trouble comes between a young man and a young woman that the young woman is the only one to be pitied. Well, I'm a woman and I don't. And when a young man has been cut off from the love that would have kept him right and the heavens have gone dark on him . . . . "

" But I loved him all the time, Janet."

" Then why didn't you come back, instead of leaving him to the mercy of these good-looking young vixens who will run any risks with a young man if they can only get him to marry them? "

Fenella's eyes were down again.

" But that's not all. Not content with deserting him for so many years, you must try to disgrace him also."

" Janet ! "

" Oh, I saw what you said at the trial."

" But nobody knows whom I . . . . "

" Don't they indeed! The men may not—most of them are so stupid. They may even think you meant somebody else. But you can't deceive the women like that. And then *he* knew that you intended it for him. Just when you were about to become his wife, too, and you were the only woman in the world to him ! "

" I was so shocked. I thought he wasn't the man I had taken him for."

" Perhaps he wasn't, perhaps he was, but thousands of women have lost faith in their men and clung to them for all that, and they're the salt of the earth, I say. I'm only an old maid myself, but to stand up for your husband, right or wrong, that's what *I* call being a wife, if you ask me."

Fenella could bear up no longer. She flung her arms about Janet's neck and buried her face in her breast.

The darkness was gathering before they broke from their embrace and then it was time for Janet to smooth out her silvery hair and go. Fenella saw her to the carriage and whispered as she kissed her,

" Tell him to come back to me."

And then Janet went home with shining eyes.

III

Day after day Fenella waited at home for Victor, denying herself to everybody else. Every afternoon she dressed herself in some gown he had said he liked her in. She dressed her hair, too, in the way he liked best. But still he did not come.

At length she determined to write to him. Writing was a terrible ordeal. Her pride fought with her love and she could never satisfy herself with her letters. First it was—

> " DEAR VICTOR,—Don't you really think you've stayed
> away long enough? Remember your ' Manx ones '—espe-
> cially your lovely and beloved Manx women—won't they
> be talking? "

But no, that was too much like threatening him, so she
began again—

> " DARLING,—Did you really think I meant all I said
> that day? Don't you know a woman better than that? I
> suppose you think I am very hard-hearted and can never
> forgive, but . . . . "

No, that was wrong, too.

> " VICTOR,—Don't you think I have been punished
> enough? It has been very hard for me, yet I love you
> still . . . . "

But the trembling of her handwriting betrayed the emotion
she wished to conceal. At last, after a long day of solitude and
abandonment, two little lines—

> " VIC,—I am so lonely. Come to me. Your broken-
> hearted—FENELLA."

But all her letters, with their cries and supplications, were
torn up and thrown into the fire.

Why did he stay away? Did he expect her to bridge *all* the
gulf between them? At length she thought he must be ill. The
idea that he could be suffering (for her sake perhaps) swept down
all her pride, and she determined to go to him.

But just as she was setting out for Ballamoar somebody
brought word that Stowell was staying at Fort Anne. That
quenched her humility. So near, yet never coming to see her!
Oh, very well! Very well!

For two days she felt crushed and abased. Then she heard
that Stowell was constantly to be seen at the Law Library, and
that brought a memory and an explanation. She remembered that
she had said (in that wild moment when she didn't know what
she was saying) that she would never forgive him while the girl
Bessie lay in prison.

That was it! He was finding a solid legal ground on which
the prisoner could be liberated, and when he had convinced the
law officers of the Crown that this was a proper case for the exercise of mercy, he would come up to her and say, " Bessie Collister
is free!—the barrier between us is broken down."

For a full day after that her heart was at ease. Nay more, she was almost happy, for hidden away in some secret place of semi-consciousness was the thought that the measure of Stowell's efforts for Bessie Collister was the meter of his love for herself.

At length her impatience got the better of her tranquillity and she became eager to know what was going on. There was only one person who could tell her that—her father.

Coming down to breakfast on the sunny morning after the storm, she saw, among the letters by the Governor's plate, a large envelope superscribed, "*HOME SECRETARY.*" When her father had opened it she said, as if casually,

"Any news yet about that poor thing in Castle Rushen?"

"Yes, there's something here."

"Of course she's pardoned?"

"On the contrary, her death-sentence has been confirmed."

"Confirmed?"

"Yes, she's to die, and it only remains for me to fix the date of the execution."

The sun went out as before a thunderstorm, and, rising from her unfinished breakfast, Fenella fled from the room. A great wave of pity seemed to sweep down every other feeling. She determined to go to Castle Rushen again and break the news tenderly to the unhappy woman.

On her way to the railway station her mind swung back to Stowell. After all he could have done nothing to save the girl's life. It was inconceivable that the authorities in London could have been indifferent to the opinion of the Judge who had tried the case.

"No, he can have done nothing—nothing whatever."

Then came a shock to her also.

As her carriage dipped into the hill going down to the station she saw Stowell coming up from the bridge with rapid strides. Something told her that, having heard the news, he was going to Government House to protest. But what was the good of going now? Useless! Worse than useless!

One glance she got of his face before she dropped her own. It was whiter and thinner than before, as if from sleepless nights and suffering. She wanted to stop; she wanted to go on; she did not know what she wanted.

At the next moment her coachman, who had seen nothing of Stowell, being occupied with the difficulties of the hill, had swept into the station-yard.

When she got out of the carriage her heart was burning with the pangs of mingled love and rage.

"If that girl dies in prison there shall never be anything between us—never," she thought.

But deep in her heart, almost unknown to herself, there was a still more poignant cry,

"He does not care for me—he cannot."

CHAPTER THIRTY-FOUR

THE MAN AND THE LAW

WHEN Stowell reached Government House he found the Governor in the garden, bareheaded and smoking a cigar of which he was obviously trying to preserve the ash, while he watched his gardener at his work of repairing the ravages of last night's storm among the flower-beds.

"Ah, you've come at last! But you have just missed Fenella. She has gone to Castletown—that girl again, I suppose."

"I know. I saw her. That's the matter I've come to speak about."

"So? Oblige me then by walking here so that I may keep an eye on the gardener."

Stowell winced, but stepped to and fro on the path by the Governor's side while in a low tone he broached his business.

"Deemster Taubman told me at Tynwald that you had reported against the Jury's recommendation."

"Well?"

"I thought perhaps you would permit me to explain the exact legal position."

"Yes?"

"It is fifty years at least since the prisoner has been executed on this island for that crime."

"Fifty, is it?"

The Governor blew his light blue smoke into the lighter blue air and watched it rising.

"Deemster Taubman seems to think that a prisoner who has wilfully taken life is necessarily a murderer. That is wrong, Sir."

"Wrong?"

"Quite wrong. It is established by the laws of this and every civilised country that it is the reason of man which makes him accountable for his action and the absence of reason acquits him of the crime."

"And is there any ground for thinking that this girl was not responsible?" said the Governor.

" Every ground, Sir. No woman in her position ever was or can be responsible."

" No? . . . . Gardener, don't you think those tulips . . . . "

" That's why the law of England," continued Stowell, " has ceased to look upon infanticide as a crime punishable by death. In some foreign countries it is not looked upon as a crime at all. The woman who kills her child within five days after its birth is thought to be suffering from temporary mania and therefore not guilty of murder. Besides . . . . "

" Besides—what? "

Stowell breathed heavily and then said,

" There are exceptional circumstances in this case which call for merciful treatment."

" You mean . . . . "

" I mean," said Stowell, speaking rapidly and in a vibrating voice, " that the girl had no bad motives such as usually inspire murder—no greed, no lust, no desire for revenge. In fact, she meant no harm to anybody. On the contrary it is conceivable that she meant good—good even to her child—to save it from a life of suffering in a world in which it would have no father, no family, and nobody to care for it but its shamed and outcast mother."

The Governor looked at Stowell for a moment and thought.

" He's ill, and he's trying to unload his conscience."

Then he said aloud,

" So you've come to ask me to . . . . "

" I've come to ask you, Sir, to withdraw your objection to the recommendation to mercy, so that the death sentence may be commuted to imprisonment."

Again the Governor looked at Stowell's heated face and thought, " Yes, he'll ill, and doesn't see that I am fighting his own battle."

" Do it, Sir," said Stowell. " Do it, for God's sake, before it is too late, and there is such an outcry throughout the kingdom as will shake the very foundations of justice in the island."

The Governor was still smoking leisurely and keeping his eye on his flower-beds.

" Gardener, don't you think that bed of geraniums . . . . " he began, but Stowell could bear no more.

" Good God, Sir, isn't this matter of sufficient importance to merit your attention? "

The Governor turned sharply upon him, threw away his half-smoked cigar and said,

" Come this way."

21

Not another word was spoken until, returning to the house with a certain pomp of stride, with Stowell behind him, the Governor reached his room and closed the door behind him. Then, unlocking his desk, he took out a large envelope (the same that Fenella had seen at breakfast) and handed the contents of it to Stowell, saying,

"Look at that."

Stowell saw at a glance what it was and uttered a cry of astonishment.

"Then it's done."

"Yes, it's done. And now sit down and listen to me."

But Stowell continued to stand with the paper crinkling in his trembling fingers.

"You say Taubman told you I reported against the Jury's recommendation. Quite true! As President of the Court and head of the Manx judiciary, I told the Home Secretary I saw no justification for it—no justification whatever."

Stowell was silent.

"You say it is fifty years since such a crime has been punished by death. Perhaps it is, but the fact that the Statute remains is proof enough that the law contemplates cases in which it may properly be exercised. This in my view was such a case and I had every right to say so."

Still Stowell remained silent.

"You say the prisoner may have acted from a good motive. I see no good motive in a mother who takes the life of her child. You speak of her shame, but shame is no excuse for crime. Why shouldn't such women suffer shame? Shame is the just consequence of their evil conduct, and to try to escape from it by making away with their misbegotten children is crime."

Stowell was trembling but still silent.

"Pity for women of that sort is sentimental weakness. Worse, it is a danger to public safety. The sooner such people are put out of the world the better for the public good."

There was a palpable silence on both sides for some moments. The Governor glanced at Stowell's twitching face and began to be sorry for him. "Good Lord!" he thought, "why can't the man see that it's best for himself that the girl should die? As long as she lives the wretched scandal may break out again and his own share in it may come to light. And then Fenella! How could I allow her to marry him with that danger hanging over his head?"

Stowell's fingers were contracting over the paper that crinkled in his hand. At length he threw it on the desk and said,

" Your Excellency, if you carry out that sentence you will be committing a crime—a monstrous judicial crime."

The Governor returned the paper to his desk, and then rose and said, with a ring of sarcasm in his voice,

" So I am the criminal, am I? Well, I am responsible for public security in this island, and as long as I am here I am going to see that it is preserved. Offences of this kind have been too frequent of late and they can only be put down by law. The prisoner in the present case has been justly tried and rightly condemned, and it shall be my business to see that she pays the penalty of her crime."

Stowell's pale face had become scarlet, his lower lip was trembling. Outside the sea was sparkling in the sunlight; a band was playing far off on the promenade.

" Your Excellency," said Stowell, quivering all over, " it will be a life-long grief to me to resist your authority, but I must tell you at once that if you order that girl's execution it shall never be carried out."

" What do you say? "

" I say it shall never be carried out."

" Why not? "

" Because *I* shall prevent it."

The Governor rose. His face was red, his throat had swelled; his lips were compressed.

" Do you mean that you will go over my head . . . . "

" I do . . . . "

The Governor brushed Stowell aside in making for the bell.

" There's no heed for that. I'm going, Sir," said Stowell, and at the next moment the Governor was alone in his room, speechless with astonishment and wrath.

Going down the corridor Stowell passed the open door of the library—the room in which he had parted from Fenella. In quarrelling with her father had he burnt the last bridge by which Fenella and he could come together?

" But, God forgive me, I could do nothing else—nothing whatever."

II

Fenella found that the tragic news had reached Castle Rushen before her.

Bessie had received it at first with increduility. Her expectation of pardon had reached the point of conviction, and every morning as she rose from her plank bed, she had said to herself, " It will come to-day."

When Tommy Vondy went into the condemned cell, blowing his nose repeatedly and talking about death, how it came to everybody sooner or later, Bessie looked at him with terror and screamed, " Oh, God help me! God help me! "

For a while she raved like a madwoman.   Everybody had lied to her and deceived her, and the Deemster had done nothing to save her, because he wanted her out of the way.

But after a while an idea occurred to her and she became calm. Alick Gell! If Alick would go up to London and see the King and tell him that she had never intended to kill her baby he would forgive her. And then Alick would come galloping back, at the last moment perhaps, waving a paper over his head and crying, " Stop! "

She had seen such things in her illustrated *Weekly Budget*— the story paper she used to read on Sunday mornings at home, while the dinner was cooking in the oven-pot and her mother was singing hymns in the Primitive chapel and her father was poring over the " Mistakes of Moses."

But would he do it? She had deceived him twice. And then his sisters had always been trying to drag him away from her.

All at once, like the echo of a bell through a thick mist over the sea, came the memory of his cry as she was being carried out of Court: " Never mind, Bessie, I would rather be you than your Judge! "

Yes, he loved her still, and (out of the cunning which the air of a prison breeds) a scheme flashed upon her. She would write a letter to Alick Gell, not telling him what she wanted him to do, but plainly pointing to it.

Fenella was amazed to find Bessie apparently reconciled to her end. She had expected torrents of tears and even the coarse language of the farmyard.

" The suspense was the worst. I shall be glad when it's all over," said Bessie.

The only thing that troubled her was to die while Alick was thinking so hard of her, and if her hand did not shake so much she would write to ask for his forgiveness.

" I'll write for you," said Fenella.

"And will you give the letter into his own hands, miss, so that his sisters may not see it? "

" I'll try, dear."

Sitting by the door of the cell, under the light from the grill, Fenella wrote with the prison paper on her lap, while Bessie, without a vestige of colour in her forlorn face, dictated from the bed:

" DEAR ALICK,—You will have heard what they are going to do to me. It is dreadful, isn't it? I thought perhaps you would have written me a few lines, though I know it is too much to expect after all the sorrow and shame I have brought on you.

" Oh, if I could only have lived to make it up to you! We could have gone away, as you always said, to America or somewhere. I should have been so good, and we should have been so happy and nobody to cast all this up to us.

" What I did was very wrong, but I don't see what good it will do to the King to take my life, and me a poor girl he never saw in the world. I still think if there were anybody to speak for me he would forgive me even yet and everything would be all right. But that's more than anybody would do for me now, I suppose—even you, though I have always loved you so dear."

Bessie paused.

" Is that all? " asked Fenella, in a husky whisper.

" Not quite," said Bessie, and she began again.

" Mother was here last week and brought me your photo. It got wet in my bag on the way from Derby Haven, and it is cracked and smudged. But I kiss it constant and it is such company.

" Good-bye, Alick! My last thoughts will be of you and my last prayer that God will bless you. If I could only see you for a minute I think I should be satisfied. But if you can't come, write and say you forgive me. It has been all through my love for you that I am here, so think the best of me."

Bessie signed the letter, filling up the remaining space with crosses, and then wrote with her own hand—

" P.S.—It's a week to-day, so if anything is to be done there's no time to lose."

Fenella saw through the girl's pitiful subterfuge, but knew well that Gell could do nothing. There was only one man in the island who could have saved Bessie, and that was the Judge who had tried her.

Why hadn't he?

All the way home in the train Fenella asked herself this question. The only answer she could find was that Stowell was afraid of offending the Governor, owing so much to him. But oh, if he had only resisted her father in this case—standing up against him and fearing no one—how she would have loved him!

She found Government House shuddering with awe, as if a tornado had swept through it and gone. At length Miss Green explained what had happened. Mr. Stowell had called to see the Governor and been turned out of the house!

Hardly had she reached her room when her father followed her into it.

" I suppose you know that Stowell has been here? " he said.

" Yes. What did he come for? "

" To threaten me—that's what he came for. To threaten me that if I attempted to carry out the sentence of the law on that girl in Castle Rushen he would prevent it."

Fenella tried to conceal the joy that was rising within her.

" What do you think he intends to do? " she asked.

" Appeal to the Home Secretary against me, I suppose. I shouldn't wonder if he leaves the island in the morning. And if he does, and brings back a pardon, it will be a vote of censure upon me—nothing short of it."

The Governor strode across the room in his wrath, and then suddenly drew up on seeing that Fenella was smiling.

" But I see who is the cause of the man's insane conduct," he said.

" Who? "

" You! You've broken with him, haven't you? Because he had the misfortune to encounter that woman long ago you hold him responsible for everything she has done since. So to satisfy your ridiculous qualms he falls back upon me. The fool! The damned fool! And you are no better! I don't know what's taking possession of women in these days. I'm sick to death of their feminist imbecilities and the braying of their male asses! "

" But father . . . . "

" Don't talk to me," said the Governor, and with blazing eyes he swept out of the room.

Then Victor *had* done something! He *did* care for her! And now he was going to take some great risk to save the life of the girl in prison.

A momentary qualm about her duty to her father was swept down by the tide of her love for Stowell. After all, he *was* the man she had thought him to be! God bless and speed him!

CHAPTER THIRTY-FIVE

" AND GOD MADE MAN OF THE DUST OF THE GROUND "

STOWELL had travelled far by this time.

When he left Government House in the heat and flame of his anger he was at war with God and man. There was a kind of self-defence in thinking that, however deep his own wrong-doing, the whole world was full of infamy.

He found that news of the forthcoming execution had reached Fort Anne before he returned to it. To avoid the whispering groups in the public rooms he packed his bag and took the afternoon train to Ballamoar.

Alone in the railway carriage he had time to review the situation. His visit to the Governor had been a wretched failure. But even if it had been a success what would have been the result to Bessie Collister? Substitution of the jail for the gallows. Instead of death, three years, five years, perhaps ten years' imprisonment. Thank God he had not succeeded!

" But what am I to do now? " he asked himself.

Appeal to London? Useless! The Home officials would support the resident authority, and, having made a hideous error, they would be reluctant to correct it.

" Then what can I do? " he thought.

Suddenly he saw that every argument he had used with the Governor against putting Bessie to death applied equally to keeping her in prison. This was not a question of degrees of guilt— of murder or manslaughter. Either Bessie was guilty of murder and ought to be executed or she was not guilty (not being responsible) and ought to be set at liberty.

" Then the law under which she has been condemned is a crime," he thought.

This terrified him. All his inherited instinct of reverence for the justice and majesty of the law revolted.

" The law a crime! Good heavens, what am I thinking about? "

And yet why not? Why had there been so much misery in the world? Was it because of the crimes committed *against* the law? No, but chiefly because of the crimes committed *by* the law. Yes, *that* was the real key to the long martyrdom of man throughout the ages.

" If a law is a crime it ought to be broken," he told himself.

But how! There was only one proper way in a free country— through Parliament and by the slow uprising of the human conscience. But that was a long process, and meantime what would happen in this case? Bessie would be dead and buried! That must not be! No, the law that had condemned Bessie Collister must be broken at once—now!

"But who is to break it?"

He trembled at that question, but found only one answer. It shivered at the back of his mind like the white water over a reef at the neck of a narrow sea, and it was not at first that he dared to think of it. But at length he saw that since he had been the instrument of the law in dooming Bessie to death it was he who must set her free.

When he reached this point on his dark way he was horrified.

"What? A Judge break the law!"

He thought of his oath as Deemster and of the execration that would fall on him if found out. He remembered his father's motto: "Justice is the most sacred thing on earth." No, no, it was impossible! His honour as a Judge forbade it.

But, as the train ran on, the call of nature conquered and he asked himself what, after all, was his honour as a Judge compared with that poor girl's life?

"Nothing! Nothing!"

Bessie Collister must not die! She must not remain in prison! She must escape! He must help her to do so. Secretly, though, nobody knowing, not even the girl herself or Fenella.

At St. John's, a junction between the north of the island and the south, the Bishop of the island stepped into Stowell's compartment. He had been holding a confirmation service at a neighbouring church, and a company of young girls, in white muslin frocks, were seeing him off from the platform. While the carriages were being coupled he stood at the open door and said good-bye to them.

"And now go home, dear children, and have your suppers and get to bed. Home, sweet home, you know!"

But the children would not go until they had sung again in their sweet young voices the hymn they had just been singing in church —"Now the day is over." By the time the engine whistled and the train was moving out of the station, they had reached the verse—

> "Comfort every sufferer,
> Watching late in pain,
> Those who plan some evil
> From their sin restrain."

Stowell dare not look at them. He was thinking of the girl in Castle Rushen and picturing to himself a similar scene of joy and innocence which might have taken place only a few years before in the station by the glen.

"Ah!" said the Bishop, settling himself in his seat.

He was a short, dapper, almost dainty little man, who talked continually like the brook that often runs behind a Manx cottage and fills it with cheerful chatter.

"I suppose you've heard the news, Deemster?"

He produced a small evening newspaper.

"That poor young person in Castle Rushen is to be executed after all! Terrible, isn't it?"

Stowell bent his head.

"I really thought that after your address to the Jury she would have been pardoned. But who am I to set up my opinion against that of the King's advisers? And then think of the effect of bad example! Those dear children, for instance, they are not too young to remember. And if that unhappy girl had got off who knows what effect . . . . "

Stowell, nursing the fires of his rebellion, hardly heard the running stream of commonplace.

"And then Holy Wedlock! I always say that every act of carnal transgression is a sin against the marriage altar."

The train was running along the western coast; the sun was setting; the Irish mountains were purple against the red glow of the sky behind them.

"And then think of the poor soul herself! It may be best for her too! God knows to what depths she might have descended!"

Stowell wanted to burst out on the Bishop, but a secret voice within him whispered, "Hold your tongue! Say nothing!"

"All the same, I'm sorry for the poor creature, and only yesterday I was using my influence to get her into a Refuge Home for Fallen Women across the water."

The train drew up at the station for Bishop's Court, and the Bishop, after a cheerful adieu, hopped like a bird along the platform to where his carriage stood waiting for him, with its two high-stepping horses and its coachman in livery.

Stowell's heart was afire.

"Refuge Home! Send some of your fashionable women to your Refuge Homes! Holy Wedlock! There are more fallen women inside your Holy Wedlock than outside of it!"

At the station for the glen Stowell got out himself, and there he saw a different spectacle—an elderly woman in a satin mantle, surrounded by a group of other elderly women in faded sun-bonnets.

It was Mrs. Collister again. In one hand she held her black-thorn stick, and in the other she carried a small bundle in a print handkerchief—probably containing her underclothing.

Stowell understood. The news about Bessie had reached her home, and the heart-broken (almost brain-broken) old mother was waiting for the south-going train to Castletown.

A hush fell on the women when Stowell stepped out of the rail-way carriage, but as he made his way to his dog-cart at the gate, he heard one of them say,

" It's a wicked shame! But you'll be with the poor bogh at the end and that will comfort her."

A kind of savage pride had taken possession of Stowell.

" Not yet! Not yet! " he thought.

The law was wrong, therefore it was right to resist the law. It was more than right—it was a kind of sacred duty.

II

From that time forward the Judge went about like a criminal.

He stayed at home the following day to think out his plans. All his schemes revolved about Castle Rushen. The great, grey, bastioned fortress—how was he to get the prisoner out of it?

His first idea was to use the jailer, who was a simple soul and had obligations to his family. But he abandoned this thought rather from fear of the old man's garrulous tongue than from qualms of conscience.

It was Tuesday, and Bessie's execution had been fixed for the Monday following, but the day passed without bringing any better thought to him.

Somewhere in the dark reaches of Wednesday morning an idea flashed upon him. It was usual for one of the Deemsters to make an annual examination of the prisons of the island, the time being subject to his own convenience. Stowell determined to make his examination of Castle Rushen now.

At eleven o'clock he was going round the Castle with the jailer. There were two sides to the prison, a debtor side and a criminal side, and they went over both—the jailer complaining of decaying doors and rusty padlocks, and the Deemster, with a sense of shame, pretending to make notes of them, while his eyes and his mind were on other matters.

" Not much chance of a prisoner escaping from a place like this, Mr. Vondy."

" Not a ha'porth! Those old Normans knew how to keep

people out—and in too, Sir. But there's one cell you haven't looked at yet, your Honour—the girl Collister's."

"We'll leave her alone, Mr. Vondy. How is she now, poor creature?"

"Wonderful! That cheerful and smart you wouldn't believe, Sir."

"Then she doesn't know . . . . "

"'Deed she does, Sir. But she thinks Mr. Gell, the advocate, is up in London getting her pardon, and she's listening and listening for his foot coming back with it."

Stowell went to bed on Wednesday night also without any scheme for Bessie Collister's escape. But in the grey dawn of Thursday morning, when the world was awakening from a heavy sleep, another idea came to him. The Antiquarian Society of the island had made him a Vice-President when he became a Deemster, and having opened up certain portions of the Castle that were outside the precincts of the prison, they had asked him to inspect their discoveries.

With another spasm of hope, Stowell returned to Castletown.

"Give me your lantern, and let me wander about by myself, Mr. Vondy."

"'Deed I will, Sir. Your Honour knows the Castle as well as I do."

There was said to be a subterranean passage under the harbour for escape in case of siege. Stowell found it (a noisome, slimy, rat-infested place, dripping with water) but the further end of it had been walled up.

There was a foul dungeon in which a Bishop had been confined when he came into collision with the civil authorities, and tradition had it that he had preached through a window to his people on the quay. Stowell found that also, but the window was narrow and barred.

There were ramparts round the four-square walls, but on one side they looked down into the back yards of the little houses that lay against the great fortress and on the other three sides they were exposed to the market-place, the Parliament-square and the harbour.

For the second time Stowell went home in the lowering nightfall with a heavy heart. As the time approached for the execution his agitation increased, and on Thursday night also he tossed about, thinking, thinking. At length he remembered something. He had a key to the Deemster's private entrance to the Castle, and though the door was always bolted on the inside, a plan of escape occurred to him.

On Friday morning he was in the jailer's room. It had been the guard-room of the Castle and was hung about with souvenirs of earlier times—maps, plans, a cutlass that had been captured in a fight with Spanish pirates, a blunderbuss that had been used by Manx Fencibles, a keyboard, a line of handcuffs, and a rope, in a glass case, that had been used in the hanging of a Manx criminal.

"You haven't many prisoners in the Castle now, Mr. Vondy?"

"Aw, no! Didn't your Honour discharge all but one at the last General Gaol?"

"And not much company?"

"Only Willie Shimmin, the turnkey, and he's a drunken gommeral, always wanting out, and never sure of coming back at all."

"What about your female warder?"

"Mrs. Mylrea? A dying woman, Sir. Not been here since the trial, and if it wasn't for Miss Stanley . . . . "

"Does she come often?"

"Nearly every day now, Sir."

At that moment there was the clang of a bell.

"There she is, I'll go bail," said the jailer, and snatching a big key from the keyboard he turned to go.

In the collapse of his better nature Stowell was afraid to meet Fenella, knowing well she would see through him.

"Don't trouble about me, or mention that I'm here," he said, and picking up his lantern he made a show of going on with his researches.

But as soon as the jailer had disappeared he turned rapidly to the Deemster's door and had opened it and stepped out and closed it behind him, before the jailer and Fenella (whose voices he could hear) had emerged from the Portcullis into the court-yard.

It was done! Light had fallen on him at last. Now he knew how Bessie Collister was to escape from Castle Rushen.

But it was not enough that Bessie should escape from her prison; she must escape from the island also; and to do so by means of the regular steam packet from Douglas to England was impossible. Was this to be another and still greater difficulty?

The tide was up in the harbour and the fishing-boats were making ready to go out for the night. As Stowell walked down the quay he saw a blue-coated and brass-buttoned elderly man coming up with unsteady steps—the harbour-master. A sudden thought came to him. Why not by a fishing-boat?

He remembered his night with the herrings on the Governor's yacht, when, lying off the Carlingford sands, he had seen the lights of Dublin. Why could not a fishing-boat steal away in the darkness and put Bessie ashore in Ireland?

It was the very thing! Only it must not be a Castletown boat, lest she should be missed when the fleet came back to port in the morning. Why not a Ramsey boat, or, better still, a boat from Peel?

After dinner that night he walked on the gravelled terrace in front of the house. The moon was shining in a pale sky and the bald crown of old Snaefell was visible through the motionless trees. He drew up on the spot on which he had first parted from Fenella, and a warm vision of the scene of so many years ago returned to him. Then came the memory of their last parting and of the scorching words with which she had driven him away from her.

" But wait! Only wait! " he thought.

He was satisfied with himself. He was sure he was doing right. He even believed God was using him as an instrument of His divine justice, to correct the infamy of the world by a signal action. It was one of those lulls betwen the wings of a circling storm which come to the soul of man as well as to nature.

He was almost happy.

III

Next morning, under pretext of the Deemster's fortnightly Court at Douglas and of important business to do before it, Stowell breakfasted by the light of a lamp and the crackling of a fire, and set out in his car for Peel.

Soon after six he was descending into the little white fishing-port that lies in the lap of its blue circle of sea, with the red ruins of its Cathedral at its feet and the green arms of its hills behind it.

The little town was still half asleep. Middle-aged women were gutting herrings from barrel to barrel, while blood dripped from their broad thumbs; old men were baiting lines with shell-fish; cadgers' cart were standing empty at the foot of the pier, with their horses' heads in bags of oats and chopped hay; a hundred fishing-boats by the quay, with their sails hanging slack from their masts, were swaying to the ebbing tide, and an Irish tramp steamer, the *Dan O'Connor,* was lazily letting down the fires under her black and red funnel.

But at the pier-head, close under the blind eyes of the Cathedral, there was a scene of real activity. It was the fish auction for the night's catch. The auctioneer, an Irishman, was standing on a barrel, with a circle of fish-cadgers around him, and an empty space, like a cock-pit, in front, to which the long-booted fishermen, one by one, with ponderous agility, were carrying specimen baskets of herrings and dropping them down on the red flags with a thud.

"Now, gintlemen, here's your last chance of a herring this week. We're a religious people in the Isle of Man and sorra a wan more will ye get till Tuesday."

Stowell, who had drawn up his car, and was standing at the back of the crowd, was startled. How had he come to forget that Manx fishing boats did not go out on Saturday or Sunday? Was this going to defeat his plan?

The fish auction went on.

"Now, min, what do you say to forty mease from the *Mona*? Thirty-five shillin'! Thank you, Mr. Flynn! Any incrase on thirty-five?"

"Thirty-six and a quid for yourself if you'll lave me to put a sight up on the wife," said a voice from the back of the crowd.

During the laughter which the rude jest provoked, Stowell looked at the speaker. He was the skipper of the Irish tramp steamer—a grizzly old salt, spitting tobacco juice from behind a discoloured hand, and having rascal written on every line of his face.

Turning away, Stowell walked slowly to the further end of the bay, and as slowly back again. A new scheme had occurred to him—something better than a fishing-boat, far better. He was now more sure than ever that the Almighty was using him for His righteous ends since even his failures of memory were helping him.

By the time he returned the auction was over. The pier was empty and nobody was in sight except the Irish Captain who was standing on the deck of his ship by the side of the cabin companion. After looking to right and left, Stowell saluted him.

"Where are you going to when you leave Peel, Captain?"

"To Castletown, Sir."

"And from there?"

"To wherever the dust" (the money) "looks brightest."

"May I come aboard, Captain? I have something to say to you."

"Shure!"

After another look to right and left, Stowell stepped on to the steamer and followed the Captain to his cabin.

When he came on deck, half-an-hour later, his face was flushed.

"Then it's settled, Captain?"

"Take the world aisy—it's done, Sir."

"At what time will it be high water on Sunday night?"

"Elivin o'clock, Sir."

"You'll sail immediately your passengers come aboard?"

" The minit they put foot on deck, Sir."

" What about the harbour-master? "

" Him and me are same as brothers."

" And the turnkey? "

" Willie Shimmin? He's got a petticoat at the " Manx Arms.' "

" You have no doubt you can do it? "

" Divil a doubt in the world, Sir."

Stowell, back in his car, was driving to Douglas. The Judge had bribed a blackguard, but he was still sure that he was doing God's service.

Only one thing remained to do now, and through the long hours of an uneasy night he had thought of it. It was not even enough that Bessie Collister should escape from the island. If she were not to be tracked and brought back it was essential that somebody should go with her. Who should it be? There was only one answer to this question—Alick Gell.

Would Alick go? He must! Betrayed and deceived as he had been, if he did not see that he must forgive the woman who had faced death for him, and save her from an unjust punishment, Stowell would feel like taking him by the throat and choking him.

But would Gell forgive him also? That was a different matter. Memory flowed back, and he saw again the fierce yet broken creature who had come stumbling into Ballamoar on the night after the adjournment, crying in the torment of his betrayal, " Damn him, whoever he is! Damn him to the devil and hell! "

" No matter! I must face it out," thought Stowell.

He must unite those two injured ones. And perhaps some day, when they were gone from the island, and safe in some foreign country, the Almighty would accept his act as a kind of reparation and cover up all his wretched wrongdoing in the merciful veil which is God's memory. But meantime he must go about for a few days longer, a few days after to-day, warily, secretly, unseen and unsuspected by anybody.

Driving into Douglas, he came upon the Chief Constable, Colonel Farrell (a cringer to all above him and a bully to all beneath), who hailed him and said,

" Just the gentleman I wished to see, Sir. It's about Mr. Gell. Ever since you sentenced that woman of his he has been threatening you, and we've had to keep a close watch on him. But he seems to be going out of his mind, and I've been warning the Speaker that we may have to put him away. The other night he gave us the slip and we believe he went to Ballamoar."

" Well? "

"We wish you to allow a plain-clothes man to go about with you for the next few days."

Stowell was startled.

"No, certainly not.   It is quite unnecessary," he said.

"Well, if you say so it's all right, Sir.   Still, with a madman about, who may make a murderous attack on you . . . . "

"Where is he now?"

"In his chambers."

"Good-morning, Colonel!" said Stowell, and before the Chief Constable had replied he was gone.

A few minutes later the policeman who, for the protection of the Deemster, was on point duty outside Gell's rooms was astonished to see the Deemster himself go up the carpetless staircase.

At a door on the second landing, with Gell's name on it in white letters, he stopped and knocked.   The door was not opened, but he heard shuffling steps inside and knocked again.

CHAPTER THIRTY-SIX

OUT OF THE DEPTHS

ALICK GELL, also, had travelled far.

After his temporary detention at Castletown, he had returned to Douglas in a frenzy.

For four days everything had fed his fury.   Having no housekeeper he took his meals in a neighbouring hotel which was frequented by his younger fellow-advocates.   Sitting alone in a corner he spoke to none of them, but they seemed to be always speaking at him.   In loud voices they praised Stowell—his eloquence, his knowledge, above all his impartiality, his superiority to the calls of friendship.

This was gall and wormwood to Gell.   He wanted to come face to face with Stowell that he might charge him with his treachery.   He knew the police were watching him, but one day he eluded them and took the train to Ballamoar.

It was evening when he got there.   The cowman, who lived in the lodge, told him the master was out in his car and might not return until late.   To beguile the time of waiting Gell walked in the lanes and woods about the house.   These evoked both kind and cruel memories, the worst of them being the memory of the day when he stammered his excuses for loving Bessie Collister, and Stowell had said, "Good-bye and God bless you, old fellow!" What a scoundrel!

The darkness gathered.   There was the last bleating of the

sheep, the last calling of the curlew (like the cry of a bird without a mate), and then night fell, dark night, without a star, and still Stowell did not come.

Where was he? Gell thought he knew. He was at Government House with Fenella Stanley. They were reconciled, of course; they were kissing and caressing, while Bessie . . . . but no, he dare not think of that.

What stung him most was the thought of the money he had taken from Stowell. It had been neither more nor less than the price of Bessie's honour. He remembered the Peel fisherman who had burnt his boat. How he wished he had the money now that he might ram it down Stowell's throat!

There had been rain and the frogs were croaking, but otherwise the air was still. All at once the silence of the Curraghs was broken by a low hum. Stowell's car was coming! Looking down the long straight road Gell saw its two white headlights opening the darkness like a reversed wedge. Then in a moment, unpremeditated, unprepared for, his wild thirst for personal vengeance returned to him.

"Now, now," he thought, and he closed the gates to give himself time.

But when Stowell came up and got out of his car to open them, and his lamps lit up his face, a mysterious wave of emotion heaved up out of the depths of Gell's soul. Something took him by the throat and cried "Stop! What are you doing?" and he dropped back into the deeper darkness of some bushes behind one of the gate-posts. He must have made a noise, for Stowell cried,

"Who's there?"

But Gell made no answer, and at the next moment Stowell was back in his seat and gliding up the drive.

After that, horrified by the homicidal impulse which had so suddenly taken possession of him, Gell kept to his rooms for several days, going out only at night, with the collar of his coat up to his ears, to eat and drink in the tap-room of a low tavern on the quay.

He had been denying himself to everybody who called at his chambers, but one morning there came an unsteady knock, followed by a peremptory voice, saying,

"Alick, let me in!"

It was his father, and an inherited instinct of obedience compelled him to open the door. He was shocked to see the change in the Speaker. His burly figure had become slack, his clothes (especially his trousers) baggy, his long beard thinner and more white, the crown of his head bald. Only his red eyes, with their unquenchable fire, remained the same.

22

The old man sat down heavily with his stick between his knees, and his trembling hands on its ebony handle.

"I didn't expect that I should have to come here, but Farrell says that since that trial at Castletown you have not been responsible, and if things go farther he'll have to put you away."

"Put me away?"

"Don't you understand?—the asylum."

"He doesn't know, father, and neither do you . . . ."

"I don't want to know. If you had listened to me long ago this wouldn't have happened. But I'm not here to reproach you. I'm here to advise you to do something for your own good—mine, too, everybody's."

"What is that, father?"

Gell had expected the usual storm and his father's emotion was moving him deeply.

"Leave the island before anything worse happens. Look" (the Speaker drew a stout envelope from his breast pocket), "I've just been to the bank for you. A thousand pounds in Bank of England notes, and if it's not enough there's more where that came from. Take it and go away at once—to America—anywhere."

Alick drew back and his lips tightened. "This is a trick to get me to desert Bessie," he thought.

"I can't do it," he said, and he pushed back the old man's trembling hand.

The Speaker fixed his red eyes on his son, and said,

"Alick, I must tell you something. I've heard on good authority that they are going to hang that girl."

"They can't. Some of them would like to, but they can't."

"They can and they will, I tell you."

"Then I'll . . . . I'll murder . . . ."

"There you are! That's what Farrell says. A little more and you'll be capable of anything. Go away, my boy. Think of me. It has taken me forty years to get to where I am. I was born neither an aristocrat nor a pauper, but I've got my hand on all of them. That's just the kind of man both sorts would like to pull down. If my son disgraced me I should have to give up everything. Go, my son, go."

"I can't, father, I can't."

The old man passed his hand over his bald head and in a low voice he said,

"Perhaps I've not been a good father exactly, but there's your mother. Bad as it would be for me it would be worse for her. She has only one son—one child you might say—and since that affair at Castletown she has never been out of doors—just creep-

ing over the fire with her feet in the fender. If you don't want
to bring your mother to her grave . . . . "

Gell felt as if his heart were breaking.

" But I can't, I can't! "

" You mean you won't? "

" Very well, I won't."

The old man's voice thickened—the storm was coming.

" And for the sake of this woman who killed her brat . . . . "

" Call her what you like. I'll stay here until she comes out
of prison, and then . . . . then I'll marry her."

" You fool! You damned heartless fool! God forgive me
for bringing such a fool into the world."

Struggling to his feet the old man made for the door. But
having reached it, and while tugging at the handle, he stopped
and said,

" Look here, I'll give you one more chance."

He took the stout envelope out of his breast pocket again and
flung it on to Alick's desk.

" There's the money and this is Monday. If you are not off
the island by this day week I'll not leave matters to Farrell—I'll
have you put into a madhouse myself to prevent you from plunging
us all into disgrace and ruin. Idiot! Fool! Madman! "

He screamed like a sea-gull until his breath was gone, and
then, gesticulating wildly, went downstairs with heavy thudding
steps like a man walking on stilts.

A few minutes later Gell, going to the window with wet eyes,
saw his father on the opposite side of the street, looking up at
the house as if half minded to return. His stick fell from his
nervous hand, and with difficulty he picked it up. It dropped
again, and a passer-by handed it back. Then he went off in the
direction of the railway station, dragging his feet after him.

II

Frightened by what his father had said about the intention of
the Chief Constable to have him arrested as insane, Gell stayed
indoors altogether.

This meant days without food. At first he drank a great deal
of water, being very thirsty. Then his thirst abated and his head
began to feel light. After a while he became dizzy, and even in
the darkness everything seemed to float about him.

On the morning after his father's visit he heard a woman's step on the stairs, followed by her knock at his door. He thought it was his sister Isabella and that she had come, with her sharp tongue, to remonstrate, so he made no answer.

On the day following he heard the same light step. Isabella again! But no, she had always railed against Bessie, and he was not going to give her another opportunity of doing so.

Meantime, without food or drink, he was travelling fast towards the borderland of the desert realm of Insanity, with its cruelly-beautiful mirages.

Lying on his sofa with eyes closed he was picturing to himself the day of Bessie's release, when he would go to Castletown to bring her away, and then the day after, when he would marry her, and then the day after that when they would leave the island for America—Bessie walking along the pier with head down, but himself with head up, as if saying, " There you are—I told you so! "

The knock came again, and again he did not answer it. " No, no, Mistress Isabella! You shan't speak ill to me of the woman who cared so much for me that she went to prison for my sake."

He had still travelled farther by this time. He was out in the middle-west, on one of the high plains of that free continent. He was working at his profession. He was not a great lawyer, but he could speak out of his heart, and when he defended injured women juries heard him and judges listened.

He saw them coming to him from far and near—that long trail of the broken followers after the merciless army of civilisation. They were nearly always poor and could pay him nothing. But what matter about that? At home, at night, wet or cold, there was a bowl of soup, a cheerful fire and . . . . Bessie!

On the Saturday morning he awoke from a dizzy sleep, with the sun shining into his room and the sea outside the breakwater singing softly. He was in his shirt sleeves, for he had thrown himself on the bed in his clothes; his boots were unbuttoned; his fair hair was tangled; he had not shaved for many days.

Again he heard the light step on the stairs. But something in the rustle of the dress seemed to say that after all it was not his sister. He listened. There were two knocks, louder and more insistent than before; then the rattle of the brass lid of his letter-box, and then something falling on the floor.

A letter! After the light footsteps had gone downstairs he crept over the carpet on tiptoe, picked up the letter and looked at it. There were two lines at the top, partly printed, and partly written—

" *Castle Rushen Prison—Number 7.*"

Gell stared at the blue envelope, and then with trembling fingers tore it open. It was the letter which Bessie had dictated to Fenella Stanley. She was to die, and was calling on him to save her. Through her heart-breaking words he could hear her cries and supplications. The letter had been written five days ago, and in two days more she was to be executed!

Whatever he had been before, Gell was no longer a sane man now. He was thinking of Stowell and cursing him. Oh, that God would only put it in his power to punish him!

Then he remembered that this was the Deemster's fortnightly Court-day. The Court began to sit at eleven, and it was now half-past ten.

He would go across to the Court-house. Why not? He was an advocate—nobody dare refuse him admission to a Court of Law. And as soon as Stowell stepped on to the bench he would rise in his place and cry, " You scoundrel! Come down from the Judgment seat! Because you were rich you thought you could buy a man's soul and a woman's body. But take that, and that! " and then he would fling his father's money into Stowell's face.

At that moment, having parted from the Chief Constable, Stowell was driving down the street.

Gell dragged his black bag from the corner into which he had thrown it on returning from Castletown, and put on his gown without remembering that he was in his shirt-sleeves, and then his wig, without knowing that his hair was dishevelled.

He was staggering from weakness and the pictures on the walls were going round him with an increasing vertigo, but he was struggling to regain his strength.

He heard a step on the stair (a man's step this time) and then a firm knock at his door.

" Farrell! " he thought. The Chief Constable was coming to arrest him. But nobody should do that yet—not until he had come face to face with Stowell.

The knock was repeated.

" Go away! " he cried.

Then he pulled open the door, and found Stowell himself standing on the threshold. He fell back breathless. Stowell entered the room and closed the door behind him.

III

" Alick! "

" Go away! "

" I have something to say to you."

"Go away, I tell you."

"But I have something to tell you."

"There's only one thing you can tell me. Is it true—is she to die?"

"It . . . . it is so appointed."

"Then take that," cried Gell, and flinging himself upon Stowell with the fury of madness he struck him in the face and laid open his cheek-bone.

There was an awful silence. Gell had staggered to a bookcase behind him, expecting Stowell to strike back. But Stowell remained standing, and then said, with a break in his voice,

"I have well deserved it."

That was too much for Gell. He began to stammer incoherently and when he saw a streak of blood begin to flow down Stowell's cheek he broke down altogether. Out of the depths of a thousand memories of their friendship, all the way up since they were boys, a great tide of tenderness came surging over him, and he dropped into a chair and cried,

"Then it's true—I'm mad."

But after another moment he was up and hurrying into the next room for a sponge and a basin of water.

"It's nothing! Nothing at all," said Stowell. "See, it has stopped already. And now sit down and listen."

A few minutes later they were sitting side by side on the sofa— Gell sniffling, Stowell talking quietly.

"Alick!"

"Yes?"

"Bessie is waiting for you. She thinks you are trying to obtain her pardon."

"I know. She has written. But what can I do? Nothing!"

"If I can help her to escape from Castle Rushen will you take her away from the island?"

Gell's eyes glistened. "Only give me the chance," he said.

"She could never come back. Therefore you could never come back either."

"What do I care?"

"You would have to give up everything—your inheritance, your family, your . . . . !"

"I . . . . I can't help that."

"You are sure you would never regret the sacrifice?"

"Never! Only show me the way . . . ."

"I will," said Stowell.

And then he explained his scheme and the motives which had inspired it. He had been compelled to condemn the girl, according to law, but he had come to see that the old Statute was a crime, and that it was his duty to break it.

" Do *you* say that, Victor—you? "

" Listen."

An Irish tramp steamer would be lying in Castletown Harbour on Sunday night. She would berth in front of the Castle, not more than fifteen yards from the gates. At eleven o'clock Stowell would open the Deemster's private door and bring Bessie out. Gell must be there to take her aboard. The tide being up, the vessel would sail immediately. She would sail north, past the Point of Ayre, to give the appearance of going to Scotland; but in the morning, when out of sight from the land, she would steer south and land her passengers at Queenstown. Atlantic liners called there twice a week and Gell and Bessie must take passages to New York. On reaching New York they must travel west—far west . . . .

" But can it be done? Can you get Bessie out of the Castle? "

" I've counted every chance," said Stowell. " Whatever happens, I must not fail."

" What a good fellow . . . . " began Gell, but Stowell dropped his head and hurried on with his story.

" I've given the Irish Captain a hundred pounds, and you are to give him another hundred when he puts you ashore at Queenstown. I'll find you the money."

" No, no! I've enough of my own—see," said Gell, and he showed the bundle of banknotes given to him by his father.

" Your father gave you that? "

" Yes, to pay my way to America."

Stowell's face glowed with a kind of superstitious rapture. More than ever now he was certain he was doing right, that the Divine powers were directing him. But all the same he kept up the cunning of the criminal.

" I must see you again to-morrow night in some secret place. Where shall it be? "

" Why not the Miss Browns' at Derby Haven? They'll hold their tongues. They owe me something."

" Very well, eight o'clock, Sunday night," said Stowell, and he rose to go.

" What a good fellow . . . . " began Gell again, but Stowell looked at him and he stopped.

The Deemster's Court had to wait for the Deemster. When he arrived with a patch of plaster on his cheek-bone, he told Joshua Scarff that he had accidentally knocked his face against

a gas-bracket and had had to go to a chemist to get the
wound dressed.

It was an intricate case he tried that day, but the advocates
engaged in it said he had never before been so cool, so clear,
so collected.

"After all, the Governor knew what he was doing," they
told themselves.

That night, Saturday night, after a furtive visit to the tavern
on the quay, Gell slipped through the back streets to the railway
station and leapt into the last train for the north as the carriages
were leaving the platform.

He was going home to say good-bye to his mother—not with
his tongue, for he had no hope of speaking to her, but with his
eyes and his heart. If he could only see her for a moment before
leaving the island!

It was late when he reached the lane to his father's house, and
the night was dark, for it was the time between the going and
the coming of two moons.

At length the blacker darkness of the house stood out against
the gloomy sky. There was no light in any of the windows—the
family had gone to bed. But Alick had been born there, and he
thought he could find his way blindfold.

For some time he walked stealthily about, trying to discover
the dining-room window, for he remembered what his father had
said about his mother sitting with her feet in the fender. He
found it at last, but, peering behind the edge of the blind, he saw
nothing except the dull slack of the fire dropping to ashes in
the grate.

Groping about in the darkness on the gravel his footsteps had
made a noise and presently a dog inside began to bark. It was his
own dog, Mona, and he remembered that when he was a boy he
had bought her as a pup for five shillings from a farmer and
brought her home in his arms, licking his hand.

The dog's clamour awakened the household, and presently,
through the long staircase window, he saw his sisters on the
landing, in their nightdresses and curl-papers, carrying candles
and looking frightened.

Then the sash of a window went up with a bang and his
father's voice came in a husky roar through the night,

"Who's that?"

With a chill down his back, Alick turned about and hurried
away, feeling that he was being driven from the home of his
boyhood as if he were a thief.

CHAPTER THIRTY-SEVEN

THE ESCAPE

NEXT day was Sunday. It was a blind day at Ballamoar, with a chill air and white mists sweeping up from the sea.

In the morning Stowell went to church. In the afternoon he sat in the Library, reading in many volumes the stories of prison-breakings and escapes. He saw that in nearly every case of failure chance had played a part at the last moment, and he thought hard to foresee every possible contingency.

Towards evening he brought his car round from the garage and told Janet not to wait up for him. She had delivered Fenella's message (" Tell him to come back to me ") and thought she knew where he was going to. He was going to Government House. The sweet old soul was very happy.

" I'll leave the piazza door on the catch, dear," she said, as he was going off into the moving shadows of the trees.

By the time he reached Castletown the mist had deepened to a fog. The broad tower of the Castle looked monstrously large and forbidding against the gloom of the sky, and the fog-horn of the light-house on Langness was blowing with a measured and melancholy sound across the unseen sea.

Coming upon a tholthan (a ruined cottage) by the roadside he ran his car into it, and then walked into the town.

The little place was once the capital of the island, and still retained many of its primitive characteristics. There were no lamps in the streets, which were therefore quite dark. Only a few of the houses gave out light, for the younger children were already in bed, and their parents were trooping to church or chapel.

The church bells were ringing. Save for that, and the footsteps of his fellow pedestrians who walked in the darkness beside him, Stowell heard nothing but the blowing of the far-off fog-horn. Everything favoured his design. " It was meant to be," he told himself.

Nevertheless he was conscious of making his steps light and of trying to escape observation. He took the least frequented thoroughfares, so that he might walk fast and not be recognised, but in a narrow lane that ran along under the Castle he came upon a pitiful spectacle and was compelled to stop.

An elderly woman, wearing little except her nightdress, with her feet bare and her long grey hair hanging loose, was kneeling on the paved way and praying.

" Oh Lord, as Thou didst send Thine angel to take Peter out of prison, send him now to take my poor girl out of the Castle."

By a dull light from a curtained window, Stowell saw who the poor demented creature was. It was Mrs. Collister. Little as he desired it, he had to pick her up and take her home.

" Come, mother," he said, raising her to her feet.

She looked into his face with awe, and permitted herself to be led away by the hand like a child. A group of boys and girls who had gathered round told him where she lived and that she was the mother of the woman who was to be " hangt " in the morning.

Just then the people, a man and his wife, with whom she lodged, came hurrying up, saying they had left her in bed while they went into their yard on some errand and on returning to the kitchen they had missed her.

In a few moments they were all at the open door of the house, a tiny place two steps down from the street, with a lamp burning on the table.

Finding the light on his face Stowell said Good-evening and hurried away, but not before the man and his wife had seen him.

" That must be the young Dempster," said the man.

" It was his father," said Mrs. Collister.

" But his father is dead, woman," said the wife.

" It was his father, I tell thee," said Mrs. Collister, and they let her have her way.

Still the church-bells rang, the fog-horn blew and Stowell stepped lightly through the dark streets of the little town. He passed the new Methodist chapel with the dark figure of the pew-opener against the coloured glass screen of the vestibule; the barracks, with the sentinel pacing outside and a number of red-coated soldiers in a bare room within, smoking and playing cards. The market-square was ablaze with light from the windows of the church (the same at which Bessie had kept Oie'l Verree) and the shadowy forms of the congregation were passing in at the porch.

At length he reached the quay with its smell of rock-salt and tar. The *Dan O'Connell* was lying under the Castle gates, lazily getting up steam, and the Captain was smoking by the gangway.

" Everything right, Captain? "

" Everything, Sir."

" Will the fog interfere? "

" Not a ha'porth, yer Honour."

" What about the Harbour-master? "

" In church with the wife, but I'm to have supper with him after the sarvice and take a bottle of something."

" And the Turnkey? "

" Blind polatic at the ' Manx Arms,' Sir."

There came a dull hammering from the inside the Castle. Stowell shivered.

" Will they be gone in time ? "

" Going back by the last train they're telling me."

" You'll whistle when you're clear away ? "

" Shure ! "

As Stowell crossed the foot-bridge at the back of the Church, he heard the congregation singing the opening hymn (" Nearer, my God, to Thee ") and thought he knew the subject of the forthcoming sermon. The melancholy blowing of the fog-horn was coming through the blindness of the sea; the revolving light was blinking in and out on Langness.

A quarter of an hour later he was at Derby Haven. Most of the houses of the little port were dark, but the window of one of them gave out a faint light. Stowell tapped at it and Gell opened the door.

For two hours they sat together in the old maids' stuffy sitting-room, talking in whispers. Stowell gave Gell his last instructions.

" You remember that there are two gates to the Castle ? "

" Yes."

" At eleven o'clock exactly, the moment the clock has ceased striking, you'll ring at the big gate, and then step round to the Deemster's."

" Yes ! "

" Somebody will open the gate. It will be the jailer. If he calls you'll make no answer."

" Yes ? "

" Yes ? "

" As soon as he has closed the big gate the little one will be opened and Bessie will be brought out to you."

" Yes ? "

" That's all. You know the rest."

After that there was a cold silence, quite unlike the warmth of yesterday. Each was thinking of the cruel thing which had come between them, and neither dared to talk about. At length Gell, taking something from his pocket, said,

" I owe you some money."

" No, you don't. Remember the terms I lent it on."

" Then take this anyway," said Gell, handing Stowell a sealed envelope.

After that there was another long silence, and then Gell said, in a thick voice,

" When we're far enough away I'll write."

" No, no! "

" Do you mean that I'm never to write to you? "

" Never."

" But I will . . . . I must . . . . "

" Don't be a damned fool, man. Can't you see you never can? "
There was a pause.

" Victor," said Gell, " that's the first unkind word you have
ever said to me."

" Alick," said Stowell, " it shall be the last."

The wash of the tide (it was near to the flood) on the stones of
the shore, the monotonous blowing of the fog-horn and the deliberate ticking of the clock on the mantelpiece were the only sounds
they heard except the irregular heave of their own breathing.

The two men were alternately watching the fingers of the clock
and gazing down at the pattern of the carpet. At a few minutes to
ten Stowell got up and said,

" I must go now."

" I'll walk down the road with you," said Gell.

They walked side by side in the mist until they came to the
ruins of Hango Hill (where long before Alick had had his fight
with the townsmen) and were breast to breast with King
William's College.

" You had better go back now. We must not be seen together," said Stowell.

They stood for some moments without speaking. The clock
in the school tower was striking ten. The school itself was in
darkness. Another generation of boys were lying asleep in it now.

" I suppose we've got to say good-bye," said Gell.

Stowell made no reply, but he took Gell's hand and there was a
long handclasp. Then they separated, Stowell going on towards
the town, and Gell turning back to Derby Haven. Each had
walked a few paces when Gell stopped and called,

" Vic! "

" What is it? "

There was a pause, and then, in a thick voice,

" Nothing! S'long! "

And so they parted.

There was loud laughter and a voice with a brogue from a
house on the quay with the blind down but the top sash of the
window partly open. The church was dark and the market-place
silent, save for the measured tread of the sentry.

But as Stowell crossed the square he heard a light step and
saw through the thick air the shadowy form of a woman coming

from the direction of the Castle and going towards the hotel opposite.

He hung back until she had passed, and when the door of the hotel opened to her knocking, and the light from within rushed out on her, he saw who it was.

It was Fenella. Stowell understood. She had come from the cell of the condemned woman, and was sleeping in Castletown that night in order to be with her in the morning.

" But wait! Only wait! "

In spite of his certainty that Providence was on his side he stepped more lightly than ever as he went down to the quay.

The funnel of the Irish steamer was now throbbing hard, and a few sailors on the forward deck were swearing. Save for this and the wash of the tide against the sides of the harbour, all was still.

Stowell looked around and listened for a moment. Then he stepped up to the Deemster's door and pulled the bell, and heard its clang inside the walls.

II

" Ah, is it you, Dempster? You've come for Miss Stanley? She's just gone, Sir."

" I know. I saw her. Are you alone, Mr. Vondy? "

" Alone enough, Sir. It's shocking! The night before an execution too! That Willie Shimmin, the drunken gommeral, went off at four and isn't back yet. I wouldn't trust but I'll be here by myself until the High Bailiff and the Inspector and long Duggie Taggart come at six in the morning."

" How is your prisoner to-night, Mr. Vondy? "

" Wonderful quiet, Sir."

" Still expecting her pardon? "

" 'Deed she is, poor bogh, and listening for Mr. Gell's feet to fetch it. Now she thinks he'll come in the morning. ' Something tells me he'll come at daybreak,' she said, and that's the for she's gone to sleep."

They had reached the guard-room, where a fire was burning, and an old oak armchair (once the seat of the Kings of Man) was drawn up in front of the hearth.

" Gone to sleep, has she? I must see her though. I have something to tell her."

" Is it the pardon itself, Sir? Has it come then? "

" Not yet, but a telegram may come from London at any moment."

" You don't say? "

" Give me your key, and sit here and make your supper "
(a kettle was singing on the hob), " and if you hear the bell you
will go off to the gate immediately."

" I will that, Sir."

At the end of a long corridor Stowell stopped at a cell that
had a label on the door-post (" *Elizabeth Corteen. Murder.
Death* ") and looked in through the grill. In the dim light he saw
the prisoner lying on her plank bed under her brown prison
blanket. With a tremor of the heart he opened the door quietly
and closed it behind him.

" Bessie ! "

It had been hardly more than a whisper, but through the mists
of sleep Bessie heard it. There was a cry, a bound, and then a
rapturous voice saying in the half darkness,

" Ah, you are here already ! I knew you would come."

But at the next moment, seeing who her visitor was, she stared
at him with wide-open eyes, and then fell on him with reproaches.

" So it's you, is it? What have you come for? Is it only to
tell me that I'm to die in the morning? "

Stowell stood with head down, feeling like a prisoner before
his Judge. Then he said,

" You are not to die, Bessie."

She caught her breath and put up her hands to her breast.

" Do you mean that I am . . . . "

" You are pardoned and have to leave this place immediately."

For a perceptible time Bessie stood silent, save for her breathing, which was loud and rapid.

" Is it true? Really true? "

" Quite true."

There is something childlike in sudden joy; Paradise itself
must be a place of children. Bessie dropped back on her bed,
clasped her hands together like a child, and said,

" I see it all now, and it has been just as I thought at first.
You wrote a letter to the King and he has pardoned me. The
law is hard but the King is so tender-hearted. ' Poor girl,'
he thought, ' she didn't mean to kill her baby—not after it
came, anyway.' "

Her eyes, which had been glistening, suddenly became grave,
and lifting them to the ceiling, with her hands clasped before her
face, she began to pray.

" Oh God, I've not been a good girl and I don't know how to
pray right, but . . . . " and then came a flood of words too sacred
to be set down.

When she had finished her prayer she said,

" But *you* have been good too, and I have been insulting you! That's the way with a girl when she has been in trouble. You'll forgive me, won't you? "

Her face lit up and she went on talking, more to herself than to Stowell.

" Did you say I was to leave this place immediately? That means first thing to-morrow, doesn't it? I'll go to mother. She's staying with some Methodist people in Quay Lane. Poor mother, she won't be able to believe it. We'll go home by the first train."

Thinking of home she found a kind of proud revenge in triumphing over her enemies.

" Dan Baldromma will have to hold his tongue now. And those Skillicornes will never be allowed to show their ugly old faces again. And Cain the constable will have to find another beat, too, and those impudent girls who stared at me at Douglas station—they'll never have the face to sit in the singing-seat again."

But the smiling background of her thoughts was love.

" Alick will hear of it, won't he? I wrote to him but he didn't answer. Perhaps his sisters prevented him—they've always been casting me up to him. Poor Alick! He'll forgive me—I know he will. It was for Alick I did it. And just think! Next Sunday, perhaps, when people are walking about, we'll go down Parliament Street together! And me on Alick's arm, and nobody to say a word against it, now that the King has forgiven me! "

Stowel hardly dared to look at the girl. For a long time he could not speak. But at length he compelled himself to tell her that she was not to go home. It was a condition of her pardon that she should leave the island.

" Leave the island? "

" Yes, there's a steamer in the harbour, and you are to sail by it to-night."

" To-night? "

" Yes, to Ireland, and from there, by another steamer, to New York."

" To New York? "

" Yes, but Alick is to go with you. I've just left him. We have arranged everything."

She looked searchingly into his agitated face and the radiance died off her own.

" But are you telling me the truth? " she said. " Am I really pardoned? You are not helping me to escape, are you? "

He pretended to laugh—It was hollow laughter.

"What an idea! A Deemster helping a prisoner to escape! Who would believe such a thing?"

"No! People wouldn't believe such a thing, would they?" she said, and her eyes again began to shine.

"At eleven o'clock the big bell will ring," said Stowell. "That will be Alick coming for you. You must give me your hand and I'll take you down to him."

"Oh, how happy we shall be!" she said. "We shall go far away, I suppose—where nobody will know what has happened here?"

"Yes, but you must make no noise on going out, and not call to anybody."

"But Mr. Vondy—he has been so good—I may stop and thank him?"

"He wont be there. I'll give him your message."

"But mother—if I'm going so far away I must say good-bye to her."

"No, I'm sorry the steamer will sail immediately."

She looked again into his agitated face and then, raising her voice, she said,

"Mr. Stowell, you are deceiving me. I have *not* been pardoned. You *are* helping me to escape."

"Hush!"

But (again in a loud voice) she cried,

"Don't lie to me any longer. Tell me the truth."

He hesitated for a moment, and then he told her. Yes, he *was* helping her to escape. He had tried to procure her pardon and failed, so he had determined to set her free.

While she listened to his tremulous voice she became a prey to a strange confusion. For days she had felt as if she hated this man, and now a mysterious feeling of warmth from the past came over her.

"But what about you?" she asked.

"I can take care of myself," he answered.

"But if anything becomes known after Alick and I have gone . . . ."

"Nothing *will* become known."

"But if anything does, and you get into trouble . . . ."

"Bessie," said Stowell (he was breathing hard), "I did you a great wrong a year ago . . . ."

"No, that was as much my fault as yours. I have been praying and praying for pardon, but rather than run away now and leave you to . . . . No, I won't go!"

There was a moment of uneasy silence and then Stowell said,

" Alick is waiting outside for you, Bessie. He is ready to give up everything in the world for your sake. Are you going to break his heart at the last moment? "

" But I can't! I can't! I . . . . I won't! And you shan't either. Mr. Vondy! Mr. Von— . . . . "

" Be quiet! Be quiet! "

She had tried to reach the door, but he had thrown his arms about her and was covering her mouth to smother her cries. Ceasing to shout she began to moan, and then he tried to coax her.

" Come, girl! Trust me! I know what I'm doing. Pull yourself together. Stand up! It's nearly eleven o'clock. You'll have to walk to the gate presently. Come now, be brave."

But her eyes had closed, and by the dim light from the grill he saw that she was insensible.

" Bessie! Bessie! " he whispered, but she was lying helpless in his arms.

For a moment he was bewildered. Of all the chances that might prevent success this was the only one he had not counted with. But at the next instant his mind, which was working with lightning-like rapidity, saw a new opportunity.

" Better so," he thought, and laying the unconscious woman on her bed he hurried back to the jailer.

II

" Mr. Vondy! Mr. Vondy! Your prisoner is ill."

The jailer, who had fallen asleep after his supper, staggered to his feet.

" God bless my soul! And the doctor living at the other end of the town too."

" Never mind the doctor! Brandy! Quick! "

" There isn't a drop in the Castle, Sir."

" Yes, there's a flask in my room. Take these " (giving him a bunch of keys) " and go for it."

" Where will I find it, Sir? "

" I don't know. I can't remember. Look everywhere—in every drawer, every cupboard."

" I will, your Honour."

" Don't come back without it."

" I won't, Sir." And still in the mists of sleep the jailer picked up his lantern from the table and staggered off.

Stowell listened to the sounds of the old man's retreating footsteps until they had died away.

23

"This will give more time," he thought—he had sent the jailer on a fruitless errand.

It was then five minutes to eleven. Returning to the cell he lifted Bessie in his arms and carried her out of the prison. At first he was no more conscious of her weight than he had been of the weight of the sheep on the mountains.

But outside it was very dark, and at every uncertain step his burden became heavier. In the open space between the main building and the outer walls the fog lay thick as in a well, and it was as much as he could do to see one foot before him.

Over the wooden drawbridge his feet fell with a thudding sound, but he groped for the grass at the bottom of the stone steps, so that he should not be heard on the gravel path.

There was no sound in the court-yard except that of the fierce belching from the funnel of the steamer, the wash of the tide in the harbour, the boom of the sea in the bay and the monotonous blowing of the fog-horn.

He was making for the Deemster's private entrance and had no light to guide him except the borrowed gleam from the door to the Deemster's rooms, which the jailer in his haste had left open. As he passed this door he heard the sound of the rapid opening and closing of drawers. The weight of the woman in his arms was becoming unbearable.

At one moment he saw the shadowy outlines of a white thing which the carpenters had erected against the walls. He shuddered and went on.

The damp air was chill and Bessie began to revive under it. At first she breathed heavily, and then she made those low, inarticulate moans of returning consciousness which are the most unearthly sounds that come from human lips.

"Mr. Von— . . . . Mr. Von— . . . . "

Both arms being engaged, Stowell had to crush the girl's mouth against his breast to stop her cries. They ceased and she swooned again.

His burden was becoming monstrous. With a savage strength of will and muscle he struggled along. At length he reached the Deemster's door. It was fastened as he knew, not only by the lock of which the key was in his waistcoat pocket, but also by three long bolts. With the unconcious girl in his arms it was as much as he could do to open it. At last he did so. A pale face was outside. It was Gell's.

"Take her—she has fainted." Not another word was spoken.

Gell, breathing rapidly, took Bessie into his arms, and carried her across the quay. Stowell watched him until he reached the gangway, and then the sea mist hid him. He heard Gell walking on the deck and then going, with heavy footsteps, down the cabin companion.

He closed the Deemster's door, locked and bolted it, and then turned back to the prison. Again he kept to the grass and was conscious of an effort to make his footsteps light.

On reaching the drawbridge he looked back and listened. The opening and closing of drawers was still audible. The funnel of the steamer was still belching invisible smoke, and red sparks from the fires below were shooting through it. The tide was still washing in the harbour, the sea was still booming in the bay, and the fog-horn was still blowing on Langness. Save for these sights and sounds, everything was dark and silent within the great blind walls.

Then the clock in the tower struck eleven. Every stroke fell on the clammy air like a blow from a padded hammer.

III

Five minutes passed.

Stowell had returned to the cell, stretched out the brown prison blankets so as to give the appearance, in the dim light, of a body on the bed, and was now sitting in the armchair before the fire in the guard-room. His work was not yet done, and he was listening to the sounds outside. Until the steamer sailed he must remain in the Castle to keep watch on the jailer. He was more sure than ever that he was doing God's work, but he was still behaving like a criminal.

Footsteps approached. The jailer entered, mopping his forehead.

" I can't find it, your Honour, and I've searched everywhere."

" Never mind, Mr. Vondy. Your prisoner recovered from her attack and is now sleeping peacefully."

" Sleeping, is she? I'll take a look at her."

" Don't! I mean don't go into the cell and disturb her."

" I won't, Sir," said the jailer, from half-way down the corridor.

Stowell listened intently. Presently the jailer returned.

" Aw, yes, she's fast enough! Wonderful the way they sleep on the last night. Something you told her, perhaps. Has the telegram come, your Honour? "

" No, and it won't come now. Eleven o'clock, they said. If it didn't come then I was not to expect it."

" Poor bogh! It will be a shocking thing when Duggie Taggart comes in the morning. I wouldn't trust but it will be a dead woman itself we'll be taking out of the cell, Sir."

" I wouldn't trust," said Stowell.

Insensibly he had dropped into the Anglo-Manx. He was trying to find some excuse for remaining.

" It'll be a middlin' cold drive home, old friend—couldn't you make me a cup of coffee? "

" With pleasure, Sir," said the jailer. And while the old man stirred the peats and hung the kettle on the slowrie, Stowell, listening at the same time to the voices without (the husky brogue of the Irish Captain and the guttural croaking of the half-tipsy harbour-master) got him to tell the story of his appointment.

" It was thirty years ago, when I was coachman at Ballamoar in the ' Stranger's ' days—a wonderful kind woman your mother was, Sir."

" Hurry up, boys. Bear a hand with that crank "—the swing-bridge was being opened; the steamer was to go out in spite of the fog.

" I used to be taking her for drives in the morning, and it was always ' Thank you, Mr. Vondy! A beautiful drive, Mr. Vondy! ' Aw, gentry, Sir, gentry born! "

" Damn your eyes, let go that forrard rope "—the Captain was on the bridge.

" We had a young Irish mare in them days, Sir, and coming home one morning in harvest, not more than a month before your Honour was born, Illiam Christian (he was always a toot was Illiam) started his new reaper in the road field just as we were passing the Nappin, and the mare bolted."

" Why the divil don't you take in the slack of that starn rope? Do you want me to come down and dump you overboard? "—the funnels had ceased to roar and the paddles were plashing.

" I was a middling strong young fellow then, Mr. Stowell, Sir, and if the mare pulled I pulled too, until one of the reins broke at me and I was flung off the box."

" Aisy does it! Take in that breast rope, bys "—the steamer was passing through the gate.

" I wasn't for letting go for all. Not me! Just holding on like mad, though it was tossing and tumbling on the road I was like a mollag in a dirty sea."

" Half-steam below there "—the steamer was opening the bay.

" I bet her at last, Sir, and up she came at the Ballamoar gates blowing like a smithy bellows and sweating tremenjous, but quiet as a lamb."

" Heave oh and away ! "

" I was ragged and torn like a scarecrow, and herself was as white as a sea-gull, but never a scratch, thank God ! "

" Bravo ! "

" The Dempster had heard the yelling on the road and down the drive he came in his dressing-gown and slippers, trembling like a ghost. And when he saw it was all right with herself, ' Mr. Vondy,' says he, with the water in his eyes, ' I'll never forget it, Mr. Vondy,' he says."

" And he didn't ? "

" 'Deed no ! Aw, a grand man, the ould Dempster, Sir. Middlin' stiff in the upper lip, but a man of his word for all. And when Capt'n Crow pegged out and this place was vacant he put me in for it."

Straining his powers of listening Stowell was still waiting for the whistle that was to tell him the steamer was clear away.

" Crow ? That was Nelson's Crow, wasn't it ? "

" Nelson's Crow it was, Sir. One-eyed Crow we were calling him. He was boatswain on the *Victory*, and when the big man went down he was in the cockpit holding him in his arms. ' Will I die, Mr. Crow ? ' said Nelson. ' We had better wait for the opinion of the ship's doctor, Sir,' said Crow."

There was a long shrill whistle from a distance. Stowell leapt to his feet and laughed—the steamer had gone.

" Ah, a rael Manxman, wasn't he ? Wouldn't commit himself, you see."

Then he slapped the jailer on the shoulder and said,

" So you've been here thirty years, old friend ? "

" About that, Sir," said the jailer.

" But do you know you wouldn't be here thirty hours longer if I were to tell the Governor what you've done to-night ? "

" Why, what's that, your Honour ? "

" Left a condemned prisoner without guard, or even without remembering to lock her up and carry away the keys "—and he threw the keys of the cell on the table.

" God bless me, yes ! I never thought of that. But it was yourself that sent me out, and your Honour will not tell."

" Not I, old friend. But listen ! Nobody in the island knows that I've been trying to get your prisoner's pardon, and now that it hasn't come, it's better that nobody should know. So you'll say nothing to anybody about my being here to-night ? "

" Not a word, Sir. But you've done your best for the poor bogh, and it's Himself will reward you."

It was not until Stowell was outside the Castle that he reflected that whatever else happened in the morning the jailer must certainly fall into disgrace.

"I must find a way to make it up to him," he thought.

IV

The quay was deserted and the berth of the tramp steamer in the harbour was an empty space, but in the fever of his impatience Stowell walked to the end of the pier to make sure that the ship had gone.

The fog had lifted a little by this time, the fog-horn was no longer blowing, and against the dark sea he could just make out the darker hull of the steamer leaving the bay. Farther away he saw the revolving light from Langness, which was shooting red vapour into the sky like breath from fiery nostrils. The night air was still cold, but his forehead was perspiring.

Bessie would be recovering consciousness by this time. "Where am I?" she would be saying. And then she would hear the throb of the engines and the wash of the water, and see Alick by her side.

For a moment he lost sight of the ship's stern light (a mist was sweeping over the surface of the sea) and his anxiety became agony, but it reappeared at the other side of the light-house and his spirits rose again. Yes, she was steering north.

"Sail on! Sail on! Sail on!"

He returned to the town. In the thinning fog everything looked immensely large and frightening. He walked slowly in order not to attract attention. Passing through the narrow streets he found nearly all the houses dark. Only two or three of the upper windows showed light, and from one of them, partly open, he heard the cry of a sick child.

But in a winding lane, close under the Castle, he came upon a cottage that was lit up in the lower storey, and loud with many voices. He recognised it as the house at which he had left Mrs. Collister, and understood what was happening. The old woman's Primitive friends were holding a prayer-meeting by her bedside in the kitchen to comfort her. A man was praying and many women were shouting responses.

"Save the sinner, O Lord!" (*Hallelujah!*) "She may be inside prison walls to-night, but show her the Golden Gates are always open." (*Hallelujah!*) "Remember Thy servant, her mother!" (*Aw yes, remember her!*) "Her soul is passing through deep waters." (*'Deed it is, Lord!*) "Stretch out Thy hand as Thou didst to Peter of old and suffer her not to sink."

Outside the town Stowell had an impulse to run. He found his motor-car where he had left it and pushed it into the road. While lighting his lamp he thought he heard sounds from the direction of the Castle. Had the escape become known? He listened for anything that might denote alarm. There was nothing.

The Castle clock struck twelve. The fog had nearly gone now, and looking back he saw the gloomy and forbidding fortress towering over the sleeping town. A few stars had appeared above it.

All was quiet. The condemned woman had escaped from Castle Rushen. There was nothing to show that he himself had been there.

With a last look back he started his engine and released his levers, and his car shot away.

CHAPTER THIRTY-EIGHT

THE GRAVE OF A SIN

NEARLY three hours later Stowell was at the Point of Ayre, where the head of the island looks into the sea. Leaving his car at the end of the last paved road he walked over the bent-strewn plain to where the tall, white, brown-belted light-house stands up against sea and sky. The light-houseman, who had just put out the light, seeing the Deemster approach, went down to meet him.

" May I go up to your lantern, Light-houseman? I've always wanted to see the sun rise from there."

" With pleasure, your Honour," said the Light-houseman, and he led the way up the circular stone stairway, through the eye of the light-house, with its glistening columns of bevelled glass, to the iron-railed gallery that ran like a scalf round its neck.

For a long half-hour Stowell walked to and fro there. He felt as if he were on the prow of some mighty ship, with the sea racing in white foam along the rocks on either side. Far below were the booming waves; the sea-fowl were calling in the midway air; the sky to the east was reddening; the day was striding over the waters and driving the trailing garments of the night before it, and the sea was singing the great song of the dawn.

At last, straining his sight to the south, he saw what he had come to see—a steamer with a red and black funnel. Kept back during the dark hours by the fog on the coast, she was now coming on at full-speed.

There was a pang in thinking that this was the last he was to see of the two who were aboard of her. but there was a boundless joy in it also. They were united; they were happy; they were safe; he had wiped out his offence against them.

He watched the vessel as she passed. She lurched a little as she went through the cross-current of the Point. But now she was out in the Channel; now she was heading towards the Mull of Galloway; now she was fading into the northern mist and seemed to be dropping off into another planet.

At half-past three Stowell was back in his car. He could go home now with a cleaner heart, a surer conscience. It was a beautiful morning. The sun had risen. It was slanting over his shoulder as he drove along the grass-grown road on the north-west coast, with the sea singing and dancing by his side over a stretch of yellow sand. The lambs were bleating in the fields and the larks were loud in the sky.

What relief! What joy! His car was bounding on—past the Lhen, the Nappin, the old Jurby church with its four-square tower on the edge of the cliff—going faster than he knew, faster and still faster, like a winged creature, parting the way as it went, making the road itself to fly open, and the hedges, the trees, and the sleeping farm-houses to slant off on either side, and coming round at last, as with the heart of a bride, to the big gates of Ballamoar.

Home once more!

As he slackened speed and slid up the drive the rooks were calling in the tall elms and the song-birds in the bushes were singing. As silently as possible he ran his car into the garage and crept into the house.

The blinds were down and the rooms were dull with a yellow light, like sunshine behind closed eyelids. The grandfather's clock on the landing was striking four. Only four hours since he had left Castletown!

The servants were not yet stirring, and he stepped upstairs on tiptoe, hoping to reach his room unheard, but as he passed Janet's door she called to him.

" Is that you, Victor? "

He answered, " Yes."

" How late you are, dear! "

" Don't waken me in the morning."

In his bedroom he was partly conscious that familiar things looked strange—or was it that another man had come back to them? He undressed rapidly and got into bed, drawing a deep breath. It was all over. Bessie Collister was gone. It was nearly impossible that she could ever be traced and brought back. A monstrous judicial crime had been prevented. *He* had been permitted to prevent it. And now for the long, long rest of a dreamless sleep.

But in the vague, intermediate half-world of consciousness before sleep comes, he was aware of another, a warmer and more secret motive. Fenella! " Tell him to come back to me! " Ah, no, not until he had wiped out his fault. But *now* he could go to her! He had broken down the barrier between them. He had buried his sin in the sea.

Thank God! Thank God!

And then sleep, deep sleep, and the breathless day coming on.

END OF FIFTH BOOK

SIXTH BOOK
THE REDEMPTION

CHAPTER THIRTY-NINE

THE BIRTH OF A LIE

AWAKENING in the " George " in the early hours of morning, Fenella heard a noise outside her window that was like the running of a shallow river over a bed of small stones. She knew what it was. It was the sound of the feet of the people who were coming in crowds to stand outside the Castle walls and watch the slow-moving fingers of the clock, until the hoisting of the black flag over the tower should tell them that the invisible presence of Death had come and gone.

When, as the clock was striking six, she crossed the market-place on her way to the Castle, she found this crowd in great commotion, hurrying to and fro and calling to each other in agitated voices.

" Is it true? "

" So they're saying."

" God bless my soul! "

The Castle gate was open and people had penetrated as far as the Portcullis. An Inspector of Police, coming out hurriedly, commanded them to go back.

" Away with you! Is it play-acting you've come to look at? Smoking your pipes, too! "

But without waiting to see his orders obeyed he hastened away himself, shouting to somebody that he was going to knock up the telegraph office.

The court-yard, when Fenella reached it, though less crowded was as full of agitation. A blear-eyed man, who looked as if he had just awakened from a fit of intoxication, was walking aimlessly to and fro. It was Shimmin, the turnkey, but when Fenella asked him what had happened, he stared vacantly and made no answer. A very tall man, wearing a cloth cap over his head and ears and carrying a carpet-bag, was standing by the scaffold. This must be " long Duggie Taggart " and when Fenella, shuddering at sight of the man, asked him the same question, he shrugged his

362

shoulders and turned away. At the foot of the draw-bridge the High Bailiff and the jailer were in fierce altercation.

" I know nothing about it, I tell thee, Sir."

" Then you are a blockhead and a fool! "

At length two elderly men, the Chaplain and the Doctor, came down the Deemster's stairs, and then the truth, which Fenella had partly surmised, became fully known to her. The condemned woman had escaped during the night. There would be no execution that day.

Through a tumult of mixed feelings, Fenella was conscious of a sense of immense relief. Her first thought was of Bessie's mother, and she turned back to take the news to her.

The little house in Quay Lane had its door still closed, but through the kitchen window, whereof the upper sash was partly down, came the singing of a hymn in tired and husky voices,

> " Jesus, lover of my soul,
> Let me to Thy bosom fly."

It was not immediately that Fenella could get an answer to her knocking, but at length the man of the house, in his ganzie and long sea boots, opened the door, still singing.

The little low-ceiled kitchen was full of people, and the close air of the place seemed to say that they had kept up their prayer-meeting the night through.

On a chair bedstead against the opposite wall, Mrs. Collister in her cotton nightcap, from which long thin locks of her grey hair were escaping, was rocking her body to the tune, while fumbling with bony fingers a Methodist hymn-book which lay open before her on the patchwork counterpane.

Fenella, with a warm heart for the old mother in her trouble, pushed through to the foot of the bed, but Mrs. Collister was terrified at the sight of her, thinking she was bringing bad tidings,

" Have they deceived me? " she cried. " Seven o'clock they said. Is it all over? "

" Be calm," said Fenella, and then she delivered her message. Bessie had gone from Castle Rushen. She was not to die that day.

A moment of vacant silence fell upon the room, such as seems to fall on the world when the tide is at the bottom of the ebb. With difficulty the old woman grasped what Fenella had said. Her watery eyes looked round at her people as if asking them to help her to understand. At length one of these cried,

" Glory to God! It's the answer to our prayers."

And then the truth seemed to descend on the poor broken brain like a healing breath from heaven. Stretching out her match-like arms, she seized Fenella's hands and said,

"I know who thou art. Thou art the Governor's daughter. Is it the truth thou'rt telling me?"

"Indeed it is."

"My Bessie is out of prison?"

"Yes, and nobody knows what has become of her."

A wild cry of joy burst from the old woman's throat.

"Liza! Liza Killey, wilt thou believe me now? Didn't I tell thee it was the old Dempster himself that the Lord had sent to take my child out of prison?"

A wave of new life seemed to come to her, and throwing back the clothes she struggled out of bed (her blue-veined legs and feet showing bare under her cotton nightdress) and went down on her knees to pray. But her prayer was drowned by the husky voices of her companions, who had by this time raised a hymn of thanksgiving.

Fenella turned to go, and the man and woman of the house followed her to the door.

"What was that she said about the Deemster?"

They told her what had happened the night before—how the old woman had escaped into the streets and the Deemster had brought her back to the house.

"Are you sure it was the Deemster?"

"We thought so then, but she thrept us out it was his father who is dead and buried, and now we don't know in the world if it was or wasn't."

The singers were singing in triumphant tones—

> "God moves in a mysterious way,
> His wonders to perform."

Fenella, who had begun to tremble, turned back to the hotel. The market-place was full of people, who were pouring into it from every thoroughfare. On reaching her room she locked the door, pulled down the window-blind, sat on the bed, covered her eyes, and tried to think out what had happened.

The noise outside was like the surge of the sea, and like the surge of the sea was the tumult in her heart and brain.

Could it be possible that Victor Stowell had helped Bessie Collister to escape? She remembered what he had said to her father—that if any attempt were made to carry out the sentence *he* would prevent it. She remembered what she had said to him—that never could there be anything between them while that girl lay in prison. He had been in Castletown the night before, and he was the only man in the island who could have access to the Castle without an order from the Governor or the Chief Constable.

But a Judge to break prison! What would be the end of it? *Why* had he done this incredible thing, risking everything? Was it solely because he could not allow that unhappy girl, who had suffered so much for him already, to go to the gallows? Or was it, perhaps, because she herself had said . . . .

Suddenly a great quickening of her love for Stowell came over her. If she had stumbled upon his secret she would protect it.

" But what can I do? " she asked herself.

At one moment it occurred to her to run back to Quay Lane and warn the good people there to say nothing more about the Deemster. But no, that might awaken suspicion. They thought Bessie's escape was due to supernatural agencies, that it had come as an answer to their prayers—let them continue to think so.

At seven o'clock she was in the train for Douglas and the telegraph poles were flying by. She must know what the Governor was doing. But whatever her father might do her own course was clear.

She must stand by Victor now, whatever happened.

II

In the cool sunshine of the early May morning Government House lay asleep. The gardener was mowing a distant part of the lawn when he saw a carriage drive rapidly up to the porch. Two gentlemen got out of it, and in less time than it took him to empty his grass-pan into his wheelbarrow they rang three times at the door.

Inside the house nobody was yet stirring except old John, the watchman, who was drawing the curtains and opening the windows. He heard the bell and thought the postman had brought a registered letter. In his cloth shoes he was shuffling to the vestibule when the bell rang again and yet again.

" *Traa de looiar* " (" Time enough "), he growled, but his voice fell to a more deferential tone when he opened the door, and saw who was there.

" Our apologies to His Excellency, and say the Attorney-General and the Chief Constable wish to see him immediately on urgent business."

The two men stepped into the smoking-room, which was still dark with the blinds down and rank with last night's tobacco smoke.

A few minutes later, the Governor entered in his dressing-gown over his pyjamas and with his bare feet in his heelless slippers. And then the Attorney told him—the young woman who was to have been executed that morning had escaped.

" Good God, no ! "

" Only too true, Sir. Colonel Farrell has had an urgent telegram from his Inspector at Castletown."

" When did it happen? "

" During the night. The jailer says he locked her up at eleven and when he opened the cell at five the prisoner was gone."

" Where is the jailer? "

" At the Castle still," said the Chief Constable, " but I've told the police to send him up immediately."

The Governor rose from the seat into which he had dropped and walked to and fro.

" Such a blow to the authority of the law—the escape of a prisoner on the eve of her execution ! " said the Attorney.

" Such a handle to the disorderly elements, too ! " said the Chief Constable.

" Good Lord, don't I know? Let me think! Let me think! "

The Governor drew up one of the window blinds and his eyes fell on a steamer lying by the pier with smoke rising lazily from her black and red funnels.

" If the woman escaped only a few hours ago," he said, " she cannot have left the island yet. Have you given orders that the passengers by the morning steamer shall be watched? "

" Not yet, sir."

" Do so at once. If that fails, telegraph to your police in every town and parish. Good gracious, in this pocket-handkerchief of an island it ought to be possible to re-capture an escaped prisoner in a day, even if she lies like a toad under a stone."

" We'll leave no stone unturned, sir."

" A woman! A mere girl! Unless the jailer or his people deliberately opened the doors for her she must have had assistance."

" That's what *I* say, your Excellency."

" Have you any idea who helped her? "

" No . . . . that is to say . . . . "

" Where's young Gell, the Advocate? "

" In his rooms in Athol-street . . . . I presume."

" Find out for certain. Come back at four this afternoon and bring that blockhead of a jailer with you. And listen " (the men were leaving the room), " try to keep this ridiculous thing quiet. If it gets into the papers across the water all England will be laughing at us."

The Governor was again at the window, watching the Attorney-General's carriage going rapidly down the drive, when he saw a hackney car, containing Fenella, coming up to the house.

That sight started a new order of ideas. He remembered Stowell's threat—" If you order that girl's execution, it shall never be caried out, because *I* shall prevent it." For three days he had understood this to mean that the Deemster would appeal over his head to the Imperial authorities. But Stowell had not done so—he wasn't such a fool, he had remembered the bedevilments of his own position. So the Governor had dismissed the thought, and his anger at the son of his old friend had subsided. But now the threat came back on him with a new interpretation. Could it be possible? Such an unheard-of thing?

As soon as Fenella entered the house he called her into his room and shut the door behind her.

" You have just come from Castletown? "

" Yes, father."

" Then you know what has happened? "

" Yes."

" Can you throw any light on it? "

" Light on it? "

" I mean . . . . have you seen anything of Stowell since we spoke of him last? "

" Nothing."

" Nor heard from him? "

" No."

" Do you think it likely that . . . . But it is impossible. No responsible person in his sense could do such a thing. It must be the other one."

" What other, father? "

" Young Gell, of course. He is the only man in the island who could wish that girl to escape—the only one who would be fool enough to help her to do so."

Fenella went to her room with a heart at ease. She was sorry for Gell, very sorry, but in the consuming selfishness of her love for Stowell she found a secret joy in the thought that suspicion was being diverted from the real culprit.

Victor was safe thus far. But what would he do himself? What was he now doing?

III

It was near to noon when Stowell awoke at Ballamoar. His bedroom (formerly his father's) faced to the south and flashes of sunshine from the chinks of the window curtains were crossing the bed on which he lay with his head on his arm.

It was a startling moment.

His long sleep had washed his brain as in a spiritual bath, and with the awakening of his body his conscience had awakened also. The events of the previous night rolled back on him like a flood, and now, for the first time, he saw what he had done.

To prevent the law from committing a crime he had committed a crime against the law! He, the Judge, sworn to uphold Justice, had deliberately betrayed it! Had anything so monstrous ever been heard of before?

After a while, through the deafening buzzing of his brain, he became aware of the droning sound of voices in the room below, and then of their sharp clack as the speakers (they were Janet and Joshua Scarff) stepped out of the house to the gravel path in front of it.

" No, don't waken his Honour, Miss Curphey. He hasn't been well lately, and sleep does no harm to anyone. Besides he'll hear the bad news soon enough."

" 'Deed he will, Mr. Scarff."

" It will be a terrible shock to him—especially if my suspicions about a certain person prove to be justified. But that's the way, you see—one act of wrong-doing leads to another. Pity! Great pity! "

It was out! Stowell felt as if the bed under him were rocking from the first tremor of an earthquake.

Half-an-hour later he was at breakfast downstairs. For a long time, Janet was trying to break the news to him. At last it came. The young woman who was to have been executed that morning had escaped. Joshua Scarff had had it from the Inspector at Ramsey—it was being telegraphed all over the island.

For the sake of appearances Stowell made an exclamation of surprise, despising himself for doing so and feeling as if the toast in his mouth were choking him.

" It's impossible not to be glad," said Janet, " that the poor guilty creature has escaped the gallows, but Joshua thinks things are not likely to end there."

" And what does he say? . . . . "

" He says she must have had an accomplice, and when the man is found out it will be the worse for both of them."

" And who . . . . who does Joshua think . . . . "

" Alick Gell. It seems he put appearances against himself at the trial, poor boy! "

Instead of going to town that day, as he had intended to do,

Stowell rambled through the trackless Curraghs. He was trying to be alone with the melancholy swish of the sally bushes and the mournful cry of the curlews. But his anxiety to know what was being done brought him back to the house. Hearing nothing there, he walked to the village for a copy of the insular newspaper. He found some excuse for speaking to everybody he met on the road—on other subjects, though, always on other subjects.

At the door of the little general store, with its mixed odour of many condiments coming out to him, he stopped and called,

" How's the rheumatism this morning, Auntie Kitty? "

" Aw, better, your Honour, a taste better to-day. But it's moral sorry I am to hear the bad newses you've had yourself, Sir. It's feeling it terrible you'll be, your Honour—you and the young man being the same as brothers. It will kill his mother—and her such a proud stomach. The woman couldn't see the sun for the boy, and she's been fighting the father all his life for him."

On his way back he met Cain, the constable, looking large and important.

" I'm sarching for them two runaways," he said, with his short asthmatical breathing, " and the Chief Constable is telling me I'll have to be finding them if they're lying like a toad under a stone."

Gell again! The report of the escape had passed over the island with the swift flight of a bird of prey—everywhere he could hear the flapping of its wings. And to the question of who could have assisted the young woman to escape from a place like Castle Rushen there was only one answer—Gell.

Towards nightfall Joshua Scarff called at Ballamoar on his way home from town. Things had turned out as he had expected —suspicion had fastened on Mr. Gell, and the Governor had ordered the police to scour the island for him.

" But everybody is sorry for your Honour. His friend! His bosom friend! Pity! Great pity! "

Gell! Always Gell! Again Stowell felt as if the earth were rocking beneath him. Where had his head been that he had not thought of this before—that in helping Alick Gell to go away with Bessie Collister he had put him into the position of the guilty man—guilty not only of the prison-breaking, but also of the earlier and uglier offence of being the girl's fellow-sinner?

He had thought he had buried his sin in the sea—had he only cast the burden of it upon Gell?

He recalled Alick' gratitude on going away, the undeserved praises which had cut to the heart, and then thought of Gell (far away in a foreign country) coming to hear of the evil name he had left behind.

24

What was Alick to think of him then? That what he had done had not been at the call of friendship, but of mere self-protection —to divert suspicion from himself, to remove the only witnesses against him, and thus to build his future life on the unprotected name of an innocent man?

"Must I let that lie run on without saying a word against it?"

And then Fenella! He had seen himself going to her and saying, "Now that the girl is no longer in prison the barrier between us is broken down." He had seen himself marrying her, and then rising higher and higher in the esteem of his people, with that brave woman by his side.

But now—what now?

Fenella would find him out! It was impossible that she could live long with a man who carried such a corroding secret without discovering it sooner or later. And when she had done so what would she think of him? A traitor to his friend and to the law! A Judge who had broken his oath! A wrong-doer, not a righter of the wronged, sitting in judgment upon others, yet himself a criminal! A man of honour to the outer world, a hypocrite in his own house; a pillar of the island in the eyes of his people, a liar in the eyes of his wife!

"No, God forbid it! I cannot let that lie run on. I cannot allow myself to be pilloried in life-long hypocrisy."

All the same he would wait to see what the Governor might do next. It was no good acting hastily.

CHAPTER FORTY

THE CALL OF A WOMAN'S SOUL

At four o'clock that day the Attorney-General and the Chief Constable had returned to Government House and were sitting, on either side of the Governor, with the jailer standing before them. Fenella stood by the window, apparently gazing into the garden but listening intently.

"Come now," said the Governor, "tell us what you know of this matter."

The jailer knew nothing. Changing repeatedly the leg on which he was standing and mopping his forehead with a coloured handkerchief, he protested absolute ignorance.

"After Miss Stanley left the Castle a piece after ten o'clock I locked the poor bogh in her cell . . . . "

"Do you mean the prisoner?"

"Who else, your Excellency?"

" Then say the prisoner."

" Well, I locked the prisoner in her cell a piece after ten o'clock last night and when I went back at five this morning to take her a bite of breakfast . . . . "

" Breakfast? Where was your female warder? "

" Mistress Mylrea? Sick of the heart since General Gaol. They're telling me she died last night, Sir."

" Where was your turnkey then? "

" Willie Shimmin? He went out on lave for a couple of hours on Sunday afternoon and didn't return on the night, Sir."

" Do you mean to tell me you were alone in the Castle on the night before an execution? "

" Aw, yes, alone enough, Sir."

" Colonel Farrell! " said the Governor, turning sharply upon the Chief Constable.

That gentleman, although embarrassed, had many excuses. He had not been made aware of the situation, and if this blockhead had only communicated with the police-station . . . .

" Well, well, enough of that now. Let us have the facts," said the Governor, and turning back to the jailer he said,

" Did anybody come to the Castle last night after Miss Stanley left it? "

" No, Sir, no! "

" And your keys? Did they ever leave your possession? "

" Never, Sir."

" After you locked the prisoner in her cell, what did you do? "

" I went back to the guard-room and sat by the fire, Sir."

" And fell asleep, I suppose? "

" I'll give in I slept a wink or two, Sir."

" Where were your keys while you were asleep? "

" On the table beside me, Sir."

" And when you awoke where were they? "

" In the same place, your Excellency."

" Were the gates of the Castle locked last night? "

" Aw, 'deed they were, Sir."

" And were they locked this morning? "

" They were that, Sir."

The Attorney-General, who had been leaning forward, dropped back.

" Extraordinary! " he said. " The whole thing has the appearance of the supernatural."

" Nonsense! " said the Governor. " Vondy, do you know Mr. Gell, the Advocate? "

" I'm sorry to say, Sir . . . . "

" Never mind about sorry—do you? "

" I do, Sir."

" When did you see him last? "

" At General Gaol, when he was out of himself, poor man, and we had to lock him up for threatening the Dempster."

" Did he never come to the Castle afterwards to see the prisoner? "

" Never, Sir."

" Will you swear that he was not there last night? "

" I will—before God Almighty, Sir."

" Then, if the cell was locked all night and the Castle gates were locked, how do you account for the escape of your prisoner? "

The jailer smoothed the hair over his forehead and then said, " Bolts and bars are nothing to the Lord, Sir."

The Governor gasped.

" Do you mean to say that while you were asleep before the fire in the guard-room an angel from heaven carried your prisoner through the Castle walls? "

" Aw, well . . . . I wouldn't say no to that, Sir. We're reading of the like in the Good Book anyway."

" Fenella," cried the Governor, " take this fool away and turn him out of the house."

When Fenella, who had been quivering all over, had left the room, followed by the jailer, the Governor turned to the Chief Constable.

" The woman was not on the morning steamer? "

" No, Sir."

" And what about Gell? "

" We broke open the door of his room in Athol Street and found he had gone."

" Ah! Have you come upon any trace of him elsewhere? "

" Yes; he slept at the Railway Inn at Ballaugh on Saturday night and took a ticket for St. John's by the first train on Sunday morning."

" Anything else? "

" The blacksmith at Ballasalla believes he saw him on Sunday evening going in the fog in the direction of Derby Haven."

" Aha! Did any fishing boat leave Castletown last night? "

" The Manx boats do not go out on Sunday, Sir."

" Any trading steamers then? "

" I don't know, Sir."

" Inquire at once. If your constables do not find the fugitives in the island we must send a ' Wanted ' across the water."

" I'll draw one up, Sir."

" Got the necessary photographs ? "

" One of the girl, which was found in the young man's rooms, Sir. Also one of the young man which we found in the girl's cell, but it is not of much use, being scratched and blurred as if it had been lying in water."

" No matter ! The Deemster is sure to have another. I'll write and ask him to meet us here at eleven on Wednesday morning. He'll be able to help you to your personal description and issue the warrant at the same time."

II

Meantime, Fenella had taken the jailer into the drawing-room and closed the door behind them.

" Mr. Vondy," she said in a low voice, " you can trust me. Nothing you may say in this room will ever be repeated. Did not somebody come to Castle Rushen last night after I left it ? "

The old man tried in vain to look into the big moist eyes that were on him, but at length he dropped his own and said,

" It is no use, miss. There will be no rest on me in the night unless I tell the truth to somebody. There can be no harm telling it to you neither—going to be the man's wife soon they're saying. It's truth enough, miss—somebody did come."

" Was it the Deemster ? "

" It was that," said the jailer, and then he told her everything that had happened.

Fenella's head became giddy and her cheeks blushed crimson. In a flash she saw what had happened. Victor had deceived the jailer. Did the old man know it ? Lowering her eyes she said,

" You didn't say this when the Governor questioned you—had you a reason for not doing so ? "

" I had. The Deemster made me promise to say nothing."

And then came the other and still more degrading story—the story of the intimidation Stowell had put upon the jailer to keep his visit secret.

Fenella felt as if she would sink through the floor in shame, but all the same she found herself saying,

" You've known the Deemster all his life, haven't you ? "

" I have. I was reared on the land," said the jailer, and then, raising himself to his full height, " I'm a Ballamoar myself, miss."

" Then you will keep the promise you gave him ? "

" Trust me for that, miss."

" But if anything should happen to yourself as the consequence of last night's escape . . . . "

"The father put me in the Castle and the son won't see them fling me out of it."

"But if he should be overruled by the Governor and unable to help you . . . . "

"I'll take my chance with him. What's it they're saying?— *the Ballamoar will out*, miss."

Tears sprang to Fenella's eyes, but her heart beat high.

"Mr. Vondy," she said, "he has not been well lately, and perhaps he doesn't always know what he is saying. If you should ever come to think that what he told you was not the truth . . . . the whole truth, I mean . . . . "

"Maybe so. I've been thinking as much myself since five this morning. But that's all as one to me, miss. Tell him *Tommy Vondy will keep his word*."

The jailer was gone, and Fenella was sitting with her hands over her eyes when she heard voices in the corridor and footsteps going towards the porch.

"You're right there, your Excellency" (it was the Attorney-General who was speaking). "The authority of law in this island has received a blow, and already the disorderly elements are stirring up strife."

"Who, for instance?"

"Qualtrough of the Keys and the man Baldromma."

"Farrell" (it was the Governor in a stern voice), "quash that instantly. If there's any rioting send for the soldiers from Castletown to assist your police."

"I will, your Excellency."

"And listen! Get rid of that blockhead of a jailer. Appoint somebody in his place and give him authority to employ his own warders. He'll have his prison full enough presently."

The closing of the outer door rang through the corridor, and at the next moment the Governor was in the drawing-room.

"Fenella," he said, "do you happen to know if Stowell has a photograph of young Gell, the Advocate?"

Before she had time to reflect, Fenella answered that he had. It was taken in America, and stood on the mantelpiece in the library at Ballamoar.

"But why?"

"Because I want him to bring it with him when he comes on Wednesday to issue the warrant."

"What warrant?"

"The warrant for the arrest of Gell, for breaking prison and aiding in the escape of the girl Collister."

"But, father, they are friends—life-long friends."

" What of that? Stowell is Deemster, and you heard the oath he took, didn't you? ' Without fear or friendship, love or gain.' His duty as a Judge is to administer Justice, and as long as I am here I'll see he does it."

III

During the remainder of that day and the whole of the following one Fenella was a prey to the cruellest perplexity. Would Victor Stowell issue that warrant for the arrest of the innocent man, being himself the guilty one?

How could he refuse? It would be his duty to issue the warrant—what excuse could he make for not doing so? And then what a temptation to let things go on as usual! Although he had broken prison, and therefore his oath as a Judge, how easily he might persuade himself that it had only been to snatch that poor girl from a wicked Statute!

Yet if Victor issued that warrant for the arrest of Gell he would be a lost man for ever after. No matter how high he might rise he would go down, down, down until his very soul would perish.

" It cannot be! It must not be! It shall not! "

She wanted to run to Ballamoar and say, " Don't do it. If you have done wrong confess and take the consequences."

Oh, what did she care about their quarrel now? It was no longer Bessie Collister's life, but Victor Stowell's soul that was in peril.

But no, she could not ask him to act under compulsion. He must act of his own free will. In the valley of the shadow of sin the guilty soul must walk alone.

" But is there nothing I can do for him? " she asked herself.

Yes, there was one thing—one thing only. She could pray. For long hours on the night before Stowell was to come to Government House Fenella knelt in her bed and prayed for him.

" O God help him! God help him! Help him to resist this great temptation."

At length peace came to her. Somewhere in the dead waste of the night she seemed to receive an answer to her prayers.

" He'll do the right, whatever it may cost him," she thought, and as the day was dawning she fell asleep.

But when she awoke in the morning she felt as if her heart would break. If Stowell confessed and took the consequences (as she had prayed he might do) he would be lost to her for ever. He would have to give up his Judgeship, be banished from the island, and become an outcast and a wanderer.

"Is that to be the end of everything between us? After all this waiting?"

Her eyes were full of tears when she looked at herself in the glass, but they were shining like stars for all that. An immense pity for Stowell had taken possession of her. An immense faith in him also. He must be the most unhappy man alive, but he was her man now; and nothing on earth should part them.

Going down to breakfast she met Miss Green on the stairs. The old lady was full of some breathless story of rioting in Douglas the evening before. How remote it all sounded! She hardly heard what was being said to her.

Coming upon the maid in the corridor she said,

"The Deemster is to call to-day, Catherine. Tell him I wish to see him before he sees the Governor."

In the breakfast-room her father was looking over a printer's proof on a sheet of foolscap paper. It was headed with the Manx coat-of-arms and the words "ISLE OF MAN CONSTABULARY," and had an empty space near the top for a block to be made from a photograph.

"But that is of no consequence now," thought Fenella, "no consequence whatever."

CHAPTER FORTY-ONE

IN THE VALLEY OF THE SHADOW

"GOOD heavens, what does it matter? A lie is only dangerous when it does some harm!"

Stowell awoke on the second day after the escape putting his situation to himself so. Where was the harm if Gell *was* suspected? He had gone with the woman he loved. He was happy. What would Alick care about the evil name he had left behind him?

"Then where's the harm?" he asked himself.

He would let things go on as usual—of course he would. Only he must make sure that the fugitives had got clear away.

Remembering that he had seen placards of the Atlantic sailings in the railway-station, he walked over to the station from the glen. It was all right—a big Atlantic liner was timed to leave Queenstown at twelve that day. It was now half-past twelve. Gell and Bessie would be out on the open sea by this time—steaming past Kinsale where the Manx boats fished for mackerel.

"Where's the harm?"

But just as he was leaving the station with a sense of security and even triumph, a train from Douglas drew up at the platform.

The guard shouted something to the station-master; and, looking back, Stowell saw a crowd gathering about a first-class carriage.

Somebody was being assisted to alight. It was the Speaker. He was utterly helpless. Between two members of the House of Keys the stricken man was half led, half carried to a dog-cart that was waiting for him at the gate.

His mouth was agape, his legs were dragging behind him, and his large hands were shaken by senile trembling. He did not speak, but as he went by he looked up, and Stowell felt that from his red eyes a mute malediction was being thrown at him.

When the dog-cart had gone, with the Speaker stretched out in it, stiff as a dead horse, and one of the Keys to see him home, the other joined Stowell and walked down the road by his side.

" Then your Honour hasn't heard what has happened? "

" No. What? "

There had been a sitting of the Keys that morning. The debate had been on some new scheme of land tenure—a thinly disguised form of confiscation. The Speaker had opposed it passionately, saying a man had a right to keep what he had earned and hand it on to his children. Then Qualtrough (a firebrand who possessed nothing) had taunted him with the unfortunate affair of yesterday. Why did *he* want to hand on his land, his son having run away with the woman he had corrupted?

A terrible scene had followed. The Speaker had had one of his brain-storms. His neck had swelled until it was nearly as broad as his face. " Sit down, Sir," he had shouted, but Qualtrough had refused to do so. At length, overcome by the clamour of his enemies and the silence of his friends, the Speaker had risen to resign. Since he could not maintain the authority of the chair he had no choice but to get out of it.

It had been a pitiful spectacle. None of them who were fathers had been able to look at it with dry eyes. The old man was trembling like a leaf and his legs seemed to be giving way under him.

" They say the sins of the fathers are visited upon the children, but maybe it's as true the other way about. I'm going blind and deaf. The sands of my life are running out . . . . "

He swayed forward and they thought he would have fallen on his face, but the Secretary of the House caught him in his arms, and then two of them were nominated to bring him home.

" Sorry to say it to your Honour, being his friend," said the member of the Keys, as they parted at the turn of the road, " but that young fellow has something to answer for."

That lie *had* done harm then! Was this the mystery of sin—

that it must go on and on, from consequence to consequence, deep
as the sea and unsearchable as the night?

On returning to Ballamoar, Stowell found Janet in great agitation. Mrs. Gell had sent across to ask if Robbie could run into
Ramsey to fetch Doctor Clucas. The doctor had come and gone.
The Speaker had had a stroke. It was his second. The third
would almost certainly prove fatal.

All that day Stowell was shaken by a chill terror. If the
Speaker died would Alick Gell come back to claim his inheritance?
If so he would hear it said on all sides that he had killed his
father by the disgrace he had brought on him.

What then? Would he tell the whole truth under that terrible
temptation, and thus bring down Stowell himself to ruin
and extinction?

" But what nonsense I'm talking," thought Stowell.

Gell could never come back, because Bessie could never do so.
Then who was to know that it was a lie that Gell had killed
his father?

Suddenly came the thought, " *I* am to know."

This fell on him like a thunderbolt. How was he to marry
Fenella with a thought like that in his heart? It would be with
him night and day. He might even blurt it out in his sleep.
" Assassin! It was I who killed the old man by letting that
lie go on."

Feeling feverish and unable to remain indoors, he went out to
walk on the gravel path in front of the house. The fresh air
revived him and he took possession of himself again.

" If the Speaker dies it will be the act of God," he thought.

He would be in no way responsible. Neither would Gell. If
rumour charged the son with killing the father it would be a lie—
a damned lie, manufactured by Fate, the great liar.

It was not as if Gell were in any danger—the danger of arrest
for instance. *That* would be different. But Gell was in no danger—none whatever.

" Therefore bury the thing! Bury it and go on as usual," he
told himself.

The evening was closing in. It was beautiful and limpid.
With a high step Stowell was walking to and fro on the path.
Visions were rising before him of Gell and Bessie Collister on the
big liner, ploughing their way through the darkening ocean to that
free continent " where the clouds sailed higher "—Archibald
Alexander and his sister Elizabeth going out to the new world
to begin a new life.

He had visions of Fenella too—how he would go up to Govern-

ment House to-morrow morning. " Tell him to come back to me,"
she said to Janet, and now he would go. How happy he was going
to be!

" Surely I've a right to some happiness after all I've gone
through."

He gave himself up to the intoxication of living by anticipation
through those most blissful moments to a man and woman who
love each other—the first moments of reconciliation after a quarrel.

Night had fallen. It was very dark. The late birds were
silent, and only the soft young leaves of May were rustling in the
darkness overhead with that gentleness that is like the whispering
of angels. All at once a red light jogged up from the gate, making
shadows among the trees that bordered the drive.

" Good evenin', Dempster! A letter for you, Sir."

It was Killip the postman.

" Thank you, Mr. Killip," said Stowell, taking the letter. He
could not see it in the darkness, but at the touch of the large
envelope a heavy foreboding came over him.

" I suppose you've heard about that affair, your Honour? "

" What affair? "

" Tommy Vondy. He's got himself kicked out of the Castle
for letting that girl escape. The gorm! He's my first cousin, and
he's in his seventy-seven, but he was always a toot, was Tommy! "

" Good-night, Mr. Killip."

" Good-night, your Honour! "

When Stowell returned to the porch he looked at his letter by
the light of the lamp on the landing. It was from the Governor.
He went into the Library and tore it open.

II

" DEAR STOWELL,—Of course you have heard what has
happened. The escaped prisoner must be recaptured and
dealt with according to law. And not she only, but her
accomplice also. You know who that is—young Gell. The
evidence against him is overwhelming. We have traced him
almost to the door of the Castle on Sunday evening, and find,
too, that a trading steamer left Castletown late the same
night. There can hardly be a doubt that the fugitives sailed
in her. We must find where she has gone to and bring her
passengers back.

" Come here to-morrow morning to issue the necessary
warrant and assist Farrell to the ' distinguishing marks '
which may be needful for Gell's identification. I know

there is a certain risk in re-opening this wretched inquiry. I
had hoped to bury it once for all when I decided on what
you thought the extreme step of sending the guilty woman
to the gallows. But law and order must be upheld, and the
sooner we can silence the people, who are saying we are
winking at the corruption of justice to spare the son of the
Speaker and the friend of the Deemster, the better
for everybody.

"Be here at eleven. We (the Attorney and the Chief
Constable are coming) will be waiting for you. Good Lord,
haven't you been long enough away from this house anyway? If there are strained relations between you and
Fenella let them be faced squarely and straightened out at
once—Yours, etc.,

"JOHN S. STANLEY,
"Brig.-Gen., K.C.B.

"P.S.—Fenella says you have a photograph of Gell
which was taken in America some years ago. It is probably
the only one on the island, and therefore invaluable to
Farrel at this moment. Bring it with you—don't forget."

Stowell was struck with stupor. Alick Gell *was* in danger,
then, and the whole situation was different.

Raising his eyes after reading the Governor's letter he saw
Gell's photograph on the mantelpiece in front of him. At that
sight a flame of passion took possession of him, and snatching up
the picture he flung it in the fire.

"No, by God!" he said aloud. And if Farrell ever asked
him for "distinguishing marks" towards Gell's identification he
would take him by the throat and choke him.

But what about the warrant? Any Justice of the peace might
issue it, but if the Governor asked him to do so the request would
be equal to a command. Suppose he did, what would be the
result? Bessie would be brought back and executed. Worse than
that, even worse in its different way, Gell would be arrested and
tried—perhaps by him, and under his warrant!

"No, no, no! It would be a crime—a base, cowardly, infamous, abominable crime!"

The veins of his forehead swelled as he thought of the trial.
It would be more terrible than the other one. To sit in judgment
on an innocent man, being himself the guilty one—not Jeffries,
or Braxfield, or Brandon or Harebottle or any of the bewigged
barbarians whose names befouled the annals of jurisprudence had
done anything so awful.

" Never," he thought. " Never in this world."

Yet what alternative had he? After dinner (he had tried to eat to keep up appearances before Janet) he drew to the fire and tried to think things out. He had sat long hours in pain, and the fire had died down, when a kind of melancholy peace came to him and he thought he saw what he had to do.

He had to get up early in the morning, reach Government House before the others had arrived, see the Governor alone and say to him in secret,

" I cannot issue this warrant for the arrest of Alick Gell for breaking prison to procure that girl's release because *I* did it."

What would happen then? The Governor (he was a just man if a hard one) would say,

" In that case, you cannot be a Judge in this island any longer."

But that would be all. Out of consideration for his daughter, and perhaps for the man who was to become his daughter's husband, the Governor would go no farther. Some show he might make of publishing the police notice, but he would never send to a foreign country.

There would be no scandal. The public would know nothing. They had heard that the new Deemster had been unwell, and would be told that his health had broken down altogether, and he had had to resign his office. It would be a month's talk, and then— Time would cover up the whole miserable story in the merciful vein in which it hides so many of our misdoings.

And Fenella? He would tell Fenella also. It would be a shock to her, but she would be on his side now. She would see that he had only tried to prevent a judicial murder, to secure the happiness of two unhappy creatures who, but for him, would have been plunged in misery. They would marry and go away from the island, to Switzerland perhaps, and live there for the rest of their lives.

" Yes, that's it, that's it," he told himself.

It was a cruel comforting—like the surgeon's knife, which, while taking away a man's disease, takes some of his life-blood also.

He thought of his father, how proud the old Deemster had been of his judicial position and how anxious that his son should succeed to it—it was pitiful. He thought of Fenella, what great things they had planned to do when he became a Judge, and now all their hopes had fallen to dust and ashes—it was agonising.

Was it necessary? Inevitable? To be cast aside on life's highway in suffering and shame everlasting; to be like a wretched ship that lies at the bottom of the sea, swaying to the groundswell below, and moaning like a lost soul to the moans of the other wrecks in the womb of the ocean?

It was not as if he had injured anybody. He had done harm to nobody and nothing. Yet he must do what he had thought of. There was no help for it.

It was late. The household was asleep. The log fire he had been crouching over had fallen to ashes on the hearth. He was shivering and he got up to go to bed. Before leaving the library he sat at the desk under his mother's picture and wrote—

"*Please call me at six. I must take the first train to Douglas.*"

He was laying this on the table on the landing, lighting his candle and putting out the lamp, when he heard wheels on the carriage drive, and then a loud ringing at the front door bell.

Who could have come at this time of night? Candle in hand he went down and opened the door.

It was Joshua Scarff.

CHAPTER FORTY-TWO

" HE DROVE OUT THE MAN "

" SORRY to trouble you at this hour, your Honour, but I had to come and tell you what has happened."

" What is it, Joshua? "

" There has been a fearful outbreak of lawlessness in Douglas this evening—breaking of shop-windows, looting of the houses of well-to-do people, assaults and outrages of all kinds."

" What is the reason of it? "

" Mob reason, and you know what that is, your Honour. They say justice in the island is corrupt. If you are rich you get whatever you want. If you are poor you get nothing. A guilty man and a guilty woman have been allowed to escape. Why? Because the man belongs to a family of 'the big ones' and is a friend of the Deemster."

" Who say that? "

" Old Qualtrough and Dan Baldromma."

" Baldromma? If his step-daughter has escaped what has he to complain of? "

" Nothing, but that's not the worst, Sir."

" What is? "

" The Governor has telegraphed for soldiers from across the water. They are to come over by the first boat in the morning. It's a frightful blunder, Sir."

Beads of perspiration were rolling down from Joshua's bald crown.

" There'll be bloodshed, and Manxmen won't stand for that. They've been their own masters for a thousand years. The Governor can't treat them as if they were Indian coolies."

" What do you think ought to be done? "

" That's what I've come to say, Sir. I had gone to bed but I couldn't take rest, so I got Willie Dawson to drive me over. The people may be wrong about justice, but the only way to pacify them is to prove it."

" How? "

" The guilty man in this case must give himself up."

" Give himself up? "

Joshua took off his coloured spectacles and wiped the damp off them.

" I thought your Honour might know where he was. He can't be far away, Sir."

" Well? "

" He ought to be told to deliver himself up to the Courts to save the island from ruin. And if he won't he ought to be denounced."

" Denounced? "

" It will be a terrible ordeal—I know that, Sir. Your friend! Your life-long friend! Pity! Great pity! "

For a perceptible time Stowell did not speak. Then, in a voice which Joshua had never heard before, he said,

" Go home and go to bed, Joshua. I'll see what can be done."

Joshua had gone, the door had closed behind him and his wheels were dying away down the drive, but Stowell continued to stand in the hall, candle in hand and stiff as a statue. At length he returned to the dining-room, put the candle on the table and sat before the empty hearth.

It was all over! The plan he had made for himself was impossible. There could be no resigning in secret and stealing away from the island.

He *had* done harm to something. He had done harm to Justice. If Justice fell down what stood up? The man who took the law into his own hands was a criminal, and as a criminal he ought to be punished.

Punished? The shock was terrible. Was he then to give himself up? To confess publicly?

He saw himself pleading guilty to having broken prison. He heard the whole wretched tale of his relation to the unhappy prisoner, and of his trying and condemning her, coming out in

open Court. He heard the howls of execration from the people
who had hitherto loved and cheered him.

" Is there no other way? " he asked himself.

He saw himself in prison, in prison clothes, in the prison cell,
on the prison bed. Above all he saw another Deemster going
upstairs to sit on the bench while he lay in the vaults below.

He thought of his father and his family—four hundred years
of the Ballamoars and not a stain on the name of one of them
until now. He thought of Fenella—the cruel shame he would
bring on her. Granted he was guilty, and deserved punishment,
had he any right to punish Fenella also?

The clock on the landing struck one. An owl shrieked in the
plantation. He got up and strode about the room. The impulses
of the natural man began to fight for safety.

" Good God, what am I thinking about? " he asked himself.

What had he done to deserve all this? He had broken a
wicked law which had no right to exist, but did that require that he
should denounce himself, go to prison, degrade his father's name,
break Fenella's heart and put himself up on a gibbet for every
passer-by to jeer at and spit upon?

" What madness! What rank madness! "

He thought of the thousands of " great " men in all ages of
the world who had broken bad laws, and yet lived in honour and
died in glory. Why should he suffer for doing the same thing?
Why he and not the others? He laughed in scorn of his own weakness, but at the next moment a mocking voice within him seemed
to say,

" Go on! Go on! Issue that warrant! Let the unhappy girl
who trusted you be brought back and executed. Let the friend
who loved you be arrested and tried and sent to jail for the crime
you have committed. Go through all that duplicity again. Let
the whole community be submerged in anarchy as the consequence
of your sin. But remember, when you come out of it all, you will
be a devil, and your soul will be damned."

That terrified him and he sat down by the empty hearth once
more. After a while he found his hands wet under his face. He
heard a soft, caressing voice pleading with him,

" Victor, my darling heart! Resist this great temptation and
peace will come to you. Do the right, and no matter how low you
may fall in the eyes of men, you will look upon the face of God."

It was Fenella's voice—he was sure of that. Across the mountain and through the darkness of the night her pure soul was
speaking to him.

The candle had burnt to the socket by this time, but a new light came to him. For more than a year he had been a slave, dragging a chain of sin behind him. At every step in his wrong-doing his chain had lengthened. He must break it and be free.

" Yes, I will go up to Government House in the morning," he thought, " confess everything and take my punishment."

It was only right, only just. And when the cruel thought came that the next time he entered the court-house it would be to stand in the dock, with the dread certainty of his doom, he told himself that that would be right too—the Judge also must be judged.

II

Groping his way upstairs in the darkness he entered his bedroom and locked the door behind him. He found a fire burning, the sofa drawn up in front of it, a lamp burning on the bureau that stood at one side, and at the other the high-backed arm-chair in which his father used to undress for bed. He was surprised to see that the fire had been newly made up, but hearing footsteps in the adjoining bedroom he understood.

" Poor Janet ! " he thought.

His thoughts were thundering through his brain like waves in a deep cavern. He was convinced that he would never survive the ordeal that was before him. When men lived through long imprisonments it was because they had hope that the beautiful days would come again. He had no such hope, so, sitting at his bureau, he began to sort and arrange his papers like one who was going away on a long journey.

After that he wrote a letter to the Attorney-General:

" Dear Master,—When this letter comes to your hand you will know the occasion for it. I am aware that it cannot have the authority of a will, but (in the absence of a more regular document) I trust the Clerk of the Rolls may find a way to act upon it as an expression of my last wishes.

" I desire that Janet Curphey should be suitably provided for as long as she lives. She has been a mother to me all my life, the only mother I have ever known.

" I desire that Mrs. Collister of Baldromma may have such a provision made for her as will liberate her from the tyrannies of her husband.

" I desire that Thomas Vondy, formerly the jailer at Castle Rushen, should be taken care of in any way you may consider best.

25

"Finally, if I do not live to return home, I desire that everything else of which I die possessed should be offered to Fenella Stanley as a mark of my deep love and devotion.

"I think that is all."

Having signed, sealed and inscribed his letter he put it in his breast pocket. Then taking a drawer out of the bureau he carried it to the sofa, intending to destroy the contents of it.

The first thing that came to his hand was the letter which Alick Gell had given him at Derby Haven. It was marked "To be opened after we have gone," and turned out to be a memorandum to his father's executors, telling them he was leaving the island with no intention of returning to it, and asking (as his only request) that in the event of an inheritance becoming due to him, seven hundred pounds, which had been advanced to him at various times, should be repaid to Deemster Victor Stowell—"the best friend man ever had."

Feeling a certain twinge, Stowell hesitated for a moment, with the memorandum shaking in his hand, and then threw it into the fire.

There were other papers of the same kind (I O U's and the like) which shared the same fate, and then up from the bottom of the drawer, came a leather-bound book. It was "Isobel's Diary." He had decided to destroy that also. As the sanctuary of his father's soul he could not allow it to be looked into by other eyes.

But, never having looked at it himself since the night of his father's death, he could not resist the temptation to glance through it once more before committing it to the flames. It fell open at the page which said,

"So it's all well at last, Isobel. Your son can do without me now. He needs his father no longer. With that brave woman by his side he will go up and up. They will marry and carry on the traditions of the Ballamoars. It is the dearest wish of my heart that they should do so."

His throat throbbed. Ah, those hopes, all wrecked and dead! Going down on one knee before the fire, and holding the book on the other, he tore out page by page and burnt it, feeling as if he were burning his right hand also. He was afraid of tears and had rarely given way to them, but he was weeping like a heart-broken woman before the last page had been consumed.

Then, taking Fenella's letters from his pocket-book, he prepared to burn them too. They brought a faint perfume, a feeling

of warmth, a sense of her physical presence. Most of them were
notes of no consequence—appointments to ride, drive, fish, skate,
all touched by her gay raillery ("eight o'clock in the morning—is
that too early for you, Victor, dear?")—he had preserved every
scrap in her hand-writing. But one was the letter she wrote to
him when he was in London, and with palpitating tenderness he
held it under the lamp to read it again:

> "Victor, when I think of the life that is so surely before
> you, and that I shall walk through it by your side, perfectly
> united with you, sharing the same hopes and aims and
> desires, enjoying the same sunshine and weathering the same
> storms, I have a vision of happiness that makes me cry
> with joy."

His heart swelled like a troubled sea, and to conquer his emotion he thrust the letter hurriedly into the flames. But before it
was more than scorched he snatched it back and was preparing to
return it to his pocket when he bethought himself how soon it
must pass into other hands with everything he carried about him.
And then, turning his head away, and feeling as if he were burning his heart also, he put it into the fire.

After that he dropped back on to the sofa with feelings about
Fenella that found no relief in tears. One by one the joyous hours
of their love returned to his memory. They seemed to ring in
his ears with the melancholy sound of far-off bells. It was a
cruel pleasure.

All at once came a moment of fierce rebellion. When he had
told himself downstairs that in making the great renunciation of
his public office he must renounce Fenella also he had not realised
what it meant. It meant that never again, for as long as he lived
(Fenella being impossible to him), would Woman take any part
in his existence.

A cold fear took possession of him at that thought. He was
a man—was he for the rest of his life, if he survived his imprisonment, to be cut off from his kind, separated, alone?

Better be dead than live such a life!

Then another and still more startling thought came to him—
why not? A letter to the Governor, exonerating Gell, and then it
would all be over. No warrant! No trial! Why not?

Outside the night was dark. Not a breath of wind was stirring. In the silence of earth and sky he could hear the "swish,
swish" of the sea on the shingle at the top of the shore. It
must be high water.

" Why not?   Why not? "

His head was dizzy.   He was thinking of a boat that lay among the lush grass on the sandy bank above the beach.   Alick and he had often gone fishing in her.   She was heavy, but he was strong—he could push her into the water.

He saw himself pulling out to sea, far out, beyond the Point, to where the Gulf Stream in its long race round half the world swept by the island to the coast of Iceland.   And then, as the dawn broke in the eastern heavens, he saw himself scuttling the boat and going down with her.

No one would know.   The boat would lie at the bottom of the sea until she fell to pieces, and he—he would go north on the way of the great waters until he came to the feet of the frozen Jökulls, where nobody would be able to say who he was or where he came from.

No scandal!   No outcry!   No vulgar sensation!   Just a pang to Fenella, and then the darkness of death over all.

Thinking the lamp was burning low he was reaching out his hand to turn up the wick when a sense came of somebody being in the room with him.   He looked round.   All was silent.

" Is anybody there? " he asked aloud.

There was no answer.   The dread of miscarrying for ever if he died by his own act began to struggle on the battle field of his soul with the fear of being cut off from the living who live in God's peace.   He shivered and was trying to rise when again he had the sense of somebody else in the bedroom.

" Who is it? "

At the next moment, raising his eyes, he thought he saw his father in the arm-chair where he had seen him so often.   The august face was the same as when he saw it last in that room, except that the melancholy eyes were now open.

" I'm ill," he thought, and he closed his eyes and put his hand over them.

But when he opened his eyes again his father was still there, looking at him with tenderness and compassion.   His brain reeled and he fell face down on the cushions of the sofa.

Then he heard his father speaking to him, gently, affectionately, but firmly, just as he used to do when he was alive.

" My son!   My dear son!   I know what you are thinking of doing, and I warn you not to do it.   No man can run away from the consequences of his sins.   If he flies from them in this life he must meet them in the life hereafter, and then it will be a hundred-fold more terrible to be swept from the face of the living God."

" Father! "

Stowell tried to cry aloud but could not. His father's voice ceased and at the next moment a vision flashed before him. A line of miserable-looking men were standing before an awful tribunal. He knew who they were—the unjust judges of the world who had corrupted justice. All the grandeur in which they had clothed themselves on earth was gone, and they were there in the nakedness of their shame crying,

" Mercy! Mercy! Mercy! "

Stowell felt as if he were falling off the world into a void of unfathomable night. Then blindness fell upon the eyes of his mind and he knew no more.

CHAPTER FORTY-THREE

THE DAWN OF MORNING

" VICTOR! Victor! "

It was Janet's voice outside the door.

" Eh? "

" Six o'clock. Didn't you want to catch the first train to town, dear? "

" Oh yes! All right. I'll be down presently."

Stowell found it difficult to recover consciousness. He was lying on the sofa, and he looked around. There was the arm-chair—it was empty. But the lamp on the bureau was still burning. He must have slept, for he was feeling refreshed and even strong.

Leaping to his feet he blew out the lamp and pulled back the window curtains. It was a beautiful morning, tranquil as the sky and noiseless as the dew. Over the tops of the tall trees the bald crown of old Snaefell was bathed in sunshine.

He was like another man. Life had no terrors for him now. It was just as if a curse had fallen from him in the night. No more visions! No more spectres! He knew what he had to do and he would do it. He had a sense of immense emancipation. He felt like a slave who had broken the chain which he had dragged after him for years. He was a free man once more.

Throwing off coat and waistcoat he washed—lashing the cold water over face and head and neck as if he were diving into one of the dubs in the glen—and then went downstairs with a strong step.

Breakfast was not quite ready, so he stepped out over the piazza to the farm-yard. The cheerful place was full of its morning activities. Cows were mooing their way to the grass of the fields before barking dogs, and milkmaids were carrying their frothing pails across to the dairy.

He saluted everybody he came upon. " Good-morning, Betty! "

" Good-morning, Mary! " The girls smiled and looked proud, but they said afterwards that the young master's voice sounded as if he were saying good-bye to them.

Unconsciously he was going about like one who was taking a last look round before setting out on a long journey. He went into the stable, and Molly, his young chestnut mare, turned her head and neighed at him. He went into the empty cow-house, and four young calves in boxes licked, with their long moist tongues, the hand he held down to them.

On the way back to the house he met Robbie Creer, who was full of another story of Mrs. Collister of Baldromma. She had taken the ground with the ebb tide, poor woman. They had put her into the asylum. The doctors said her case was incurable. She was always saying the old Dempster had come from the dead to take her Bessie out of prison.

" But what a blessed end," said Stowell. " She'll think her daughter is in heaven, so she'll always be happy."

" It's like she will, Sir," said Robbie, looking puzzled, and going indoors for his morning bowl of porridge he said to his wife,

" A mortal quare thing to say, though, and the woman in the madhouse."

Stowell ate with an appetite (Janet plying him with coffee and eggs and toasted muffins), and then young Robbie brought round the dog-cart. Janet helped him on with his light loose overcoat and went to the door with him.

He paused there, pulling on his driving-gloves and thinking what cruel pain the dear soul would suffer when she heard that night what he had done during the day. At last he threw his arms about her and kissed her, saying with a gulp,

" Good-bye, mother! God bless you! "

And then he sprang up into the cart, snatched at the reins, pulled them taut, and (after the young mare had leapt on her fore-legs) darted away.

As he approached the turn of the drive where the house was hidden by the trees he turned and looked back at it—what a home to lose!

Janet, who was still at the porch, smoothing her silvery hair, thought he had looked back at her, and she waved her hand to him. Nobody had said a word to her, yet she knew he had been suffering as a result of some terrible wrong-doing. She thought she knew what it was, too, and she had wept bitter tears over it. But he had not a fault in her eyes now.

Her boy! Hers all the way up since he was a child and used to run about the lawn in pinafores. Heaven bless him! He was the best thing God had ever made.

II

The train to town was full to overflowing. The northside people, having heard of yesterday's doings, were going up to see for themselves " what them toots in Douglas " were doing.

In spite of the guard's deferential protests Stowell stepped into an open third-class carriage. It had been humming like a beehive until then, but except for a general salutation it became silent when he entered.

A draper's assistant who sat opposite handed him an English newspaper, two days old, with an article on the escape from Castle Rushen. The incident was a disgrace to the insular administration, and if the Governor could not offer a satisfactory explanation the sooner the island's Home Rule came to an end the better for Justice.

One or two of the passengers tried to draw Stowell into conversation about the article, but he said little or nothing. Then some black-coated persons (well-to-do farmers and the like) gave the talk another turn.

" Still and for all," said one, " that doesn't justify such doings as there are in Douglas!" " Chut!" said another. " It isn't justice the agitators are wanting, it's robbery." " Truth enough," said a third, " it's the land they're after, and if the Governor isn't doing something soon, there'll be not an acre left at the one of us." " Give them a pig of their own sow," said a fat farmer. " Men like Qualtrough and Baldromma ought to be taken to say and dropped overboard."

Again the passengers tried to draw Stowell into conversation, and when they found they could not get him to speak to them they spoke at him.

" Where's the big men of the island that they're not telling the people they're bringing it to wreck and ruin? "

" When a man is claver—claver uncommon—and mighty with the tongue, he ought to be showing the ignorant gommerals the way they're going."

" Yes," said a little man (he was a local preacher), " when a man has the gift it's his duty to the Lord to use it."

" He must be a right man though," said the fat farmer,

" straight as a mast himself, same as some we've had at Balla-moar in the good ould days gone by."

There was silence for a moment after this, and then an old man by the opposite window was heard to whisper,

" Lave him alone, men; he knows what hour the clock is striking."

When the train reached Douglas, Stowell went off with a heavy face. It was remarked that he had not shaken hands—his father used to shake hands with everybody.

" He's his father's son for all," said the old man by the window.

Stowell took the cable-car at the bottom of the Prospect Hill which is at the foot of the town. Douglas was still in a state of agitation and the driver had as much as he could do to forge his way, without accidents, through the tumultuous throngs in the thoroughfare.

A cordon of red-coated soldiers from Castletown surrounded Government office, and a noisy crowd (including women with children) were jeering at them from the middle of the street, and shouting up at the windows, under the impression that the Governor was within.

The shops bore signs of yesterday's rioting—many having their shutters up, while the windows of others were barricaded with new boarding.

Stowell got out of the car at the terminus and made the rest of his journey afoot. At the top of the hill, where the road turns towards the Governor's house, he came upon a mass meeting. From a horseless lorry, decorated with banners, a burly old ruffian with shaggy grey hair (Qualtrough, M.H.K.) was speaking in a voice of thunder, while, on the cross-seat by his side, Dan Bal-dromma was sitting with the air of a martyr.

" There's a man on this platform who has gone to prison for his principles. That's what Justice in the Isle of Man is. And that's what they would like to be doing with the lot of ye, the big ones of the island. But, gentlemen and ladies, their rotten ould ship is floating on the pumps and she'll soon be sinking."

When Stowell reached the Governor's gate he paused, being out of breath and not so strong as he had imagined. From that point he could see a broad stretch of the coast, as well as the shadowy outlines of the English hills on the other side of the channel. A steamer was sailing into the bay. Perhaps she was bringing the English cavalry the Governor had sent for.

Life is sweet when death is at the door. At that last moment, although he had thought his mind was made up, Stowell found that his heart was failing him. Must he go on? Deliberately destroy himself? No outside power compelling him? The world was wide—why not leave all this wreck and ruin behind him and in some other country begin life anew?

The moment of weakness passed and he went on. Half way up the drive, where the trees broke clear and the long white façade of Government House became visible, he dropped his head. He was thinking of the last time he had been there and remembering again the stinging words with which Fenella had driven him away. But there was strength in the thought that he was about to break the chain which he had dragged after him so long, and save his people at the same time.

When the maid opened the door, he asked for the Governor.

" Yes, your Honour," said the maid, " but Miss Fenella wishes to see you first, Sir."

His heart was beating hard when he stepped into the house.

CHAPTER FORTY-FOUR

" GOD GAVE HIM DOMINION "

THREE times during breakfast that morning Fenella had seen somebody coming up the drive. The first to come was the Major from Castletown, riding at a fast trot. On being shown into the breakfast-room, with spurs clanking, he told the Governor that a mob had gathered about Government Office and were very threatening.

" Tell the Mayor to read the Riot Act, and then do what is necessary for the protection of life and property," said the Governor.

The second to come was the Chief Constable, driving rapidly in a hackney carriage. On entering the room with his heavy step, he said the steamer from England was in sight and the soldiers would be landed at the pier within half an hour.

" If the thoroughfares are still thronged with riotous mobs at that time," said the Governor, " tell the cavalry to ride through them."

The last to come up the drive was a solitary man afoot, walking slowly and pausing at intervals as if his strength had failed him.

Fenella knew who it was, and rising hastily from the table she went into the drawing-room.

When Stowell was brought in to her she was shocked at the change in his appearance. He looked ten years older. His dark hair had become white about the temples and his eyes were full of a strange light.

"How he must have suffered," she thought, and an almost overpowering desire took possession of her to put her arms about him and comfort him.

He looked at her and the same thought and the same impulse came to him. But they were afraid of each other, and with the surging ocean of their love between them they stood apart, but trembling. At length, trying not to look into each other's faces, they began to speak.

"Fenella!"

"Victor!"

"You know why I have been sent for?"

"Yes, and that is why I want to speak to you before you see my father. There are things you ought to know."

"Yes?"

"Mr. Vondy, the jailer from Castle Rushen, was here two days ago, to be examined by the Governor, the Attorney-General and the Chief Constable."

"Did he say anything?"

"Not to them."

"To you, perhaps?"

"Yes. I brought him in here. He told me what occurred after I left the Castle."

"Then you know?"

She dropped her head and answered "Yes."

"I had to do it, Fenella—I thought I had to."

A moment passed.

"He asked me to tell you that he would keep his word to you, whatever happened."

"Did he say that?"

"Yes."

A spasm in Stowell's throat seemed to be stifling him.

"I did wrong, Fenella, terribly wrong, but there is one thing I will ask of you."

"What is it, Victor?"

"Not to judge me until you know what I've come to do to-day."

Fenella, deeply affected, thought she caught a glimpse of his meaning.

"Do you intend to resign, Victor?"

"Yes, but that is not all."

"What is, Victor?" She was thinking of his exile, his possible banishment.

"Perhaps I am speaking to you for the last time, Fenella. That's why I am glad you have given me this opportunity of seeing you."

She trembled, thinking he meant suicide, and said in a choking voice,

" You don't mean that you intend to take your . . . . No, no, that is impossible. Think of your father."

Stowell did not speak for a moment. Then he said,

" I saw him last night, Fenella."

" Who? "

" My father. I was thinking of *that* as a way out of all this miserable wrong-doing, when he came to warn me."

" How he must have suffered," thought Fenella.

" But perhaps you think it was only a delusion? "

" Indeed no! If the spirits of our dear ones may not come back to speak to us in our times of temptation . . . . "

" But my father was not the only one who spoke to me last night, Fenella."

" Who else did, Victor? "

" You. I heard you as plainly as I hear you now."

Fenella's bosom was heaving. " When was that? " she asked.

" In the middle of the night. But perhaps you were in bed and asleep at that time."

" No . . . . no, I did not sleep until after daybreak. In the middle of the night I was " . . . . (she was breathing audibly) " I was praying."

He looked up at her with his heavy eyes.

" Were you praying for me, Fenella? "

She cast down her eyes and answered " Yes."

Another moment passed, and then in a husky voice he said,

" Fenella, what did you pray for for me? "

" That you might have strength to do what was right, whatever it might cost you."

He reached forward and grasped her hands.

" Did you know what that meant, Fenella—whatever it might cost me? "

" Yes," she said, raising her eyes, " and at length an answer came to me."

" What answer? "

" That if you did, and made atonement, however low you might fall in the eyes of men you would look upon the face of God."

Stowell gasped, dropped her hands and for a while was speechless. Then he said,

" And do you think I will? "

" I am sure you will, Victor. I had a sign from God."

"Do you, after all, believe in God, Fenella?"

"Indeed yes.   And you—don't you??"

"My father did.   He used to kneel by his bed like a little child every night and every morning."

She saw that he did not speak for himself, and a great wave of love and compassion for the sin-laden man stormed her heart.

"Victor," she said, tears springing to her eyes, "you must try to forgive me.   I've not been what I ought to have been to you—I see that now.   Whatever you have done I should have clung to you, not driven you away from me, and let you go on from sin to sin, doubting God's mercy and forgiveness.   Let me do so now. We belong to each other, Victor.   There can never be anybody else for either of us as long as we live.   Let us go together."

She had seized his hands.   The hands of both were trembling.

"Would to God you could, Fenella.   But it is too late for that now.   I have gone too far for you to follow me.   Where I go now I must go alone."

"Don't say that."

"Wait until I have seen your father."

At that moment the maid came into the room to tell the Deemster that the Governor, having heard that he was in the house, wished to see him immediately.

Stowell was turning to go, when Fenella put a trembling hand on his shoulder and said in a whisper,

"Victor, whatever happens with my father, promise me that you will never do *that*."

"But if the Governor . . . . "

"Never mind about the Governor now, promise me."

There was a moment of silence and then he said, "I promise," and with head down passed out of the room.

Being alone, Fenella tried in vain to compose herself.   The fear that Stowell might kill himself (as a result of the public exposure and humiliation which the Governor would impose upon him) threw her into violent agitation.

Unable to support the strain of her anxiety she could not resist the temptation to listen at the door of her father's room.   She heard the two voices within—Stowell's in tones of pitiful supplication, her father's in accents of fierce expostulation.   At length she heard her own name mentioned and then she could contain herself no longer.

Opening the door noiselessly she entered the room.   The two men were face to face, looking at each other with flaming eyes.

II

"Come in, Stowell. I'm glad you're early. I wanted a word with you before the others arrived. Sit down."

The Governor too was violently agitated. He was striding about the room. His grey hair, usually brushed down with military precision, was loose and disordered, as if he had been running his hands through it, and his pipe, still alight and as if forgotten, was smoking on the arm of his chair.

"You came by train?"

"Yes."

"Then you saw the soldiers. I had to do it. I couldn't allow this raggabash to take possession of the island. There may be casualties, but the shortest way is the most merciful—that's my experience. Sit down. Why don't you sit down?"

But the Governor went on walking and Stowell continued to stand.

"They say this rioting is the sequel to the escape from Castle Rushen. Only an excuse, of course, but that makes no difference. If we are to justify our administration of Justice in the eyes of the authorities across the water we must re-capture those runaways. The man—the guilty man in particular—must be locked up in prison. The Attorney and the Colonel will be here presently. You'll be able to help them to the personal description they want—nobody better—and then issue the warrant."

Stowell, who had been clutching the back of a chair behind which he was standing with a fixed stare, said in a quivering voice,

"I'm sorry, your Excellency. I cannot do that."

"Eh? Cannot do what?"

"I cannot issue the warrant for the arrest of Alick Gell for breaking prison because . . . ."

"Well?"

Stowell swallowed something in his throat and continued . . . . "because *I* did it."

The Governor drew up sharply and said,

"What's the matter with you? Are you ill?"

Stowell, who had recovered himself, answered,

"No, I am not ill, your Excellency."

"Then you must be mad—stark mad. It's impossible. You can never have done such a thing."

"I am not mad either, Sir. What I tell you is the truth—it is God's truth, Sir."

And then, excusing nothing, extenuating nothing, Stowell told the Governor what he had done, and how he had done it.

"I used my official position to effect the escape of the prisoner, and I arranged for her flight, with her companion, to a foreign country."

The Governor listened without drawing breath.

"But why . . . . why did you . . . . was it because I refused to remit . . . . "

"No, I did it because I came to see that the law which permitted you to order the execution of that girl was a crime, and that a higher law called upon me to undo it."

"A crime? Good Lord, what if it was? What had you to do with that?"

"I had tried and condemned her. And besides, I had my personal reasons for wishing the prisoner to escape punishment."

"But damn it all, man, when you were doing all this for the girl, didn't you see what you were doing for yourself?"

"Not then. But now I see that in preventing the law from committing a crime I committed a crime against the law, and am no longer fit to be a Judge. That's why I'm here now, Sir—not to issue that warrant, but to resign my judgeship."

"Resign your judgeship?"

"Yes, but that's not all—to ask you to order my arrest and commit me to prison."

The Governor, who had been half stupefied, took possession of himself at last.

"Commit you to prison? Good heavens, what are you saying? A Deemster in prison! Whoever heard of such a thing!"

"I am guilty of a crime against Justice . . . . " began Stowell, but the Governor bore him down.

"Tush! I don't care for the moment whether you are or are not. Neither do I care whether the law which condemned the prisoner to death, was or was not a crime. What I have to deal with is the present situation. You say you want me to order your arrest—is that it?"

"Yes, you said yourself the guilty man ought to be in prison."

"But heavens alive, man, can't you see the disgrace? Gell is a private person, while you are a Judge, the Judge who tried and condemned the prisoner. What is to happen to Justice in the island if a Judge is condemned and imprisoned?"

Stowell tried to speak, but again the Governor bore him down.

"Oh, I know what you'll say—you'll talk about your conscience. But what is your conscience to me against the honour of the public service and the welfare of the whole community?"

The honour of the public service cannot rest on a lie, Sir," said Stowell. "It would be a living lie if I continued to be a Judge, and the only way to save the island is to tell it the truth, no matter what . . . . "

" Don't talk damned nonsense."

Stowell drew himself up.

" Do you wish me, then, to issue that warrant against Alick Gell now that you know that I am myself the guilty man? "

The Governor flinched for a moment, then smote the top of his desk and said,

" I know nothing of the kind, Sir, and don't want to know. I believe you're mad—made mad by the ordeal you have lately gone through. Nothing will make me believe the contrary."

There was silence after that for several minutes. Then the Governor, who had thrown himself in his chair, said in a softer tone,

" Stowell, listen to me. I partly understand you. But even if you did this unbelievable thing, and are satisfied you did it from a good motive, why can't you hold your tongue about it? "

" I have thought of that, Sir," said Stowell, with a tremor in his voice. " I have fought it all out with myself. Believe me I would have given all I have in the world not to have had to come here on this errand. But the life of a Judge would be impossible to me with a lie like that for its foundation. My work cannot be a mockery, Sir. I cannot allow another to suffer for what I have done."

The Governor leapt up from his seat.

" You talk about others suffering for what you have done— have you forgotten how many others must suffer if I allow you to do what you want to do now? Think of your island—your native island—do you want to cover it with dishonour? Think of your profession—do you want to load it with disgrace? Think of your father, who loved you as no father ever loved a son. We put up his portrait in the court-house the other day—do you want to pull it down? And then think of me—I suppose I ran some risk when I recommended you for your position . . . . "

Stowell was trying to speak, but again the Governor put up his hand.

" Oh, you needn't thank me. Perhaps I wasn't acting altogether unselfishly. I may have been wanting somebody to stand by me now that I'm growing old, somebody like your father—able to fight these rascals who are trying to ruin everything. And when you came along, you whom I had known since you were a boy, the son of my old friend, who was to be *my* son some day . . . . "

The Governor, startled by the emotion that was coming over him, broke away and crossed the room, saying,

"But damn it all, why need I talk of myself? There's Fenella—have you forgotten Fenella?"

It was at this moment that Fenella entered the room. Neither of the men saw her. She stood noiselessly at the door.

"If I do what you want, order your arrest, what's the first question the Court will ask you—why did you help the prisoner to escape? Then the whole wretched story of your relations with the girl Collister will come out. And what will be the result? Fenella's name will become a byword. It will be the common talk of every slut in the island that she came second after your woman . . . . your offal."

Stowell flamed up with anger for a moment, and then choked with tears. After a short silence he said,

"I can never be sufficiently grateful to you, Sir, for what you've done for me. As for Fenella, I can hardly trust myself to speak. The thought of her suffering is the bitterest part of my own. I would live out the rest of my life on my knees if I could undo the wrong I have done her. But I cannot bring her down with me. I cannot take up again my life as a Judge after it has been so hideously disfigured and ask her to share it. Let me go to prison . . . ."

Sobbing in his throat Stowell could go no further. Fenella, sobbing in her heart, crept noiselessly out of the room.

The Governor, in spite of himself, was visibly affected.

"Look here, my boy," he said. "I'll tell you what I'll do. It's going far, perhaps too far for the safety of the public service, but to prevent worse things happening I'll take the risk. I'll stop that warrant and hush up this miserable scandal on one condition —that you say nothing, take leave of absence on grounds of ill-health, go abroad and never come back again."

Stowell shook his head.

"Why not? Good gracious, why not? The guilty ones have gone. Your secret is safe. Except ourselves, nobody knows it. Why shouldn't you?"

"I dare not," said Stowell.

"*Dare* not?"

"I have committed a crime. If I do not pay for it in this life I must do so hereafter. Therefore I ask for my punishment *now*."

The Governor got the better of his emotion.

"So you wish to resign your office and ask me to order your arrest? Well, I won't do it. I am the only authority to whom you can resign and I decline to accept your resignation—I refuse to transmit it to the Home Authorities. What you wish to do would undermine the stability of law and the authority of Government. It would humiliate me and destroy my daughter's happiness. Therefore I not only refuse to receive your resignation, I forbid it."

Stowell hesitated for a moment and then said,

" In that case, your Excellency, you will force me to denounce myself."

" Denounce . . . . ?   You mean in open Court? "

" Yes, it will be my duty, and I shall be compelled to do it."

The Governor's wrath became rage.   With a ring of sarcasm in his voice he said,

" Very well! Very well! I cannot prevent you.   Denounce yourself in open Court if you are so unwise, so insane.   But understand—if *you* are compelled to do your duty, *I* shall be compelled to do mine also.   After you have made your public confession and the Courts have dealt with you, I shall issue the warrant just the same.   You say the fugitives have gone to a foreign country, but no foreign country will refuse to give up a condemned murderess. The woman shall be brought back and executed according to the sentence *you* pronounced upon her.   More than that, your friend, your confederate, shall be brought back also, and dealt with according to his crime.   Therefore your public confession will be of no avail.   It will be an empty farce, ruining three lives that might otherwise have been saved."

Stowell trembled, his lips became white.

" I beg you not to do that, Sir."

" I will! I take God to witness that I will.   Now choose for yourself which it is to be—your course or mine? "

Stowell breathed hard for a moment and then smiled—but such a smile!

" Your Excellency," he said, " for your *own* sake I beg of you not to do it."

" *My* sake? " said the Governor, drawing up sharply—he had been striding about the room again.

" Yes, yours," said Stowell.   " One of those two was my victim, the other was merely the subject of my will.   I alone am guilty, and if I cannot meet my punishment without bringing such consequences on the innocent I must meet something else."

" What else? "

" Death.   Then, in the eyes of heaven, the crime against the law will be *your* crime and I shall not live to witness it."

There was a breathless silence.   The Governor was dumbfounded.   Stowell stepped towards the door and said in a low voice,

" God forgive you, Sir.   You will never see me again."

26

At that moment the maid entered the room to announce the Attorney-General and the Chief Constable, who came in immediately behind her.

"Ah, Victor, how are you?" said the Attorney. "Your Excellency, we have brought the Warrant."

"And here," said the Chief Constable, with an obsequious bow to Stowell, "is the Deemster ready to issue it."

Nobody spoke, and the Chief Constable, taking a paper out of a long envelope, proceeded to read it:

"*This is to command you to whom this Warrant is addressed forthwith to apprehend Alexander Gell . . . .*"

"That will do. Give it to me," said the Governor.

When the Warrant had been given to him he tore it up and threw it into the fire. The two men were aghast.

"Your Excellency, what . . . . what . . . ."

"This damnable thing must go no further. Let me hear no more about it."

After saying this the Governor's strength seemed to leave him. He dropped into a chair before the fire and gazed at the blazing paper.

Stowell's trembling hand was on the handle of the door.

"I thank you for what you've done, Sir," he said, "and wish to God the matter could end there. But it cannot . . . . it cannot."

He went out. The two men looked into each other's faces. A flash of understanding passed between them, and, without a word more, they stepped out of the room.

Meantime, Stowell, going down the corridor, felt a hand that had been stretched out from the drawing-room, taking hold of his arm and drawing him in. It was Fenella's. Her face was utterly broken up. Flinging her arms about him she kissed him passionately.

"Victor," she said, "do as your heart bids you. Don't think of me any longer. I am with you in life or death. If you have to go to prison I will go with you, and if . . . ."

Unable to say more she broke away from him and hurried into an inner room.

The front door rang as Stowell pulled it after him, and when he walked down the drive with a high step his head was up and his ravished face aglow.

END OF SIXTH BOOK

SEVENTH BOOK

THE RESURRECTION

CHAPTER FORTY-FIVE

THE WAY OF THE CROSS

THERE had been wild doings in Douglas since the Chief Constable's visit to Government House. Stones had been thrown and windows broken. At length the Mayor, not without personal risk, had read the Riot Act from the steps of the Town Hall.

The result had been the reverse of what the Governor expected. The police, a small force, had charged the mob with their batons, but they had soon been overpowered. Then the soldiers from Castletown, a little company of eighty, had attempted to intimidate the crowd with their rifles, but twice as many stalwart fishermen, coming up behind, had disarmed them. After that the people had surged through the streets in delirious triumph.

At ten o'clock the throng was densest outside Government Office, which stands midway on the steep declivity of the Prospect Hill. The police and the soldiers had as much as they could do to guard the doors of the building. The space in front of it was packed with people of both sexes and all ages. They were squirming about like worms on an upturned sod. There were loud shouts and derisive cries.

" Down with the Governor! "

" Tell him the steamer leaves for England at nine in the morning."

Suddenly, with the rapidity of a desert wind, word went through the crowd that mounted soldiers from England had just been landed at the pier, and were riding up the principal thoroughfares, driving everything before them.

A cold fear came, culminating in terror. Presently the cavalry were seen to turn the bottom of the hill. They were swinging the flats of their swords to scatter the crowd. The people screamed and ran in frantic haste to the parapets on either side of the street. In a moment the broad space in front of Government Office was clear.

Clear, save for one tiny object. It was a child, a little girl of four, who had been clinging to her mother's skirts and in the scramble had lost her hold of them.

The cavalry were now coming up the hill at a gallop and the little one's danger was seen by all.

"Save the child," people shouted, and more than one ran out a few paces and then ran back, for the horses seemed to be almost upon them. The mother was screaming and trying to break into the open, but women were holding her back.

At that moment a man, whom nobody recognised at first, pushed his way through the crowd with powerful arms, and darted out in the direction of the child.

"Come back; you'll be killed," cried someone, but the others held their breath.

At the next instant the man was lost to sight in the midst of the cavalry. In the confused movement that followed one of the horses was seen to rear and swing aside, as if it had been struck in the mouth by a strong hand.

When the crowd were conscious of what happened next the cavalry had galloped past, with its clang of hoofs and rattle of steel, and the broad space was once more empty.

Empty save for the man. His head was bare, his hand was bleeding, and the skirt of the loose overcoat he wore was torn as if a sword had accidentally slashed it. But in his arms was the child—unhurt and untouched.

Then the people saw who he was. He was the Deemster, and they crowded about him. He gave the little one back to its mother, who had a still younger child at her breast, and was too breathless from fright to thank him.

He tried to conceal himself in the crowd, but they followed him—down the hill to Athol Street, where the Court-house is—a long train, chiefly of women and children, with wet eyes and open mouths, crying to him and to each other,

"The Deemster! God bless him!"

They thought he was going to the Court-house to sit on the bench as Judge, but when he came to the big portico he passed it, and, turning down a side street, he stopped at a little black door and knocked.

The door was opened by a police sergeant who was not wearing his helmet. The Deemster stepped into the vault-like place within and the door was closed behind him.

It was the Douglas prison.

II

The High Bailiff of Douglas held a Court that day. The court-house was almost empty. Not more than six or seven persons sat in the places assigned to the public. Three young reporters yawned over their note-books in their box beside the wall. In the well allotted to Counsel there were only two advocates in wig and gown.

A few bare-headed policemen stood near the bench and the Clerk of the Court sat under it. There was nobody else in the court-house except the High Bailiff himself, an elderly man with a red face and a benevolent expression.

He was trying a number of petty cases, chiefly of larceny and drunkenness. The light was low and the voices echoed in the vacant chamber. But from time to time a deadened rumble came from the streets outside—the clang of horses' hoofs, the derisive cries of a crowd, the loud shout of a commanding officer, and then a scamper of feet that was like heavy rain pelting down on the pavement.

Behind the Jury-box, which was empty, there was a door that led to the prison below. The last case was being heard when this door was opened and the Chief Constable came up into Court, followed by Stowell and a policeman. The Chief Constable took a seat in the advocates' well; Stowell and the policeman sat on the public benches.

When the High Bailiff, who was a great respecter of authority, saw the Deemster enter, he sent a policeman to ask him to come up to a seat by his side on the bench, but Stowell shook his head.

The case being tried was that of a farmer who was charged with driving his country cart on the high road without a stern light. The defence was that the lamp was alight when he left town, and had been put out by a high wind that was blowing. On this issue there was a long questioning and cross-questioning by the advocates, but at length the case came to a close.

"Half-a-crown and costs," said the High Bailiff; and then reaching over to his clerk he asked if that was the last case for the day.

"Yes, your Worship," said the Clerk, and the High Bailiff was pushing back his chair, when the Chief Constable rose with an air of importance.

"Your Worship, I have a serious charge to make."

He beckoned to the policeman at the back, who opened the door of the dock and Stowell stepped into it.

"I charge his Honour Deemster Victor Stowell, on his own confession, with breaking prison on Sunday night last between the hours of ten and twelve, to effect the escape from custody of a prisoner lying there under sentence of death."

The High Bailiff seemed to be stupefied and the charge had
to be repeated to him.

"Eh? What? God bless my soul! On his own confession,
you say? Is the Deemster well? What conceivable motive . . . . "

"I will give formal evidence, your Worship, and ask for a
committal to General Gaol, when the question of motive will be
fully gone into."

"Well, well! Good gracious me! If it must be it must. It
is my painful duty to put the Deemster back for trial. But I
suggest that a doctor be asked to see him immediately. And
meantime " (the High Bailiff turned to the reporters, who were
now busy enough over their note-books), "may I request the
representatives of the press to publish nothing about this painful
matter at present? "

It was all over in a few minutes. The door behind the Jury-
box was opened again and Stowell and the policeman returned
to the cells.

In less than half-an-hour the news was all over the town.
Special editions of the newspapers (single sheets) had been run
off in furious haste, and the newsboys were shouting through
the streets,

Arrest of Deemster Victor Stowell.

The news fell on the public like a thunderbolt. It eclipsed
their interest in the soldiers.

III

Like lightning out of a thunder-cloud the news fell on Government House also. On hearing it the Governor, who had been
thinking less about the riot than about Stowell's last words to
him, broke into uncontrollable rage.

"The fool! The infernal fool! After I had given him such
a chance, too! "

With a determined step he went into the library, where Fenella
was writing letters, and broke the news to her with a kind of
fierce joy. At first her eyes filled with tears and then a proud
smile shone through them.

"You were right after all, Fenella. I see now that you must
throw the man up," said the Governor.

"On the contrary," said Fenella. "Now I must stand by him."

"What on earth do you mean? "

"I mean that Victor has justified himself."

"Justified himself? "

" Yes. The only thing I was afraid of was that he might take his life to escape from his dishonour. But now that he has made his choice I have made mine also."

" *Your* choice? "

" I cannot cut him out of my heart because he has been brave enough to face the consequences of his crime."

" But good heavens, girl, don't you see that he will be brought up for trial, and then all the wretched story of the Collister girl will come out? "

" I'm prepared for that, father."

" Fenella," said the Governor, white with the passion that was mastering him, " if you were my son instead of my daughter do you know what I should do with you? "

" You mean you would turn me out of the house? There will be no need for that—I will go of myself, father."

" Fenella! Fenella! " cried the Governor, recovering himself, but Fenella had gone from the room.

The Governor returned to his smoking-room. For a long half-hour he ranged about, kicking things out of his way, ringing bells and snapping at the servants. What was Fenella doing? Could it be possible that she was taking him at his word? Unable to contain himself any longer he sent for Miss Green. He got nothing out of the old lady except lamentations.

" Oh, dear, oh dear, what is the world coming to? "

At length, with an air of authority, he went up to Fenella's bedroom, and found her on her knees before an open trunk into which she was packing her clothes.

" Fenella," he said, " this is nonsense. It cannot be."

" I'm afraid it must be, father."

" Look here, girl, when a man's angry he doesn't always mean what he says. I never meant you were to go."

" It's better that I should, father."

The Governor struggled hard with his pride and said,

" Listen. Don't make me ridiculous in the eyes of the whole island, Fenella. I may not have acted wisely in relation to Stowell and the advice I gave him—I see that now. But if so perhaps it was because I was thinking less of the public service than of you. If you were a father you would understand that. But you cannot wish to leave me. You are my only child. I am your father, remember. What, after all, is this man to you? "

Fenella leaned back on her heels and her eyelids quivered for a moment. Then she said,

" We are told that a man must leave father and mother and

cling to his wife, and surely it's the same with a woman and her husband. Victor is my husband, or soon will be."

" Good Lord, what are you saying, girl? "

" I promised myself to him, and I intend to keep my promise."

" But he's a prisoner, and if the governing authority objects . . . . "

" In that case I'll wait until he is a prisoner no longer, and then . . . . then I'll marry him."

" That you never shall. Not in this island anyway. No clergyman here will marry you to that man against my wish."

" Then I'll go to him just the same."

" What? "

" Yes, I'm prepared even for that sacrifice."

" You're mad. You're both mad—stark mad."

Again the Governor returned to his smoking-room. After a while he heard a hackney carriage coming up the drive to the porch, and then old John, the watchman, lugging a trunk along the corridor. A moment later, looking through the window, he saw Fenella, in the blue and white costume of her Settlement (the same in which, with so much pride, he had brought her up to the house from the pier in his big landau), stepping into the coach.

Then his anger and emotion together burst all bounds. He tore open his door with the intention of countermanding Fenella's orders and driving the hackney carriage off his grounds. But before he could bring himself to do so he heard the door of the carriage close and saw its wheels moving away.

Miss Green came back to the house with her handkerchief to her eyes, saying,

" She was crying as if her heart would break, poor darling! "

The Governor went slowly back to his room once more. The masterful man, who had never known before what it was to have tears in his eyes, was utterly broken. He had lost his daughter; he was to be a childless man henceforward; he was to spend the rest of his life alone. But after a while he thought of Stowell as the man who had taken Fenella from him, and his anger rose again.

" He wants punishment, does he? Very well, he shall have it, and damned quick too."

Two hours later Fenella was at Castle Rushen, in the living-room of the new jailer and his wife.

" I hear you want a female warder, and I've come to offer myself," she said.

The new jailer, who was embarrassed, stammered something about menial labour, but Fenella was not to be gainsaid.

" I'm a trained nurse, and have experience in managing people
—will you take me? "

" Well . . . . if the Governor doesn't . . . . for the present,
perhaps."

" For good," said Fenella.

Within a few minutes she was settled in her new quarters—a
large, dark, cell-like chamber, of irregular shape, with a deeply-
recessed window, a piece of cocoa-nut matting, a deal table, a chair,
a wash-stand and a truckle bed.

Two hundred years before it had been the 'tiring room of the
greatest of her ancestors, Charlotte de la Tremouille (Countess
of Derby), when, in the absence of her husband, she held the
fortress for weeks against the siege of Cromwell's forces.

The blood of the Stanleys was in it still.

CHAPTER FORTY-SIX
VICTORY THROUGH DEFEAT

A LITTLE later Stowell was brought up for trial at a special
sitting of the Court of General Gaol Delivery held in Douglas.

" This wretched case has injured the credit of the island in
England," said the Governor to the Attorney-General. The sooner
it was over and done with the better.

For a long half-hour before the proceedings began the court-
house was dark with men. Indignation against Stowell had succeeded to astonishment. Piecing things together (from Fenella's
outburst in Court to Gell's threat of personal violence against the
Deemster) people had arrived at something like the truth. The
lips which a few days before had saluted Stowell with cries of
worshipful lover were ready to break into shouts of execration.

The scoundrel! The traitor! Poor young Gell! And then
that girl Collister was not so bad as they had thought her.

Stowell's enemies had been crowing with satisfaction. " Well,
what did I tell you? " said Hudgeon, the advocate. And Qualtrough, M.H.K., repeated what he had said in the smoking-room
of the Keys—you had only to give the rascal rope and he would
hang himself.

His friends were yet more deadly. Nearly all had deserted
him. The good things they had said had been forgotten. Every
bad thing they could remember was revived, as far back as his
reckless days at Mount Murray as a young man and his expulsion
from King William's as a boy. He was a man of straw. It was

surprising what people had seen in him, and astonishing that the Governor had recommended him for the position of Deemster.

The press had been silent, from fear of the penalties of contempt, but the pulpit (Sunday having intervened) had been loud with platitudes, inspired by the text, " Be sure your sin will find you out."

When the time came for the Judges to enter the court-house the atmosphere was rank with evil passions and the acid odour of perspiring people.

Taubman was the Deemster. Although tortured by rheumatism he had dragged himself out of bed, having scented an opportunity of gaining favour with the Governor.

The Governor presided, as it was his duty to do, but it was remarked that except for one moment on taking his seat, when he looked round at the open-mouthed spectators with an expression which seemed to say, " What a race! " he never raised his eyes.

It was a short trial, and rarely had there been a more irregular one. Taubman was notorious for his legal deficiencies. In earlier days Stowell, in one of his " Limericks," had cristened him " Old Necessity," because " necessity knew no law." He had long been jealous of Stowell's popularity and particularly of his rapid rise to a position which he had had to wait forty years for. Now he had the " upstart " in his hand at last.

When the case was called Stowell was brought up by two policemen and placed in the dock. His cheeks were very pale and his eyes heavy as with unshed tears. It was almost as if his youth had stepped with one stride into age. But suffering gives a certain sublimity, and it was said afterwards that never before had he looked so strong and noble.

The spectators saw nothing of that now. His calm seemed to them to be callousness. He did not appear to see the scorching glances they cast at him. The last time they had seen him in Court he was on the bench, now he was in the dock, and they would have been better pleased if, in the dread certainty of his fate, he had betrayed the fellness of terror. But except for one moment, when he turned slowly round to look at them, and their murmurs ceased suddenly at full sight of his face, he seemed to them to have forgotten the shame of the place he stood in.

Taubman, in a rasping voice, read out the charge to the prisoner and called on him to plead.

" How say you, are you Guilty or Not Guilty? "

" Guilty," said Stowell in a clear voice, and then, after a moment of merciless silence, there was a deep drawing of breath.

" Had you any accomplices? "

" None."

" Humph! And what was your motive in committing this crime? "

Again there was a moment of merciless silence, and then Stowell, speaking very slowly, said,

" I had seduced the prisoner and was therefore the first cause of her crime."

Ah! There was another long indrawing of breath among the spectators. It was a wonder the man didn't fall dead with shame!

" And what, if you please, was your reason for making this confession? "

" I could not allow an innocent person to suffer for my crime."

" Was that your only reason? "

The silence became breathless. After a pause Stowell said, in a low voice,

" That is a question I will answer to a higher tribunal."

" Indeed! " said Taubman, with a sneer, and then the silence was broken by a cowardly titter which passed through the court-house.

The Attorney-General rose to summarise the facts. His face was white and decomposed; his thin hair was disordered, and the linen slip under his chin was awry.

Only once before since leaving Government House had he been out of doors—to visit Stowell at the Police-station and receive the letter which had been found on him. He, too, had dragged himself from bed to come to Court, being afraid to leave the prosecution of the son of his old friend, the boy brought up in his own office, to the Deputy whom the Governor was sure to appoint in his place—Hudgeon, who sat by his side.

His speech did not please either the Court or the spectators. It gave the impression of being a plea for the prisoner. And indeed there were moments when the Attorney seemed to forget that he was there to prosecute.

Speaking in a tremulous voice, and never once looking towards the dock, he said it would seem incredible that anyone in the position of the accused could be guilty of the crime with which he was charged. But the lucidity of his confession, and its correspondence to the facts as they knew them, made it inconceivable that he had told a lie. There could be no doubt he was guilty, and being so he came under the condemnation of the law.

" Ha! "

" But," said the old man, flashing his moist eyes on the glistening eyes behind him, " the Crown stands for Justice, not revenge."

The Court would remember that the prisoner had made a

voluntary confession, that nothing would have been known of his crime if he had not of himself disclosed it, and before the sublime spectacle of a man who was making the only reparation in his power to the Justice he had sullied, it would be touched by the fire of a great renunciation.

A murmur of dissent passed through the court-house.

Again, the Court would remember that the prisoner had confessed to the secret sin which had tempted him to his crime. If he had been a scoundrel he could have concealed it, but he had put conscience before liberty, before reputation, perhaps before life.

" Oh! "

Once more the Court would remember that the prisoner had surrendered to Justice because another was in danger of arrest, and it would not be human if it were not moved by the sight of a man giving himself up to the law so that an innocent man might not suffer in his stead.

Finally, the Court would remember the youth of the prisoner, his undoubted talents, his brilliant promise, his high position, and the revered memory of his father, and if, moved by these considerations, it decided to impose a nominal penalty, the Crown would be satisfied.

" Ah! "

" But whatever the punishment the Court thinks fit to impose on the prisoner," said the Attorney, " it can be as nothing to that which he has inflicted upon himself. Never in this island has there been so great a downfall, and rarely can suffering for sin have been more terrible since the Veil of the Temple was rent in twain and darkness covered the land."

It was impossible for the spectators not to be hushed to awe by the daring words and quivering tones with which the old Attorney closed his speech, but Taubman, in the ferocity of his malice, was unmoved.

" Humph! " he said. " All that means, I suppose, that a man may be innocent and guilty at the same time."

And then another cowardly titter ran through the court-house.

The time had come for judgment. Taubman leaned over the bench, clasped his bony fingers in front of him, and said,

" Victor Stowell, stand up."

Stowell rose, and stood with his hands interlaced, and his heavy eyes fixed steadfastly on his Judge.

" Have you anything to say why judgment should not be pronounced upon you? "

" Nothing."

It needs no skill to wound the defenceless, and for the next few minutes Taubman seemed to glory in the exercise of his power.

"Prisoner at the bar," he said, "you have confessed to the crime of breaking prison to effect the escape from custody of a young woman you had first debauched and then abandoned."

"Ha!"

"It has been said on your behalf (strangely enough by the public servant whose duty it was to arraign you) that your confession was voluntary. Nothing of the kind. It was made when the hand of the law was upon you, when the warrant for the arrest of an innocent man was about to be issued, and you were face to face with the certainty of exposure and punishment."

"Ha!"

"It has been also been said that the confession of your private sin shows the operation of your conscience. But your conscience would have been better employed when you sat in judgment on your own victim—a deliberate offence that is probably without precedent in the history of criminal jurisprudence.

"Finally it has been argued that your high position and family connections ought to mitigate your punishment. On the contrary, they ought to increase it, as showing your disregard of your responsibilities, and especially your ingratitude to the head of the judiciary, his Excellency" (here Taubman bowed to the Governor), "whose favours you have so ill requited."

"Ah!"

"Your crime is clear. It is without a particle of justification. You have disgraced your name, your profession, and your island. Therefore the Court can only mark its sense of the enormity of your offence by inflicting the maximum penalty prescribed by the law—two years' imprisonment in Castle Rushen."

Hardly had the last words been spoken when the spectators broke into frenzied shouts of approval. Neither the police nor the Judge made any attempt to repress them. The Governor rose hastily and hurried off the bench, and Taubman, gathering up his papers, his spectacles and his two walking-sticks, hobbled after him.

The shouting went on. It surged about Stowell as he stepped out of the dock and passed with slow stride through the door that led down to the prison. The deadened sound of it followed him while he descended the stairs, and when he reached the cell it mingled with yet wilder shouting from the streets, where a tumultuous crowd had been waiting for the verdict. The delight of the mob seemed delirious. Some women from the meaner streets by the quay were dancing on the pavement.

Meantime, in his robing-room with the Governor, Taubman was congratulating himself on his travesty of Justice. Taking his wig off his stubbly grey hair he said,

"I think I gave my gentleman his deserts for his bad treatmen of your Excellency. Eh? What?"

And then the Governor spoke for the first time that day.

"Maybe so," he said, "but all the same you are not fit to wipe his boots, Sir."

II

Early next morning Stowell was removed to Castle Rushen.

There was a rumour (probably inspired by the police) that he would travel by the seven o'clock train, therefore at half-past six the railway station and its approaches were full of a noisy crowd. But at ten minutes to seven the prison van, drawn by two horses, drew up at the back door under the court-house and Stowell was hustled into it.

"Come, get in, quick," said the Chief Constable (all his former deference gone), and then the van rolled away, Stowell being shut up in the windowless compartment within, while the Chief Constable and his Inspector of Police occupied the outer one with the grill.

Crossing a swing-bridge which spanned the top of the harbour, they climbed the lane to the Head until they reached the cliff road, and had the town behind them under a veil of morning mist, and the open sea in front. There had been wind overnight, and a fiery sun was blazing out of a fierce sky like the red light from the open door of a furnace.

Stowell, in his dark compartment, had not yet asked himself which way he was going. The feeling of exaltation, of doing a divinely appointed duty, which had buoyed him up during the trial, was now gone. The nullity of his past life, the hopelessness of the future had left him with the sense of being already a dead man. Two years inside the blind walls of the Castle Rushen, while the sun shone and the flowers grew and the birds sang outside, and the world went on without him—how could he live through it?

At length, having a sense of physical as well as spiritual suffocation, he tapped timidly at his door, and asked, when it was opened, if it might remain so for a few moments that he might have a breath of air.

"Certainy not," said the Chief Constable, and he clashed the door back.

"Better so," thought Stowell.

He had caught a glimpse of the scene outside, and knew where they were—on the rocky shelf along which he had driven with Fenella after the oath-taking at Castletown.

The memory of that day came back to him like a stab. He could feel Fenella's warm presence by his side; he could see her gleaming eyes; he could hear her rich contralto voice as they sang together above the boom of the sea below and the cry of the sea-fowl overhead:

> " Love is the Queen for you and for me,
> Salve, Salve Regina! "

What memories! What regrets! Only now did he know how necessary Fenella had been to him—only now when he had lost her. He felt like a dead man—dead, yet doomed to remember his former existence.

An hour and a half passed. Stowell sat huddled up in the close atmosphere of the van, with the thunderous rumble of the roof above him and the crack of the driver's whip outside. He knew every mile of the way. When the van swung round at a turn of the road, or the horses slowed down at the foot of a hill, the memory of some moment in his drive with Fenella came back to him, and he told himself how far they had still to go.

At length they were entering Castletown. He knew that by the hollow sound under the horses' hoofs as they crossed the bridge over the harbour—the bridge from which Fenella had looked back and waved her hand to the crowd about the Castle gate who had raised the deafening shout—" Long live the new Deemster, hip, hip, hip! "

Groaning audibly, digging with his fingernails deep trenches in his palms, praying for strength of spirit, he waited for the ordeal which he felt was before him.

Another crowd had gathered about the Castle gate that morning.

Telegrams had been received from Douglas saying that Stowell was travelling by road, so half the people of Castletown had come down to the quay as to a funeral to see the last of the condemned man before he was buried in his living tomb.

They were of two classes. The larger and noisier class consisted of raw youths and young men to whom the trial of the Deemster had been mainly a subject for lewd jests about Bessie Collister.

One of them, with the small eyes of a sow and the thick lips of a cod, wore a butcher's apron and a steel attached to a belt about his waist. This was John Qualtrough (son of Cæsar), the lusty ruffian whose skull had been cracked in his boyhood by the blow from the stick which had been intended for Alick Gell.

The Castle walls were low by the gate, and off the shoulders of a comrade Qualtrough clambered to a seat on the battlements. From that elevation he beguiled the time of waiting by conducting a chorus of his companions on the ground, using his steel for baton. He selected the crudest of the old Manx ditties, and amid shrieks of laughter, he emphasised the doubtful lines by frequent repetition.

> " *I'm not engaged to any young man I solemnly do swear,*
> *For I mane to be a vargin and still the laurels wear.*
> *For I mane to be a vargin and still the laurels wear.*"

The other class, consisting chiefly of women, demure and severe, occupied themselves with serious talk about Fenella. That splendid young woman! It was shocking the way Sto'll had treated her—worse than the other in a manner of speaking.

"They're telling me she wasn't at the trial in Douglas yesterday."

"What wonder if she wasn't, poor thing! I wouldn't trust but she'll never show her face in public again."

"It's no use talking, the man has brought shame on the lot of us and is a disgrace to the name of a Manxman."

Suddenly, over the loud clamour there came a wild shout from the battlements.

"Here he is!"

The prison van was seen to cross the bridge, and as it came up to the gate, it was received with a howl of execration.

Stowell heard it. In his dark compartment the surging of the crowd around the outside of the van was like the breaking of a tidal wave on a sleeping town in the middle of the night. The van stopped with a sickening jolt, and he heard the Inspector of Police crying,

"Stand back! Make way!"

Then there was a flash of daylight and the voice of the Chief Constable saying peremptorily,

"Come, get out! Be quick about it."

At the next moment he was on the ground with a roar of hoarse voices and a rush of contorted faces around him. There were screams of lewd laughter and yells of merciless derision. Arms were raised as if to strike him. He felt himself being pushed and pulled by the police through the open gate and up the passage way to the Portcullis.

The crowd, not yet appeased, tried to force their way past the jailer and his turnkeys as if to lynch him. But they were checked by an unexpected sight. A young woman, in the costume of a nurse, with heaving breast, quivering nostrils, and flaming eyes, rushed through the gate with outstretched arms to stop them.

They recognised her instantly, but it was not that alone that cowed them. There is something in a brave act which pierces the noisiest crowd to the core of its cruel soul. Certainly this crowd fell back and its uproar died down.

Then in a voice which vibrated with contempt and scorn, Fenella tried to speak to them.

" You . . . . you . . . . you . . . . " she began, but further words would not come, and returning to the Castle she clashed its iron-studded gate in the people's faces.

The crowd broke up rapidly and slank away, subdued and ashamed.

" Morning, men ! "

" Morning ! "

Within two minutes nearly all were gone. The open space in front of the Castle gate was empty, save for two old women with little black shawls over their heads, who were wiping their eyes on their cotton aprons.

" Did thou see that, Bella ? "

" 'Deed I did, though."

" I belave in my heart it was the girl herself—the one they say he has done so bad to."

" Aw well, if a woman isn't willing to stand up for her man whatever he has done what *is* she anyway? "

CHAPTER FORTY-SEVEN

THE RESURRECTION

THREE days later, Fenella set out for Bishop's Court in a two-horse landau.

The island had begun to recover from its fit of moral intoxication. Sympathy was swinging round to Stowell. The pathos of his stupendous downfall had taken hold of the people. Taubman had been wrong. Nobody would have known anything of Stowell's guilt if he had not revealed it himself. There must be something great in a man who could take up his cross like that. And as for that wonderful woman who might be living in Government House but was living in Castle Rushen instead . . . .

As Fenella, in her nurse's costume, drove through the town some of the women curtsied to her, and most of the men raised their hats. She returned the salutations of none.

" So that's how they expect to wipe out what they did to Victor! Not if I know it though! "

Two hours afterwards she was at the Bishop's palace—a somewhat palatial place, partly old, partly new, sleeping in the shelter of big trees and surrounded by a blaze of rhododendrons.

The Bishop, in his dapper black clothes, received her in a room in the old part of the house. It had been the study of the most famous of his predecessors, the fanatic and saint who had ordered that Kate Kinrade, for the saving of her soul, should be dragged at the tail of a boat. Souvenirs of the dead Bishop were on the walls and tables—his portrait, his Bible, his short crozier, his tasselled staff, and his horn-rimmed spectacles.

The living Bishop was suave and voluble. He congratulated Fenella on looking so well after so much trouble.

" Such a calamity! I might almost say such a tragedy! How the island will miss him! "

He agreed with the Attorney-General. Stowell's act had been one of renunciation. When a man had sinned against God, and violated the world's law, he set a great example by submitting to authority.

" God forbid that I should excuse his crime, but already his renunciation is having a good effect throughout the island. The rioting is over. The soldiers are being sent back, and as for the agitators nobody listens to them any longer. Only this morning the man Baldromma . . . . "

Fenella, who had been beating her foot impatiently on the carpet, at length broke into her own business.

" Bishop, you have heard that I have gone to the Castle as female warder? "

" Yes, indeed. It's so nice of you to stay by the poor man's side while he is in prison, to see that his bodily comforts are being cared for."

" But more than that will have to be done for him if his soul is to be kept alive," said Fenella.

" Really? If you think there is anything *I* can do . . . . "

" There is, Sir . . . . You know that I was to have married Mr. Stowell? "

" Indeed I do. Wasn't the marriage to have taken place before very long in our chapel at Bishop's Court? "

" Well, I want it to take place now. Only it must be in the Chapel at Castle Rushen instead."

" You mean . . . . the prison Chapel? "

" Yes."

For a moment the Bishop was speechless. Then recovering from his astonishment, he rose and stepped to the hearthrug, and standing with his back to the fire, he said, as if addressing an assembly,

" Beautiful and noble, dear lady! To be ready to become the wife of the fallen man just when the whole world is hissing at him in chorus, to inspire him day by day with the hope of a great resurrection, of taking up manful work anew, of regaining all he has lost and more—yes, it is beautiful and noble."

" Then you will be willing to marry us, Sir? " said Fenella.

The Bishop hesitated, and then asked Fenella what view the Governor took of her intention.

" He disapproves of it altogether, and says no clergyman in the island can marry us without incurring his displeasure."

" Ah! "

" But I have always understood that the Bishop is a baron in his own right and therefore independent of the Governor."

" True! That's true! Still . . . . "

The river of rhetoric had suddenly stopped.

" Well? "

" Mr. Stowell is a prisoner. Why marry when you can't live together? Why not wait until he is at liberty? "

" Because he may be dead of despair before the time for that comes," said Fenella, " and the resurrection you speak of may never take place. His heart is breaking. He wants something to live for now. He wants *me*."

Her eyes had filled and the Bishop had to turn his own away. At length he said, stammering painfully, that he was sorry, very sorry, but having to live at peace with the Governor . . . .

Fenella leapt to her feet.

" Bishop," she said, " the chaplain at Castletown is a poor man with five young children and his living is in the gift of the Governor. But if I can find any other clergyman who is willing to perform the ceremony, will you permit him to do so? "

" Ye—s . . . . that is to say, if you tell him what you have told me, and he is prepared to take the risk."

Within two minutes more Fenella was back in her landau, driving towards Ballamoar across the Curragh roads, with their warm and rooty odour of the bog.

Janet came running out of the house to meet her, and in a flash they were crying in each other's arms. But, to Fenella's surprise, there was a look of joy in Janet's face, and on stepping into the house she found an explanation. An army of maidservants were in every room, with an arsenal of brushes and mops and pails.

"Why, Janet, what are you doing?"

"Getting ready for my boy coming back, that's what I'm doing."

"But, dear heart, don't you know . . . . ."

"Certainly I know. But do you think they can keep a Balla-moar in yonder place long? 'Deed they can't. He'll be coming out soon, and then those dirts of Manx ones who have been making such a mouth will be the first to run to meet him."

It would have been cruel to gainsay her, therefore Fenella described the object of her journey, told of her father's threat and the Bishop's excuses.

"So now I'm looking for a clergyman who will be brave enough to marry us," she said.

They were in the dining-room, and through the glass door to the piazza they could see, on the edge of the cliffs, a field's space from the church, a lonely house without a tree or a bush about it, looking as if it had been slashed by the rain and winds of a hundred winters. It was the Jurby parsonage—the home of Parson Cowley. Janet pointed to it and said,

"Have you been *there?*"

At that question Fenella remembered a story her father had told her about something splendid that Victor had done, before she returned to the island, to save the drunken parson of Jurby in the eyes of the parishioners. In another minute she was back in her carriage.

"Good-bye, child, and God bless you!" said Janet by the carriage door. "And don't forget to tell my boy that Mother will be lighting the fire in the Deemster's room every night of life for him."

The parsonage looked yet more desolate at a nearer view than at a distance. Sea-fowl were screaming in the sky above it and the earth was quaking from the measured beat of the waves against the cliffs below. A patch of garden in front was rank with long grass, and the salt breath of the sea had encrusted the glass of the windows with a grey scale that was like the mould on a dead face.

The door was opened by a timid, elderly woman, the parson's wife, who was her own servant and looked as if all the pride of life had been crushed out of her.

"Please come in, miss," she said. And when the door had been closed from the inside and she was taking Fenella into the study, she called at the foot of the stairs,

" John, a young lady to see you."

The dingy little room looked like an epitome of the life of the man who lived in it. Everything was faded and worn out—books in torn bindings on bulging shelves against the walls; a threadbare carpet trodden thin by the fender; a handful of earthen fire; an arm-chair upholstered in horsehair and sunk in the seat as if the springs had broken; a table laden with loose papers and sprinkled with shreds of tobacco, which seemed to have fallen from a shaking hand; and behind a mirror, from which half the silvering was worn away, two objects on the mantelpiece—a drinking glass, which had obviously contained a frothy liquor and a photograph in a mourning frame of a young man in sailor's costume with the fell stamp of consumption in his eyes and cheeks.

After a moment there was an unsteady step on the stairs and the parson came into the room, wearing a faded skull cap and a dressing-gown much patched and stained.

Fenella told him her story, as she had told it to the Bishop, and then said,

" So I've come to ask if you dare run the risk of marrying us? "

The old parson, who had been listening intently, seemed eager to reply, but something checked him, and looking across at his wife, who continued to stand timidly by the door, he said,

" What do *you* say, Sarah? "

The old lady did not reply immediately, and pointing to the photograph on the mantelpiece the parson said,

" If it had been John James's case, eh? "

" Do as you think best, John."

" Then I'll do it! Certainly I'll do it! What do I care what the Governor may do to me? Once a priest always a priest—he can't take *that* from me anyway."

It was just the chance he had been waiting for. Victor Stowell had done something for him, and before he died he wanted to do something for Victor Stowell.

" I will too! I'll give give him a good wife and that's the best thing a man gets in this world anyway. I've been publishing your banns too. Do you know I'd been publishing your banns these three Sunday mornings, Victor Stowell being one of my parishioners? "

Fenella, who was feeling a tightness in the throat, contrived to say,

" Then perhaps you'll drive back with me to Castletown and celebrate the service to-morrow? "

" Why shouldn't I? ' said the parson, and off he went upstairs (with a firm step this time) to put on his clerical clothes and pack his surplice in a hand-bag.

While his quick footsteps were shaking the ceiling above them the two women stood together in the study, the young one and the old one, face to face.

" It is very good of you, Mrs. Cowley, to take this risk with your husband," said Fenella.

" But isn't that what we women have all got to do? " said Mrs. Cowley.

And then Fenella, unable to say more, put her arms about the timid old thing, who had submerged her own life in the wrecked life of her husband, and kissed her.

II

Stowell had been four days in prison and his depression had deepened to despair. The sense of being buried alive was crushing. Even when he was taken into the court-yard for exercise, and the white birds sailed through the blue sky, he had the sensation of being in a roofless tomb.

Yet he did not spare himself. He had a right to certain indulgences, but asked for none. They put him into an upstairs room, which had once been the armoury of the Castle, but he said,

" Put me in the cell that was occupied by Bessie Collister."

He might have continued to wear his own clothes, but said,

" Give me the same clothes as any other prisoner "—a rough tweed, uncombed and undyed, just as it had come from the back of the sheep.

The silence was terrible. The first night was calm, and the only sound that reached him through the thick walls was the monotonous wash of the waves on the shore, which lay empty and alone under the dark sky.

Next morning he heard the clamour of the gulls, and knew that the boats had come in from their night's fishing and the birds were fighting for the refuse thrown overboard. A little later he heard the deadened sound of hammering at a distance—they were caulking the deck of a new vessel in the shipyard across the bay. The world was going on as usual, yet there he was in a silence like that of the grave.

" Don't people sometimes go mad in a place like this? " he asked the jailer.

On the second night the sea was loud, but over the wailing of the waves he heard a raucous voice outside. It was the voice of Dan Baldromma, who, ranging round the Castle walls like an evil spirit, was calling up his taunting message at every lancet window, not knowing which was the window of Stowell's cell.

"The Spaker is dead the day. That's the way they go, the big ones that rob the people. But there's no pocket in the shroud, Dempster—no pocket in the shroud."

On the morning of the third day Stowell received a letter from London, telling him that His Majesty the King had withdrawn his commission, having no longer any use for his services. This smote him like a blow on the brain. It was an abject degradation, like that of an officer being stripped of his decorations before the eyes of the soldiers who had served under him.

But the worst of his pains were his thoughts about Fenella. Like a man suddenly struck blind he was always living over again the scenes of his past life. Sitting on his bed, with his head in his hands and his eyes tightly closed, all the beautiful moments of their love passed in procession before him, from the moment in the glen when he had picked her up in his quivering arms and carried her across the stream, to that parting in the porch at Government House, after she had promised to marry him, and he had seized her about the waist and fastened his lips to her mouth.

Do what he would, he could not resist the intoxication of these cruel memories. But crueller still were his dreams of the future— the dead dreams of their married love, when she would be wholly his, the beautiful body as well as the beautiful soul. Nothing in the world was to have been so lovely as her bare arms about his neck; nothing so thrilling as the throbbing of her breasts when he told her how much he loved her. But when he opened his eyes and saw the blank walls of his cell about him, he felt as if some devil from hell had been tormenting him.

Was this to be his greatest punishment—that what he had lost in Fenella was to be for ever haunting him? Was he never to be left in peace, now that all hope of her was gone from him for ever?

"Better die," he thought. "A thousand times better."

Several times every day the jailer had been in to talk with him. The prison was nearly full of prisoners now, many of the rioters having been arrested ("Not the ring-leaders, they are always too cunning"), so that his turnkeys and lady warder had as much as they could do to keep things going.

This, through the thick haze of his preoccupied mind, brought back to Stowell's memory a glimpse he had got of a woman in nurse's costume who had flashed past him when he was being hustled through that furnace of wrathful faces at the Castle gate, and he asked who she had been.

"Oh, that . . . . *that's* our lady warder," said the jailer.

" Is Mrs. Mylrea better then? "

" No, she's dead. We have another one now, Sir."

" Who is she? "

The jailer hesitated and then said, " Don't you know, your Honour? "

Stowell looked up quickly and a stifling recollection of Fenella's last words (" If you have to go to prison, I will follow you ") came surging back on him.

" Is it . . . . is it . . . . *she?* " he faltered.

" Yes."

That night, when Stowell's supper was brought to him, he sent it away untouched. But the morning broke fair on his sleepless eyes, for he had made up his mind what to do.

A pale ray of reflected sunshine from the eastern wall of the court-house was on the upper part of his cell, and he could hear the voices of children who were playing on the shore.

He asked for a candle, pen and ink and paper, and sat down to write a letter.

" MY DEAR FENELLA,—They have told me what you have done and I cannot bear to think of it. When it became necessary to do what I did, I knew I should have to give up all hope of you, and since doing so I have suffered as few men can ever have suffered before. But if you remain in this place I shall never know another hour's sleep by night or rest by day. I shall feel that in surrendering to Justice I was not really doing a courageous act, as perhaps I thought, but a cowardly one, because I was throwing half the burden of my sins on to you, who are innocent of any of them. That thought would break my heart."

He paused. The sea outside was singing on the shore; the children were laughing at their play.

" Fenella, at this last moment I must tell you something. Ever since I came to care for you, it has been the dearest wish of my heart that, God helping me, I should make your life a happy one—that, whatever happened to me, in a world so full of cloud and shadow, you should live in the sunshine. And now that you follow me here, to this prison, this tomb . . . . it is too much. I cannot bear it.

" Go home, dear. Good-bye and God bless you! Don't let me regret the impulse that brought me here. If it was right and true I must bear my punishment alone. Leave me the comfort of thinking that at least your outer life goes on as if I had never shattered it. We have had many happy hours together, but they are over. Life is for ever closed against me. You can do nothing for me now. It was sweet and good of you to come to this place, and I feel as if I could give my heart's blood for one more look into your dear face, but . . . . "

He had written thus far when the key rattled in the lock of his cell. The door opened and there was a flash of the jailer's lantern. Instinctively, without looking up, Stowell covered his letter in his blotting-paper and busied himself with both for a moment. When he raised his eyes the lantern was on the table, but the jailer was gone and somebody else was standing before him.

It was Fenella. She was in wedding dress, with the veil thrown back, looking more lovely than in the most delirious of his dreams. At first he thought it was a phantom, born of the preoccupation of his tortured brain, and in a hushed whisper, trembling all over and rising from his chair, he said,

" Fenella ! "

She, too, was trembling, but she put on a brave air and even a little of her gay raillery.

" Yes, it is Fenella. She has come, as she said she would, you know."

" But *why* have you come? "

" Why? Don't you know what day this is, Victor? This was to have been our wedding-day. It shall be, too."

" Do you mean it? "

" Look at me. Do you think I have dressed up like this for nothing? "

" But don't you see it is impossible? "

" Impossible? Don't you want me any longer then? You promised to marry me, Sir—are you going to break your promise?'

She was laughing, but trying at the same time not to cry. Stowell's voice grew thick and husky.

" Go home to your father's house, Fenella. That is the only place for you."

" But my father has turned me out, so if you send me away also I shan't have a roof to cover me."

" Is that true? "

She tried to laugh again with her old gaiety.

" Well . . . . nearly."

" You cannot live in a place like this, Fenella."

"Why not? I have the apartments of a Queen, and what was good enough for her will be good enough for me, surely."

"But you forget—I am a prisoner, and if the Governor objects . . . ."

"He doesn't. He has been told and has raised no objection."

"But there isn't a clergyman in the island who would marry a woman like you to a man like me."

"Oh yes, there's one, and I have brought him with me."

"Who . . . ."

"Somebody you did a beautiful thing for long ago, and who new wants to do something for you—for me, I mean. Come in, Parson Cowley."

Then Stowell saw that the door was open and that Parson Cowley was standing in the darkness beyond it. The old parson came into the cell at Fenella's call, sober as a Judge, but with his face more broken up by emotion than it had ever been by drink, for he had heard everything.

"Parson Cowley," said Stowell, in a hoarse voice, "show her it is impossible."

The old man swallowed something in his throat and answered, "Nothing seems impossible to love, my son."

"But tell her that no good woman can live all her life with a dishonoured man like me."

Again the old parson cleared his throat.

"I know one who has been doing so for forty years, Sir."

Stowell fell back on his chair and dropped his head over his arms on the table. Parson Cowley, unable to bear more, slipped out of the cell and pulled the door behind him.

Fenella and Stowell were then alone. She knew that her last chance had come. She had to conquer him now or lose him for ever. It was the primitive man against the primitive woman, only their age-long positions were reversed, and with all the battery of her womanhood she meant to win him. Stepping closer she said, in a caressing voice,

"Victor, you won't send me away from you, will you?"

"I shall always love you, Fenella," said Stowell, whose head was still down. "I shall love you as an angel."

"But forgive me, dear, I am only a woman, and I want to be loved as a woman first."

He raised his head and looked at her. Her eyes were glistening, her lips were trembling, never before had she seemed to him so beautiful. Feeling himself weakening he rose and turned away.

"I should never forgive myself, Fenella, if I allowed you to make this sacrifice."

"What sacrifice? Everything I want in the world is within these walls."

"Don't tempt me, Fenella. Go away, I beg of you."

"Victor, I am for you. You are for me. Do you want to rob me of the only man in the world for me?"

His heart was beating fast.

"Go away, I tell you. I cannot trust myself any longer."

But the more he commanded her to go, the more her eyes glistened with a look of triumph.

"If I am to go out of this place, you'll have to carry me out," she said, "just as you carried me across the river in the glen."

He gasped, and then flung out at her in a torrent of words.

"Why do you come like this? Is it only to torture me with the thought of what might have been? Haven't I done enough wrong to you already? If I do this wrong also I shall hate myself. And the end of that will be that I shall come to hate you also. I *do* hate you. Go away! For God's sake go!"

Fenella, with gleaming eyes, took one step closer.

"Victor," she said, "you love me. You know you do. You have never loved any other woman in the world—never for one single moment."

He looked back at her again. Her arms were stretched out to him; her bosom was heaving; her lips were quivering and apart. He could struggle no longer.

"Fenella!"

"Victor!"

She had conquered. They were clasped in each other's arms.

III

Half-an-hour afterwards they were married in the prison chapel. The little place was naked enough now. No flowers, no flags, no carpets, no cushions. Only the two rows of forms, without backs, and the placards on the whitewashed walls at either side —"For Men" and "For Women."

The deal table which served for altar was covered by a kitchen table-cloth, on which nothing stood but a plain brass cross and a couple of lighted candles in kitchen candlesticks.

Parson Cowley, in his surplice, stood in front of it, with his well-thumbed prayer-book in his trembling hands. The two who were being married were kneeling at his feet—the sin-soiled man and the daughter of a line of old Manx Kings, bearing a name that had been written high in English history for five hundred years. The jailer and his wife were standing somewhere in the shadows. There was no sound except that of the parson's quavering voice within and the low rumble of the sea outside.

> "*I require and charge you, as ye will answer at the dreadful day of Judgment, when the secrets of all hearts shall be disclosed, that if either of you know of any impediment why ye may not be lawfully joined together in Matrimony, ye do now confess it.*"

Stowell made a stifled sound as of protest. Fenella put down her hand and took his hand and held it.

> "*Victor Christian, wilt thou have this Woman to thy wedded wife?*"

There was a sensible pause, and Parson Cowley leaned down to Stowell and whispered,

"Say 'I will,' my son."

Then came a slow, half-smothered murmur,

"I . . . . will."

> "*Fenella Charlotte de la Tremouille, wilt thou have this Man to thy wedded husband?*"

In a clear, unfaltering voice Fenella answered,

"I will."

*　　*　　*　　*　　*　　*　　*

It was all over. The parson and the jailer and his wife were gone. Stowell and Fenella were alone together in the prison chapel, locked in a passionate embrace. The kitchen candles were burning out, but the little dark place shone with glory. The air was stirred as with the presence of angels and lit as by a celestial torch.

In their immense happiness every trouble of life seemed to be gone. Two years? It would be like two months, two weeks, two days—it would be like a walk in the sunshine.

"We must hold together now, dear."

"Yes, until death parts us."

Their hearts swelled with gratitude. Love had taken the sting out of suffering—Love, the saviour, the redeemer. A great hymn of thanksgiving was going up from body and from soul.

They talked of the future.

"Will you leave the island when your time comes, dear?"

"Indeed no, never."

Where his sin had been there also should be his expiation.

"How great! How glorious!"

She cried a little, being so happy, and he had to comfort her. Oh, mystery of the heart of woman! They had changed places again, and now it was she who was the weak one—or pretended to be so—just to make him feel how strong he was, being the man, and that she would have to look up to him all her life to guide and protect her.

"Will you love me always, Victor?"

"Always? As sure as God . . . . "

"Hush! I know you will, dearest. But being only a woman I shall want you to tell me so every night and every morning."

He warned her of the struggles they would have to go through yet, even when the time came to leave that place and return to the world—of the many who would look askance at them for his sin's sake. But she said no, and painted for him a picture of his coming out of prison.

What a scene it would be! His people, his beloved countrymen and countrywomen, who were good at heart, would be at the Castle gates to meet him. There would be thousands and tens of thousands of them to go back with him over the hill to Ballamoar. Carriages, cars, spring-carts, stiff-carts, fishermen in their ganzies and lifeboatmen in their stocking caps—such a procession across the mountains as nobody had ever seen in that island before, his little nation taking him home.

"Oh, I see it all, Victor. When the time comes for you to go through the Castle gates it will be like passing out of death into life, out of the cloud of night into the glory of the sunrise."

He smiled, a melancholy smile, and shook his head.

"I have much to go through yet. You, too, Fenella."

But well she knew that the victory had been won, that the resurrection of his soul had already begun, that he would rise again on that same soil on which he had so sadly fallen, that shining like a star before his brightening eyes was the vision of a far greater and nobler life than the one that lay in ruins behind him, and that she, she herself, would be always by his side—to "ring the morning bell for him."

CONCLUSION

THE herring shoal, which in the early summer comes down from Norway to the western coast of Man, drifts eastward as the year advances, past the Calf Island, the Sound and the Spanish Head, with their deafening clamour of ten thousand sea-fowl, to where the big waves of the Atlantic roll to their organ music, and the porpoises tumble through the blue waters of the Channel on their way back to the frozen seas.

In the late autumn of the year of Victor Stowell's trial and imprisonment the fishermen from Ramsey and Douglas, going south to their fishing ground in the evening of the day, would find as they sailed past Castletown, and opened the Poolvaish, that the sun had set behind Castle Rushen and its square tower stood up black against the crimsoning sky.

Then they would go down on their knees on the decks of their boats, just as in old days they used to do after they had shot their nets at night, to acknowledge their Maker, and pray, in their Manx, to St. Bridget and St. Patrick to send them safely home in the morning with a full cargo of "the living and the dead."

But it was not the harvest of the sea they were thinking of then. It was of the two who lay interned within the walls of the grim fortress—the man who had voluntarily made the great Sacrifice for his sin, and the woman, who in the greatness of her love was living out his punishment beside him.

In my early manhood I used to hear old Methodist fishermen say that when they rose from their knees, after their rough hands had been held close over their eyes, and looked back at the Castle, they would sometimes see a golden cross plainly outlined in the sky above it.

Perhaps it was only another of their Manx superstitions, but it seemed to bring a certain inspiration to their simple hearts for all that, by reminding them of a story which resembled (very remotely and feebly) the great one which they told each other every Sunday in their little wayside chapels—the story of Him Who " gave the world away and died."

> " He descended into hell; the third day He rose again
> from the dead; He ascended into heaven and sitteth on the
> right hand of God the Father Almighty . . . . "

THE END